MORE PRAISE FOR NINA BANGS!

THE PLEASURE MASTER

AN ORIGINAL SIN

TEMPTATION

"Welcome to the Woo Woo Inn." That was what she said out loud.

Oooh, yes! Pant, pant, pant. Woo-hoo, come and get me, you big beautiful hottie. That welcome was from the sluts who lived in her basement.

"Thanks." He smiled.

Even if a portal to Hell had opened at her feet, she wouldn't have felt more shocked. Sure, he had sensual lips and great teeth, but that's not what his smile was about. It was about temptation. Every woman who ever saw Thrain Davis smile would wonder about the pleasure his mouth could give her, and from there go on to imagine what his mouth combined with the rest of him could accomplish. His intense blue gaze and sexy smile were an invitation that said, "Press any of my body's hot spots for sensational sex." Cindy allowed her glance to slide the length of him. Both her basic and higher-level instincts agreed that it would be fun to explore those hot spots.

Night Bites

NINA BANGS

LOVE SPELL NEW YORK CITY

LOVE SPELL®

March 2005

Published by

Dorchester Publishing Co., Inc.
200 Madison Avenue
New York, NY 10016

ISBN 0-505-52614-X

The name "Love Spell" and its logo are trademarks of Dorchester Publishing Co., Inc.

Printed in the United States of America.

Visit us on the web at www.dorchesterpub.com.

To Alicia Condon,

Thanks for taking that initial chance on an unpublished writer and a stranger-than-strange book. Since then, you've accepted each new idea, no matter how wild and wacky, with genuine enthusiasm. Ganymede, Sparkle, and I salute you.

Prologue

"There's nothing more sensual than a pile of fall leaves and the crisp bite of autumn in the air." Sparkle Stardust drew in a deep breath of October with its many erotic possibilities. "Fall is a sexy season." She climbed the wooden steps, paused beneath the porch light of the old Victorian inn, and turned to gaze at night shadows enveloping the New Jersey Pine Barrens.

"Phtt! Hiss!" The chubby gray cat she clutched to her chest was expressing his opinion.

"Hmm?" She glanced down at him. "You spoke, sweetie?"

"Every season is sexy to you. And there's nothing sensual about a pile of leaves or New Jersey. Now put me down." He wiggled in a vain attempt to leap from her arms. *"And I'm a verbal being. I have to be able to talk out loud. I hate this mental communication crap."*

She stroked his head. A warm, fuzzy moment. He was an entity with unspeakable powers, and yet he chose not to claw her when even a teensy scratch would make her drop him. Of course, if she were cynical, she might conclude that he just didn't want to be dropped. Mede was still working on the cats-always-land-on-their-feet thing. "Wrong. New Jersey is an erotic playground. I remember a time in Wildwood on the roller coaster—"

"Sweetie" stared at her in horror. *"You did it on a roller coaster? You're kidding, right?"*

"You have no imagination, Mede. Haven't you ever rolled around naked in a pile of leaves with a woman who was hot for you, and then had crazy sex as the leaves crunched and crackled under your sweat-slicked bodies?" Sparkle considered what she'd said. "In your human form, of course." She slid the tip of her tongue across her bottom lip as a particularly delicious memory touched her. "Preferably your golden-god human form."

"No. Rolling around naked in a pile of prickly and scratchy dead leaves isn't a turn-on. Now put me down. I need to be free and verbal." He wiggled some more.

"No can do, sweetie. The cat form is for heavy-duty snooping. It won't work if you don't stay in character. And I have to make sure no one hears me talking to you out loud." It was beneath her, but she felt gleeful triumph in adding, "You wouldn't let me talk when *I* was the cat." She tried to look righteous.

"Put. Me. Down." He glared up at her with angry amber eyes.

"Uh-uh." Sparkle smiled at him. Male anger was so . . . arousing. She didn't think that was the effect he was aiming for, however. "This is an inn, Mede. No cats running loose. It's either this or the carrier."

He narrowed his eyes to dangerous amber slits.

"Try to put me in a carrier and New Jersey will be nothing more than a dust cloud blowing across Pennsylvania."

Sparkle decided that maybe she'd pushed him as far as she should. "Okay, no carrier. So here's the deal: We go into the Woo Woo Inn and I tell them I'm a witch and you're my familiar." She could hear the sound of a car drawing closer.

"No." He watched with her as the car's headlights appeared around the last bend in the winding tree-lined driveway. *"You tell them exactly what we are. We're cosmic troublemakers and proud of it."*

Sparkle sighed. Mede could be so pigheaded. "No one will believe me. Witches are part of the culture. No one's ever heard of cosmic troublemakers."

"Your point is?" He looked exasperated. *"This is the Woo Woo Inn. Everyone here expects the weird and wacky. No one will care what we call ourselves."* He glanced up at Sparkle, and for the first time she saw humor in his cat eyes. *"And I'm not pigheaded."*

Sparkle couldn't help it; she smiled back. Mede could always do that to her, make her forget all the irritating little things he did. Of course, he could also do a lot of incredibly sensual things when he was in human form. And for Sparkle, sexy would always cancel out irritating.

Mede returned his attention to the driveway. *"That's Thrain parking his car. We need to make up fake names."*

"Fake names?" She frowned. Sparkle Stardust was who she *was*, and she couldn't conceive of another name having such panache. "It's been over two hundred years. Thrain won't remember our names."

"Hello? I'm Ganymede and you're Sparkle Stardust.

Trust me, he'll remember. We need dull, ordinary names." He narrowed his amber eyes, obviously having as much trouble as she was with the word "ordinary." *"Just call me Trojan while we're here."*

"Trojan? That's a condom brand." She bit her lip to keep from laughing. Mede hated anyone laughing at him.

He twitched his whiskers in irritation. *"It's a tough-guy name, and you'd think of sex no matter what name I picked."*

"I think I'll be Prada." Her absolute fave shoes.

"Prada? I never heard of anyone named Prada. Doesn't sound like an ordinary name to me." Now his whiskers *and* ears were twitching.

What a grouch. "Okay. Prada *Smith.* Is that ordinary enough for you?" She considered the situation for a moment. "And I'd suggest we completely immerse ourselves in our aliases, even when we're thinking. Thrain has enough power to slip past our thought barriers if we're careless."

Sparkle studied the man climbing from his car. "Even with our name changes, do you think he'll figure out who we are?"

"No way. The last time we met, you were a cat and I was in human form. Besides, that was back in seventeen eighty-five. It's two thousand five now."

Sparkle smiled. "You looked like Paul Bunyon."

He offered her an annoyed hiss. *"I looked like a powerful Scottish laird, and I don't have a clue why I invited you along on this job."*

"You invited me along because I bribed you, oh greedy one." She tried on a sweet smile. Okay, so sweet smiles weren't her thing. "I offered you a month of uninhibited sexual excess on an exotic island. Of course, you'll have to show up all buff and blond. Remember the last time we did this? What a yummy memory." She shivered to indicate how delicious it had been.

He chose not to comment on her yummy memory. *"Why'd you decide to come along this time?"*

Sparkle kept her attention on the man who had now pulled his travel bag from the trunk of his car. "For the same reason you're probably here. If this Cindy Harper is the person we think she is, I want to make sure Thrain does the wrong thing by her. Wrong as in sexually tempting and wicked." She glanced down at Mede and smiled. "Of course, all work and no play makes Sparkle a dull troublemaker, so I intend to create all kinds of erotic excitement in Ye Olde Woo Woo Inn."

Small travel bag in hand, the man strode toward them. Such a small bag for such a big man. *Big.* A word to conjure with. She loved the word big.

He climbed the porch steps, then paused in front of them. Sparkle had to look up a long way to meet his narrow-eyed gaze. She'd only seen two men with eyes that I'm-hot shade of blue. One of them was the man facing her, and the other was Darach Mackenzie. But Thrain wouldn't remember meeting her.

"Hi, I'm Thrain Davis. Do I know you?"

"Definitely not." Surprised, Sparkle felt him probing her mind. Her shield was in place so he'd find nothing, but the fact that he felt the need to probe was a red flag. She couldn't forget he was an immortal, too, and had survived by always being careful. "I'd certainly remember if I had." She offered him her sexiest smile, the one known to reduce grown men to whimpering lumps of throbbing testosterone. "I'm Prada Smith." She glanced down at Mede. "And this is Trojan."

Thrain smiled back at her, and Sparkle blinked. He hadn't been at his best the last time she'd seen him, so she hadn't realized the full extent of his sensual pull. Talk about a high-amp vamp. Vampires were sexual creatures by nature, but this one would take any woman's lust level to a new high.

"Great meeting you." He nodded at her, then pushed open the inn's door and went inside.

"Wow. What an erotic powerhouse. Did you feel it? Did you?" She glanced down at a glowering Mede.

"No." He glared at her.

"You're jealous." She smiled at him. "You have to know that no being is sexier than you are, sweetie. But Thrain is still special."

"Sweetie" looked a little mollified.

"I'm going to have soooo much fun here. Messing with the sexual lives of humans always gives me a buzz." She thought for a moment. "Of course, with so much talent, it would be a shame for me to limit myself to humans. I'm open to manipulating the sex lives of nonhuman entities as well."

Mede made a noise that sounded suspiciously like a groan. *"Did you pack lots of the pink stuff? I feel a tummy ache coming on."*

Chapter One

Cindy Harper had werewolf burnout. Six had checked in this week, and once a werewolf sat on your furniture, it took days to get the hair out. Why did it always have to be were*wolves?* Why not were-ducks, or werebunnies?

She stood near the front door, smile already in place and electronic organizer in hand, waiting for the last few guests to check in. She knew the organizer sort of clashed with the old-fashioned feel of the inn, but she couldn't help it. She was addicted to technology. Electronic gadgets were now, and her motto was always look forward, never look back. Looking back was useless. She hadn't found the answers she needed there.

Cindy couldn't wait to meet people who checked in after sunset. Guests who arrived at nightfall were usually the most interesting. They understood the game. Her inn only awoke when night mist crept from the surrounding forest and twined around the old inn like ghostly fingers. Travel guides always gave the Woo Woo Inn five stars for atmosphere.

"Uh, Cindy, could you tell me how to get to that cemetery you mentioned in your brochure? It's dark now, so I figure the spirits will be up and running soon." Her guest from the Dracula room offered Cindy a toothy grin showcasing his long, pointy canines.

Running *away*, if the spirits had any sense. Cindy always wondered what dentists thought when patients walked in and said, "I wanna be a vampire, Doc." She smiled at the mental picture. "No problem, Latrienne." Also known as Jim Kehoe on his American Express card. "Just take the path into the woods behind the inn. It's about a five-minute walk, and don't forget your flashlight."

He frowned. "Won't the light scare away the spirits?"

She shrugged. "It's an old graveyard, so I'm pretty sure the spirits are down with flashlights. Besides, lots of murderers, bank robbers, and worse are buried there. No wimps in that bunch."

"Worse? Oh." He swallowed hard. "I think I'll take my girlfriend along. She won't want to miss this." He scurried up the staircase, his black cape flapping as he went.

Cape? She needed to take him aside for some advice on the latest styles in vampire gear.

Cindy shook her head in wonder. Didn't these people know that none of this was real? Obviously not, because her inn was always full. With enough capital to indulge her sense of humor, she'd bought and renovated the old place, then dedicated it to all those who were fascinated by the strange and unexplained or who thought they *were* the strange and unexplained.

She'd named it the Woo Woo Inn in a moment of wild whimsy, then stepped back to see what happened. What happened was that she had a spectacular success on her hands.

During her six months in business it had been pretty easy to separate her guests into two categories—the delusional and the curious. A select few were genetic scientists she'd specifically invited to visit the inn in the hope that . . .

Her thoughts scattered as one of the final guests she'd been expecting walked in.

The impact of the man striding toward her made Cindy suck in her breath. She dealt with the weird, wacky, and wonderful on a daily basis, so she felt she was pretty much immune to anyone or anything that walked through the Woo Woo Inn's doors. But *this* man . . . It was as though every woman's darkest fantasy of the ultimate alpha male had suddenly materialized in her hallway.

She didn't need to burn any brain cells analyzing him. This was a man to be enjoyed on a strictly primitive level. Cindy let her basic instincts do their thing.

First impressions? Tall. Broad-shouldered. Long leather coat—unbuttoned. Jeans—buttoned. *Damn.* White shirt—mostly buttoned. *Double damn.* Of course, her basic instincts never spoke in complete sentences, so once her gaze wandered above his neck she had to move up a step in the evolutionary process to do justice to him.

Describing any other man, she'd simply say he had blond hair, but on this man blond didn't say it at all. Blond evoked images of all things soft and golden. No one in their right mind would describe him as soft or golden. The wind had whipped his hair into a long tangled glory lying across those incredible shoulders. Each strand was the sun rising over the icy North Sea, the swish of a longboat's prow cutting through the gray waves, the battle cries of sea-borne invaders. It was . . . Viking. He was a dark warrior no matter the color of his hair.

Dark warrior? Whoa. She was skating on the thin ice of purple prose when she usually just laid everything out in the fewest possible words. He had a great bod and sexy hair. That's all there was to it.

"You must be Cindy Harper." He stopped in front of her and offered his hand. "Thrain Davis."

His voice matched the rest of him, all husky and filled with dangerous, erotic traps for unwary women. And she definitely detected a touch of Scotland there, not so much in his choice of words, but in the cadence of them. Cindy shifted her Viking imagery to purple hills, shadowed glens, and sexy Highlanders.

"Hi." She automatically took the hand he offered but still kept her unblinking gaze on his face.

His eyes were a strangely brilliant shade of blue. Blue was an ambiguous color. It was a flame's superheated center and winter's coldest waters. She suspected he could be both.

Uh-oh. She'd just fallen through the ice.

"Welcome to the Woo Woo Inn." Her brain's welcome.

Oooh, yes! Pant, pant, pant. Woo-hoo, come and get

me, you big beautiful hottie. That welcome was from from the sluts who lived in her basement.

"Thanks." He smiled.

Even if a portal to Hell had opened at her feet, she wouldn't have felt more shocked. Sure, he had sensual lips and great teeth, but that's not what his smile was about. It was about temptation. Every woman who ever saw Thrain Davis smile would wonder about the pleasure his mouth could give her, and from there go on to imagine what his mouth combined with the rest of him could accomplish. His intense blue gaze and sexy smile were an invitation that said, "Press any of my body's hot spots for sensational sex." Cindy allowed her glance to slide the length of him. Both her basic and higher-level instincts agreed that it would be fun to explore those hot spots.

"I think you need to blink now." His smile widened.

Cindy blinked, then quickly dropped his hand. What had *that* been about? She'd learned when she was eighteen never to let a man's physical appearance affect her judgment, and she hadn't been eighteen for a very long time. But she tried to be honest with herself most of the time, and she couldn't deny that something about him touched all of *her* hot spots.

"You're a spectacular-looking man. I'm sure women all over the world have suffered dry eyeballs after meeting you." She smiled back at him.

It was his turn to blink. He was probably used to women playing coy around him. Well, she said what she thought. Within reason. She didn't think she'd share her hot spot fantasy with him.

" 'Spectacular-looking'? I don't think so." He

frowned, then raked his fingers through his hair. "At least, I hope not. I want to blend in with your other guests." He actually looked worried. "It's the hair, isn't it?"

Cindy thought about some of her other guests. No, he definitely wouldn't blend in. "It's the whole package." His response surprised her. Most men she'd known loved to have their egos stroked. "You mustn't look in a mirror often."

A smile tugged at the corners of his expressive mouth, and she had the feeling he was laughing at a private joke. "No, I don't. But you're wrong, Cindy. What you see now is the ordinary me. I save 'spectacular' for dark moonless nights."

Cindy felt a stab of disappointment. He must be just like most of her other guests, who liked to play at being something they weren't. She glanced at her organizer. For some reason, Hal hadn't entered any info next to Thrain's name. An oversight. "So are you a vampire, werewolf, demon . . . ?" She waited, ready to put in the details.

His soft chuckle mocked her. "None of the above. I'm only here to observe. Paranormal events fascinate me."

Cindy glanced up to meet his suddenly intent stare. Sheesh. She was back to the unable-to-blink thing. And she felt . . . different. She couldn't put her finger on it, but it was like something alien had touched her mind. Whatever it was slipped away before she could think about it. Probably just the beginning of a headache. She hadn't slept well today, and lack of sleep always gave her a headache.

"You don't believe any of this, do you?" Thrain swept his arm wide to encompass all that she didn't believe. "Why do you run this place if you don't believe in any of the paranormal stuff?" For some reason, he seemed really bent out of shape by his insight.

How had he known? She'd never talked about her personal beliefs with anyone. Cindy shrugged away what she couldn't explain. "I don't know what makes you think that, but I guess the truth is that I'm an observer like you. I'm open-minded, but I need proof before I believe anything." And proof was the one thing no one had ever offered.

But someday, someone might walk through the inn's door with all the answers to her questions, and she wanted to be here when it happened. "I opened the inn because I wanted to invest my money in a business, and this seemed like it would be fun." Not the only reason. *Definitely* not the only reason.

He latched on to just one part of her answer. "I think we're entirely different kinds of observers."

She sensed disappointment before he seemed to close off his emotions. His expression gave away nothing. Since she couldn't think of anything meaningful to say, Cindy simply shrugged.

"Are you really open-minded? Would you accept proof if it were standing in front of you?" He sounded sincerely interested in her answer, but his eyes remained neutral.

Now he was creeping her out. "Sure." Maybe. She shifted her attention to her organizer and carefully entered him as an interested observer. "I'll have someone carry your—"

"I can carry my own bag."

Cindy looked up from her organizer at his terse comment. Yep, she'd somehow managed to annoy him. Not a good beginning to his stay. She smiled in the hope that it would improve his mood. "Your choice. I'll have someone show you to your—"

"I can find my own room." He held out his hand for the key.

Now he was making *her* mad. She barely kept herself from slapping the key into his palm. "Fine. You're in the Incubus room. Second floor, turn right. Breakfast will be in a half hour, and then you have a choice of activities. The brochure in your room will give you the details." She forced some warmth into her voice. No matter how strange her guests acted, they were still paying for an enjoyable experience, and she'd play the happy hostess even if it killed her.

Cindy tried to look past him, but he stayed planted in front of her, his body blocking her view of the front door. Impatient, she looked up at him. "What?"

A sudden smile softened his mouth and actually reached his eyes. "You deserve some good memories. I do great memories."

Memories? What did memories have to do with anything? He left her staring after him as he strode past her, then climbed the stairs. Mmm. He looked just as wow going as he did coming. She smiled. What a totally sexual animal. Within that context, she understood the great memories thing perfectly.

Only when he was out of sight did she return her attention to the front door. What had just happened? Because *something* had definitely happened.

Okay, she wouldn't think about it now. At least there was one thing she knew for sure: No way could the last guest top Thrain Davis.

A woman pushed open the door and walked toward her. No, walked was the wrong word. This woman stalked with a sinuous sway that said sexual huntress loud and clear.

Cindy sighed. Fine, so the possibility existed.

She studied her last guest. Incidentals? Black leather pants. Black silk top. Waist-length black leather jacket. Cat cradled in one arm. Hmm. A witch? Maybe. A succubus? More likely. Whichever non- or semi-human entity this woman was playing, it would be convincing. Tall, with a body that should be labeled made-for-men, the woman had perfect features and the most arresting amber eyes Cindy had ever seen.

While Cindy was busy staring, the woman tossed back long, flame-colored hair and smiled at her. "I think my sister made a reservation for me."

Cindy glanced down at her organizer. "Right. A Ms. Stardust made the reservation, but she didn't give my assistant your name." How had that happened? She had to remind Hal to always get a name. Stardust? Did anyone really have a last name like Stardust?

"My sister's name is Sparkle Stardust. The Stardust family has a long and unique history." The woman's smile never wavered. "I'm Prada Smith."

Cindy frowned. Had she asked her Stardust question out loud? She didn't think so. Prada? Like the shoes? "Welcome to the Woo Woo Inn, Ms. Smith. I hope—"

"Call me Prada." She glanced down at the cat she held in her arms. "And this is Trojan."

For the first time, Cindy really looked at the cat. Big. Gray. Scary. *Scary?* Where had that thought come from? She reached out to pet the cat's head.

"Hey, kitty." Most cats would've watched her hand. Not Trojan. His unblinking amber gaze never left her face. "Is he like the Trojan Horse? Bring him in and bad things happen?" Cindy smiled just in case Prada didn't get that she was kidding.

Prada's answering smile was a sly lift of her lips. Not a comforting smile. "You know, I never thought of Trojan that way. I think you nailed it."

Nailed what? Cindy was confused. Oh, well, nothing new there. A lot of her guests confused her. Once again, she glanced down at her guest information. "Hal didn't make a note about whether you were a nonhuman entity or just someone interested in exploring the paranormal." Hal had a lot to answer for when he showed up tomorrow. He'd really dropped the ball with these last two reservations. Cindy slept during the day so she could stay awake at night when her guests were exploring the supernatural, so she needed someone responsible to take care of the inn then. Up to now, Hal had been fine.

"We're cosmic troublemakers. We generally raise hell wherever we go in the universe. I'm more specialized than Trojan. I provoke stimulating sexual situations that always end with climactic satisfaction. Trojan is more into chaos and destruction, although he's mellowed out a lot since the old days." She sighed as she gazed down at her cat. "Too bad. Mellow isn't half as exciting as ultimate evil."

"That's so fascinating." Not the cosmic troublemaker part; she'd dealt with weirdness before. But the stimulating sexual situations and climactic satisfaction parts were high concept. Personally, she hadn't experienced any climactic satisfaction lately. She was open to the possibility, though. She wondered about Thrain Davis's ability to deliver climactic satisfaction. *Don't go there now.*

Cindy studied her information. She had a category for every possible type of guest. None of the categories said cosmic troublemaker. She quickly entered CT into her organizer. Prada and Trojan would probably be the only ones to ever appear in that category.

"I'll get someone to bring in your bags and . . ." Cindy trailed off as Trojan hissed at her, then snarled at Prada.

Prada looked mildly amused. "Don't mind him. He's just telling me to cut the crap and get the key to our room."

She leaned toward Cindy as if to offer a confidential insight. Cindy wasn't sure she wanted to hear it.

"Typical male. Trojan's just ticked because he has to be the cat this time. But that's only fair. I was the cat last time. Don't you think it's fair?" She looked to Cindy for confirmation.

"Sure. Fair." Good grief. Where did the weirdness end?

Prada shrugged to indicate her bewilderment with the male mind. "He was a black cat once before, and it was an okay experience, so he wanted to be black again." She smiled at Trojan, and he lifted his lips from his teeth in a silent snarl. "I can understand the color thing, because black symbolizes all that we are."

She offered Cindy a playful grin. "Yeah, I admit I was feeling a little bitchy because he forced me to be a white cat last time out, which was so not me. White made my butt look huge. We fought about his color and finally decided to compromise between black and white."

"Gray." Cindy couldn't force her lips to form more than one word at a time. "Bags?"

Prada reached into the pocket of her coat, pulled out her car keys, and handed them to Cindy. "Black Porsche. License HOT. What room are we in?"

Cindy frowned as she stared at the CT she'd entered. She liked things tidy and organized, so the new cosmic troublemaker category hanging all by itself bothered her. She took a deep breath and found her voice. "I've put you in the Troll room. Hmm. After what you've told me, I think you might fit in the shape-shifter category." She liked to keep her entity groups organized so that she could plan activities specific to their interests. What could she plan for a CT group with only two members? She started to delete the CT.

"No." Prada touched her wrist with the tip of one long red fingernail, and Cindy felt as though her hand was frozen in place.

Cindy lifted her gaze from her organizer to meet the angry gazes of both Prada and Trojan. The combined force of their wills almost made her step back. No, that was impossible. She was letting Prada's nonsense mess with her mind.

"We're so much more than shape-shifters, sister. You put that CT right back in, because there's no one in your little organizer that belongs in our league." Prada smiled and removed her finger from Cindy's wrist.

"Sure. No problem." At least there wouldn't be as soon as she sent Prada off to her room. She beckoned to Tom, who had been hovering nearby. "Tom will take you to your room and then get your bags. I've left you an itinerary of interesting activities at the inn and places to go within a short walking distance. All of the inn's activities take place at night, so I recommend you sleep during the day." Cindy dredged up one more perky smile. "If you have any questions, I'm always here."

"The Troll room? How totally inappropriate." Prada's frown slowly changed to a thoughtful smile. "I've never known any trolls personally, but I've heard that their sexual equip—" She cocked her head toward Trojan as if she were listening. "He wants to know when we eat."

"Breakfast is in half an hour." Cindy didn't smile, perky or otherwise.

Prada nodded and followed Tom up the stairs. Sighing, Cindy headed down the hall to the back of the inn, where she had her apartment. She needed a couple of Advils to get her through the night. Even when you've lived over seven hundred years, you sometimes needed to pop a few pills to kill a headache.

Thrain still sat on the big four-poster bed long after he probably should have been downstairs meeting and mingling. He'd showered and changed his clothes, but none of that provided the inspiration he needed. He'd waited more than seven hundred years for this moment, and now he wasn't sure how to handle it.

During those years, he'd followed Cindy across continents, tracking her down each time she changed her identity, wondering if the woman he sought really was Darach Mackenzie's daughter.

Now he knew. Tonight was the first time he'd seen her face-to-face, and she'd looked at him with her father's eyes. Blue eyes that all in their clan shared. But her delicate face with that sexy, vulnerable-looking mouth was her mother's legacy.

Thrain didn't for a minute believe that Cindy Harper was any more vulnerable than her mother, Aesa, had been. He knew from bitter experience that beneath Aesa's seeming weakness had lain the icy determination of her Viking ancestors.

Did Cindy have any suspicions about him? Probably not. She'd been too focused on his "total package." Thrain smiled. He sought out only female vampires for pleasure, and they closed their minds to him. Cindy's mind was refreshingly open.

If she had the ability to root around among his thoughts, she might be interested to find that he thought her "total package" was pretty great, too. From her long black hair—another of her father's legacies—all the way down her curvy body, she was a complete sexual temptation.

A temptation he couldn't indulge. Because joining with her would awaken other, darker needs, and that would seem like another betrayal of Darach. He'd already betrayed his friend once when he'd helped a pregnant Aesa flee from Darach, her husband.

He exhaled sharply. Dredging up old hurts wouldn't get done what needed doing. Somehow, he had to convince Cindy she was the daughter of a powerful vampire. And he wanted to do it before Darach left the clan's ancestral home in Scotland. He had two weeks. It wouldn't be easy, considering the resistance he'd found in his brief probing of her mind.

So what should he say? "Let's take a look at your family tree, Cindy. A few of your branches have some real kinks in them. For example, on your father's side, you're part of a vampire clan with some unusual family traits. We're born human but become vampire somewhere around our thirtieth birthday. No need to panic, though, because we can't feed too often or we'll dilute the purity of our vampire blood and turn into mindless bloodlust-driven monsters that have to be hunted down and destroyed. I knew you'd want me to be straight with you about your heritage. Welcome to the clan." Sure, that would work.

You can make it easy. He had the power, and its siren call tempted him. Each of his clan developed the mental abilities he or she felt would be most useful. Haunted by his own memories, Thrain had honed his power to change the memories of others. If he chose, he could erase Cindy's memory of her real past and instead fill her mind with happy memories of a childhood spent with Darach, memories that didn't include disbelief in vampires.

But that wouldn't be right, and Darach wouldn't accept the gaining of a daughter through manipulation of her mind. Too bad, because Thrain thought it would probably be easiest on Cindy in the end. He allowed a bitter thought to intrude: He only wished he could change his own memories.

Standing, he went to the door and pulled it open. He glanced at the clock on his bedside table. Everyone should be finished with breakfast and gathered in the parlor for the nightly get-together mentioned in Cindy's brochure. They'd be sharing last night's experiences with each other.

He grinned as he walked down the stairs and headed toward the murmur of voices coming from the front of the inn. Something evil inside wanted him to stand up when it was his turn to speak and announce that he was a centuries-old vampire. And wow, was he hungry tonight. He *never* skipped breakfast.

But he'd control himself. Cindy wouldn't thank him for scaring all her guests.

When he reached the archway leading into the crowded room, he paused . . . then froze. Waves of power flowed over him, power that those in the room hadn't bothered to hide, because they hadn't been expecting him, and because they'd been busy trying to impress each other.

Thrain stood under the archway and watched unease register on many of the faces in the room. They didn't know him or how much power he had, only that he was nonhuman like they were. And those who moved silently around the edges of humanity learned early that a healthy dose of suspicion was the key to a long life.

But there was one in the room who *wasn't* uneasy, one who had power equal to his. Thrain's enhanced senses felt the subtle throb of energy and knew the others didn't have the capability to even realize what was in the room with them.

Thrain knew. He scanned the faces turned toward him and tried to isolate the source of all that power. Puzzled, he studied each face in turn. He paused when he reached the darkened corner farthest from the fire.

Four night feeders stared back at him from the shadows. Thrain frowned. What were they doing here? A loosely knit group of the most vicious vampires, night feeders lived only to hunt and kill. Individually, they didn't have impressive powers, so they traveled in packs in order to bring down their prey. They hated Thrain's clan but weren't powerful enough to do much about it. Their presence didn't bode well for any humans in the area. He'd have to keep an eye on them.

But he still hadn't found the powerful entity he knew was somewhere in the room. Puzzled, he continued his scan. *None of them.* Prada Smith offered him a smile and a little finger wave.

Where the hell was the source? It had to be someone in this . . . His gaze dropped to the large gray cat in Prada's lap. The cat stared back at him from enigmatic amber eyes.

The cat. What had Prada called him? Trojan. Who would've guessed? Thrain smiled as he attempted to slide into the animal's mind. He stopped smiling as the cat rejected his attempt with the force of a body slam. Thrain narrowed his gaze. He didn't know what the cat was, but he intended to find out. Nothing would interfere with what he'd spent seven centuries working toward.

Someone touched his arm. *Cindy.* He didn't need to look to know she stood beside him. His senses recognized her—the faint scent of lavender, the soft sound of her breathing, the warmth of her fingers on his skin. *And the strong beating of her heart.* At the thought, something dark, primitive, and needy pushed everything else aside. *No,* he wouldn't let his entwined hungers for sex and nourishment sidetrack him now.

Turning his head, he met her gaze, then let his glance skim the length of her body. Dressed in worn jeans that hugged the curve of her hips and molded slim legs that went on forever, she called to the elemental male in him. Her red top clung to her full breasts, and he swallowed the low growl forming in his throat. The others in the room were a study in black. He guessed they figured that black was cool for creatures of the night. Well, he was one creature of the night who was turned on by sexy red tops.

"Hey, everyone. Listen up." She removed her fingers from his arm and stepped into the center of the room. "We have another new guest in the Woo Woo Inn." She turned to smile at him. "I'd like you to meet Thrain Davis. He's here as an interested observer, and I'm sure he'd like to join some of our discussion groups on the paranormal. I know you'll make him welcome."

The humans in the room called out greetings. Those who were not human simply stared. Prada obviously didn't feel threatened by him. She blew him a kiss. Trojan shifted his unblinking stare from Thrain to Prada. He snarled.

Interesting. Jealousy? Thrain stored that thought away for future use.

"Come in and have a seat." Cindy chose a large overstuffed couch near the blazing fireplace and sat down between an old man wearing a tweed jacket and a woman who watched Thrain from pale, predatory eyes. "Before we break up for our night's activities, we always report anything interesting that happened the night before."

Thrain smiled grimly as he purposely chose Prada's couch. He squeezed himself in between Prada and a sallow, balding man who looked like an ordinary mid-management type. Thrain knew he was much more than that.

An angry hiss drew his attention to Trojan. The cat stared balefully back at him. Thrain's smile widened. He opened his mind and spoke to the cat. *"You'll need to express yourself in more than hisses and growls if you want me to understand you."*

Trojan looked ready to burst with his need to *express himself*, but he evidently chose to remain silent. Thrain mentally shrugged away the mystery that was Trojan in favor of more important things.

Like Cindy's choice of a seat. She'd wedged herself between the old man and the woman so that Thrain couldn't sit next to her. Interesting. He made her nervous. And even though her nervousness wouldn't help his cause, it made him feel good on a purely male level.

"Okay, who wants to start?"

Cindy sounded bright and cheerful, but Thrain didn't miss the crease between her eyes. A headache? He might be able to help with that.

"I'll go first." A man sitting in one of the wing chairs stood. His round face and stomach were testaments to good living. "After our run last night, all of us werewolves were sitting around arguing about which of our forms was the more dangerous—pure wolf or semi-human." He rocked back on his heels, a study in self-importance. "We finally agreed that the semi-human form was more dangerous. Like, it's bigger and has the benefit of human intelligence."

Thrain glanced at the pale-eyed woman. Her gaze was coldly expressionless, but the slight curl of her upper lip could be interpreted as either amusement or a snarl. It didn't look as if she intended to stand up for her pack in front of this stupid human and his friends, who were giving a bad name to all werewolves.

Thrain decided someone should set this guy straight. He relaxed against the cushions and stretched his legs out in front of him. "That's not true." Surprised, the man turned toward him. "Nothing is more deadly than the pure wolf form. It hunts its prey with preternatural speed, cunning, and savagery."

The man narrowed his gaze, making his dark, bushy brows almost meet. "What do you know about it?"

Thrain drew in a deep breath. *Remember, you're trying to blend in here.* "Right. What do I know about it?"

Mollified, the man sat down.

"That was really interesting, Clark. And thanks, Thrain, for your input." Cindy was looking a little harried, and the crease between her eyes was growing more pronounced. "Oh, Clark, when you and the guys are just lying around on the furniture after your runs, would you watch the shedding?" She smiled at the man. "Maybe you could change before you come inside."

Clark looked confused. "But then we'd be naked."

Thrain could tell from Cindy's alarmed expression that she was getting the same visual of a naked Clark as he was.

"Anyone else?" Her lips still smiled, but her eyes said she hoped everyone would shut up so she could nurse her aching head.

"Me, me." A thin woman in her twenties waved her hand in the air, then jumped to her feet. "Last night was a full moon, and you all know that vampires just love to hunt by a full moon. Anyway, I

changed into bat form and spent the night hunting."
She frowned. "I had to fly a long way to find a few
cows, but I never feed from humans." Her expression turned militant. "Vampires should *never* feed
from humans. I belong to the Vampires Against Human Blood Consumption Association, and we're going to initiate legislation to—"

Now it was Thrain's turn to curl his lip. *Cow's
blood?* He couldn't listen to one more second of this
nonsense. He forgot about keeping a low profile.
"That's garbage. Why would a vampire ever take the
form of a bat? Give me a break. Shape-shifting is
tough, so if you're going to go to all that trouble, at
least make it worthwhile. Take the form of a large
predatory bird if you want to fly, and if not, go the
large carnivore route. And about the cow's blood . . ."
Odin's beard! What was he saying?

He glanced at Cindy's startled expression and the
rapt interest of the rest of the guests. His youth spent
as a Viking and later years as a Highlander
should've taught him that he who speaks the loudest
often dies first. Why couldn't he remember that?
Life in this modern age had softened his brain cells.
"Never mind." He hated having to guard what he
said, but over the centuries he'd seen too many immortals destroyed because they couldn't keep their
mouths shut.

Some of the other humans stood up and reported
their experiences, but Thrain purposely tuned them
out. He didn't want to hear anything that would
compel him to speak out in defense of the truth. He
noted that all the nonhuman guests sat quietly and
offered nothing. Smart. If he'd followed their lead,
Cindy wouldn't be looking at him the way she was.

Her gaze was a mixture of amusement and disbelief. And that made him mad. She was more than seven hundred years old and yet she dismissed even the possibility that any of her guests could be from the nonhuman realm. She thought the whole thing was funny. What was her problem?

The man next to him leaned over. "You need to vent, pal. I'm going hunting, but not for cow's blood. Want to come along?"

Thrain took a deep calming breath. "Thanks, but not tonight." The vampire was not from his clan, but that wouldn't have mattered if Thrain didn't want to stick around for a few words with Cindy the nonbeliever. "I fed last night, so I won't need to hunt again for a few weeks."

The vampire raised one brow. "That old, huh? I figured as much." He smiled, then stood. "Anyway, I'm Stan. I'll be here till the end of the week. The two others of our kind always hunt together. You know, young love and all that stuff. They can't be more than a hundred years old." He glanced at the night feeders and grimaced. "I don't count them as any of our kind."

Thrain watched Stan leave and then glanced at Prada, who still sat beside him. "What's your cat when he's not busy being a cat, and why are you here?"

"Mmm. I love a man who's direct. It's an incredibly sensual alpha male characteristic." She smiled at him, a completely sexual smile. "And we're here for the same reason all the nonhuman beings are here. It's a sanctuary where we can relax and be ourselves without fear of discovery. The humans are so far out there that they make us seem normal." She glanced down at Trojan, who was obviously one pissed kitty. "And if Trojan wants you to know what he is, I'm sure he'll tell you himself."

She wasn't going to reveal anything else right now, so Thrain nodded before standing and going in search of Cindy.

He found her sending the happy pack of fake werewolves off to howl at the moon. Right behind the werewolves was the phony vampire with her two equally phony female friends. All of them were dressed in black from head to toe. All of them ignored him. Good.

Finally, Cindy closed the door on the last of the night's adventurers. He heard her relieved sigh and watched her shoulders slump.

"I sure hope we're a few miles away from any town, because most of the bunch that just left are certifiable." He purposely stood close so his arm brushed her shoulder for the pure pleasure of watching her edge away from him.

Cindy turned her head to study him. "I don't get it. You sounded really passionate about the whole myth thing back in there, and yet you're saying they're all crazy." She still had the crease between her eyes.

For a moment he felt guilty about fueling her headache. His guilt fled when he thought about her deliberate denial of what she was. "The ones who just left are children playing at being grown-ups. But there are some here with real power. Oh, and be careful of the four who were sitting together back in the corner. They're dangerous." He leaned closer as she leaned away from him. "Don't you feel the power of the beings who're here, Cindy? Or don't you *want* to feel them?"

She eyed him warily out of huge blue eyes. Thrain tried to ignore the instinctive tightening of his body as he watched her swallow hard. His enhanced senses duly recorded the hot flow of life just beneath the smooth skin of her neck, and he suspected that placing his mouth against the warm flesh of her throat would bring incredible pleasure. After so many centuries of life, she'd taste like sweet aged wine. Luckily, his enhanced brain cells overruled his senses. He was making her nervous right now, and he'd guess that if he leaned down and slid his tongue across her throat, his senses would be duly recording intense pain in a particularly aroused organ.

Over the centuries, he'd thought that finding her would be the hardest part. After meeting her, he wasn't sure.

She lifted her chin and offered him what she probably thought was a fierce glare. It would've been more effective if she reached higher than his shoulders.

"I don't know what you are, Thrain Davis, but you're not the impartial observer you said you were." Her hard stare dared him to contradict her. "I don't know who you are."

Ah, but I know who you are, Elina Mackenzie.

Chapter Two

"So, what do you think of the Woo Woo Inn?" Cindy held Thrain's gaze while she shamelessly changed the subject. She wouldn't use her headache as an excuse for what she'd just said to him. It was none of her business what he believed or didn't believe.

"I think you have a bunch of idiots running around outside in the dark along with some very powerful entities. That's a situation made for disaster."

He dropped his gaze to her lips, and it was as though he'd touched them with his fingertips. The sensation was too real, too intense to be comfortable. Right now, her reaction to him seemed merely another part of tonight's general weirdness. Uneasy, she edged away from him.

"And I never said I was impartial, only interested." The corners of his mouth tipped up, acknowledging her attempt to distance herself from him. But his eyes promised that she would not succeed.

Okay, pull it together. She was getting way too analytical about a great-looking guy who happened to have some strange beliefs. Without people like Thrain, her business wouldn't be booming. Time to go in a different direction. "Maybe I'm wrong, but I think I hear a ghost of Scotland in your voice." She still didn't understand why she thought that, because on the surface his speech was pure USA. "Did you ever live in Scotland?" *Hint, hint. Tell me something about your life so I can move you from my strange-and-unusual column into my ordinary guy one.* Fine, so he'd never make it as an ordinary guy.

"Very perceptive." His eyes gleamed with amusement he didn't try to hide. "I left Scotland when I was young and I never went back. I thought nothing of the Highlands remained in me."

Cindy felt really good about that tidbit of information. At least she now knew he hadn't sprung full-grown from some demon's lair. But as much as she wanted to keep digging, duty called. "I have to start my rounds of the discussion groups. Why don't you tag along? Maybe you'll find a subject that interests you." Once he was settled with one of the groups, she could close her eyes and relax for a moment, maybe get rid of her lingering headache. She turned toward the parlor.

"I've already found a subject that interests me." His soft murmur stopped her as effectively as the hand he put on her shoulder. "Sit."

Surprised, she sank onto the straight-backed chair placed by the small hallway table. Her instant obedience had more to do with the shock of his touch than his one-word order.

What she'd felt when he put his hand on her shoulder went beyond sexual awareness, and heaven knew she'd recognized that feeling from the first moment he stood in her hallway. It was the impression of his hand on her bare flesh when he'd only touched the material of her top, the instant sensation of heat and hunger that didn't seem to originate from her but *had* to come from her unless the headache was making her a little crazy.

"You have a headache." Thrain moved behind her chair. "Let me help you." He placed his fingers on each side of her head. "Relax."

Sure. Relax. Like she could possibly relax with his hands on any part of her body. "How did you know I have a headache?"

His soft laughter seemed to stimulate all of her senses. Could you taste the flavor of dark amusement, feel it touching your emotions, see it in your mind's eye? Probably not. But whatever his laughter was or wasn't doing, she was sure his touch would *never* relax her.

"You have a crease the size of the Grand Canyon between your eyes." He started a slow massaging of the sides of her head then moved on to her forehead.

Against her will, Cindy felt her eyes drift shut. She would not relax. She would *not* relax. She relaxed.

Somewhere in a dusty corner of her mind, her instinct was jumping up and down, waving madly, and shouting words like *careful*, *alert*, and *dangerous*. But her instinct couldn't compete with whatever magic he wielded through his fingertips. Her whole body seemed to be collapsing into itself, every part of her growing pliant and loose.

"What do you know about your mother's family, Cindy?"

He must be leaning over her because she could

feel his words ruffling her hair, moving inside her head, compelling her to answer. Something about the compulsion seemed wrong, but she was too relaxed to think about it now.

"Not much. My parents never talked about Mom's life before she married Dad. We lived in England when I was a child, but I knew Mom wasn't born there." She frowned, trying to retrace those many years, those many *centuries*. "My mother never came out and told me, but I got the impression she had a Norse heritage. I don't remember why I thought that. Probably because of the way she spoke."

And because of Loki. Mom had once told her about Loki the Trickster, the Norse god who caused the other gods so much trouble. Mom had actually looked happy while she spun her tales of Loki. And for one of the few times in Cindy's life, she felt that her mother was sharing a piece of her past with her daughter. So when Mom had given her a young injured raven, she'd named him Loki.

Cindy smiled at the memory. Like the legend that said at least six ravens must remain at the Tower of London or both the Tower and the monarchy would fall, Cindy believed she must have a Loki in her life to give it some kind of continuity.

She believed that for a hundred years. During that time she had four Lokis. Each time one would grow old and die, she would get another to take his place, all the time trying to fool herself into believing they were one and the same because they all bore the same name.

Finally, when she couldn't take the sadness of burying yet another Loki, another friend who reminded her everyone and everything she cared about eventually disappeared, she simply hadn't replaced him. She'd never had a pet since.

"What about your father?" His fingers continued their magic, bringing a sensation of energy threading along the paths of pain in her head, drawing out the discomfort along with her tension.

"Strange, but I don't remember much about him. He took care of the stables at the manor of some bigwig with a long title in England." She shrugged, and the effort was almost too much for her. "We were never close." Something about the way Thrain was touching her head seemed to demand she tell more. "He wasn't my real father. I don't know who my real father was. Mom never talked about him."

"Do you ever wonder about your real father?" His fingers stilled for a moment, as though her answer was important to him. Of course it wasn't; there was no reason it should be.

Don't stop. Don't ever stop. His touch on her head was a soothing flow of inhibition releasers. She frowned. How stupid was that thought? Releasing her inhibitions around a man like Thrain Davis would be like walking down a dark alley at midnight waving hundred-dollar bills.

She sensed his amusement, mocking her words even as his fingers once again began their wonderful rhythmic stroking of her head. Okay, she had to stay semicoherent here. First, he couldn't be mocking her words because she hadn't said anything out loud. Second, no way could she *sense* his amusement. No empaths in her family history. But then again, what did she know about her family history? She was living proof there'd been some strange skeletons in her family's closet.

Cindy tried to force her lethargic mind to find some kind of reason for all she'd felt since Thrain had walked through the inn's door, but the effort was too much. She'd think about it later.

"You haven't answered my question." He must have leaned closer, because his warm breath moved across her cheek. "Do you want to know more about your real father?"

The tiny suspicious corner of her brain that hadn't melted into a relaxed puddle of goo ordered her to shut her mouth. She didn't discuss her family with *anyone*.

Oh, why not? Her headache was gone, and she felt right with the universe. She would beat herself up later over her security lapse. "Not really. Mom only mentioned him to me once. They were planning to marry when she found out she was pregnant. He abandoned her, and her family disowned her because of the disgrace. Why would I want to know about that kind of a jerk?"

"Why indeed, Elina?" His response was a bare whisper of sound.

The name she thought he'd uttered ripped apart her woolly euphoria. She turned to look at him as his hands fell away from her. "What did you call me?"

His smile was exactly the right mix of innocent puzzlement and relaxed calm. "I didn't call you anything. What did you think I called you?"

She shook her head to clear away the fuzzies. At least now it didn't feel like there was a bowling ball rolling around in her head when she moved it. And he probably hadn't said a thing. Talking about the past must have conjured the name from the dark recesses of her memory.

"Never mind." She stood, then touched her head. "Thanks. I know who to go to with my next tension headache."

"I can ease all kinds of aches." He paused to slide his gaze the length of her body. "In all kinds of places." His eyes gleamed with sexual intent just in case she misunderstood his message.

Message received. Cindy sucked in a deep, fortifying breath. Her body absolutely thrummed with a need to experiment. What would his fingers do to the ache pooling low and hot in her belly?

She blinked and backed away from him. Whoa, this was too fast and entirely too weird. "I'll keep that in mind." How to escape without looking as if she was fleeing from the devil? And why did she even feel the need to run away? Men had hit on her before without exciting this kind of reaction.

Cindy had no more time to mull over whether he was sexual evil incarnate before Latrienne slammed open the front door and barreled into her. She fell against the immovable wall that was Thrain Davis. He wrapped his arms around her to steady her, and his deep laughter vibrated to all the interesting places vibrations could reach.

"I saw it. Ohmigod, I saw it!" Latrienne bounced up and down like a demented kangaroo. "I saw the Jersey Devil." His cape flapped with every hop, and the powder he'd used to make himself vampire pale ran down his face with his sweat.

"Calm down. Sit here." She guided him to the seat she'd just vacated, and he collapsed onto it. "Would you—" She turned to Thrain and found him holding the glass of water she'd been about to request. She gave only a passing thought to how he'd known what she would ask for and how he'd gotten it so fast.

She handed it to Latrienne. "Okay, tell us what happened."

He held the glass in shaking hands and stared up at her with terrified eyes. His face was flushed and he was still breathing hard. "It came at me while I was looking at one of the tombstones in the old cemetery. It just swooped out of the sky."

Cindy did some mental eye-rolls. People came to the Woo Woo Inn primed to see supernatural beings, so in the dark a stray dog became a werewolf, an owl became a vampire, and something as simple as a piece of white paper caught in a tree branch became a ghost. She'd heard it all, and even though she didn't like to see guests frightened, this was the kind of tale that would bring tons of new guests to the inn. People loved to be scared.

"Feel like describing what you saw?" She offered him what she hoped was a soothing smile as he gulped down the water and then handed the glass back to her.

Latrienne nodded and sucked in a deep breath of courage. "It was about ten feet tall and it had a head that was sort of the shape of a horse's head. But when it opened its mouth, it had long, pointy teeth instead of a horse's teeth." He gazed past Cindy, obviously seeing the creature in his mind's eye. "It had a long, thin neck, and it stood on its hind legs. Its front legs were small, kind of like a T-Rex's, and it had huge bat wings and cloven hooves."

He bit his bottom lip and narrowed his eyes as though trying to dredge up any important details he might have left out. "Its eyes glowed, it looked really pissed off, and I think you need to find Patty."

"Patty?" Cindy and Thrain spoke in unison.

Latrienne nodded. "My girlfriend. She's still out there."

"Why?" Cindy could hardly get the word past her shock.

"She can't run as fast as me." He blinked as he seemed to think about how that sounded. "I mean, the fastest person had to run for help. We didn't have a gun or anything to protect ourselves."

Thrain's hiss of anger said it for Cindy, too. Latrienne glanced at Thrain and seemed to shrivel inside his black cape. "Look, I'd go back out there with you, but I'm done in, man." He struggled to his feet and then scuttled up the stairs. Didn't look too done in to Cindy.

"If *Latrine* were a true vampire, I would've separated his head from his shoulders for leaving his mate unprotected." Thrain's expression said he was considering expanding his head-separating routine to fake vampires.

Even among all the jumbled experiences tonight had brought, something about Thrain's words bothered Cindy. His speech pattern had changed, become more in tune with a past time. And who in heaven's name called a girlfriend his *mate*? It was one more thought to put aside and take out later when she had time to put everything into perspective. Right now, she had a missing guest.

"You pronounced his name wrong. It's Latrienne. And I have to find his girlfriend. It doesn't take much to get lost in these woods if you wander off a path." She didn't for a minute think they'd met the Jersey Devil. The Devil was a legend born of overactive imaginations and mass hysteria. The last rash of sightings had been back in 1909, and even though a cameo appearance would be good for business, Cindy doubted the couple had seen anything more demonic than an old tree trunk or a sandhill crane. The night darkness played tricks with people's eyes.

Thrain's expression was grim. "A latrine is a toilet. Latrine suits him." He turned toward the stairs. "Wait while I get my weapon and I'll go with you."

Weapon? What kind of weapon? And why had he brought it into her inn? The thought of a guest with a gun was way more disturbing than a possible Jersey Devil sighting. She kept a small handgun for protection, but she didn't take it with her when she was looking for a lost guest. There weren't any dangerous predators in the Pine Barrens.

Maybe there was now. Fear touched her for the first time. What did she really know about Thrain Davis except that he was a super-heated nova in her sexual universe? She ran to her apartment, threw on her jacket, and put her cell phone in one pocket. Then, reluctantly, she fished the small gun from her kitchen drawer and shoved it in the other jacket pocket. Maybe she was overreacting, but she hadn't survived so many centuries by being careless. On her way out the door she grabbed her flashlight.

By the time she got back to the hallway, Thrain was waiting for her. He'd also taken time to put on the leather coat he'd worn earlier. She did a quick body scan. No semiautomatics sticking out anywhere. She should leave well enough alone, but her curiosity wouldn't be denied. "Do you have your weapon?" Too late, she remembered that curiosity was known to kill cats and innkeepers with big mouths.

Don't say it. She won't think it's funny. He said it anyway. "Which weapon? You'll have to be specific."

With a small huff of annoyance, she turned from him to reach for the door. He got there before her and held it open. She strode past without even glancing at him, but he slipped into her thoughts as she paused on the porch. He knew his smile must be all hungry predator, because his sexual innuendo hadn't flown right past her. She was thinking about it. So was he.

Turning on her flashlight, she led him down a wooded path. Every few minutes, she'd shout Patty's name. The sound echoed in the darkness as wisps of mist twined around the black silhouettes of trees. He noticed a strange absence of normal night noises. Other than the crunch of dead leaves beneath their feet, all he could hear was a distant chorus of shaky, high-pitched howls.

"That isn't . . . ?" The howls skittered along his nerves like dozens of fingernails scraping across a chalkboard. There were times when his enhanced hearing wasn't a plus.

Thrain caught the brief flash of her smile. "Yep, that's our pack of bloodthirsty werewolves serenading the moon. The fact that they can't see the moon tonight is an unimportant detail."

He didn't have to read her mind, because he could feel the question she wanted to ask him. If he asked one first, she might feel free to ask hers. "What do you think happened to Patty? Even if she sat down to take a breather, we should've met her by now." *Ask me, and always know that I'll tell you the truth.*

41

Well, maybe not right away. If he told her now that her dad was an ancient vampire and that he was her dad's best buddy, she'd probably laugh at him or go ballistic. But soon, very soon, she'd believe.

"If she was scared, Patty might've run off the path. By the time she stopped running, she'd be lost. If we don't come across her in a few minutes, we'll find our friendly werewolf pack to see if they saw her. Patty might even be back at the inn by now." She cast him a sideways glance. "Why are you carrying a gun? What did you think you'd find here that would warrant that kind of weapon?" She didn't turn to look at him as she kept her flashlight focused on the trail in front of her.

He frowned. She was uneasy with him because of his weapon. She didn't realize that something as puny as a gun was a zero on the danger scale compared to the power wielded by some of her guests.

"I don't have a gun." Something niggled at his senses, something nearby that was deliberately trying to cloak its presence. "But you do. Why?"

Startled, she glanced at him before returning her attention to the trail. "How did you know that?"

"You have a bulge in each pocket. It makes sense that one of the bulges is a phone, and you're holding your flashlight. Considering that you're afraid of me because you think I'm carrying a gun, I figure the other bulge must be your own gun." The thing he sensed was behind them and drawing closer. Even cloaked, the entity's power touched him.

"You're right." She sounded matter-of-fact. "I don't think there's any supernatural evil prowling these woods, but I definitely believe in human evil. I wasn't about to take a chance being alone with a stranger carrying a gun. What do you have, pepper spray or something like that?"

"Something like that." If whatever was following them got any closer, she'd find out exactly what he carried. "Don't the people in the area complain about the howling and your guests running through the woods?"

She shrugged. "We don't have any close neighbors, and the nearest town is five miles down the road. I was lucky to find this place. There's an old deserted church close to the cemetery and a few abandoned estates nearby that I've hinted are haunted. Everybody loves this place. It's the creepiest."

And about to get creepier. Whatever was stalking them had just invaded his personal space. The entity must feel pretty confident; it wasn't bothering to cloak its power anymore. From the sheer force of its energy flow, Thrain suspected what he'd see even as he spun in one motion and pushed aside his coat to draw the sword sheathed at his left hip.

Cindy's frightened yelp echoed in the thickening mist as Thrain stood with his sword poised, staring down at Trojan.

"A sword?" Cindy's voice was a horrified squeak. "You brought a sword with you? Hello? Do you see any dragons that need slaying, St. George? I don't think so." Cindy took a deep breath and fired another salvo. "I mean, what's wrong with a little container of pepper spray?" She glanced down at the cat. "And why is Prada's cat following us?"

Good question. Even as he'd guessed what followed them, Thrain recognized that the cat posed no

43

threat. At least not now. He felt no aggression from Trojan. Thrain's sword was a nonverbal warning to whatever entity hid behind the cat's form.

Thrain knew he shouldn't smile, knew that it would just tick her off more, but he couldn't help it. Cindy was cute when she was steamed.

She stood with legs spread, one hand on her hip, glaring at him with narrow-eyed intensity. "I don't get it. No one carries a sword around. Okay, I take that back. The first month that the inn was open I had a guest who thought he was the second coming of the Highlander. I hated the idea of your having a gun, but at least a gun makes sense. What can a sword do that a gun can't do better?"

"It can separate a head from a body."

"Oh." She swallowed hard.

He'd finally managed to strike her speechless. "Bullets wouldn't do much harm to some of your guests, but even they'd have trouble hot-gluing their heads back to their bodies." Thrain shrugged. "Besides, it's the weapon I've always used."

"Sure. It's a great weapon. How about putting it away?"

He felt her withdrawal and knew she'd mentally put him in the same category as her off-key werewolves. Too bad, because if seeing his sword rattled her cage, she was in for a long, hard journey to self-discovery.

He slid the sword back into its scabbard. "Let's get moving. If we haven't found Patty in a few minutes, you might want to call back to the inn for help." Thrain didn't think any of the inn's nonhuman visitors would take a chance on destroying their nice, safe haven by hurting a human guest, but with the four night feeders in residence, you never could tell.

"Right." She raked her hair away from her face, and he didn't miss the slight tremor of her fingers. "What about Trojan? Shouldn't we—"

She got no further, because suddenly a woman stumbled into view. Thrain decided that this must be the elusive Patty. Other than wearing half the pine needles in the forest and looking a little wild-eyed, she seemed okay.

"Oh, God, I thought I'd never find anyone." The woman stopped in front of Cindy and stood breathing hard. "Can you believe that jerk ran away with our only flashlight and left me to be eaten by the monster?"

Ah, the jerk. Also known as the intrepid Latrine. Thrain made believe he didn't see Cindy's pointed glare promising that really bad things would happen to him if he laughed. "Did the . . . monster follow you?" He forgot about laughing as he noticed the swelling on Patty's forehead. "What happened to your head?"

The woman winced as she touched it. "I was looking behind me to see if it was coming after us and I ran into a tree. I fell down and couldn't get up for a few minutes because the dumb tree knocked me silly. Jim didn't even look back to see what happened to me. When I finally got up, I must've still been woozy because I lost the trail. I was getting really scared when I saw your flashlight." Energized by the telling of her story, she shook some of the pine needles off, then lifted her lips in a vicious snarl. "Let's get on back to the inn so I can wrap that stupid cape

45

around Jim's chicken neck and watch his face turn purple."

Thrain decided watching Patty wring the life from Jim-the-jerk would probably be the most fun he'd have that night. Or maybe not. He riveted his gaze on the sway of Cindy's round little behind as she started back toward the inn with Patty beside her. As a reward for all he'd endured tonight, he allowed the sexual hunger he'd held tightly reined loose for a moment to play in the darkness. Unfortunately, it brought a friend.

He felt the slide of his fangs preceding a hunger that was not only about nourishment. It was part sensual pleasure, a total feeding of the senses, and now that it was loose it didn't want to say good night.

"Not now, bloodsucker. Get rid of the fangs. Think about something gross—worms, rats, tuna casserole." The male voice in his head surprised Thrain, but it wasn't totally unexpected. Thrain had figured that Trojan wouldn't be able to keep his thoughts to himself forever.

Thrain glanced down at the cat padding along beside him and then at the two women walking ahead of him. Cindy and Patty weren't close enough to hear his conversation. "Well, well. I guess playing the strong, silent guy gets tough after a while."

But Trojan was right. No more self-indulgence tonight. He couldn't afford to have Cindy turn around and see his vampire form. She wasn't ready yet. Would she ever be ready? He firmed his resolve even as he willed his return to human form. He had to help her accept who she was, who her father was. Thrain owed Darach that much.

"So why don't you tell me who you are? I got that you're deep undercover, so that's why your lips are sealed."

The cat stared up at him, its amber eyes eerily brilliant against the gray backdrop of the mist, the darkness, and its own body. *"Hey, I'm nothing special, just your ordinary demon out for some fun with his lady."*

"That's a bunch of crap. I've known all kinds of demons, and none of them came close to having your power." What was it about Trojan's voice? Had he ever heard it before? No way of telling. After more than seven hundred years of life, it was hard to remember individual voices. "Are you sure I don't know you and Prada?"

He would've sworn the cat's eyes widened in alarm.

"Nope. Absolutely not. Never saw you before." Trojan broke eye contact to glance back the way they had come. *"Do you feel something?"*

They both stopped walking. Thrain watched Cindy and Patty disappear around a curve in the path and then turned to look behind him.

Suddenly, the darkness shimmered with energy like the static electricity preceding a storm. Thrain had lived long enough to recognize something powerful coming, and he'd bet that whatever it was didn't have a friendly chat in mind.

"Pick me up. I'll merge my power with yours." Trojan's gruff and grouchy house cat persona was gone, and in its place was pure, cold intelligence.

Thrain scooped Trojan into his arms as the shimmer became waves of fury that battered at his mind, tempting him to raise all his psychic shields in defense. But he needed to project strength now, and he wouldn't achieve that by going into a defensive mode. Trojan and he were the only things standing between whatever was coming and the two women.

Suddenly, he *felt* Trojan, his immense power flowing over Thrain, *into him*. Thrain almost staggered as he attempted to not only focus his own power but also control the incredible energy of the being that was Trojan. Intuitively, he knew the part of Trojan he now held within himself was thousands of years old. Maybe he should be more afraid of Trojan than whatever unknown was almost upon them. But whatever happened, they could now attack with one overwhelming force instead of two separate and less powerful ones.

The air around them surged and exploded with wind and sound. Tops of trees whipped back and forth even as shrieks pitched so high that no human could hear them made Thrain want to cover his ears. He'd just bet that dogs for miles around were in a frenzy right now. For a moment, Thrain considered drawing his sword, then dismissed the idea. He'd wait to see what they were facing first.

And then it was on them. It swept down from above the trees on bat wings with a twenty-foot span. With eyes glowing and mouth open to showcase razor-sharp teeth, it was a nightmare horror meant to freeze the blood.

But it would take more than a showy entrance to freeze Thrain's vampire blood. He'd been around long enough to know it wasn't the fierce exterior that mattered, but the power within. In a straight-up battle, he'd bet on Trojan in his cozy-kitty form over all the sound and fury of the creature threatening them.

Focusing, Thrain projected their combined energy

in front of the swooping creature. The resultant explosion of blinding light and heat was a shot-across-the-bow sort of thing, a warning of what might come next. Thrain avoided killing unless he had no other option. The creature aborted its dive and instead landed a short distance away to study them.

Thrain opened his mind to the creature but received only primitive feelings of confused anger—so many unknown creatures, so many unwanted ones invading territory it considered its own. Thrain understood the territorial thing because his clan felt the same about their ancestral castle in Scotland. His instinct told him this was a primal being who normally would be fairly placid, content to remain hidden from humans. But Cindy's Woo Woo Inn had lured a potent mixture of powerful entities and human crazies to this one spot, and now the Pine Barrens' native had risen to protect its home. Thrain couldn't fault it.

The creature oozed menace, but beneath its aggression, Thrain sensed uncertainty. Finally, with a last scream of defiance, it swooped into the mist-shrouded forest. Thrain waited until he was sure it was returning the way it had come before exhaling deeply.

He sucked his breath back in almost immediately as Trojan reclaimed his impressive power. Thrain glanced down at the cat he still held in one arm.

The cat offered him a slit-eyed warning. *"Drop me and you'll never live to see your thousandth birthday. Put me down gently."*

Thrain bit his lip to keep from smiling as he set Trojan on the ground, then flexed the arm he'd used to hold the cat. "Guess I understand why you don't want me to drop you. With all that weight you're packing, you'd probably land like a plane without its landing gear down."

"You have a smart mouth, vampire." Trojan padded beside Thrain as they started toward the inn. *"And this isn't fat. This is all well-toned muscle."*

"If you say so." Thrain's thoughts drifted to Cindy. How to tell her she'd stirred up the Jersey Devil, and that maybe she shouldn't let her guests wander around in the dark for a while?

"You know, that was kinda fun, bloodsucker." Trojan glanced up at Thrain, his eyes gleaming with wicked glee. *"We make a kick-butt team. Prada's going to be getting her chuckles by raising hell in the sexual realm, so while she's tied up . . . or while she's doing the tying—she likes it both ways—we can see that everything runs smoothly."* He paused for thought. *"Or not."*

Another round of quavery howls from the werewolf pack rose in the distance. Trojan hissed his opinion. *"Any chance of the Devil chowing down on them?"*

Thrain shook his head. "Don't think so. The furry costumes would choke it." He knew he sounded as regretful as Trojan felt.

"Guess you're right. Maybe they won't stay long." Trojan's eyes indicated he was going to work on encouraging the pack to check out early. *"Anyway, we can hang together and see what shakes out at the Woo Woo Inn. Maybe generate a little chaos and destruction just for the hell of it."*

Thrain glanced down at his new mini-partner with the incredible power pack and a thirst for evil.

"Chaos and destruction. Great."

Chapter Three

Cindy had an ice cream flavor for every emotion. Right now, as she sat at the hallway table wondering how long she should wait before rushing back into the woods to look for Thrain, she'd opted for a big bowl of Ben & Jerry's Vanilla Caramel Fudge. It was a flavor to complement semi-worry. Very symbolic. The vanilla was confidence while the swirls of caramel and fudge were varying degrees of unease. She liked to think that her pigging out helped her to resolve issues. Goal-oriented gorging wasn't fattening.

Sure, she'd been a little nervous when she reached the inn and found that Thrain wasn't right behind her, but she'd figured he'd either had to chase after Trojan or had decided to investigate Patty and Jim's claims. Nothing to panic over. *Yet.*

"We're checking out. This place is way too weird." Jim Kehoe, alias Latrienne, stopped beside her and dropped his room key on the table. A silent Patty stood behind him, her narrow-eyed glare drilling a hole in his back.

Cindy paused in her ritualistic stirring of the ice cream. It had to have the perfect mushy consistency to express her growing unease.

She noted the weak smile exposing his pointed canines, the streaks of white powder making interesting patterns on his thin face, and the black cape he still wore. Her inn wasn't the only thing that was "way too weird."

But Jim and Patty were guests of the Woo Woo Inn. She couldn't let them leave without expressing her profuse apologies and regrets. "I'm so sorry you didn't enjoy yourselves. We'll all miss you." *Not.* "I feel terrible that your visit was ruined. You won't be charged for the time you spent here, and I hope you'll consider another stay with us in the future." The no-charge thing hurt, but it was good for business.

"No charge, huh?" Jim immediately perked up. "Gee, thanks."

She waved as they opened the door to leave. "When you tell all your friends about the Jersey Devil, don't forget to say that I'd love to see them." Word of mouth was her best advertisement.

She'd barely had time to shovel the first huge spoonful of ice cream into her mouth before Thrain pushed open the door. Trojan padded beside him.

Her relief was way out of proportion to the situation. She shoved back her chair and rushed to meet him. "Where were you? I was getting ready to come after you. Why didn't you call me on your cell phone?" Relief was always best expressed by nagging the object of one's semi-worry.

"I don't have a cell phone." He seemed distracted. "We have to talk."

"No cell phone? Why not? Everyone has a cell phone. Anything could happen on the road or out in the woods. You could have an accident or—"

"Shh." He put his finger across her lips. "I've survived a long time, so there's nothing in your little woods I couldn't handle. And we still have to talk."

The touch of his finger on her lips derailed her rant. She moved smoothly from ice cream symbolism to another kind of symbolism. What if she parted her lips, then closed them around his finger? What if she slid her tongue slowly, lingeringly, around it, then gently nipped his fingertip? What if . . . She met his gaze.

He knew. She watched the pupils of his eyes grow large in the now dim light of the hallway, and if the eyes were indeed windows to the soul, then his blinds were open and a sensually aroused male waited within.

Cindy sighed as he withdrew his finger but not his sexual invitation. She would accept his invitation. Eventually. It had been a long time since she'd enjoyed that particular rush of combined emotional and physical completion. As the centuries passed, fewer and fewer men seemed able to make her burn with the intense blue flame of sexual hunger. She burned for Thrain. No doubt about it.

He exhaled sharply, and his gaze grew shuttered. "Let's go into the parlor for our talk."

Talk? Why? Oh, yeah. She'd just lost two guests, and from Thrain's serious expression, he must've found something scary in the woods. Business first, fun later. "Fine, I'll just bring my ice cream along with . . ." She turned to pick up her bowl of ice cream and froze.

It was gone. Okay, so the bowl was still there, but all the ice cream was gone. And the bowl had that just-licked shine to it. "He ate my whole bowl of ice cream! I only got one spoonful."

He sat on the table beside the empty bowl. Vanilla ice cream ringed his mouth and clung to his whiskers. Trojan looked happier than any cat had the right to.

Cindy leaned down until her nose was inches from Trojan's fuzzy gray face. "You are a little glutton, kitty. Look at your tummy. If I were you, I'd run, not walk, to the nearest Weight Watchers for Fat Cats meeting." She whipped the empty bowl from the table and headed toward the kitchen with it.

She fumed about her ice cream all the way to the kitchen and back to the hallway. Thrain was still there, but Trojan had made a clean getaway. Cindy threw Thrain a warning glance to discourage the smile she saw forming at the corners of his mouth. "Don't even think about laughing. Great ice cream is my passion, and I show no mercy to ice cream thieves."

Thrain walked with her into the parlor. "You have a fan for life. Trojan thinks you're his ice cream goddess. He's convinced that anyone who shares his taste for ice cream has to be a special lady." He slid her a sly smile.

She raised one eyebrow as he looked for a seat away from the others in the room. "Trojan said all that, huh?"

"Sure did." Thrain started to pull two chairs into a

corner. "I . . ." He stopped in mid-sentence to stare at the group of women gathered close to the fireplace. His face turned pale. "Who're they?"

"What?" She dragged her gaze from his face to glance at the group. "Oh, those are all scientists involved in studying human longevity. It isn't a paranormal subject, but it's a big interest of mine. I invited them to stay here free for a few weeks so they could relax and discuss human aging with others in their field." She sat in one of the chairs and pointed to another across from her. "Have a seat."

It was as though he hadn't heard her. His attention stayed riveted on the women. A shiver of apprehension threaded its way down her spine. Cindy would never claim any kind of special abilities, but it didn't take psychic power to feel the danger radiating from Thrain.

"Where did they come from?" He remained still, his gaze never wavering from the women.

Cindy tried to shake off the impression of a predator crouched and ready to spring. "I don't know. Everywhere, I guess." What was the matter with him?

An older woman in the group looked over, and then rose to join them. She took Cindy's hand in both of hers. "This is an incredible place, Cindy. It's great to be able to get together in a casual setting to discuss all the wonderful things going on in research." The woman glanced at Thrain.

Cindy's puzzlement grew as she watched Thrain's eyes change. Cold and expressionless, they turned him into a stranger. *Uh, he is a stranger. Remember?* She didn't know any more about Thrain than she knew about most of her other guests.

"I'm thrilled that you like it here." Cindy's smile was sincere. Jane was a friend. When Cindy had started to study the findings of scientists interested in extended human life research, she'd wanted to meet the best in the field. And Jane was the best. A common interest had brought them together, but Cindy valued the friendship that had sprung from it. "Jane, this is Thrain Davis. He's here to sit in on some discussions and see what's happening in the world of the strange and unusual."

Cindy looked at Thrain, willing him to offer Jane a friendly smile. "Thrain, Jane is a leader in the research to find a way to extend human life. Because of her work, humans could someday live for hundreds of years." *Some of us already have and would like to know why.*

Thrain smiled and took the hand that Jane offered, but his eyes remained cold and watchful. "Sounds like fascinating stuff. How long have you been working on it?"

"At least thirty years now." She cast Cindy a playful glance. "Pretty soon, I'll have to include Cindy in my research. I've known her for ten years and she doesn't look a minute older than when I first met her." Jane glanced back to her group. "It was great meeting you, Thrain. I hope you find what you're looking for here."

"Oh, I have," Thrain's gaze followed Jane as she returned to her friends.

Cindy didn't even bother to think about Thrain's reply. She was too busy being sad for herself. It always happened this way. Now that Jane was starting to notice that Cindy didn't age, their association had to end. Cindy would have to start making excuses not to see Jane again.

Not for the first time, Cindy thought about telling Jane the truth. Maybe Jane could find an answer to why she'd lived for 738 years. But the fear was still there—the fear that Jane would think she was crazy, the fear of becoming a human lab rat surrounded by hordes of scientists, *the fear of finding out what she truly was.* Cindy tried never to go near that last thought. She was simply a human being with an unusual genetic mutation.

And so she'd do what she'd always done, sever the friendship. There was something incredibly lonely about never being able to have a close friend, someone she could share her centuries of experiences with.

"I don't think now is the right time to talk. We can discuss things later." Thrain turned with no other explanation and strode from the room.

Cindy blinked. What was that all about?

A blink was as far as she got before Prada swayed into the room. All conversation paused for a moment in homage to Prada's overwhelming sensual presence, then proceeded unabated. As Prada made her way over to Cindy and sat in the chair across from her, Cindy noticed that Trojan was nowhere in sight. Had Prada left the cat in her room? She hoped Trojan wasn't wandering around the inn somewhere. Cindy never let pets run loose. She thought about the werewolves. Fine, so sometimes she did.

Prada sighed as though the weight of the world bore her down. "You know, sister, if you're not careful, you'll blow your chance with him."

"Blow what? With whom?" Cindy stared, mesmerized, at Prada's gold medallion, which looked as though it was resting only an inch or two north of her navel. Wow, what a dress. Black, silky sin.

Prada's low sexy chuckle drew Cindy's attention back to her face. "If you don't know the answer to 'Blow what?' then you're worse off than I thought."

Centuries ago, someone like Prada would've confused and embarrassed Cindy. Okay, so Prada still confused her, but no way would she embarrass Cindy. "You're sitting here because you want to tell me something." She smiled at Prada. "Let me guess; it has to do with sex."

"Everything has to do with sex." Prada crossed her legs, and the short dress rode high on her smooth thighs.

Cindy felt it was inevitable that the dress's plunging neckline and high-riding hem would eventually meet. "And this is about what?" Prada was a guest, so Cindy would smile and listen to her, but what she really wanted to do was chase after Thrain to see why Jane and her fellow scientists bothered him.

"This is so about you." Prada frowned as she glanced down at one perfect nail. "It's going to break. I hate a broken nail. It makes me feel . . . incomplete." She turned her attention back to Cindy, and her brow smoothed out. "Anyway, Trojan and I will just hang around until you discover your roots. I'd help in the discovery process, but it's really not my game."

An icy frisson of fear touched Cindy. No one knew about her roots. *No one.* "Explain."

Prada made a small moue of apology. "I probably

shouldn't have said anything. It's really nothing. Just forget about it." She smiled a perfect smile.

A perfect smile that said, *"I hope you're not stupid enough to believe it's really nothing."*

Prada leaned over to tap Cindy's jeans-clad knee with her fingertip. "Hey, things are getting too tense. Let's talk about your sex life."

"What sex life?" Prada's thought processes were like a bunch of jackrabbits, leaping great distances and taking unexpected turns.

"Exactly." Prada looked at her as though Cindy had said something brilliant. "You have no sex life. I can help. It's what I do." She nudged Cindy and pointed to a darkened corner where two people huddled. "I love a sexual challenge. See those two over in that corner?"

As if sensing that they were the subjects of conversation, the two glanced in Cindy's direction. She recognized the pale-eyed woman, Andrea Combs. The other was Darren Henson, a tall, loose-limbed man whose intense, unblinking stare made her want to look away. "Yeah, so?"

"Andrea is a werewolf and Darren is a werecat. The normal course of true lust would have Andrea patiently waiting for the alpha male of her pack, who will arrive tomorrow. And poor Darren would have no one." Prada tried to look sad for Darren, but her gleeful triumph seeped through. "I couldn't let that happen to Darren, could I?"

"Well, I guess not." Escape. She needed to get out of here.

"So I did a little of this and a little of that, and now the two of them will share an erotic week filled with unimaginable sexual pleasure." She glanced at her nail again, as though her will alone could keep it from breaking. "You know, this nail really ticks me off."

Cindy did *not* believe one word of Prada's crazed ramblings. And she did *not* want to know how the story would end. And she definitely would *not* ask. She asked. "So what's going to happen when the leader of the pack shows up tomorrow and finds out what's going on? If Darren's only a little cat, won't he get hurt?" *Listen to what you're asking.*

Prada lowered her lids so Cindy couldn't see her expression and offered a small cunning smile. "No, Cindy. Big cat. Darren's a very big cat."

"Oh." Sheesh, he'd tear her place apart. At least the werewolves didn't claw the furniture. "Just wondering, don't really need to know this, but since Andrea and Darren are different species, can they really do it with each other?" Was this the question of a sane person?

Prada leaned back in her chair, her expression thoughtful. "Everything's a go in human form, but the canine and feline forms could be problematic."

Cindy understood now how some of the people who visited the inn could get sucked into their fantasies. Prada made everything sound perfectly logical and real. She was good, very good.

"That was all really fascinating, but I have to—" She started to rise.

"Sit down."

Prada didn't raise her voice, didn't touch her, but suddenly Cindy felt as though she didn't have the energy to rise from her chair.

"I'd say your sex life has been pretty sucky now

for a lot of years." Prada studied her as if she were a particularly long to-do list.

"A lot of years? I'm not ancient." It wasn't fair. Prada was hitting her in her weak spot. Her sex life *had* been sucky for the last fifty years.

Prada shrugged. "If you say so. I'm not here to argue with you. I just want to help you fulfill your potential as a sensual being. You're going to have to work with me on this."

Against all reason, Prada fascinated her. And it didn't hurt that when Prada mentioned sensual potential, Thrain's face popped up on Cindy's wish-list screen. "Not that I'm admitting you're right about anything, but just supposing some of what you say is true, what's your take on how I could improve things?" Prada was the sexiest woman Cindy had ever met. Cindy was open to some expert advice.

Prada's amber eyes glowed with the inner passion of a true zealot. "You have to want sensational sex with every fiber of your being, be willing to open all of your senses to the joy of joining, and fling off all inhibitions until only naked want remains."

Cindy bit her bottom lip. "All that, huh? Sounds tough." She hadn't thought this whole lust thing through to its obvious conclusion. Just because she'd felt a major jolt of desire with Thrain when all the men before him had been nothing more than mini-sparks on her sexual power grid, that didn't mean she had to act on her desire. In fact, Cindy was sure there must be something in the official innkeeper's handbook warning about getting it on with a guest. It was probably a professional no-no of major proportions.

"You're thinking. Don't think. *Feel*." Prada's voice vibrated with evangelical fervor. "Visualize Thrain stretched naked on your bed, or any other place of interest. All that hard muscle sheathed in warm golden skin, all that hungry male need calling to you, all that—"

"Okay, okay. I get the idea." Understatement. Her whole sexual being was clenching around the concept of a naked Thrain in her bed, and in her shower, and on her kitchen table, and she was starting to sound just like Prada. Like Prada? That was certainly a cold splash of reality.

Whatever else she was, Cindy was not like Prada. She'd survived the centuries by keeping everything in perspective, never letting one aspect of her life make her oblivious to everything else. Because immersing yourself in one thing, like sex, made you careless. And since Cindy didn't have family or friends to watch her back, she'd always erred on the side of caution.

"Oh, good grief." Prada flung up her hands in disgust, calling attention to several spectacular bracelets and one ring with a diamond the size of Rhode Island. "You know, you're really going to have to work on all that thinking. When you find six feet of hot, sexy male orbiting your sun, you'd better grab him or you'll end up colder than Pluto."

Cindy raked her fingers through her hair. Prada was exhausting and should only be experienced for short periods of time. "I really appreciate your trying to help me, but I guess I'm having more trouble with the flinging-off-all-inhibitions thing than I thought I would. When I met Thrain, my first impulse was to go for it." She smiled at Prada, but Prada didn't smile back. "But I'm not an impulsive person, and I *always* have second thoughts. Those second thoughts have kept me alive on more than one occasion."

Prada shook her head. "Ultimate sexual pleasure has to be impulsive, sister. It's the nature of the beast. I'd think you would've learned that by now." She bent down and picked up a red velvet box by the side of her chair.

Cindy frowned. She didn't remember Prada carrying the box into the room, but maybe she hadn't noticed because her attention had been on Thrain.

Prada handed her the box. "Take this. I put a few little girly things together to keep you happy while we're dealing with your impulsivity issues."

Cindy took the box. She didn't open it. She wouldn't open it. Knowing Prada as she was beginning to, Cindy wasn't sure if she'd survive what was in the box. "Thanks. I'll take a look at it later." She stood and started to edge toward the doorway.

Prada offered Cindy her I-know-something-you-don't smile. "You think you won't open it, but you will. Every woman eventually opens it. I call it my First Aid Kit for Women Who Waffle. Have fun with it until the real deal comes along."

"Uh-huh. Can't wait to see what's inside." She would *never* open that box. She was outta here. But as she hurried from the room, Cindy realized she didn't need to rush, because Prada had already joined Jane's group of women scientists. Probably scoping out new victims.

Cindy heaved a relieved sigh as she moved on to another room where discussions were going on. The worst was over for the night. She'd make the rounds, then indulge herself by going back to her apartment early. It would feel great just to kick back and think fluffy thoughts about nothing. *Thoughts about nothing? Right. And you are such a huge liar.*

Thrain hated to admit he was running away from a group of women, but that's exactly what he was doing. How many years would it take before he forgot—a thousand, two thousand? How many powers would he need before he felt invincible? The truth? No amount of power could ever rid him of that cold, sick, helpless feeling when he saw a group of women watching him. And in his mind, this one weakness canceled out all the incredible abilities he'd gained through the centuries.

"Yo, bloodsucker, in here."

Trojan. Great. Just what he needed, the feline gnat. Thrain stood for a moment, trying to figure out where "here" was, and how much hassle he'd get if he tried to ignore the cat.

"Lots. And I'm in the kitchen."

Too late, Thrain raised his thought shield. It would probably be easier to just go and see what Trojan wanted. If he didn't, the cat would follow him around endlessly.

He entered the kitchen to a bizarre scene. Trojan was hanging by his front paws from the door of Cindy's fridge, swinging back and forth like a feline pendulum. "What the hell are you doing?"

"I'm hungry and I can't open the frickin' door." He hissed his anger at the concept of doors that cats couldn't open. *"While Prada's out there trying to convince Cindy to do the deed with you, I'm in here starving."*

"Maybe I was hallucinating, but I could've sworn that you just slurped down a whole dish of ice cream." He offered Trojan a pointed stare. "You can't be hungry."

"I'm big-boned. I need lots of food to keep up my strength. Now open the door before I . . . bite your ankle."

"I live in fear." He'd better keep talking, because if he stopped, he'd start thinking about covering Cindy's hot body with his own. And what was the deal with Prada trying to turn Cindy on to him? "You have the power to open any door in this house, so what's the problem?"

"Take a good look at me, vampire. I'm supposed to be a cat. Even though it's between meals and the cook isn't here, I can't take the chance of someone walking in while I'm using my powers. Now open the damned door for me." Trojan dropped to the floor and waited with twitching tail for Thrain to do his bidding.

Thrain couldn't help it: Trojan amused him. And because he hadn't had much to laugh about in a long time, he opened the door and then started to walk away.

"Whoa, big guy. You're not finished. I want that thick, juicy steak on the top shelf. Medium rare."

Thrain lifted one brow. "You want me to cook it for you?"

Trojan sat down, wrapped his gray tail around himself, and gave Thrain a long-suffering look. *"Whatta you think? I should cook it myself? Let's look at the possibilities. I use my power to put the steak on the grill, and just as that big, old steak is floating through the air, Cindy walks in. Busted."* Trojan stopped, either to consider the consequences of getting caught, or maybe just to think about "that big, old steak." *"Anyway, Cindy freaks out and wants to know what's going on. I'd have to tell her about me . . . and about you, since you're my buddy. I'd guess you don't want her to know about you. Right?"*

"Is that a threat, cat?" The dark violence that always waited just beneath the civilized face Thrain wore writhed and coiled.

"Hey, don't get all hostile. This is just a little blackmail between friends. So how about it?" Trojan blinked, and for the first time, Thrain noticed the cat's eyes were the same color as Prada's.

Thinking logically, Thrain knew Trojan wouldn't say anything to Cindy. Because Trojan also had an agenda. Prada and Trojan were making a point of involving themselves with Cindy and him. Coincidence? Thrain didn't think so. Distracted, he put the steak on the grill and turned on the heat.

"The more I listen to you, the more I think I've met you before." He narrowed his gaze on the cat.

"No chance." Trojan glanced up at the microwave. *"There's a bag of potatoes in that bin next to the fridge. How about nuking one for me? I like tons of butter on my potatoes, and I think I saw a container of sour cream in the fridge."*

Thrain didn't argue as he took care of Trojan's potato. Trojan was a shape-shifter, and he'd bet that Prada was, too. So if he'd met them before, they would've been in different forms. And it must've been a brief meeting a long time ago or else he wouldn't be having so much trouble placing them. Trojan had probably cloaked his full power during the meeting, because Thrain would've remembered that kind of ability. He'd make the connection soon, and when he did, he'd know what to do with Trojan.

After putting the steak and potato on a plate, he

placed the plate on the floor behind a door so no one would see Trojan consuming his illicit meal. "When you're ready to tell me why you're really here, let me know." He quickly cleaned up the evidence of his cooking. The plate was Trojan's problem.

Trojan offered him a long stare, and once again Thrain caught a glimpse of something quite different from what the cat was choosing to show him.

"Yeah, sure. Now let me eat." He turned his attention to the steak, and Thrain knew he'd been dismissed.

As he started to leave the kitchen, he saw Cindy heading back toward her apartment. He still needed to talk to her about the Jersey Devil, but beyond the Devil, he had to start working on her belief system. He hadn't quite figured out how he was going to do that. Once again, he pushed aside the temptation to change her memories.

He gave her a few minutes' head start, then rapped on her door. It took her a few minutes to answer his knock, but when she did he could only stare.

"Hi. Was there something you needed?" Her smile was welcoming, but her eyes looked cautious.

What he needed? It would take hours to tell her and would involve many erotic buzz words. He'd better not even think about what he needed. "I have to talk to you about what happened in the woods tonight." She wore a plain, cream-colored nightgown that showed no cleavage and hung straight down to her ankles. It was the stealth fighter of nightgowns. Nothing showed. But it was still the sexiest nightgown he'd ever seen because *she* was inside it.

"If you think it's important, then I guess we need to talk." She held the door open for him, but her whole attitude said she didn't believe he'd seen squat in the woods. "Have a seat." She curled up on a sleek leather chair with her feet tucked under her so the only body parts showing were hands, neck, and head.

Thrain's gaze slid across the smooth skin of her neck. He thought it was kind of ironic that she hadn't covered her neck—so vulnerable, so seductive. As she picked up the remote to turn off her TV, Thrain tried to distract himself from his endlessly erotic thoughts of sex and the warmth of her throat against his mouth, along with the incredible orgasmic pleasure both could bring.

He glanced around the room, anywhere but at her neck. "Does this apartment belong to the same person who furnished the inn?" The whole room was a triumph of glass, chrome, and modern technology. Thrain was surprised she'd let anything as soft as leather through the door. He sat on the gray leather couch and surreptitiously ran his fingers across it to make sure it wasn't the newest synthetic material masquerading as leather. "Is there anything in this place older than five minutes ago?" He studied the abstract paintings hung on the white walls.

"Yes."

He heard her *me* loud and clear in his mind. She was amused. Too bad he'd have to ruin her enjoyment of the moment.

"I furnished the inn with old and comfortable and threw in a few antiques, because that's what guests would expect to see." She swept her hand to encompass the room. "But this is me. I don't dwell on the past. I embrace the now."

"Now isn't very warm." It wasn't just the furnishings and the paintings, it was the feeling that she was rejecting anything that other hands might've touched before hers, anything that might have a past. "I like the windows."

"I'm glad you approve of something." She turned her head to stare out the French doors. "I like to keep the blinds up even at night. There's something about the forest and the darkness that calls to me."

You get that from your father's side of the family, sweetheart. "Well, after I tell you about tonight, you might want to shut those blinds when it gets dark."

She sighed and shifted her attention back to him. "Okay, shoot. But I wouldn't put much stock in anything Jim or Patty told you. I've taken walks in these woods almost every night for six months and never met anything scary."

Thrain frowned. She was going to be a hard sell. "It wasn't just Jim and Patty who saw the Jersey Devil tonight. I saw him, too."

He felt her unwillingness to believe him, to think there might be anything out there that didn't fit into her neat little view of reality. "You don't believe me, do you?"

She shook her head, and he allowed his gaze to follow the slide of her dark hair across her shoulders, allowed his thoughts to conjure images of what it would look like sliding across his bare body.

Thrain fought to rid himself of all sexual images. He had to stay focused. Since she wasn't going to help him in her self-discovery process, it was up to him to get things started. He hated to use a compulsion on her, but he had to make her admit to something that would get the conversational ball rolling. He slipped into her mind.

She shifted uneasily, as if aware of something alien in her mind, but unable to identify it. "Look at it from my point of view: What would you say if I told you I was seven hundred thirty-eight years old? You'd say I was crazy, right?" Cindy widened her eyes as she realized what she'd admitted.

Thrain sincerely regretted her shocked look of disbelief. She had no idea he could compel her to say things. And she didn't recognize him in her mind. She would, eventually. But right now she hadn't a clue he was manipulating her. *Manipulation.* He hated it and his need to employ it now.

"No. I'd say, how about going for a walk in the woods with an older man."

Chapter Four

"You're an honest woman, Cindy Harper." Thrain looked serious as he rose to retrieve her jacket from where she'd flung it over the back of the couch. "A lot of women would've been tempted to lop off a few hundred years, but not you. I admire that in a woman."

What had made her blurt out the secret she'd guarded for centuries? Something wasn't right, but she didn't have time to think about it right now because she had damage control to take care of.

Cindy forced herself to smile as he brought the jacket to her. "I was only joking about my age. Joke's over. You can laugh now."

He didn't laugh. "And because you've been honest with me, I'll return the favor." He leaned toward her, his hair framing that hard face with those blue eyes she figured had told too many lies, and that hot mouth which had probably made those lies okay with a whole bunch of women. "If you'll stand up and put on your jacket, we can take our walk in the woods."

"Sure." She stood, but kept her gaze fixed on his face. "But we won't see anything." As he helped her on with her jacket, she almost missed the wicked gleam in his eyes. "And what did you mean about returning the favor?"

He picked up her flashlight, then opened the French doors leading out to the back porch. They walked across the backyard and found the path into the forest. Finally, Cindy couldn't stand the silence any longer.

"You didn't answer my question." The mist had thickened, and she hoped her werewolves didn't get lost on their way home.

"If the Jersey Devil is still around, the night will hold its own revelation for you. If we don't meet him, then at least we'll have found out a few things about each other." He kept the flashlight's beam fixed on the path in front of them, and the trees on either side of the trail were nothing more than shadowy silhouettes.

"Like what?" She moved a little closer to him. Even though she'd often walked these woods alone, tonight the mist made everything look a little scarier. Maybe there *was* such a thing as too much atmosphere.

"I'll know you're really seven hundred thirty-eight years old, and . . ."

He paused, and for a moment she thought he wouldn't finish his thought.

"You'll know I'm really seven hundred fifty-five years old." He didn't look to see how she'd taken his bombshell.

Even though she knew he was kidding, her heart still reacted with a hard thump. "Yeah."

Thrain stopped and turned to face her; then he handed her the flashlight. "Shine the light on my face so you'll be able to see if I'm telling the truth."

No amusement gleamed in his eyes, and suddenly Cindy was afraid. More afraid than when she'd suspected he had a gun in every pocket. "You're getting weirder by the minute, Davis." Her shaky laughter wouldn't fool anyone.

"I was born in twelve-fifty, and I spent my early years as a Viking raiding the coast of Scotland. When my clan settled in the Highlands, I took the clan name of Mackenzie. I've been a Viking, a Highlander, and many other things you probably aren't ready to know about right now." He paused to give her a chance to react.

Cindy couldn't force one word past her paralyzed vocal cords, and she knew her eyes must have the round and unblinking look of a startled owl. *It's not true. I don't believe you.*

"But I have one advantage over you, Cindy. I know why I'm still alive. You don't. I guess that's why you have those women meeting back at the inn. You're hoping they can use their scientific knowledge to find out why you never aged or died."

He leaned toward her, and she moved the flashlight's beam away from his face. The light skittered and jumped across the misty forest, creating strange patterns in response to her shaking hand. She didn't want to see truth in his eyes. She *wanted* him to be lying. Which was crazy, because she'd spent her entire adult life wishing she could find someone like herself, someone she could *talk* to. But what if he told her something she didn't want to hear?

And so Cindy reacted the way she'd always reacted when faced with uncertainties about her past. She denied everything. "Get this straight, because I won't repeat it. I'm a twenty-eight-year-old human female, and you have a scary sense of humor." Why did she feel a need to add the human part? *Because deep inside, you've always wondered.* She hated self-honesty.

He took back the flashlight from her nerveless fingers, and in the shift of light she caught a shadowed glimpse of his expression. It wasn't comforting. "You know, I finally think I've got it. You can't deny your age to yourself, but you can deny everything else. Not only won't you consider the idea that nonhuman entities exist, but you'll deny with your undying breath that you have anything in common with them."

"I'm *human*." She'd stopped thinking about how silly this argument was, how stupid she was even to respond to him. Her affirmation of her humanness sounded a little too loud, a little too tinged with hysteria. The word *human* echoed eerily in the cold, mist-shrouded woods.

Without warning, she felt the same strange sensation in her head that had preceded her earlier headache. Great. Just what she needed to finish off this horrible night: another headache.

"You're afraid of *not* being human." He sounded thoughtful. "If the idea of being nonhuman scares you so much, I wonder why you chose to run an inn that attracts the very guests you fear." They'd reached the cemetery, and he swept the flashlight's beam over the old worn and tilted tombstones.

"I can't believe we're having this conversation." Terror clogged her throat. She didn't want him to know the truth. Exactly because she was so different, she had an almost compulsive need to belong, to be a part of some group.

She'd been part of the human family her whole life, and the thought of finding out she was something entirely different scared her witless. The inn served two purposes. It confirmed her belief that there were no real ghosts, ghoulies, or things that went bump in the night. Because who could take the fake vampires and werewolves who showed up at the inn seriously? It also confirmed that since she had none of the weird behaviors of the so-called nonhuman entities, she was simply a genetic anomaly. Ergo Jane and the other longevity scientists she invited to the inn.

And of course, there was always the hope she might meet someone like herself, just so she wouldn't feel so alone in the universe.

If she could stop her hands from shaking and her teeth from chattering, she'd laugh at the irony of this whole thing. For more than seven centuries she'd hoped to meet someone who could understand the uniqueness of her existence, and now that she might have succeeded, she wanted to run screaming from him.

"Ah, I understand now." He started to turn toward her, then grew completely still.

"Understand what?" She hadn't said anything for him to understand.

Finally, she noticed his stillness. It was a complete cessation of all movement. And right now, in this place, she could almost believe even his breathing and heart had stopped. There was something not quite natural about his stillness. Of course, he was a not-quite-natural kind of guy.

He'd focused his complete attention on the dirt road leading away from the cemetery. Just as the narrow footpath they'd followed led to her inn, the dirt road led to a paved highway. The dirt road was only wide enough for one vehicle. No one ever used it, though, because no new burials had taken place here for at least fifty years. And the relatives of those already here had long since died. The only ones who ever visited the cemetery were her guests.

She watched him slowly relax, and he grinned as he shone the flashlight down the dirt road. "People are coming. Fast."

How could he tell? She didn't hear a thing, and with all the mist, the flashlight's beam didn't do much good. "I don't hear . . ."

She didn't get a chance to finish before she heard the distant sound of shouts and frightened screams, followed soon after by the pounding of running feet.

Suddenly, six werewolves in fuzzy costumes burst into sight. Without even slowing down, they charged past Cindy and Thrain, heading for the inn.

Clark shouted at her as he ran past. "Demon chasing us." Pant, pant. "Huge." Pant, pant. "Saw the glow from its eyes as it came around a curve." Pant, pant. "Run!"

Cindy watched, openmouthed, as they disappeared into the mist. Thrain's amused chuckle drew her attention back to him. "Is that the Jersey Devil you wanted me to see?"

"Not unless the Jersey Devil is a car." His chuckle grew to outright laughter.

"A car? How could they mistake a car for a demon? And how do you know it's a car?" *How do you seem to know everything?*

"This mist isn't mist any longer, it's fog. And fog can convince people predisposed to believe in scary creatures that they're seeing a lot of things they aren't. You said that yourself. Besides, they were too far away to hear the motor. I could hear the motor."

He must have extraordinary hearing, because she couldn't hear anything. But this time she didn't doubt him. Sure enough, in a few minutes she heard the soft purr of an engine. "Who would be coming to the cemetery at this time of night?" If she were by herself, she wouldn't be hanging around to find out. But Thrain and the gun in her pocket gave her courage.

The car finally emerged from the mist and stopped. A white police car. The perfect color to blend into the fog. She almost sagged with relief when Terrell James climbed from the car and walked toward her.

"Hey, Cindy. What the hell were those six furry things that ran this way?" Terrell's gaze shifted to Thrain.

"Terrell, this is Thrain Davis. He's one of my guests."

The men nodded at each other.

"We're out here because a couple of my other guests reported seeing something strange." She smiled at the officer. "And those furry creatures were supposed to be werewolves."

"Werewolves?" Terrell's booming laugh echoed in the forest's silence. "I bet in real life they're accountants, librarians, and just plain people who're bored

77

out of their skulls with their daily routine. Your place is great for relaxing and letting your imagination go crazy. Always wanted to be a vampire. Have anyone at the inn who can help me?" He grinned at Cindy.

"I can."

Thrain's matter-of-fact response drew Terrell's attention. "Sounds great. I'll hold you to it." His wink-wink grin suggested they were all in on the joke.

Cindy wasn't so sure. Thrain had sounded way too sincere. But when she glanced at him, his mocking smile was in place. She was too much of a wuss to check out his eyes and see if they, too, said he'd meant his words.

"What brings you out here?" Cindy wouldn't add that she was pitifully grateful he'd shown up because he brought a little reality to a night that up till now had been completely surreal.

Terrell leaned down to rub the dirt from the worn lettering on the tombstone next to him. "Joshua Clemmons. Horse thief. Legend says an angry mob lynched him. He was hanged from one of these trees next to the cemetery. Made it handy for burying. Didn't have far to drag the body." He looked thoughtful. "Legend also says he rises from this grave every once in a while looking for another horse to steal. Don't have any horses at your inn, do you?"

Cindy smiled, if a little weakly. "No horses. Any chance good old Joshua might've moved into the twenty-first century and be looking for cars now?"

Terrell smiled back. "Uh-uh. Josh was set in his ways." He drew in a deep breath before changing subjects. "Anyway, that doesn't have anything to do with why I'm out here. Two of your guests, a Jim Ke-hoe and Patty Cole stopped by the station a little while ago to report a Jersey Devil sighting." Terrell's sigh was long-suffering. "Just between you and me, this Kehoe character beats the Jersey Devil hands down when it comes to strangeness. But Kehoe made an official report, so I had to investigate. Seen anything out here?"

Cindy shook her head. "Only my werewolves."

Terrell nodded. "Then I'll get back to the station." He paused in the act of turning toward his car. "Why were your werewolves running like they'd seen the Devil?"

She smiled at him. "They thought they *had* seen the Devil."

His shrug said he sure couldn't account for the way some people thought. She watched him return to his car, turn around in the small parking area, and disappear in the fog.

Reluctantly, she looked at Thrain. While Terrell was here, she'd been able to push their conversation to the back of her mind. Now it was once again front and center. "Look, it's been a long night. I don't care what kind of fantasy you want to weave around yourself, but leave me out of it."

"No problem." He offered her an easy smile, but his eyes held the same strange stillness she'd sensed earlier.

She had the momentary feeling someone else lived in Thrain Davis's house, someone she hadn't met yet. But whoever that someone was, he didn't come out to visit often. That might be a good thing; she sort of liked the sexy alpha someone he was showing her now. She started walking back toward the inn, and Thrain fell into step beside her.

"Do you have your sword under your coat?" *Great way to change subjects, Harper.*

He nodded. "I always keep my sword with me."

The visual leaped fully fleshed, so to speak, into her mind—a deliciously naked Thrain wearing only his sword. Hard muscle versus hard steel. Uh-oh. She'd better say something before the image put down roots in her mind. "It's very old."

"*I'm* very old." He turned his head to look at her, and this time she saw laughter in his eyes. "We could never live together. Most of the stuff in my home is at least a hundred years old, and everything in your place was manufactured last week."

"Well, there you go. Since *I'm* very young, I like new things untouched by human hands. We just weren't meant for each other. Good thing we weren't planning to live together." Damn. The naked-Highlander-with-big-sword image was back.

"If you've run around the subject of your age long enough, feel free to stop. You're making me dizzy." He held up his hand to halt her retort. "I promise not to talk about your age."

She relaxed. "Good."

"I'll talk about mine."

They'd almost reached the inn, and she wondered if he'd think she was a coward if she broke and ran. Probably.

"One of the advantages of living to our ages—"

"*Your* age." She tried to ignore the arm he laid across her shoulders.

"Is that you develop powers."

"I don't have any powers." She tried to ignore how

safe and comfortable she felt with his arm across her shoulders.

"But you're only twenty-eight, so I guess you wouldn't."

"Oh. Right." She tried to ignore how much she wanted him to move his arm from her shoulders to around her waist. Then he could pull her close to his side, where she'd be all toasty and warm.

"But since I'm a lot older than twenty-eight, I've accumulated some interesting abilities."

Don't ask. You'd be playing right into his hands. He wants you to ask. "What kinds of abilities?" For over seven hundred years, her common sense had been a faithful friend, keeping her out of all kinds of trouble. Now, in one night, she'd kicked Old Faithful out the door in favor of Insatiable Curiosity. Insatiable Curiosity had made her ask that question, and she didn't think it gave a damn about keeping her out of trouble.

They'd reached the back porch, and he took his arm from her shoulders. She mourned its loss. As he watched her, the porch light seemed reflected in his eyes, making them shine like a predator's eyes in the night. Cindy shivered. She hoped those weren't the eyes of the other person living in his house.

"You want proof."

His husky murmur touched her on a thousand different levels. She wondered if that also was one of his abilities.

Cindy shrugged. "Not really."

Thrain shook his head, and her gaze was drawn to his hair as it lay heavy across his muscular shoulders, all sexy, shining, and *Viking*. "You might be old in wisdom, sweetheart, but you can't lie worth a damn." Smiling, he drew a sizzling line with the tip of his finger down the side of her face, and then rested his finger against the spot on her neck where her pulse beat hard and probably loud enough to irritate the Jersey Devil all over again. "This gives you away."

She couldn't stop her laughter. "I guarantee that pulse beat has nothing to do with lying."

He looked intrigued, but she didn't intend to give him a chance for any in-depth questions. "So what's this proof you seem so anxious to show me? I warn you, I'm not easily impressed."

"How about something subtle and understated? I could go for spectacular, but I don't think you want Officer James back here checking out another paranormal happening." He grinned at her, and she couldn't help it, she grinned back. She'd applaud whatever hokey little parlor trick he was going to show her, then go inside and try to get some sleep. At least her headache hadn't developed into anything.

His smile faded and his gaze grew shuttered. "I can change your memories, Cindy. I can give you new ones or take away old ones. You'll believe any memory I give you, no matter how unusual, for the rest of your life if I choose. I wouldn't really have to prove anything to you. All I'd have to do is put the memory of our long friendship into your mind, and you'd believe everything I told you. But that wouldn't be fair, would it?"

Prickles of unease raised goose bumps along her arms. "I give you points for originality, Davis. And here I thought you were just going to pull a rabbit out of a hat."

He shrugged. "No hat, so we'll go with the memory."

She relaxed into the game, because no way could he deliver what he promised. "If you give me a memory, how will I know it's from you? I mean, I'll just think it's part of my past."

His lips lifted in a sensual smile she felt all the way to her toes. "Don't worry, you'll know it's from me." Turning, he faded into the darkness.

How had he done that? She hadn't heard his footsteps moving away; he'd simply disappeared into the mist. But that was the least of her problems. All the things he'd told her about his life, and the things he seemed to know about hers had shattered her comfortable feeling of security. She needed time to think things out logically, and then she'd be back in control.

Cindy went inside, but before settling down in her apartment, she checked to make sure everyone had gotten back to the inn. Luckily for her, the werewolves had been exhausted by their race from the *demon* and were all tucked into their beds. No fur on her furniture tonight. *Let's hear it for demons.*

Finally, she made it to her apartment, flung off her clothes, climbed into her nightgown, and settled onto her couch. Since she was still keyed up, she decided to put on her DVD of the *Taken* miniseries until she relaxed enough to sleep. Dawn was near, and she needed a good day's rest before facing Thrain again.

As she watched a scene showing the alien spaceship, she smiled. Wow, that brought back some incredible memories. A few years ago, she'd been driving along a back road in East Texas about sunset when her car stalled. She'd just gotten out to lift her hood before calling for help on her cell phone when she'd noticed some cows in a cornfield.

They were acting weird, and when she'd moved closer to the fence to get a better look, she'd realized the cows were making . . . crop circles. They were actually lined up shoulder to shoulder stomping down the corn. She was standing there openmouthed when one of the cows saw her watching.

She still remembered the cow's telepathic message. *"Ach, lass, 'tis sad I am ye've stopped here. We canna let ye return to the others of your kind to report what ye've seen."* Definitely a Black Angus.

Before she'd even had a chance to punch 911 into her phone and yell that there were Scottish cows making crop circles out here, she was whisked onto an alien spaceship in a blinding flash of light.

The ship's commander was there to meet her. She smiled at the memory. It was Thrain, naked except for his sword strapped to his side.

Cindy hadn't lived all those years without learning something about naked men. The surest way to freedom lay in seduction.

She'd swayed over to him in her silky red Victoria's Secret teddy. Cindy wore nothing but a teddy when she drove anywhere in Texas during the summer; otherwise the heat wasted her.

She still remembered everything like it was yesterday. When she'd actually stood in front of him, she'd had to look up a long way to meet his gaze. She didn't have to look quite so far down to study his . . . sword. Since he hadn't said anything, she'd started the conversation. "That sword is magnificent."

His smile had been slow heat and endless promise. "It's made for hard, dangerous use."

Mmm. She could see he was a man who told the truth. Reaching up, she'd rested her palm against his bare chest and rubbed sensual circles on his warm skin. He'd put his hand over hers, stopping her gentle massage.

"Let's start at the top and work down, sweetheart." He'd turned to dismiss his assembled crew, all of whom looked exactly like Prada.

Putting his arms around her, he'd pulled her to him. She'd drawn in a deep breath of air to regain her sexual equilibrium after the shock of feeling his hot naked length pressed against her.

She'd barely recovered from first contact when he'd lowered his head and covered her mouth with his. Her lips had still been parted while she tried to draw in enough oxygen for her brain to be at least semifunctional, and he'd taken full advantage. Alien commanders were sneaky.

His lips were hot and firm against her mouth, and his tongue seduced every sensual cliché into vibrant life. He'd tasted of wild, decadent nights, and his scent was all about sin. Cindy had run her hands up and down his arms, reveling in the feel of smooth skin over powerful biceps. She'd closed her eyes to savor all her other senses more fully, because sight had already had its fifteen minutes of fame while she'd admired his . . . sword.

But, wait—what about hearing? No erotic exploration of the senses would be complete without all five senses, and maybe a few no one had yet discovered.

While she'd pondered the question, Thrain had

solved her dilemma by abandoning her mouth to kiss a path down the side of her neck. Somewhere during the kissing process, her teddy disappeared. She really didn't care, because now she could moan her pleasure, thereby fulfilling her need to involve all five senses in the erotic experience.

"I want to release your *big, thick* . . . belt." It was strange how certain words used in proximity to Thrain's body had taken on a life of their own and made it difficult for her to complete an ordinary thought. "The belt interrupts the glorious flow of sinew and muscle."

"Do it, sweetheart. Just do it." He'd circled her nipple with the tip of his finger and then closed his lips over the hard nub.

Unbuckling his belt, she'd let it and his sword slide to the floor and then thrown back her head to try to control her body's anticipatory clenching. Too soon, way too soon.

She'd reached up to grasp a fistful of his hair so she could hold him to her breast while he did all those magical things to her nipple with his lips, tongue, and teeth.

But he'd foiled her by sliding his hands down to her waist and bending her back over some kind of machine. She'd gotten a fleeting impression of the words MATTER TRANSPORTER on the machine, but what did words mean when need churned hot and demanding low in her belly?

He'd kissed a searing trail down her arched body and then shoved her legs apart with his knee. "I wanted this to be slow and sweet, but I can't wait. You excite me more than any other woman in the explored universe, even more than the Meevian females who have foot-long tongues and exceptionally strong lip muscles. I thought their ability to generate indescribable sexual pleasure was unmatched." He'd loomed over her, his bare, muscular body glistening with sweat. "Until you."

"I can't wait any more either." She'd needed to prove to him that she was superior to the Meevian females in all ways. Fine, so maybe the foot-long tongue would be a stretch. Reaching up, she'd pulled him down to her. "Now."

He'd growled low in his throat, and as she'd felt his sex start to slide into her, she'd closed her eyes and given herself over to her building orgasm.

Everything had been perfect until she'd felt the pressure of his teeth against her throat. Teeth? No, something bigger. These had felt like the slide of fangs along her neck.

Okay, orgasm-building shot to hell. She'd opened her eyes, but instead of looking at him, she'd frantically searched around her for escape. She'd beat a tattoo on his bare back while expressing how really *not* sexy the kinky fangs-in-neck thing was. "No biting! I don't do biting. Let me up."

He'd started to lift himself from her, but by this time she was flailing away at everything around her and had accidentally hit a button on the Matter Transporter. Suddenly, there'd been another flash of light, and she'd been plunked back down beside the herd of cows, which were still busy with their crop circles.

Trying not to call attention to herself, she'd crept into her car, called for help on her cell phone, and then wrapped herself in her copy of the *Wall Street Journal*. Damn, she'd had to leave her teddy behind. That really steamed her.

Cindy smiled as she stopped the DVD. What a great memory. Over time, she'd thought things through and realized she'd overreacted. All she would've had to do was to quietly tell him she didn't find biting erotically stimulating and he would've stopped. Instead, she'd gone ballistic. Standing, Cindy yawned and headed into her bedroom. Of course, Thrain had no way of knowing she was terrified of being bitten.

Crawling into bed, she pulled the covers over her and promised herself she'd explain the reason for her hysteria to him tomorrow.

And as she drifted off to sleep, she smiled at the thought of how shared memories could bring people together.

Chapter Five

"How crappy is it when I can't find one rotten thing to do to anyone? Where's the fun in making people's lives miserable when they're already doing it to themselves? I tried to interest Thrain in a little friendly mayhem, but he didn't seem too motivated." Trojan narrowed his eyes and glared at Prada, who leaned against the kitchen counter staring down at him. Where the hell did she find her dresses? This one was a black sex trap that plunged so far a man could get the bends if he swam to the surface too fast.

"Oh, stop making slitty-eyes at me and explain why you dragged me down here at four in the afternoon. Breakfast isn't until seven, so I could've caught a few more z's." She covered her mouth as she yawned.

"I'm depressed. And when I'm depressed, I eat." Yeah, yeah, so he ate when he was happy, too. But a guy needed his comfort food even when things were going great so he could store up all those warm cozy

89

feelings for when things went down the toilet again. Like now. *"And I had to come down early because the cook will be here in another hour. I don't want to get caught. Open the freezer."*

Not bothering to argue, Prada pushed away from the counter and lifted the freezer's lid. "I feel for you, sweetie. Lucky for me, I've found my main marks. Most of them are almost too easy. I won't even have to break a sweat."

"Don't gloat. You know I hate it when you gloat." He put his front paws up against the freezer's side and peered up at her. *"Get me one of those containers of Ben & Jerry's ice cream. I don't care what flavor."*

Prada bent over to get a good look at what was in the freezer. "You told me last time how the Big Boss grounded you after you got a little out of control. Now be honest. Three volcanic eruptions, a meteor strike, and a plague of locusts all in one week was a bit much. No wonder he got ticked. But you're creative enough to come up with a small evil that'll slip under the Big Boss's radar."

She reached deep into the freezer and emerged with a container of ice cream. Trojan was sort of sorry she'd found it so quickly. Admiring her perfect ass in that tight black dress went a long way toward improving his mood.

"This is sooo my kind of ice cream." She looked down at him in triumph. "Karamel Sutra. I think I'll have a small dish with you."

He watched her fix a small bowl for herself, but when she started to spoon his into another bowl, he stopped her. *"Whoa. No bowl. Just put the carton on the floor. And help me think of a 'small evil' that won't get me a butt-kicking from the Big Boss."*

She looked at what was left in the carton. "You're going to eat the whole thing?"

"Yeah. So?" He kept his gaze fixed on the carton as she set it on the floor, and then he shoved his face into it. Yes! Instant happiness. But he couldn't forget about getting Prada's input. She'd always had a devious mind. *"Sowhtshdido?"* Oops, he'd forgotten and spoken out loud. But what the heck, no one was around.

"I didn't quite get that, sweetie." She paused with her spoon poised delicately in midair.

He pulled his face from the carton. "I said, 'So what should I do?'"

Her eyes widened. "Uh, you have ice cream over every inch of your face. That's really gross. And I wouldn't speak out loud, because Hal is always wandering around."

"Okay, okay." He sat down and started to clean his face with one gray paw.

Prada put the spoon of ice cream into her mouth and savored it as her lids slid almost shut. She licked her lower lip with the tip of her tongue. "Oooh. Yummm. Soft caramel. Chocolate. Fudge chips. Aaah."

Okay, a few more "Aaahs" and he was going to spontaneously morph into his golden-god form and take her right on the kitchen floor of the Woo Woo Inn. *"Stop sounding like you're having an orgasm and help me with my problem."*

Prada blinked those big amber eyes at him. "Oh, sorry. What can I say? You know how I get into my senses. Let me think for a minute."

While she thought, she finished off her ice cream. She didn't make any more sounds of pleasure, but he could see the sensual enjoyment in her eyes. Sheesh, she did everything but purr. Prada should've been the cat; she was the one with the feline nature.

"I think I have it." She smiled at him with that small wicked grin that signaled trouble for some poor jerk. "We want to cause the most problems for the greatest number of people, so we use the local legend to help us."

Trojan whipped his tail back and forth. *"That would be the Jersey Devil."* He wasn't too sure about anything involving the Devil. *"Look, Thrain and I met him, and he's not open to civilized discussions. In fact, I think Thrain and I are the only ones here with enough power to control him. The Big Boss will be really pissed if I'm responsible for hurting any humans, and I've kinda gotten used to existing."*

"This will be perfect." She wasn't paying very much attention to what he was saying. "You can slip into a few of the human minds and hint about how much fun they could have if they used a summoning spell to call the Jersey Devil to them. With the human herd mentality, they'd figure they were safe if they did it as a group."

"And they're going to do this, how?" Trojan made his response skeptical as a matter of principle, but the idea had possibilities. He could picture the humans screaming as they scattered in all directions while the Devil spread terror among them. Get rid of all the nonhuman guests who might interfere and it was a go. Sounded cool to him.

"I'll scatter a few spell books around Cindy's library, not that any of the humans could make a spell work." She glanced at Trojan. "You could summon him and then send him away after we had our fun."

Trojan nodded, then frowned. *"What about Cindy and Thrain? Cindy would go ballistic if she found out, and Thrain has enough power to stop us."*

Prada looked thoughtful. "I'll warn the guests to keep quiet, and we'll make up some excuse to get Cindy and Thrain away from the inn that night. I don't want to take the chance of getting kicked out of here." She smiled a small secretive smile. "Because I have such delicious plans for them."

Thrain wasn't sure what to expect. He fingered the mini-recorder in his palm as he strode toward Cindy's apartment. He'd risen a little before sunset so he could catch her before she began work. Things should be okay. He'd planted a memory ridiculous enough so that when she heard herself telling him about it, she'd believe in his power.

It was what came *after* belief that was making him a little uneasy. Things could go one of two ways. Once she accepted his age and power, he might be able to move her gradually toward an acceptance of her own vampire roots. Or, she could be so horrified she'd sink deeper into denial and try to throw him out of her inn.

The dangerous part of him that remembered well his Viking and Highlander past seethed impatiently just beneath the relatively harmless surface he chose to show Cindy. He was still a warrior of the night and would do what needed doing to make her believe.

He steeled his resolve as he knocked on her door. Thrain had two incentives now. No matter what her reaction was, he still had to press forward for Darach's sake. Darach deserved to know his daughter. And beyond Thrain's duty to Darach was his own interest in Cindy.

Interest was such a weak word. What he felt for Cindy stirred the dark hunger in him, the one that merged with his sexual hunger and became part of it. He didn't think Cindy would be excited by the complete joining he had in mind.

Thrain had enjoyed many female vampires over the centuries, but he hadn't craved a mortal woman since 1785. After what a group of mortal women had done to him, he'd never expected to feel desire for one again. He'd been wrong.

Even his loyalty to Darach couldn't quell his primitive reaction to Cindy. Could he convince the insatiably hungry part of him that he should leave the Woo Woo Inn before his hunger overwhelmed his common sense? He didn't think so. Before he could consider the consequences of what he'd admitted, Cindy opened her door.

"Hey." She grinned at him. "Come in. You won't believe what I remembered last night." Moving aside, she allowed him into her living room.

Cindy had no idea what she invited into her home—darkness, danger, and a sexual need that shocked him with its strength. Since 1785, he'd prided himself on being cold, analytical, and always in control.

But his control had developed a few cracks since yesterday. As a vampire, he never dreamt during rest, but he'd been thinking about Cindy before sleep claimed him, and when he awoke, she was the first thing he remembered. His body's reaction to that remembrance was immediate. Could their joining wipe away the horror of what those other women had done to him?

No, *nothing* could erase that memory. He reminded himself that his sexual reaction to Cindy wasn't the entire picture. She was a strong woman and fun to be with. He'd push aside his darker need and focus on the strength and fun-to-be-with parts. *For now.*

"Have a seat. Would you like something to drink?" She paused, waiting for his response.

Yes. I'd like to cover your naked body with mine and then thrust deeply inside you. I'd like to put my mouth on your neck and share your life force. I'd like you to make me whole again. What an incredibly selfish thought. *What an incredibly arousing thought.* So much for pushing aside his darker need.

"Well, do you want that drink?" She looked a little impatient.

He shook his head. "No, not now."

Thrain forced himself to focus on all the state-of-the-art technology she'd managed to cram into her entertainment center. Not only was she a woman of this age, but she must spend a lot of time at home if she felt the need for all of this. Personally, he enjoyed going places and doing things too much to bother with any of it.

Okay, so he wasn't being honest with himself. Outside of his home, he accepted a few of the modern toys he really needed, like his car and even the tiny recorder he held in his hand. But inside his home, he wanted the feel of a past he could never recapture anywhere else. A past he missed yet cursed. A past that held him captive. And that was about all the self-honesty he could stomach tonight.

He lowered himself onto her gray leather couch. Her chrome and glass world still didn't touch him emotionally. "You have a lot of stuff." He nodded toward the stuff in question.

She sat down on the couch with him, her long black dress swirling around her. Evidently, she'd decided to blend in with her guests tonight. The interesting little dip at the top of the dress conjured some hot images, but Thrain still preferred her red top from the night before.

"No more stuff than most people." She looked puzzled. "TV, DVD player. I like to watch movies. And I made sure I had a great sound system, because I love music." Her expression brightened. "Then there're the video games. Do you play?"

Depends on the game. He shook his head. "Tell me about your memory." He pushed the record button on the mini-recorder still in his palm.

Happily, she launched into the telling.

Thrain winced a few times before she finished. "Are you sure I said all those things?" She'd done some creative embellishing on the basic memory he'd given her. He'd have to make sure she got a dose of what he'd really say during sex. *Uh-uh. Bad idea, hotshot.*

She looked puzzled. "Sure. I remember every detail of it." Cindy bit her lip, and her expression grew pained. "Look, Thrain, I wasn't going to mention what happened at the end, but I figure you have a right to know why I went sort of crazy on you."

The end wasn't the only crazy part, and he didn't want to prolong this any longer than he had to. "You don't have to explain anything." He surprised himself by reaching over and taking her hand. Thrain glanced down at their joined hands and wondered where that urge had come from. He didn't comfort women. Ever. But he didn't drop her hand.

She glanced away from him. "Everything was fantastic until I thought you were going to bite my neck."

He tensed. This wasn't going to be good.

"I realize it was only part of your sex play . . ." Nervously, she ran her index finger back and forth on the arm of her couch.

Part of his sex play? He didn't think so. Play had nothing to do with that final moment of joining, the sharing of a mate's life force. "Go on. I'm listening." Thrain frowned. Mate? Wrong term. She wasn't and never would be his mate. She was simply an interesting woman. But that didn't sound right either.

"I have a real phobia about being bitten." She drew in a deep breath and forged onward. "When I was about seven, a neighbor's dog attacked me. He put some serious teeth marks on me, but the worst bite was on my neck. Believe it or not, even after seven hund . . . I mean, even after twenty-one years, I can still feel his teeth in my neck." She abandoned her nervous stroking of the couch to rake her fingers through her hair. "Even the thought of teeth near my neck throws me into a panic. I never watch movies or read books that involve biting." She shrugged. "It's a weakness. What can I say?"

"So, no secret lusting after vampires?" He grinned at her.

She shuddered. "Never. Thank heaven vampires and werewolves are only myths. The fakes staying at the inn are as close to the real deal as I ever want to get."

Thor's bloody hammer! Now what should he do? "Don't worry about it. I understand." What he understood was that his problems had just quadrupled. Disgusted, he pressed the rewind button on his recorder. He'd worry about her bite phobia after he'd convinced her of his age and power.

"Everything you just told me, Cindy, was a memory I planted in your mind. It never happened." He only wished the dog had never happened either.

"Of course it happened. I remember it." But she sounded a little uncertain.

Thrain dropped her hand, then put the small recorder on the couch between them. The symbolism was obvious and disturbing. "Right now, you don't recognize how impossible your memory is because I've made everything seem logical in your mind."

Cindy stared at him, fear joining her uncertainty.

Well, hell. "I'm removing the memory now."

Suddenly, she put both hands to her head. "That feeling. It's the same feeling I had last night. I thought it meant I was getting a headache. In fact, I did get one after . . ."

For just a moment, her gaze went blank as he removed the memory. And when it was gone, her eyes widened. He saw the exact moment she put everything together. "That was you in my head last night, wasn't it?"

He simply nodded. "Want to tell me about the spaceship and telepathic cows again?"

Puzzled, she stared at him. "What're you talking about?"

Thrain exhaled sharply. Here it came, ready or not. He pressed play.

For five minutes, Cindy sat frozen listening to her

voice recounting her "memory." And when it was finished, the tiny click of the STOP button sounded way too final.

"Sorry I had to do it this way, but I guess any proof I gave you would've been tough."

Thrain watched her expression change from one of shocked horror to one that said, "I can deal with this." He sure hoped so, because he couldn't do much without her basic belief in what he was.

She picked up the small recorder and turned it over in her hand, but he knew she wasn't seeing it. "You've made your point. So what are you?" She did a great job of keeping her voice and hands steady.

He could definitely *not* be a vampire. "I'm like you." Give or take a few minor differences, like diet choices and dental anomalies. "But unlike you, I've accepted what I am and worked to develop my powers."

He'd surprised her into meeting his gaze. "I don't have any powers."

You'd be surprised, sweetheart. "How do you know? You've been so busy trying to be like everyone else, I'll bet you've never even tried."

She bit her bottom lip again, and when she released it, he had to slam the cage door shut on his hungers. Both of them. The full wet sheen of her lip was a temptation almost beyond enduring.

"Look, last night was rough, and tonight isn't starting out much better." Cindy reached up to rub her forehead.

He watched her expression as she put a few more pieces of the puzzle into place. "You made me admit my age by messing around in my mind, didn't you?"

Thrain nodded.

"So I guess it won't do any good to keep denying it."

"No." He probed her thoughts and for the first time felt the beginnings of resistance there.

"Then I might as well tell you how I feel about it. I've waited centuries to find someone like you. That's one of the reasons for the Woo Woo Inn. Sure, some wackos show up, but it also draws people who're interested in subjects outside the mainstream. I hoped it would attract someone who'd lived as long as me. If you know why we've lived so long, I want to know, too." Excitement and hope gleamed in her eyes.

He shook his head. "Uh-uh. Not tonight. Your guests are probably getting anxious. We need more time to talk." *He* needed more time to figure out how to reveal her vampire connections without freaking her out.

She looked disappointed but nodded her agreement as her expression turned grim. "I want you to stay out of my head. What's in there belongs to me."

She unfolded herself from the couch with catlike grace and walked toward the door. Then she stopped and turned to stare at him. "Wait. You were wearing nothing but your sword in my fake memory. You got that image from my thoughts, didn't you?" She narrowed her gaze to outraged blue slits.

Unrepentant, he grinned. "Sure did. You surprised me. Great mental images. Want to see some of mine?" He tried to look hopeful.

"No." She flung open her apartment door and strode toward the front of the inn.

Thrain caught up with her but didn't say anything as he walked beside her. Something about Cindy's reaction to the memory he'd planted intrigued him. She'd changed the ending of her memory because she feared being bitten. That was proof of a strong latent power; not many beings could reject his memories. He smiled at the thought of reinventing the Pygmalion legend. By the time he was finished, she'd be confident in who she was and what powers she could wield. If only he could get past the vampire thing.

They'd reached the front desk, where a tall, thin man with a wild shock of red hair was waiting for them. "Good, you're here, Cindy. I can't wait to go off-duty. You've got your work cut out for you tonight." He gathered up his wool coat and slipped it on.

Thrain sensed Cindy's inner groan and smiled.

"Let me have it, Hal. I'm tough." Cindy didn't look tough. She still looked shell-shocked from her discoveries.

Something protective stirred in him, but he firmly rejected that response. It was one thing to feel sexual attraction for Cindy, because there were no deep emotions involved. He wanted no feelings that might bind him to her once he handed her over to Darach, feelings that might make it hard for him to walk away when this was finished.

"Two potential problems checked in today." He handed her the clipboard. "First problem, Adolfo Sarducci. Says he's a werewolf. Alpha male. Big dude. Looks mean. When he asked where Andrea Combs was, I told him that she'd gone for a walk in the woods with Darren Henson. He sort of growled, left his luggage sitting at the desk, and ran off into the woods. Could be trouble."

Cindy looked worried. "How long ago?"

Hal shrugged. "About ten minutes. And problem two is up in the Warlock room. Says he's a freelance writer checking out a report of a Jersey Devil sighting."

"Latrine didn't wait long before running off his mouth." Thrain didn't need a nosy writer hanging around.

"Latrienne." Her correction was automatic as she ran agitated fingers through her hair. "Go home, Hal. I'll take care of everything."

Once again, Thrain pushed back a need to help her "take care of everything." Cindy was a strong woman, and she wouldn't thank him for butting into her business. She was at a disadvantage, though. She didn't believe in werewolves, so she didn't realize how ugly things could get if Adolfo was the real thing.

Cindy glanced at Thrain. "Why don't you go get some breakfast?" She sounded distracted as she headed toward the dining room. "If Andrea, Darren, and this Adolfo character aren't back by the time everyone finishes eating, I think I'll give Terrell a call."

Eat breakfast? Nope, couldn't do that. "I'm never hungry right after getting up, so I'll—"

"Yo, bloodsucker. Down here."

Thrain glanced down with a sense of foreboding.

"I'm starving, and if anyone thinks I'll touch that cat food crap, they can think again." Trojan stared up at him with an expression that said if Thrain valued his ankles, he'd better get with the program. *"Breakfast is a buffet, so I want you to go in and load up your plate. Then we'll find a nice quiet corner and you can share."*

Cindy frowned. "I haven't seen you eat anything since you checked in last night. You should be starving."

Uh-oh. "I got up during the day and hit the fridge. I've changed my mind, though. Maybe I will get something to eat."

She smiled her satisfaction that one of her guests wasn't going hungry. Problem was, she didn't know which guest was stuffing his little face.

Thrain went into the dining room and piled his plate high, then wandered into the parlor, where Trojan waited for him. He set the plate on a low table. "Why isn't Prada taking care of you?"

"She's busy causing sexual trouble. It's a passion with her. I think she's in one of the other rooms hooking up two Celtic faeries who hate each other." Trojan sat down and eyed the food with ferocious anticipation. *"I don't want to be anywhere near her when all hell breaks loose."* He leaped onto the table and prepared to chow down.

Thrain needed all his preternatural speed to whip the plate from under Trojan's greedy mouth. "Whoa, tiger. Let's not be too obvious. You don't think someone will notice you eating from my plate?" He grabbed a magazine from the table without looking at it. "Sit on the floor and I'll try to look like I'm reading this magazine while I'm handing stuff down to you."

Trojan growled low in his throat but leaped back to the floor. *"You don't look like a GQ kinda vampire, but whatever floats your boat. There's a copy of* House Beautiful *when you're finished with the GQ. After that you'll be all set to start your own TV show, 'Dead Eye for the Live Guy.' Hand me down a sausage."*

Thrain swallowed his laughter. No use encouraging him. "I'm not dead." He put down the magazine and picked up a book. This time he looked at it. *The Jersey Devil* by James F. McCloy. Well, if McCloy could give him some insights into the Devil, it was worth a read. "Did you get a look at this Adolfo Sarducci?" He handed Trojan a sausage and jerked his hand back just in time to save his fingers.

"Yeah. He's pure mean werewolf. If he mixes it up with the werecat, that writer who checked in today will have himself some story. Bacon."

Distractedly, Thrain tossed down three strips. "So that means if they get into a fight around here, we'll have to intervene."

Trojan stopped chewing and stared up at Thrain. *"Are you crazy? Have you ever gotten into the middle of a fight between a werewolf and a werecat? Bet you haven't. You'd have teeth marks where you never guessed you could get teeth marks. Nope. Won't catch me interfering. Toast."*

Thrain dropped two pieces of toast onto the floor, where the feline shop vac sucked them up. "If the writer and the human guests see that fight, the media will be crawling all over this place. I don't think Cindy wants that kind of exposure. She might even close the inn and move." He picked up his plate and set it on the floor so Trojan could scarf down the eggs. "I need everything to run smoothly. No distractions."

"Yeah. You're right. She can't concentrate on what you're laying down if she has shape-shifters fighting on her lawn."

Thrain narrowed his gaze. "What makes you think I'm *laying down* something with Cindy?" Once again, Thrain wondered why Trojan seemed to be sticking to him. And why did Trojan assume Thrain's concern was only for Cindy? Thrain could just as easily be worried that once the mainstream press got wind of what was happening here, the place would no longer be a sanctuary for nonhuman entities like him.

Trojan blinked up at him, and for a moment Thrain thought he saw panic in the cat's eyes.

"What Trojan is trying to say in his own unique way is that he knows you're sexually attracted to Cindy." Prada folded herself gracefully onto the recliner across from Thrain. "And the group on the other side of the room is starting to notice your one-sided conversation."

Thrain glanced over. It was Jane and the same women who were with her last night. Jane smiled at him. Thrain forced himself to smile back, but once again he couldn't push away a cold slide of unease.

Thrain returned his attention to Prada. "What makes you think I'm sexually attracted to her?"

Prada's smile was ageless sexual wisdom. "You're a vampire, and vampires are more sexually powerful than other creatures. And—"

"Hey, hold it. Stop right there." Trojan leaped into Prada's lap. *"Remember me, your golden god of erotic ecstasy?"*

Prada scratched behind Trojan's ears. "Oh, sweetie, of course you're sexually powerful, too."

"Hmmph." Trojan didn't sound mollified.

Prada looked over Trojan's head at Thrain. "I can sense your heat and need when she's near, your desire to bury yourself deep inside her while—"

"Enough. We get it." Trojan refused to meet Thrain's gaze. *"So how did things go in the other room?"*

If Thrain wasn't so worried about what might be unfolding between Sarducci and Henson, Trojan's embarrassment would've amused him. He needed to find the shape-shifters before the Woo Woo Inn became a headline in some newspaper's morning edition.

"I'm really excited about the sensual possibilities between Finvarra and Aibell." Prada licked her lower lip as though savoring the taste of her success. "They're so wrong for each other they're right." She frowned. "Did that make sense?"

"No." Thrain had to get out of here. Where the hell was Cindy? She should be in here by now.

Prada leaned toward him, her full breasts resting on Trojan's head. Trojan looked euphoric. "For over a thousand years, I've dedicated myself to bringing together people who have nothing in common. If I'm really lucky, they might even hate each other. The sound and the fury of their mating rituals have shaken continents, brought down nations." She flung her arms wide to indicate the cataclysmic results of her sexual meddling. "Antony and Cleopatra, Lancelot and Guinevere—"

"Barbie and Ken. Give us a break, Prada." If cats could roll their eyes, Trojan's would be spinning. *"Get back to Finvarra and Aibell."*

Prada glared down at Trojan, and Thrain decided maybe Trojan should keep his mouth shut or he'd have more than crappy cat food to worry about.

Prada chose not to claim one of Trojan's nine lives. She smiled at Thrain and ignored the cat's continued grumbling and growling. "Finvarra and Aibell are so much fun. Finvarra is a faery king with an unusual talent. He uses the game of chess to gain power over his foes. And Aibell is absolutely delicious. She's an Irish faery goddess whose harp brings death to those who hear it. The best part?" Prada looked as though she expected a drum roll. "They loathe each other. But I sensed the sexual tension crackling between them as soon as I walked into the room."

"Maybe that wasn't sexual tension you felt. Maybe it was just indigestion." Trojan sank back into his sulk.

Prada ignored him. "I can help you and Cindy find sexual ecstasy. I've already started working on Cindy."

Thrain was wasting time here. He should be . . . "What did you say?"

All discussion ended as Cindy joined them. "Well, at least one thing is going right. I thought those two guests who claim to be faeries hated each other. But they're sitting together in the other room, so I guess everything is okay." She paused to pick the plate up from the floor. "In fact, Finvarra is setting up his chess board and Aibell is getting ready to play her harp."

He watched Prada's eyes widen in alarm, and Trojan made an inarticulate cat sound that Thrain interpreted as feline horror.

Prada stood, dumping Trojan onto the floor. "Oops, sorry, sweetie. Have to practice my intervention skills. You'd think everyone would just let sensational sex happen without bringing his or her old baggage to the bed. See you later." Her final comment trailed behind her. "I hope."

"See, this is the kinda stuff she pulls all the time. She's always looking for a new sexual challenge, but one of these days she's gonna crash and burn. When it happens, guess who'll be in the cockpit with her?" Trojan proceeded to wash his face with one gray paw.

Thrain figured the washing process must be a cat coping skill. And since the answer to Trojan's question was pretty obvious, Thrain felt no need to answer.

"What was that all about?" Cindy played with the silver chain around her neck.

"Who knows?" The lie came easily as his gaze followed the path of her fingers. *Sensational sex*. Prada was right. Why couldn't he have sensational sex with Cindy without all his old memories wedged between them in the bed? But it wasn't just about his memories. It was about her desire. And there was no way she'd ever want the *him* she didn't know, the one who came with fangs optional.

While he was busy contemplating the many facets of sexual desire, Jane and her fellow scientists rose from their seats and headed for the door.

Jane waved at Cindy. "It's a gorgeous night, so we decided to get some exercise by walking to the old church."

Cindy returned Jane's wave and then looked back at Thrain. "Almost everyone except the help is out in the woods tonight, and I guess I need to be there, too. Adolfo and the other two haven't come back. I've already called the police, and they said Terrell would swing by in a little while." She bit her lip, and he figured she was trying to decide what to say next. "Want to come along?"

Every time she bit her lip like that, the caged beast inside him rattled its bars. "Sounds like fun."

She nodded, then walked toward the kitchen. "I'll drop off this plate and pick up my jacket."

Thrain took the steps two at a time as he went to his room, strapped on his sword, and flung on his coat. He'd made a decision a few minutes ago. Finessing Cindy Harper wasn't going to work. And if by chance it did, they'd both be a few centuries older by the time she got the whole picture.

He'd have to sit her down and administer some tough love. First he'd tell her that he knew exactly who she was, then he'd tell her what he knew about her. Up to a point. Even he didn't have the guts to admit that he and her dad were vampires. He'd have to save that until she'd recovered from his first round of disclosures.

The truth? He wanted to see how far sexual attraction would take them before the word *fangs* slithered into the picture. He'd use all the sensual knowledge he'd gained over the centuries to draw her to him. Then, if he was lucky, she'd care for him too much to go "Ugh" when she found out he was a vampire. *Care?* No, he definitely didn't want her to care for him. Lust? Sounded kind of shallow, and for some reason he didn't like the thought of Cindy's feelings for him being shallow. Odin's revenge, what *did* he want?

Thrain went back down the steps more slowly than he'd gone up. What had happened to his determination not to betray Darach? Cindy had managed to blur the lines between loyalty and desire.

He'd reached the bottom of the stairs before he heard the noise. Cindy joined him, and they stood listening for a moment.

"That sounds like animals fighting." She paused to listen for another moment. "They're behind the inn." Without waiting to see if he followed, she ran toward a rear exit that bypassed her apartment.

Thor's wrath! The situation called for one of the

old curses. The werewolf and werecat must be trying to tear each other apart out back, and Cindy was going to go charging into the middle of them shouting, "Nice doggy, nice kitty." He ran after her.

When he reached the back porch, he found her standing gape-mouthed as Sarducci and Henson tried to rip each other's heads off.

A few others were standing around, but none of them was human except Cindy.

"My bet's on the cat." Prada stood beside the two warring faeries, who had abandoned their hostilities in favor of more exciting entertainment.

"Don't know about that. The wolf looks pretty motivated." Trojan sat beside Prada, for the moment not thinking about food.

Thrain glanced around at the others. Three of the real vampires were there—Stan, Lisa, and Carl—plus the two faeries, Prada, and Trojan. None of them looked ready to take a shot at breaking up the fight. Smart.

Guess that left him. Thrain drew his power to him and prepared to fling the combatants apart with an explosive projection of force. No way would he get between those two physically. Cindy would be horrified by his show of power, but someone had to do something.

He glanced toward Cindy to tell her to stay where she was. Too late; she was gone. Frantically, he scanned the porch, and when he didn't see her, he shifted his attention to the lawn.

During his many centuries of life, there were few sights Thrain could honestly say froze him in place. This was one of them.

Cindy Harper was dragging her garden hose toward the two very angry and very powerful alpha male shape-shifters. What the hell did she think she was going to do?

The hose? It would be like spitting on a forest fire. He leaped from the porch.

Chapter Six

Cindy jerked the hose, trying to work some slack into it so she could take dead aim. She'd just see how mad they'd be with each other after they got faces full of cold water. *Note to brain: then they'll be mad at you. That might not be a good thing.* No matter; this was her property and she intended to defend it against carnage and mayhem.

But just beneath her militant determination to protect hearth, home, and business reputation lurked screaming mindless fear. The music from *Jaws* played out in her brain. She pulled up the last few pitiful strands of logic left in her terror-stricken thoughts. The animals were completely focused on killing each other, and if they changed their focus to her, Thrain was nearby. Now why did that thought bring comfort?

Questions formed in her mind and then drifted away with her panic. Why weren't people screaming and running around? Why were they simply standing on the porch watching? Hello? She was trying to break up a fight between a wolf and a panther, and she could damn well use some help. Where had the wolf and panther come from anyway? Did they escape from somewhere nearby? Out here in the woods, no one would ever know if someone kept exotic pets. Had anyone called the police, who would hopefully call Animal Control?

Above the growling and snarling of the animals, she thought she heard Thrain's voice shouting at her. He could shout all he wanted, but what she really needed were a few of his vaunted powers brought to bear on the situation. Like how about giving them memories of being friendly gerbils?

Clenching her teeth, she took aim and turned on the hose. No gentle spray here. She was going for a single powerful stream of water that would knock both of them on their butts.

Her first shot got the wolf right in his snarling face, and the second hit the panther in mid-scream. The two animals leaped apart.

In the sudden silence, she could hear someone running toward her, probably Thrain. But the footsteps were drowned out as the pounding of her heart escalated to sonic boom volume. Cindy stood for the second time that night with her mouth hanging open.

Ohmigod! Right in front of her, the two animals morphed into human shapes. Naked human shapes. Naked *male* human shapes. She recognized Darren, and the other man with the shaggy red-brown hair must be her new guest, Adolfo.

The hose dropped from her nerveless fingers and

whipped around like a demented snake, spraying her with each pass. She didn't notice.

"What happened?" She coughed to get rid of her frightened-frog croak.

"Well, hell. I think you sprayed all the hair off them." Thrain's voice came from right behind her.

"Not funny, Davis." She'd barely had time to close her mouth before another wolf trotted from the woods, paused in front of the two men, then went around them to stop beside Thrain. Bemused, Cindy stared as Thrain talked to the wolf. *Talked to the wolf?*

"Now would not be the best time to return to human form, Andrea. Go up to your room and I'll take care of everything here." Thrain looked toward the porch. "Prada, open the door for Andrea, and go with her to her room to make sure everything's okay."

Prada nodded, opened the door, and let the wolf into the Woo Woo Inn.

There was a wolf in her inn and two naked men on her lawn. Maybe she'd better check to make sure there weren't any cows making crop circles nearby.

Cindy tried to think of something to say, but words eluded her. The guests on the porch drifted back into the inn as though nothing cataclysmic had happened. Meanwhile, Thrain walked toward the two men, who still glared at each other.

"Both of you just took stupid to a new level." Thrain's smile was friendly, his voice conversational. "This place is a sanctuary, and the first rule is *never* to change in plain sight."

Adolfo transferred his attention from Darren to Thrain. "Andrea is part of my pack. She's mine." He emphasized his ownership with a snarl.

Darren hissed his anger. "She's not your mate, so leave her alone. She wants to be with me."

Thrain made no comment, but Cindy recognized his stillness, a stillness she now knew indicated complete concentration on something. And that something didn't bode well for the two combatants.

Cindy caught the momentary blankness in both men's eyes, a blankness she suspected she'd had several times herself. Then Thrain relaxed and moved back to her side.

"They'll be fine now." His smile said he'd done a little mind tinkering, and she should forget about the whole thing.

Forget. Sure. "What did you do to them?"

He didn't have to answer.

"Hey, Darren, old buddy. It's great seeing you again. I think it's awesome that you and Andrea are finally hooking up. She always had the hots for you." Adolfo slapped Darren on one bare shoulder. "Let's get inside, grab some clothes and a few beers, then catch up on old times."

Darren grinned. "I was thinking the other night about the hunts we used to go on together when we were in college. Those were the days. Remember all the blood brother stuff? We should've kept in touch more."

Neither man seemed uncomfortable with his nakedness. That was okay, because Cindy felt enough discomfort for both of them.

Cindy watched silently as the men entered the inn; then she turned to Thrain. "What's going to happen when Andrea doesn't go along with their version of reality?"

Thrain didn't seem concerned. "She'll go along

with everything. She's not stupid, and she wants Darren. Don't make the mistake of thinking Andrea is weak. In a claw-to-claw fight with either of those men, I'd bet my money on her."

Cindy swallowed hard before broaching the next subject. In just a few minutes, the world as she knew it had crumbled around her. "So there really are werewolves and werecats." She didn't phrase it as a question. She didn't have to.

Thrain didn't answer, only stood as if waiting for her to make the next leap of logic.

She drew in a deep breath of courage. "Then that means a lot of the other legendary creatures might exist, even . . . vampires." She couldn't suppress her instinctive shudder at the thought of vampires, because they spoke to one of her greatest fears. Other creatures bit, but vampire bites seemed so neck-specific.

"Even vampires." Something in his tone bothered her, but she was still too shocked to think about it.

"Let's get you inside and into some dry clothes." He guided her into the inn.

For the first time Cindy realized she was shivering. Looking down, she noted her soaked dress. She glanced at Thrain. "The demon hose got you, too." *Not funny, Harper.* After what she'd seen tonight, the existence of demons was well within the realm of possibility.

"Believe me, I'll live." He smiled as he stopped outside her apartment door. "I'd better go up to my room and—"

"No." Cindy put her hand on his arm just in case he tried to leave. "Come in. I want to talk. Now." She opened her door and stepped inside, drawing him in behind her. "You can get out of those wet jeans and I'll throw them in the dryer. I'll give you a blanket to wrap around you until they're dry."

"Wait." He stood in the middle of her living room, dripping on her plush carpet and looking sexy enough to dry her clothes using only the sensual heat he generated. She had no idea why she wasn't enveloped in a cloud of steam. "How many people do you have working now?"

Cindy widened her eyes. She'd forgotten about the help. What if they'd seen what had happened? "The cook and a few maids."

Thrain nodded. "I'll be back."

He left her standing there as he closed the door quietly behind him. Cindy was starting to appreciate having someone around who could rearrange memories. She certainly didn't need Mimi, her cook, quitting, or the maids racing home to spread the tale over all of South Jersey. Sure, she appreciated a little notoriety, but it was possible to have too much of a good thing.

Cindy went into her bedroom, stripped off her wet dress, and slipped into a clean pair of jeans, a blouse, and her fuzzy slippers. She probably should go right back to work. Her guests would expect her to be there when they returned from the woods, but she needed some recovery time.

While she was changing, she thought about the people on the porch. Would Thrain be able to alter their memories? And what about Prada? She hadn't even blinked when she'd let the wolf into the inn.

Deep in thought about the ramifications of the fight, she walked back into her living room to find Thrain leaning against the closed door that led to the hallway connecting her apartment with the inn.

He'd hung his coat, along with his sword in its scabbard, on the coatrack by the door. Didn't he go anywhere without that sword? His jeans and shirt were still wet.

Cindy paused to stare. "I thought you might go up to your room to change before coming back here." Instinctively, she walked over to close the blinds over the French doors leading to the porch.

His slow, wicked smile said she should know better than that. "Why would I change in my room when I can take off my clothes here? Besides, you said you wanted to talk. Now."

"Fine. You can undress in the bathroom, hand out your wet clothes, and I'll hand in a blanket." If she remained cool and untouched by his sexual heat, she'd win. What would she win? Nothing. Hmm, wasn't winning by its very nature supposed to include a prize? She thought about his bare body covered only by a blanket. Okay, that worked for her.

Outside the closed door of her bathroom, she waited with a blanket clutched in her hand. When he opened the door a crack and handed out his clothes, she didn't look at them as she handed in the blanket. All the way to the dryer, she didn't peek. She really didn't want to know for sure what he'd taken off, because her imagination didn't need any encouragement.

Once back in the living room, she curled up on her couch and waited nervously for him to join her. This was so dumb. Men didn't make her nervous. She was the ultimate older woman, so what was the big deal? The big deal was, if he was telling the truth, Thrain Davis was the first older man she'd dealt with since hitting her eightieth birthday. And that had been a long time ago.

When he finally returned to the living room, she had to bite her lip to keep from reacting. Somehow, she'd expected him to wrap the blanket around his shoulders. He hadn't. Instead, he'd simply wrapped it around his waist. Everything above was bare.

Her fake spaceship memory couldn't begin to compete with the real deal. When a man like Thrain took off his shirt, it was a lightning strike to a woman's hormonal system. Muscular everything covered by smooth golden skin. Warm. Just by looking at the smooth slide of muscles beneath all that wonderful wrapping, Cindy knew he'd be warm beneath her fingers, *beneath her mouth.*

She watched the heat gather in his eyes and knew he understood exactly what she was thinking. He didn't have to be in her mind to figure that out. She was probably sending out all kinds of signals announcing, "Single white female hunting buff male body for primitive pleasure."

"Why didn't you wrap the blanket around your shoulders? Aren't you cold?" *She* certainly wasn't cold. All toasty warm here.

"If I wrapped it around my shoulders, it would fall a little short in the cover-up department. And no, I'm not cold." He lowered himself onto the couch beside her. *Right* beside her. No end of the couch for him.

No way could she move farther away from him unless she wanted to straddle the arm of the couch. And she believed him when he said he wasn't cold, because she could feel his heat. Or maybe it was just her own body warming up the old reproductive system.

Because this *was* all about sex. No matter that she would be discussing some serious issues, underlying whatever they said aloud would be the unspoken dialogue of sexual attraction. And wow, was she attracted.

"Did you take care of everything?" Strange, but she felt reluctant to talk directly about his powers, as though by talking around them she could pretend everything in her world was the same as it had been yesterday before he arrived.

Thrain nodded, and she couldn't help it, she just had to reach out to push a strand of his hair away from his face. He reacted as though she'd slid her hand over his bare flesh. She could feel the tension thrumming through him, affecting her even though no part of his body touched hers.

"What about the people standing on the porch?" She frowned. "They didn't seem surprised about what happened. Maybe they thought I'd staged the whole thing to entertain them." Which made no sense at all; they had to know she didn't have the technology to make the change from animal to human look real.

"Let's be honest: You're keeping your mind busy imagining what everyone else will think so you won't have to come to grips with it yourself." He relaxed back against the couch.

Hey, distraction was an art form. For example, his movement had drawn her attention to his taut stomach and the way the edge of his blanket slipped lower and lower, igniting hopes of possible sensual revelations. Was she good, or what?

"But I'll let you get away with it this time." He rested his hand on his thigh. "You don't have to worry about the people on the porch because none of them were human."

She eyed his blanket-covered thigh. Was he all bare under that blanket, or had he kept on . . . "*What?* Did you say *none* of them were human?"

Thrain would've laughed at her wide-eyed shock if so much wasn't riding on how she accepted the things he was about to reveal. "You already know about Andrea, Adolfo, and Darren. Finvarra and Aibell are Celtic faeries, just as they said. Stan and the couple who probably didn't even see what happened because they were too busy kissing—"

"Lisa and Carl." She seemed to grow paler by the minute.

Thrain couldn't stop now. "Right, Lisa and Carl. They're all vampires." He paused, waiting for the expected exclamation of horror.

Cindy didn't disappoint. "*Vampires?* They—"

"Look normal? Is that what you meant to say?" No matter how much he tried to hold it back, anger washed over him. "Stan looks like an ordinary middle-aged businessman and Lisa and Carl look like any young couple in love. Well, guess what? That's exactly what they are."

She didn't say anything, just stared at him. Good, because he wasn't finished.

"Maybe you thought they should look like Latrine? No, wait: I bet you expected them to have foot-long fangs and be slavering at the throats of other guests." Thrain sounded a little out of control even to himself. Taking a deep breath, he tried to calm down. He couldn't figure out why her opinion made him so mad when for centuries he hadn't much cared what anyone thought.

"Are you done?" Her voice was calm, her gaze steady.

"For now." His spate of temper had shaken him. He never lost it like that. Emotional blowouts were deadly. You said and did things during moments of strong emotion that killed you down the road.

"What I was going to say before you went on your rant was that they seemed like nice people." She bit her lip, a habit that signaled deep thought on her part and sexual torture for him. "And, yes, I'll admit when you mentioned vampires, free association pulled up the words *neck, bite,* and *pain.* But I recognize my fear is something I'll have to deal with if I intend to keep this inn open." Cindy offered him a weak smile. "I mean, how do you tell tourist agents you won't accept reservations from vampires?"

"You're an amazing woman, Cindy Harper." He meant the compliment. Not only was she accepting what he told her without racing to her bedroom and locking the door, she was even trying to joke about it.

"Not really. From what you've said, I assume none of them will be setting their sights on my neck, but I still won't be spending any quality one-on-one time alone with them from now on." Her smile faded. "I can't deny the existence of something when it rears up and slaps me in the face. When I opened the inn, I was hoping to attract someone like . . ." She took a deep breath. "Someone like you. Or at the very least, make it a place where Jane and scientists like her would want to gather." She shook her head. "I never thought the inn would attract mythical creatures. I didn't even *believe* in mythical creatures. But I'm determined to keep the inn open, so I'll cope."

Thrain nodded. She'd given him a lot to think

about. Even though she'd accepted the things she'd seen and his explanations, there was still a long way to go before he could reveal everything. And he now had less than two weeks to convince her to fly with him to Scotland to visit the Mackenzie castle, where she'd meet Darach for the first time. For some reason, it was important to him that her first exposure to her family take place at her clan's ancestral home. Darach would be leaving at the end of the two weeks, and he wouldn't be returning for another twenty years.

"Since you're on a roll, tell me about Prada. She's the only other one on the porch you haven't mentioned." Her gaze darkened. "And then you can tell me why I've lived for over seven centuries."

Not tonight. He needed a little more time to gain her trust before revealing who she was. That meant he had to keep her attention on other things. "I don't know what Prada is, but you haven't asked about the most powerful entity of the whole bunch." He shouldn't be getting such childish glee from telling her this.

"No one else was on the porch." A small line formed between her brows as she tried to think.

How could her mannerisms fascinate him so when he'd convinced himself that nothing about a human female would ever interest him again? "Trojan was there."

"Trojan? You're kidding. He's just a—"

"He's not just a cat, Cindy. I don't know what he is, but he's powerful and he's always hungry." He smiled at the memory of Trojan's voracious appetite.

"They're cosmic troublemakers." Cindy seemed definite about that. "When they checked in, Prada told me a lot of things that rolled right over me." The line between her eyes deepened. "Okay, I remember she said that cosmic troublemakers raise hell throughout the universe, and that she and Trojan had argued about what color Trojan should be. I think she said Trojan wanted to be a black cat, but since he'd forced her to be white the last time, they'd compromised with gray. Didn't make much sense to me then. Still doesn't make any sense."

"It makes lots of sense to me." For a moment he was back in 1785 at the Mackenzie castle with Darach. He'd come to the castle prepared to die, but Darach and Blythe had saved his life. Blythe had been visiting from the future as part of a time travel tour, and the tour rep was Ganymede. He'd had a white cat with him named Sparkle Stardust. Darach had said they were cosmic troublemakers.

"It would help if you explained things to me." Cindy sounded impatient.

"You wouldn't want to hear it." *And I wouldn't enjoy telling it.* "Let's just say I knew Prada and Trojan a long time ago. They went by different names then, but they always had an agenda." Thrain might've forgotten many things over the course of several hundred years, but he'd never forgotten the short time he'd spent at the castle during that horrific year. And he'd definitely never forget names like Ganymede and Sparkle Stardust. When he left Cindy, he was going to hunt down Trojan. He'd probably find him in the kitchen hanging from the fridge.

"Well, since you don't want to tell me about Prada and Trojan, let's talk about my age." She uncurled her legs from underneath her and stretched them out.

Thrain tensed. "Let's not. I'd rather help you begin discovering your powers."

Suspicion touched her. "You keep avoiding my questions about our ages. Why?" *Maybe what he'll tell you is so horrific, he doesn't think you can take it.* She firmed her resolve. She'd waited centuries for an answer and she didn't intend to wimp out now.

He shrugged and smiled at her. "You're imagining things. I promise to tell you tomorrow. It's a long story, and I don't have the energy tonight after wiping everyone's memories clean. I'm your guest, and I'm paying to have fun. Helping you to discover your powers would relax me."

If she thought nagging him would change his mind, she'd go for it. But instinct told her that he wasn't the kind of guy who caved under nagging attacks.

Her powers? Cindy wasn't sure she trusted the gleam in his eyes. But since she was pretty sure she didn't *have* any powers, she might as well let him knock himself out. "So I'm going to learn how to do what—fly, disappear, get a tax refund out of Uncle Sam?"

He shook his head, and gleaming strands of that Viking hair spread across his bare shoulders. "You have to harness the power within yourself before you can project it outward."

"Wow, that sounds really deep." She grinned at him. "Before we dip into the heavy stuff, would you like a drink?"

"Sure." He shifted on the couch, and the blanket moved a little lower on his hips.

She hurried to the kitchen with visions of a massive blanket slide spurring her on. There were some things, like Haley's Comet, that swung past you only once in a lifetime. And if you missed it, well, you were out of luck. If that blanket shifted any farther south, she intended to be there for the moment. Cindy noticed the dryer had stopped. She could give his dry clothes to him now so he could dress. Or not.

Cindy focused her attention on the wine and glasses she was carrying into the living room. She put them on the coffee table, looked up, and then stopped breathing as she stared around her.

Finally, she drew in a deep breath before she keeled over from oxygen deprivation. "There's a real fire blazing in that fireplace." She moved toward it until she could feel the heat. It wasn't a hallucination. "I don't have a fireplace, blazing or otherwise."

"You have one for this time that we're together." His smile was warm, suggesting that most things worth doing should be done in front of a crackling fire.

Cindy turned toward the French doors. The blinds were open, and she could see snowflakes drifting past the glass. "Snow? What will I see if I go look out?" Her voice quavered, and there didn't seem to be anything she could do to make it stop.

"Why don't you go and see?" He'd leaned over to look at the wine bottle.

With steps that felt a little shaky, she walked to the doors. A blanket of snow covered the back lawn and coated the pine trees. "How?"

"A demonstration of what I just told you. Your power starts within your mind, and once you control that, you can move it outward." Thrain grinned at her, and for the first time she noticed the creases on each side of his mouth. Not dimples, but something much more masculine. He picked up the wine bottle to look at the label. "Vampire Wine?"

"I keep it in stock because it fits the inn's theme. It's really pretty good." She started to walk back toward the couch.

"No, Cindy." He stood, still holding the blanket in place with one hand and the bottle of wine in the other. "Get the glasses and we'll have your first lesson in front of the fire."

Right. The fire that couldn't exist because she didn't have a fireplace. Silently, she obeyed him.

He sat facing her, and she turned her head to stare into the flames, seeing her life in their heated flickering. No, that wasn't right. Most of her long life had been more like a smoldering ember craving fuel so it could burst into flame. She glanced back at Thrain. Maybe she'd found her fuel, because she'd felt more alive during the last two nights than she could ever remember feeling before.

She watched him pour the wine, then hold his glass up for a toast. Obliging, she touched her glass to his.

Thrain gazed at her across their glasses with the stillness that had become an early warning signal for her. Uh-oh.

"Here's to knowledge and the door it can open. May we step through that door with no regrets." He lowered his lids, hiding his expression.

"That's a little too cryptic for me, but if releasing my powers involves rooting around in my brain, then maybe you need to ask permission first." Cindy didn't think of herself as a weak person, a person who needed a crutch, but oh, what the hell . . . She took a sip of the merlot. Fine, so it was a gulp.

His smile was easy, sexy but reassuring. Cindy raised her gaze to his eyes. They were hot, intense, and hungry. She believed his eyes.

She had to gain some control over what was about to happen, be a little proactive. "What power will we be exploring, and can I yell stop at any time?"

"We'll start with the most basic power." He reached over and took her glass from her hand, then set both glasses on the flagstones in front of her nonexistent fireplace.

His glass looked untouched, hers was half empty. Whoa, awesome symbolism. The glasses obviously spoke to their individual levels of confidence. Hers wasn't looking too terrific.

"And I'll stop at whatever point you want me to stop." His expression said he didn't think she'd be yelling cease and desist any time soon.

Sounded fair enough. But she was still worried about the mind thing. She hadn't forgotten the spaceship. "You haven't asked permission to enter my mind yet."

This time his smile was open and his eyes held only amusement. "Why would I want to be in your mind? I can have a lot more fun right where I am."

Hmm. He still hadn't promised anything. And was he a little too happy? "Okay, let's do it."

"I want you to recognize your enhanced senses, Cindy." He didn't move, but it was as though his words flowed over her, seeping into her and filling her with exciting possibilities.

Was the excitement hers or his? She wasn't sure she trusted him not to meddle with her emotions.

"My senses have worked just fine for a lot of years."

He offered her a knowing smile that said he understood her distrust and applauded her caution. "Time to take your senses to the next level, sweetheart."

Cindy recognized a con when she heard it. "Sure. Let me guess how this'll go down: I bet you'll tell me that interacting with your body will enhance my senses. How am I doing so far?"

His eyes warmed with laughter. "You always have a choice. You can choose what you wish to see, touch, taste, smell, and hear." He shrugged. "Some sensual experiences bring more pleasure than others."

"In other words, I can touch this," Cindy reached over and rubbed her fingers across the rough fabric of his blanket. "Or I can touch this." She smoothed her fingers across his flat abdomen and felt him suck in his breath under her caress. Oh, wow, she'd definitely felt enhancement possibilities with that last touch.

"Exactly." He challenged her with the slight lift of his lips, the excited gleam in his eyes. "Personally, I'd come down on the side of body interaction."

Cindy didn't know if she really believed Thrain intended to show her how to enhance her senses. But her take on the whole thing was that it didn't matter, because she was positive anything Thrain did to her would feel enhanced. He had female-pleasure-machine programmed into every hard-muscled inch of his body, every hot suggestion in his gaze, every curve of his deceptive mouth.

Oh, yes, this would be a power trip worth taking. And Cindy wasn't going to need Prada's First Aid Kit for Women Who Waffle tonight. For most of these last two nights, things had seemed to be spiraling out of her control. This was a situation she *could* control. Maybe Prada was right. Maybe ultimate sexual pleasure had to be impulsive. She was going to find out, because tonight there would be no second guesses.

"Before the lessons begin, I think you need to understand something. I might look twenty-eight years old, and my sexual needs may be those of a twenty-eight year old, but my sensual experience is seven hundred years old." She wasn't quite sure where this little speech was headed, but she wanted him to understand he didn't have to dress everything up with a lie about enhancing her senses.

"And your point is?" His smile widened.

"I married when I was eighteen. It didn't work out." Understatement. "I never married again, but I still needed sexual release. As the years passed, I met a few men who made me feel comfortable, and after we got to know each other for a while, we made love."

"Comfortable? They made you feel *comfortable?*" He looked offended by the word.

"I'm chucking my usual waiting period with you." She smiled, hoping to erase his frown. "I'm going with impulsive tonight. I wanted you from the moment you walked through my front door. And since you're the first human I've met in seven hundred years who's like me, I figure I'd better grab you while I can. Once you leave, I might have to wait another seven hundred years." Somehow that hadn't come out as sexy as she'd hoped. She needed to get a few more lessons from Prada.

"You don't believe I can help you enhance your senses." It was a statement, requiring no answer.

If she were into self-humiliation, she could tell him that after the sucky sex life she'd had for more years than she cared to count, he wouldn't have to do much of anything. All he'd have to do was stand in front of her nonexistent fireplace naked with his sword strapped to his side and she'd have an orgasm.

His smile was slow, erotic, and terrifying. "Welcome to your future, Cindy Harper."

He reached out to touch her gold loop earring, then paused. "And if at any point you begin to feel comfortable with me, feel free to take my sword and lop off my head."

Chapter Seven

Thrain watched the flare of alarm in her eyes, the nervous twisting of her fingers in her lap, and the longing glance she cast toward her glass of wine.

Good. He didn't want her relaxed and at ease with him. Incredible sex was always a sensual explosion, and the erotic exploration leading up to it should be a burning fuse.

And what the hell was he thinking? He'd walked through the inn's doors yesterday determined to restore Darach's daughter to him. Nothing more. Thrain could've revealed Cindy's heritage to her without taking this path. So why? *Because you have never in all your existence wanted a woman more than you want Cindy Harper.* How was that for self-honesty?

But he did retain one bit of decency. He'd guide her along the path of sensual joy, but he'd stop short of opening the door to the final fulfillment. It would probably kill him, but he owed Darach and Cindy that much.

"You've looked at life through a fogged window, Cindy, with everything on the other side distorted and dulled." Casually, he allowed the blanket to fall away from his body.

She couldn't control her tiny gasp, but he gave her credit for not turning her gaze from his bared body. "Come to me. Touch me. And we'll open that window so you can see things as they really are." Holding her stare with only his will, he lay back on her carpet. Putting one hand beneath his head, he held the other out to her.

He watched her swallow hard, calling attention to the smooth temptation of her exposed throat, awakening the dark lust that wrapped itself around his sexual desire.

Thrain would control his urge to savor the hot flow of her life force, a need that grew stronger in direct proportion to his sexual excitement. And Cindy excited him almost beyond his ability to resist. But resist he would—for her, for him.

Only those of his clan with the strongest wills survived as long as he'd survived, because to surrender to the dark hunger and feed without control destroyed both predator and prey. And even though he was determined that Cindy would never be his prey, it didn't change the fact that he was most definitely a predator. But tonight he would be only her teacher. He smiled at the thought.

"I'm not sure that I trust your smile." But trusting or not, she moved close to him and clasped his outstretched hand.

Her symbolic willingness to put herself in his hands pleased him beyond what was reasonable.

That was *not* a good sign, because it signaled the beginnings of an emotional attachment when he wanted only the physical.

"For all your life, you've allowed yourself to experience your senses only in isolation. If you look at the fireplace, you see the fire, feel the heat, smell the burning wood, and hear the crackle of the flames. All separate sensations. If you close your eyes, you see nothing. If you cover your ears, you hear nothing. To fully open yourself to the sensual, you must realize that all are intertwined. Once you allow your senses to act as one, they become a powerful emotional stimulus." Uh-oh. Her eyes were starting to glaze over.

"Look at me, Cindy." He could easily compel her to meet his gaze, but he allowed her the freedom to make her own decision.

Reluctantly, she met his eyes. "This is sounding pretty complicated. Maybe we should put it off until tomorrow night."

She didn't mean what she said. He could feel the heat of her interest as she dropped her gaze to his cock, assessed it, and then slid her tongue across her lower lip. His body's reaction was the same as if she'd put that hot, luscious mouth around his sex.

"Instead, you can explain why we've lived so long." She looked hopeful, but behind that hopeful expression he saw the heated shadow of sexual arousal.

He wouldn't tell her what she wanted to know until they'd formed a sensual connection, until she liked him enough, *trusted* him enough to accept what he told her. *Listen to yourself. You better than anyone*

should know that sex is the great betrayer. Why should
she trust you just because you've touched her body?

He should at least be honest with himself, even if
he was being less than honest with Cindy. *He* was
the one with trust issues. When he led her through
the door of sensual arousal, it would be the first time
he'd trusted a human female sexually in seven hundred years.

"It would be a shame to put off something so
pleasurable. Besides, tomorrow brings other lessons." His conscience warred with his increasing desire. The desire won.

"Great. Other lessons. I live to learn." She returned his smile, but she didn't look convinced.

"I have to touch all your body, the same way you'll
touch mine." He tried not to look too happy about
that. He failed miserably. "For demonstration purposes, of course."

"Why am I not surprised?" She looked a little
grouchy. "Do I have to take my own clothes off?"

Thrain lowered his lids while he fought to control
the hungry glitter in his eyes. "Who better? I'd enjoy
it if you took each piece off slowly with provocative
body movements." He lifted his gaze but allowed
her to see only his sexual need as he smiled at her. "I
have to feed my own enhanced senses occasionally."

"Hmmph." She dropped his hand and started to
reach for her blouse. "Aren't you supposed to seduce
my clothes off me? I mean, shouldn't you be so
smooth that I don't even realize my clothes are gone?
You disappoint me, Davis."

Thrain tried to look thoughtful, unmoved by her
complaints. "If that's what you really want." He

shifted his gaze to the fire until he heard her panicked screech.

"My clothes! They disappeared. What did you do with them? That was a new pair of jeans. And my favorite red bra. Gone!" She sat next to him, eyes wide with shock, lips slightly parted, and dark tousled hair framing her suddenly pale face. Naked. Completely and vampire-temptingly naked.

He drew in his breath at the wonder of her. "They're all folded neatly on your bed." The creamy skin of her Norse ancestors, full breasts, small waist, curved hips, and long legs made him want to murmur endless words of deep appreciation. He'd bet she had a cute, round bottom he could grasp as he buried himself in her. She was sitting on it right now, but he'd see it soon enough.

"I meant to *slowly* seduce my clothes off. That's part of the foreplay. You skipped the damned foreplay." She pushed her fingers through her hair, and he could see the slight tremor in them. "And how did you *do* that? You can't be like me; I could practice for the next thousand years and not be able to do that."

"It might not take you that long. It only took me six hundred years." His playfulness faded as he slid his gaze the length of her body, and knew she felt its touch as surely as if he'd smoothed his fingers over her bare flesh. Sexual hunger stirred in him, its low growl warning that it would put up with no more nonsense. "And removing clothing doesn't count as foreplay. Only what comes after."

"And that would be?" She was recovering, the shock fading from her eyes, and the sensual interest returning.

"That would be tonight's lesson." Thrain admired her strength. If he slipped into her mind now, he knew what he'd find. She would've pushed the unconventional disappearance of her clothes into a small compartment in her brain, closed the door, and put a sign on the outside that said TO BE DEALT WITH LATER. Unfortunately, if she kept doing that every time he revealed a new power, she'd run out of compartments by the end of the week.

"Lie beside me." He wouldn't insult her by suggesting she relax. Only a very foolish woman would relax when he was near. Cindy wasn't foolish.

She obeyed without questioning, but her gaze was still wary.

Rolling onto his side, Thrain propped himself up on one elbow. She lay on her back staring up at him, vulnerable in a way she couldn't understand because she didn't know him, or what he represented. Once she knew what he was, he doubted she'd ever rest naked beside him again. The thought saddened him.

"I'll touch you only with my fingertips, Cindy. But with each touch I'll memorize the heat and texture of you to be joined with all my other senses. I'm opening my mind so you can understand what I do, and then do it yourself."

Closing his eyes, he skimmed the contours of her face with the tips of his fingers, lingering for a moment on the soft fullness of her lower lip, tasting her sexual excitement through his touch, before moving on to her hair. He let the strands slide through his fingers, *feeling* their shining darkness, the scent of almonds in her shampoo flowing through his fingertips to become part of the total oneness that was Cindy Harper.

"I'm touching your mind, feeling what you're feeling," she murmured, her voice sounding breathless with the newness of it. "How do you experience so much with just the skimming of your fingertips?"

He paused for a moment before answering. His combined hungers were roaring their need to escape, to rampage through his body, compelling him to possess Cindy in every way. With strength forged through centuries of practice, he held both at bay, refusing to let them shatter his mind's barriers while Cindy was viewing his thoughts. One glimpse of what he wanted to do with her would destroy the tenuous threads he was attempting to weave into a binding cord between Cindy and her vampire heritage.

She'd asked him a question. He forced himself to answer, when all he really wanted to do was to abandon his lesson and have hot sex with her while he tasted her life force. "I funnel all my senses through my sense of touch. In my mind, I merge them, and then open my mind to experiencing all through my fingertips."

"I can't—"

"You *can*." He slid his fingers over her neck, pausing at the spot where her life pounded strong and sweet just beneath the surface of her skin. His thoughts turned blood red with his need to feel the slide of his fangs filling his mouth, his need to lean over her and taste . . . He swept the thought from his mind, but not quickly enough.

"I don't understand your thoughts now. They're all jumbled. But for just a moment I felt . . ." She sounded puzzled, but not upset. "I don't know what I felt, but it was incredibly strong."

Thrain laughed softly and hoped it sounded natural. "I want you, Cindy, and it's getting pretty hard to finish this lesson without involving body parts other than my fingertips."

"Then don't finish the lesson." Her suggestion was soft, husky, and filled with the same excitement threatening to engulf him. Well, maybe not exactly the same.

"I have to." *I need time.* He needed time to defeat the almost overpowering need to change, to become the dark predator she feared so much. "I promised." *Promised myself I'd return you to Darach, not drive you away from him forever.*

Using the immense power of his mind, he calmed his body, but only for the moment. Abandoning her neck, he drew an imaginary line around one breast and felt her deep, sensual shudder. When he touched her nipple, the soft moan she tried to suppress made his fingers unsteady even as they absorbed the faint scent of vanilla and reveled in the deep, rich red of sexual arousal.

"Too slow. You're going too *slow.*" She sounded as though she wanted to grab his hand and proceed with the lesson at her own pace.

He thought that might not be a half-bad idea. Because while he'd been involved in his lesson, a hard and determined organ had taken advantage of his mind's distraction to prepare itself for what it was absolutely sure would happen next. Things were going to get ugly fast, because his cock didn't take disappointment well.

Concentrate. He had to remember that Cindy was in his mind. Thank Odin she was focused on hot, sweaty sex and had probably missed that last thought.

Thrain trailed his fingers over her stomach, not lingering even as he felt her draw in a deep breath. He sensed her readiness for him, felt the slight shift of her body as she opened to him.

With eyes still closed, he slid one finger between the swollen lips of her sex to touch the sensitive nub that would drive her toward those final climactic spasms.

Her cry was harsh, needy. If he'd had a human heart, it would have been a drum roll in his chest, his breathing raw gasps of uncontrolled want.

"Lesson over." She reached up to grasp his hair so she could pull him to her. "Now, Thrain. Now!"

Even as he shifted to a kneeling position between her spread legs, he tried to understand. It wasn't supposed to be like this—so fast, so urgent. He'd been able to prolong the pleasure with all the female vampires who'd come before Cindy, enjoying their bodies but always knowing he controlled the pace.

He'd lost that control, and it scared the hell out of him. Thrain could only pull one last power from the depths of his immense will. He clasped Cindy's bottom, lifted her to meet his thrust, and prayed to the gods of his youth that she would keep her eyes closed as the change washed over him—unchecked, unbridled.

He felt the slide of his fangs accompanied by the ravenous need to sink them into her neck and drink deeply, while his sexual hunger demanded he plunge into her again and again. The convergence of his senses shook him.

She would experience this powerful merging, the complete clarity of the senses, through his mind. The explosive oneness that was the scent of sex, the inner sight of sexual truth, the taste of passion, the sounds of sensual pleasure, and the orgasm's supreme moment of primitive ecstasy.

As Thrain pulled all these into one euphoric moment in which only one sense existed, he gathered the last of his strength and power to move away from Cindy.

And then he gave her the *memory*.

Cindy felt the head of his sex sliding into her, the incredible sensation of his smooth possession, and the feeling of fullness that was completely right.

With eyes tightly shut, she knew in the part of her that didn't think but only reacted to physical stimulus that nothing that had come before or might come after could ever compare to this moment of unspeakable sensual pleasure.

She dug her fingers into the taut flesh of his buttocks, felt his cheeks clench beneath her grasp as she moaned with her effort to take more of him, to help him thrust hard enough, deep enough, to touch a spot instinct said only he could reach.

The power and speed of his thrusts increased, shaking her, stretching her beyond what she thought possible, and dragging cries she barely recognized as her own from her. She arched her back, meeting his plunges as he pushed her ever closer to that one primal moment when he would stroke her so deeply that she would hold the memory of him within her body forever. She knew it would happen as surely as she knew the primitive drive for sexual completion ruled her now.

Suddenly, she was there. She stopped breathing as his final plunge touched something so elemental in her that she screamed her triumph. She expelled her breath on a shuddering moan as spasm after clenching spasm shook her. And as the spasms gradually weakened and her reasoning power returned, Cindy knew that this virtual stranger had not only rocked her sexual world but brought it tumbling down around her.

Cindy lay quietly with eyes closed as her breathing slowed and her senses once again became her own. Her mind kicked into high gear as the first cold tendrils of doubt wrapped around the sizzling core of heat Thrain and she had generated together. She fought back the lethargic feeling of satiation that demanded she just lie there and bask in orgasmic afterglow.

He'd done what he'd said he would do. Cindy knew she could never again enjoy sex without comparing it to what she'd just experienced. And nothing, absolutely nothing, would ever measure up to it.

But why hadn't she heard any sounds of pleasure from him? She was woman enough to know he'd been into the moment as strongly as she had. She'd felt him climax. Then why . . . ? She opened her eyes.

He lay beside her, his eyes closed, and she sensed the tension thrumming through him. No postorgasm smile on *his* face. She slid her gaze the length of his sweat-sheened torso and stopped when she reached the proof she was looking for, the proof even he didn't have the power to hide. His erection was so massive and hard that it looked painful.

The strength of her outrage and fury shocked her. "My orgasm was fake. You planted the memory." She wanted to yell more at him, but emotion clogged her throat.

Thrain opened his eyes and turned his head toward her. His eyes looked unutterably weary, as though he'd fought a battle with an enemy he'd barely defeated. Looking at the strength of his arousal, she decided the enemy hadn't been completely crushed.

"You're wrong. Your orgasm was completely real. The only fake part was my participation." He turned his face from her again.

"You coward." It was the most hurtful accusation she could think to fling at him. "You cheated me. Damn you! You cheated me." And then, to her complete and utter horror, tears slid down her face.

Cindy hadn't cried since she was a child. She hadn't cried when her husband fled. She hadn't cried as she'd continued to live when those around her died. Good grief, she hadn't even cried when Bambi's mother died. And now she was sobbing over a simple orgasm? No, not simple. *Never* simple.

Once again, Thrain turned his face toward her. And what Cindy saw in his eyes immediately dried her tears.

Rage. Pure, focused rage.

"Coward? It was torture not taking you." His words were an angry snarl.

"Why didn't you? I wanted *you*, not some fake memory." Beneath her anger was hurt and confusion.

"You don't know what could've happened if I'd taken you. I kept my promise. I showed you the power of your enhanced senses." His fury seemed to be fading into weariness again.

"Could've, would've. You had no right to make the decision for me." Her frustration beat at her. "Tell me *something*, dammit. Explain why you didn't want to complete our lovemaking." Her voice softened. Maybe his weariness was transferring itself to her. "Explain who you are and why we've lived for seven centuries. Please." The *please* was rung from the heart of her long, uncertain life.

She heard the soft expulsion of his breath. "I wanted you, Cindy. A man can't hide that."

"Then let me finish it. You said I could touch you in the same way you touched me. I didn't get my turn." She didn't give herself time to think, or else she knew she'd find reasons not to do this. Quickly, she knelt, and then straddled his hips.

But as she started to lower herself onto his erection, he grasped her arms tightly, holding her in place. She met his gaze, prepared to argue.

Cindy forgot her argument as she stared into his eyes. Eyes she knew could express any emotion he chose, hide things from her or lie to her with equal ease. The emotion she saw in his eyes now was honest. She knew it on a level that needed no explanation.

Fear. Deep, intense fear. "Get off me. Now." His anger was gone, replaced with an urgent need to be free of her.

For some reason, Cindy had assumed that Thrain, with all his power, was beyond fear. Really stupid. Every human had fears. It was just that this fear didn't make any sense.

She shifted off him, then sat beside him. Waiting.

He sat up, then rubbed his hand over his face. When he finally looked at her, his panic was gone. "That wasn't about you, Cindy. It was about something that happened a long time ago."

"Maybe someday you'll tell me about it." There it was. She'd verbalized what her subconscious already knew. She wanted more from Thrain than just the reason for her long life. She wanted to know about *him*—why he'd denied his own satisfaction, why the idea of her completing their lovemaking terrified him. Wanting to know personal things about him was scary. Because at the end of his stay he'd be gone, and she'd be left with a lot of unanswered questions. Caring about the answers was the dangerous part.

"Maybe I will." He rose in one lithe motion and helped her to her feet. "Let's go get our clothes." At ease with his nakedness, he left the blanket on the floor.

Not as easy with *her* nakedness, Cindy scooped up the abandoned blanket and wrapped it around herself. Her legs still shook with reaction as she took his clothes from the dryer. While he was dressing in her bathroom, she went into her bedroom. Sure enough, her clothes were folded on her bed.

As she slowly dressed, the growing unease she'd pushed aside in favor of wild and crazy sex would remain silent no more. Her whole life's search for a reason why she didn't die was predicated on the belief that she was human, but just a tiny bit genetically skewed. Only tonight she'd been given irrefutable proof that other entities besides humans existed.

Thrain said he was like her. But Thrain's power was *not* human power. *Okay, here it comes. Take a deep breath and don't hyperventilate.* If she was like Thrain, and Thrain wasn't human, what did that make her?

Even the thought made her a little nauseous. Cindy took a deep calming breath and tried to think logically. She didn't exhibit any of the characteristics of her nonhuman guests, ergo she wasn't a werewolf, werecat, cosmic troublemaker, faery, or . . . vampire. *Thank God.*

But all this conjecture was driving her crazy. She would march right back out into the living room and demand that Thrain explain—

A frantic knocking on the hall door scattered her thoughts. She hurried to answer it. With everything that had just happened, she'd forgotten that she had a business to run.

Thrain reached the door before her. As he pulled it open, a man Cindy didn't recognize stepped into the room. She did a quick scan to make sure the fireplace and snow were gone, then tried to greet the man with some semblance of composure. She pasted a smile on her face and stepped forward.

"Hi, I'm Cindy Harper. And you're . . . ?"

"Sam Pierce. Freelance writer. Just checked in today. Word's out that there's a great Jersey Devil story here waiting to be written." He looked like Danny DeVito—short, balding, and determined—in search of a hot story to sell for some cold cash. His eyes gleamed with barely suppressed excitement. "Someone just took a cell phone call from a vampire who's trapped with two of her friends out in an old cemetery."

"Trapped?" That would be Kim, Gerry, and Donna. And the last person she needed in her inn right now was a nosy writer. But she'd worry about him later.

"Yeah. There was a lot of screeching and crying, but it sounded like they were saying that all the spirits had risen from their graves and wouldn't let them leave the cemetery. They sound like a bunch of fruitcakes to me." He actually rubbed his hands together. "Fruitcakes always make great stories."

Her night was complete. "I want to talk with the person who took the call before I go searching for them." She pulled on her jacket, grabbed her flashlight, and checked to make sure her phone and gun were still in the pockets. Her casual acceptance that the gun *should* be in her pocket disturbed her.

"I'm going with you." Thrain strapped the belt with his sword around his waist and put on his coat.

Sam watched with unblinking interest. "I can't believe it. I've hit the mother lode of fruitcakes." He grinned his joy at the realization.

Cindy locked her door, then trailed the two men down the hallway. What was happening to her quaint, colorful inn? It was as if a hellhole had opened beneath it, disgorging an army of night creatures intent on making themselves royal pains-in-the-butt. And talking about a pain in the butt, what was she going to do with Sam Pierce?

By the time she reached the front of the inn, Thrain was already talking to Clark, who was still in full furry costume.

"How about if me and the guys go along to help?" Clark's words lacked a certain enthusiasm, and his expression said that if he had to go with them to the cemetery he'd wet his pants.

"No. Absolutely not." The word LIABILITY was emblazoned on her brain in neon caps. If by chance there *was* something dangerous in the cemetery and it injured any of her guests, she'd be open to a lawsuit. "Did Officer James stop by?"

Clark nodded. "He came by right after me and the

guys got back from doing our thing. We told him we didn't know where you were but that everything was cool here. He said if you didn't show up soon to give him another call." His expression turned eager. "Should we call him again?"

"No. Thrain and I will take care of things." She cast Clark a worried glance. "Would you tell everyone you can to stay inside the inn until we check out the cemetery?"

Clark nodded, and then hurried away to spread the word.

"Yo, I'm going with you." Sam inserted himself between Cindy and Thrain.

Thrain frowned. "I thought you were looking for the Jersey Devil."

"Hey, I'll do a story about anything. People love weird stuff. Let's get moving." Sam hurried out the front door, leaving Cindy and Thrain to trail after him.

Thrain caught up with him in a few strides and they waited for Cindy. Once she joined them, Cindy laid down a few ground rules.

"Here's how it's going to be, Sam. Thrain and I will go ahead in case there's any danger. You stay far enough behind us so that you can run back to the inn if anything happens." *So that your eager little ears can't hear what we're saying.*

"But I—"

Cindy held up her hand to stop his complaint. "You're on my property. If you don't want to do it my way, feel free to go back to the inn and choose somewhere else to stay." She sighed her fake regret. "I hate the thought of disappointing a guest, but if that's what it takes to ensure your safety . . ." Cindy offered him a resigned shrug.

Mumbling complaints about suppression of free speech and freedom of the press, he fell behind them on the narrow wooded path.

Thrain smiled at her. "You're a cold woman, Cindy Harper."

Because she was still steamed at him, she controlled her urge to remind him of exactly how hot she really was.

"I'm curious." Casually, he draped his arm across her shoulders.

She wouldn't give him the satisfaction of shrugging his arm away.

"You didn't warn your guests to stay out of the woods because of the Jersey Devil, but now you're telling them to stay inside because of some possible spirits. Why?" He didn't turn his head to look at her, but she could tell he was smiling.

He knew the reason, but he got some warped enjoyment from making her spell it out. "Last night I didn't believe in the Jersey Devil. Tonight I'm open to the possibility." She paused for effect. "Last night I thought you might be like me. Tonight I think you might be something very different."

She glanced up at him. Good. He'd stopped smiling.

Chapter Eight

"You know, this cemetery thing is getting old. Been here, done this. At least there's some moonlight tonight to help us see."

Cindy's words sounded flip, but Thrain noticed she kept close to his side. There was no mist tonight, but that didn't lessen the menacing feel of these woods. She'd chosen a good spot for her business—if she could find a way to appease the Jersey Devil—because the memories of many past lives lingered among these trees. Nothing that would harm her guests, but the pure power of their numbers would give even the dullest human senses a creepy feeling.

She frowned up at him. "Maybe it's just me, but it seems that all of this weird stuff didn't start happening until you showed up."

"Ouch." She had no idea how weird things were going to get. "I didn't make Adolfo or Sam show up. If you're going to suspect anyone, why not take a closer look at Trojan or Prada? They checked in at the same time."

"Shh, we're almost there." Cindy turned off her flashlight as she slipped off the path and into the woods just before they reached the cemetery.

He could hear Sam mumbling and cursing as he thrashed around in the underbrush. Thrain smiled. Cindy knew the area well enough to make her way around in the dark on a clear night, and his night vision was sharper than any human's. Sam had neither advantage.

Cautiously, Cindy peered from among the trees at the scene in the cemetery. He heard her small gasp of horror echoed by Sam's as the man stumbled to their side. Thrain could understand their reaction, but personally he wasn't that impressed.

The three vampire impersonators stood in the middle of the cemetery. Their expressions said they'd moved from terror to outrage. The women's all-black clothing was a nice contrast to the pale white forms of the ghosts hovering above each grave.

An older man wearing a tweed jacket and looking a little like someone's aging butler stood on the edge of the cemetery watching everything. Thrain remembered the man had been sitting next to Cindy last night in the parlor. Ignoring the three women, he slipped into the man's mind.

"Well, well." Thrain smiled as he glanced at Cindy. "I'm going over to talk to our tweedy friend."

"He's Leo Varinski, and I'm going with you. Those women are my guests." She stared at Sam. "You stay here."

Sam nodded, evidently not eager for a one-on-

one interview with any of the cemetery's ghostly residents.

Thrain strode toward Varinski with Cindy by his side. As soon as the women saw Cindy, they bounced up and down, shouting their personal concerns.

"If I don't get out of here right now, this mud'll ruin the third best pair of black shoes I brought. The Woo Woo Inn owes me a new pair of black shoes." The first woman lifted her foot to show the dire condition of her shoes.

"Fine, fine. We'll take care of the shoes, Gerry." Cindy's soothing assurance didn't quite ring sincere.

"This is *not* reasonable behavior for spirits. I've done tons of research on them and they absolutely would never react this way." The next woman glared at the hovering ghosts as though they were a personal affront to her vast research.

"Calm down, Donna. I'm sure there's a logical explanation." Cindy sounded ragged around the edges.

"Every time we try to leave, they start floating toward us." The last woman looked as though she thought Cindy was personally responsible for everything. "I write vampire fiction and I'm way past my deadline. I told my editor I'd e-mail him the last two chapters of my book yesterday. I haven't even *started* the last two damn chapters, and he's going to be totally pissed. I don't have time for this hostage stuff." She paused for breath. "I'm so stressed I'll need tons of chocolate to calm me down. Make them go away. Now."

"Got it, Kim. Chocolate and make them go away." Cindy turned to glare at Thrain and the old man.

"Getting really cranky here. What's going on and how do we stop it?"

Thrain glanced at Leo. "Don't you think this has gone on long enough?"

Leo clasped his hands behind his back, rocked back on his heels, and raised one eyebrow at Thrain. "No. I'm having quite a good time, actually."

Cindy turned her attention to Leo. "You're responsible for this? Why?" Her "How?" remained unspoken.

Leo sighed as though the weight of the world rested on his aged shoulders. "They called me an old fart, among other things. Now, really. I can't allow that kind of disrespect."

Thrain thought Leo had a point, but he wasn't about to stand around in the woods for the rest of the night. He turned to shout at the women. "Ignore the ghosts. Just leave."

Gerry put her hands on her hips and shouted back. "Who died and made you an expert on ghosts? You didn't have a clue about vampires last night, and I don't think you got any smarter in one day." She glanced down at her ruined shoes. "I'm suing the inn for a whole truckload of new shoes."

Thrain knew he shouldn't say anything, knew that goading the woman wouldn't solve anything. Oh, what the hell. "I don't get it. All you have to do is change into a bat and fly away. You *can* do that, can't you, ladies? And by the way, I've changed my mind about the bat form. Bats are you."

"That was a big help, Davis." Cindy sounded weary.

"As entertaining as all of this is, I really must be going." Leo glanced at his watch. "Dinner is about to be served." Without another word, he turned and ambled away.

Cindy looked horrified. "Come back. You have to—"

Thrain put his hand on her shoulder. "I can take care of this."

She stared at him and then glanced at the still-hovering ghosts. "Okay, but do it fast. Joshua is scoping out the area for a horse to steal."

A sound made Thrain and Cindy turn in time to see Sam aiming his camera at them. How many pictures had he taken? Was that a digital camera or would Sam have to develop the film? Thrain didn't own a camera, so what the hell did he know about them? What he *did* know was that he couldn't allow Sam to discover he wasn't visible in the pictures and then pass that information on to Cindy. *Not yet.* Not until she understood her vampire roots. Thrain controlled his need to rip the damned camera from Sam's hand. He wouldn't make a big deal about it now, but he'd definitely have to do some damage control with Sam. First, though, he'd better get rid of the ghostly images.

Thrain stilled as he focused his powers, visualized the images gone, and then projected his visualization outward. The spirits disappeared. He thanked the gods that nothing he'd had to do in the last two nights had been difficult. The Jersey Devil could've been a problem, but joining with Trojan had made it fairly painless. In order to exert a lot of power, he'd have to change forms, and he wanted Cindy well prepared before she saw that.

The three women didn't stop to ask any questions or offer any thank-yous as they hurried out of the cemetery and back to the inn. Sam, clutching his camera along with his juicy story, trotted after them.

Cindy sighed as she stared after her fast-disappearing guests. "I suppose I should be gleeful about the free publicity this will bring, but instead, all I can do is worry about someone getting hurt. I mean, I didn't worry about that before because I didn't believe in the paranormal. Between this and the Jersey Devil sighting, I'll have all kinds of people tramping through these woods. Some of them won't even be guests. There's no way for me to stop curious people from parking their cars on the blacktop and hiking into my woods. I own a lot of acres and I can't police all of them at night." She turned shadowed eyes up to him. "Who is Leo?"

Thrain knew he shouldn't touch her, not when he was still sexually charged from the aborted lesson back in her apartment. But she was worried, and he had this crazy urge to comfort her when he hadn't felt the need to comfort a human female in centuries.

Before he could apply logic to the urge, he wrapped his arms around her, pulled her against him, and then put his hands under her jacket so he could run his hands up and down her back while he explained what she'd just witnessed.

"Leo is a wizard. Not a particularly gifted one. Just your run-of-the-mill wizard."

Cindy rewarded him with a shaky laugh. "Even a run-of-the-mill wizard is pretty much a wow for me."

"And what you saw tonight weren't ghosts in the sense that you usually think of spirits." He continued his soothing rhythmic motions on her back.

Startled, she looked up at him. "Ghosts are ghosts, aren't they?"

Cindy felt the vibration of his soft laughter, the heat of his body through her clothing, and the intensely sensual slide of his fingers up and down her back.

"No. Every place holds the memories of people who lived and died there. This place is no different. Leo simply made manifest a few of those memories. You saw a glimpse into the past tonight." He removed one hand from her back to gesture at the forest surrounding them. "Your forest is filled with similar memories—people who hunted and played here—you just can't see them." He leaned down to whisper in her ear. "But you can feel them if you become completely still and reach for them with your senses."

Cindy was acutely aware of the warmth of his breath against her ear as she tried to achieve the inner quietness he asked of her. And as she gazed into the woods, she felt them, *she actually felt them.*

Suddenly, though, she realized she was feeling more than just the forest's memories. It was as if she had never seen the woods, the night sky, or the man who held her before. She was experiencing all her senses with a clarity that brought tears to her eyes. Every tree, every shadow, every star in the sky stood out as if she'd turned a knob on her inner camera and brought everything into perfect focus.

She turned back to Thrain and knew her eyes were wide with wonder. "I can hear small animals moving in the brush. I can smell the earth, the plants, in a way I never did before." She closed her eyes and concentrated. "I can *taste* the night."

"Now bring it all together within you and experience the one."

Even his husky command took on a deeper,

clearer reality for her. Drawing in a deep breath, she visualized all her senses merging, entwining like a single braid, and then she became part of that entwining. She gasped at the sudden explosive impact.

"Ohmigod, it's like an orgasm of the senses." She grinned up at him.

Thrain laughed as he kept his arm around her waist and guided her toward the path leading back to the inn. "Good description. I've never heard it described that way before."

As she walked beside him, she turned on her flashlight. The harsh beam of light somehow seemed to disturb the darkness. It didn't belong. She drew in a deep breath. *Whoa, reality check. Darkness is not a living thing.* These last two nights were making her crazy.

"Wait." She stopped walking, forcing him to stop, too. "I don't want to get back to the inn too soon and have to face everyone's questions."

He nodded, his eyes gleaming in the darkness as though they held their own light. A night hunter's eyes. Impossible? Not really. So many strange things had bombarded her over the last two nights that glowing eyes didn't seem like any big deal.

They were alone, and here among all the cemetery's collected memories, she intended to add another. "I want to know about myself. No more evasions. No more interruptions." She waited breathlessly to see if he'd try to avoid telling her.

He didn't. Silently, he led her back to the cemetery, looked around, then chose a low, wide tombstone to sit on. He drew her down beside him. "I don't think Molly Carson will mind our using her headstone for a little while."

Without knowing why she did it, Cindy turned off her flashlight. The darkness closed in around her—warm, comforting. She felt as though the night welcomed her. The thought made her a little uneasy. "I'm ready."

"I know more about you than you think I know, Elina Mackenzie."

His low voice flowed over her, calming and assuring her there was nothing strange about his knowing the name no one had spoken in almost seven centuries.

"How did you know my name was Elina? And my last name has never been Mackenzie." She knew she was speaking in a hushed whisper, but shock seemed to have affected her volume control.

He wrapped his arm more tightly around her waist and hugged her to his side. "You belong to a Viking clan. Those who belong to the clan don't die, as you've already discovered. Your father, Varin Kylandsson, was a Viking warrior. He married your mother, Aesa, and soon after she became pregnant with you."

Distress made her voice harsh. "Mom said my biological father abandoned her. She never mentioned marriage."

"Varin would never have abandoned you or your mother." He held up his hand to keep her from interrupting. "Your mother didn't belong to the clan. She was a normal human and lived a normal span of years. Aesa knew what your father was when she married him, but once she was pregnant with you, her fears must've grown stronger than her love for him." He shrugged. "Only Aesa knew what her thoughts were, and she took them to her grave."

"Why didn't she ever tell me about my father?" Cindy could have avoided so much conjecture and fear if she'd only known.

She saw his faint smile. "Maybe she thought if you didn't know about him, you wouldn't *be* like him. People try to fool themselves in all kinds of ways. Besides, she still had a husband when she married your stepfather. Your stepfather wouldn't have been too happy to find that out."

"Why didn't my father find her?" Find *me*?

His silence stretched on a little too long. She sensed that for some reason this part of the story would be hard for him to tell.

"Your father had gone away for a short trip to gather winter supplies, and while he was gone your mother approached his best friend. She asked him to take her to visit an acquaintance while your father was away. Aesa assured the friend that your father knew about her intended visit and would bring her home once he'd gathered the winter supplies." Thrain paused, and Cindy could feel his tension. "Your father's friend was a fool. He took Aesa where she asked to go, and no one ever saw her again."

"What happened when my father came home?" Why had her mother kept this from her? She'd known on her deathbed that her daughter was like her father. Her mother had lived to fifty-eight, an old age for that time. Cindy had been forty when her mother died, but Cindy had still looked twenty-eight, while her younger brothers and sisters looked far older.

"Your father searched for Aesa but never was able to find her. He was furious with his friend, and rightly so." Thrain shrugged. "They parted in anger.

Your father spent many years raiding the coast of Scotland. Eventually, the clan settled in the Highlands, built a castle, and changed their names to Mackenzie so they wouldn't be associated with the hated Vikings. Your father became Darach Mackenzie."

"He never knew about me." The sadness of that truth brought her close to tears.

"On her deathbed, your mother sent word to the remaining members of her family. She confessed that she'd remarried and had other children, but she took the secret of your birth to her grave. Aesa told her family that her flight from Darach had caused her to miscarry. The child was dead." Thrain grew quiet, his thoughts his own for that moment. "Your father always mourned your loss. He felt guilty, trying to think what he could have done differently to keep Aesa with him."

Cindy stared into the darkness. It didn't take much hard thinking to connect the dots. "*You* were my father's friend."

He nodded. "Even though your father and I reconciled centuries later, I always blamed myself. And so I started investigating. Eventually, I found where your mother settled and married. From there I found records of the deaths of everyone in the family except for you. I've followed you through the centuries, always one step behind because each time you moved you changed your identity."

Cindy sat quietly, listening to her heartbeat, feeling her childhood beliefs crumbling and slipping through her fingers like sand. Once gone, they would be gone forever, and she would have to build new beliefs based on the truth.

"Where is my father?" Of all the questions clamoring for answers, this was the most important.

"Darach is at our clan's ancestral castle in Scotland, but he'll only be there for twelve more days." He raked his fingers through his hair, a sign that what he was telling her wasn't easy for him either. "He doesn't know about you because I didn't want to say anything until I was sure things would work out."

She smiled because that seemed the appropriate facial expression, but she could just as easily have burst into tears. The tears would probably come later. "You mean until you knew I was really his daughter and that I'd want to meet him."

He nodded.

"I've waited seven hundred years to meet him. I'd say my answer is yes." She'd changed her mind about the darkness. It was a living, breathing extension of her anger, her sadness at all the lost years. What had her mother been thinking? She'd never given Cindy the chance to make her own decision about her father. She'd never thought about the disconnection her daughter would feel—never knowing why she didn't die, never knowing where she belonged.

"I know you have more questions, but a lot has happened tonight. Why don't you sleep on it, and I can tell you more tomorrow?" His tone said he'd told her all he intended to tell for the night.

Cindy could have argued with him, but for once she agreed. Tonight, not only had she learned who she was and that her father was still alive, but also that she was playing hostess to a bunch of nonhuman entities.

Besides, he'd probably told her the good part

first. Because of her human mother, she wasn't a full-blooded member of the clan. Thrain had given her a sneak preview of the clan's power. Any group that wielded so much power must have a name, and she had the sinking feeling that *human* wouldn't be part of their title. In true ostrich fashion, she would enjoy the good part and ignore everything else until tomorrow.

But she wasn't ready to go back to the inn just yet. Excitement and nervous energy thrummed through her. And with it came sexual awareness. So what else was new? She'd felt that from the first moment she'd seen Thrain Davis. But this was different. This was unfinished business. He'd cheated her tonight out of an honest-to-goodness orgasm. He owed her.

With her newly enhanced senses hooking up with her hip-hopping hormones, there were some raunchy raps rattling around in her mind. And each verse began with the word *Thrain* and ended with the word *sex*.

Cindy wondered if he felt this way, too, with everything larger, more powerful, more irresistible. Nothing she'd learned so far had tempered her growing desire for him—not his admission of his part in her mother's deceptions and not her knowledge that he still had secrets. Secrets she sensed he didn't want to tell her.

"So what do you think?" He waited patiently for her answer to a question she couldn't remember.

"I think you owe me an orgasm." Well, that should knock him off his tombstone.

His soft laughter warmed her. "Great minds think alike."

Thrain could have told her that mentioning the word *orgasm* to a vampire while darkness surrounded them, and his hunger was at its strongest, was not a wise thing to do. But wisdom played no part in what he intended for Cindy Harper. She had tempted him in every way while his vaunted restraint stretched thinner and thinner.

"My rubber band just snapped." He would feed part of his craving for her here in the darkness, but he would somehow manage to control the other part, the one she wouldn't accept. *At least not now.* Thrain's determination that there would be, at some future time, a complete joining between them startled him. How could he have gone so quickly from his promise not to touch her for Darach's sake to this? She shouldn't be that important to him, but on a level that wouldn't be denied, he knew she was.

"Your rubber band?"

Even her laughter made him hard. Thrain decided it was serious lust when his body translated everything Cindy did into the word *sex*. "Don't laugh. I thought I could stretch it all the way back to your bed, but it snapped right here on Molly Carson's tombstone." He slid his coat off, let it drop to the ground, and then placed his sword beside it.

She widened her eyes as he reached over and slipped her jacket off. "Here? We can't make love here! It's cold and—"

"It's warm. Don't you feel the warmth?" He planted the suggestion and watched it take effect.

She stopped shivering and stared at him. "You're right. It's warm. How did you do that?"

Thrain shrugged as he reached for her shirt. "You're very open to suggestion." The word *open* conjured all kinds of mental pictures. He growled low in his throat.

She gripped her shirt so that he couldn't slide it over her head.

He exhaled impatiently. "I'm trying to seduce your clothes from you. You have to work with me on this."

"We can't do it here because—"

"It won't be prickly and uncomfortable. You can lie on my coat." Uh-oh. His inner Neanderthal was starting to grunt demands involving words like *club*, *hair*, and *cave*.

"How did you know what I was going to say?" She narrowed her gaze on him. "You read my mind." Now she looked downright steamed. "Let's get one thing straight right now: Stay. Out. Of. My. Mind. I don't want you reading my thoughts, and I don't want you messing with my memory."

Thrain rubbed the back of his neck with his hand and pulled the pieces of his scattered control together. She was right. "I'm sorry." He met her gaze. "I won't enter your mind again without your permission and I won't change your memories."

While she sat quietly thinking about what he'd said, Thrain used the moment to remind himself why this night had to be so sensually powerful that Cindy would never forget it. He had no idea where he would fit into her future life, but he was selfish enough to want every one of her future lovers to fall far short of this memory. Future lovers? Even the thought of other men touching her started a slow, furious burn in his gut. Jealousy? He didn't know because he'd never felt the emotion before, and he definitely didn't want to feel it again.

"Does the cemetery make you feel uneasy?" Seven hundred years of sensual knowledge had shaped him, and Thrain intended to use that knowledge to make sure that within a few minutes she wouldn't remember where they were.

Her smile flashed whitely in the pale moonlight. "I've lived too long to be superstitious, and you've explained what I saw here. So no, I'm not afraid of this cemetery. It's probably one of the few places tonight where I won't be hassled by questions from curious guests.

"And since we're dealing with the preliminaries, don't bother telling me you don't need to use protection. I know we're immune from disease." Cindy's smile faded, and her expression turned wistful. "And I know I won't get pregnant. I was pregnant once, a long time ago. But I miscarried, and that was that."

Her tone might sound matter-of-fact, but he sensed her sadness, and once again felt a need to comfort. "After a certain age, we lose our reproductive powers. But who knows? In a few hundred years, scientists might come up with a way for you to have children."

"I guess that's one of the things you'll explain tomorrow." Her smile returned.

"Tomorrow." He leaned over and slid her shirt over her head. Obligingly, she lifted her arms to make it easier for him. "But tonight, we'll only think of pleasure."

"Mmm. And pleasure has taken on a whole new meaning since I've discovered my enhanced senses." Her arms gleamed palely as she slowly unbuttoned his shirt and then slipped it off his shoulders.

He shrugged out of it and flung it to the ground while he fixed his gaze on the wonder of her smooth shoulders and the soft swell of her stomach. Her red bra tempted and teased until his blood heated and forged its inevitable path to his cock, which was still feeling pretty ticked at him after its earlier disappointment. But ever optimistic, it swelled hard and demanding, making him shift to ease the discomfort.

Her smile was innocent anticipation and knowing seduction. "We didn't kiss last time. You owe me a sensational kiss, Davis." With the tip of her finger, she traced the contours of his lips.

Holding her gaze, he gripped her finger so he could slide the tip of his tongue across its pad. As she drew in her breath at the sensation, he pulled her close and covered her mouth with his.

He held nothing back. His tongue explored and savored the heat and taste of her, even as he firmly rejected his body's screaming desire to change. *Not tonight. Not with Cindy.*

His need was barely controlled ferocity, and at some point he realized her eagerness matched his. As she broke the kiss to trail her tongue down his neck, he unhooked her bra. She didn't notice when it fell away from her.

Her lips lingered for a moment on his throat. Heat and desire that was almost pain shuddered through him. Thor's thunder, but every cell in his body screamed for the feel of her teeth sinking deep into his flesh, knowing that she shared his life. It wouldn't happen. Only those born of two clan members knew the blood hunger.

Can you live without that part of your sexual fulfillment? If he'd asked the question of himself while he

YES! ☐

Sign me up for the **Historical Romance Book Club** and send my THREE FREE BOOKS! If I choose to stay in the club, I will pay only $13.50* each month, a savings of $6.47!

YES! ☐

Sign me up for the **Love Spell Book Club** and send my TWO FREE BOOKS! If I choose to stay in the club, I will pay only $8.50* each month, a savings of $5.48!

NAME: _____

ADDRESS: _____

_____

TELEPHONE: _____

E-MAIL: _____

☐ **I WANT TO PAY BY CREDIT CARD.**

☐ VISA ☐ MasterCard ☐ DISCOVER

ACCOUNT #: _____

EXPIRATION DATE: _____

SIGNATURE: _____

Send this card along with $2.00 shipping & handling for each club you wish to join, to:

Romance Book Clubs
20 Academy Street
Norwalk, CT 06850-4032

Or fax (must include credit card information!) to: 610.995.9274. You can also sign up online at www.dorchesterpub.com.

*Plus $2.00 for shipping. Offer open to residents of the U.S. and Canada only. Canadian residents please call 1.800.481.9191 for pricing information.
If under 18, a parent or guardian must sign. Terms, prices and conditions subject to change. Subscription subject to acceptance. Dorchester Publishing reserves the right to reject any order or cancel any subscription.

JOIN NOW!

mated with the many female vampires he'd known, his answer would have been no. But to be with Cindy and experience all the other sensations and emotions she evoked, he would forgo this one pleasure. The scary part? Thrain knew of no other female he'd ever been willing to make this concession for.

He stood and pulled her to her feet. Frantically, they tore at each other's clothing until they were both naked, and then Thrain lowered her to his coat.

Forcing himself to grow still, he tried to gain control of his need, the almost agonizing want that demanded he spread her thighs and bury himself inside her right now. "This isn't what I had in mind." He lay beside her while he drew circles with his fingertip on one tempting shoulder. "I planned this to be a slow, erotic peeling off of clothing to make up for earlier."

"Umm. I've changed my mind." She leaned over him, her long dark hair trailing multiple paths of sensual torture across his chest. "Peeling is for onions. Really overrated." Slowly, lingeringly, she slid her tongue over each of his nipples.

Thrain bit his bottom lip to keep from moaning his pleasure. But when she teased his nipples with that talented tongue before kissing a searing path over his stomach, the moan slipped out anyway. Through a growing haze of sexual excitement, he watched her press her lips to the head of his erection. The harsh animal sound of enjoyment he made at the brief touch of heated pressure on his sex made her look up at him and smile.

Her smile was wicked enticement and female triumph. "You excite me, Davis. Your body is hot and beautiful, and I could feed all day off your pleasure."

She smoothed her fingers down his arousal and then cupped him in her palm. "But I'm beginning to see a down side to my enhanced senses." Her hands never left his body as she gently massaged his inner thighs. "They make the fire blaze too hot, too fast, here." She put her hand between her legs, pressing against her sex as if trying to slow the burn. "That scent of man and sex, the taste of aroused male, the sounds you make when I do this . . ."

She paused to demonstrate. Pushing her dark hair out of the way, she slid her mouth over his cock. The all-enveloping heat and unbearable friction dragged a groan from him. He arched his back, and when she circled the head with the tip of her tongue and nipped gently, Thrain knew he'd reached his personal limit. Before she could become more creatively involved in what she was doing to him, he rolled her onto her back and knelt between her open thighs.

"I can't take anymore." He knew his smile was hungry, his pupils enlarged as his body prepared for the change. But he couldn't let it happen. There would be no slide of fangs, no feeding tonight. "Touching my body with your mouth and your hands guarantees that you can forget the foreplay."

"Bummer." She made a small moue of pretend disappointment. "No hands? No mouth? What's left? Maybe my toes, but . . ."

Thrain leaned down to kiss the sensitive skin behind her ear before whispering, "You touch me sensually in every way possible—the way you bite your bottom lip while you're thinking, and that sassy, sexy smile you give me when you think you've won."

He paused to draw her nipple between his lips and then run the edge of his front teeth lightly across the sensitive nub. She sucked in her breath and clasped a fistful of his hair.

Releasing her nipple, he smiled down at her wide, unblinking stare. "I could even get excited about your toes. I bet there're lots of places you could put your toes that—"

Unexpectedly, she laughed. And he discovered that her laughter touched him, too.

"I'd say we're at an impasse. If I touch you, I'll push you over the edge. And if you keep doing things to my body, I'll go off like a firecracker. I think we'll have to postpone the long, languorous foreplay until another night." She stretched her arms above her head while she studied his body. "Has anyone ever told you that you're incredibly yummy?"

He frowned. "No, I think you're the first." Why were they talking?

"Smile." Since he was still leaning over her, she didn't have far to reach to tickle his stomach.

With a surprised bark of laughter, he leaned back on his heels so she couldn't reach him without sitting up. "You're amazing, lady. No one has ever tried to tickle me in my whole life." There had *never* been any playfulness in his matings with other vampires. Sex had been hot, intense, and over.

"Good. Everyone should be tickled at least once in his life, even those of us with very, very long lives." Her gaze turned serious. "What do you want from tonight, Thrain?"

He smiled down at her. "I wanted this to be my most powerful seduction in seven hundred years so no man who comes after me will ever be able to measure up." Why the hell had he told her that? "But I think I've blown it."

For just a moment, he could've sworn her eyes misted. Sitting up, she cupped his face between her palms. "Don't you get it? Anyone can touch another person's body. That's not what makes for great sex. It's what's going on up here while the other person is touching you that makes it beautiful." She tapped the side of his head. "The whole sexual attraction thing is a mixture of the physical and the emotional." She lay back down and studied him. "It's the head-and-heart connection."

Since he didn't have a human heart, that probably left him out of the equation. For him, it had always been the cock-and-blood connection. But he had to admit his emotions were involved this time: a first in his long sexual history.

She smiled at him. "Besides staying gorgeously naked, the most seductive thing you can do is to be yourself, someone I can joke with, tickle, or ask what you were doing during the Revolutionary War. Someone I can finally feel at ease with because we've had similar life experiences."

Not really, sweetheart. Guilt held him silent, and that surprised him. After so many centuries, he'd thought he was pretty pragmatic. If lying made life easier, he lied. But this time, he couldn't perpetuate the lie by agreeing with her. Instead he'd continue their interrupted journey toward the promised orgasm.

"I think you're right about the foreplay." He curled one dark strand of her hair around his finger. "Let's go for some mutual touching until we can't stand it anymore. That should take . . . oh, maybe three, four minutes."

"That long, huh?" She smiled at him.

For just an instant, he thought about what it would

feel like to wake up to that smile for the rest of his existence, and then pushed the thought away.

Thrain touched her then. Not the slow, erotic exploration he'd planned, but one driven by barely contained sexual need. He slid his hands the length of her warm, tempting body, promising himself he would remember the way her smooth skin gleamed in the pale moonlight, the way her full breasts filled his palms.

And even as his sensual excitement sizzled along every nerve ending, he couldn't get enough of her. As he kissed the skin right behind her knee, then slid his tongue up her inner thigh, he promised himself he'd eventually touch every inch of her with his mouth. Maybe not tonight, but there *would* be another night for them.

There was one spot, though, that he couldn't leave untouched for another time. As she instinctively spread her legs for him, he lingeringly slid the tip of his tongue over her most sensitive spot. He got no further.

She cried out as she arched her hips and then grabbed his hair, forcing him to slide higher on her sweat-sheened body. "Okay," she said between gasps, "I've reached my limit. Probably hasn't even been two minutes, but you overestimated the time thing badly."

Pulling his face down to hers, she looked at him with all of the heat and desire she was feeling. "I want to be touching your sex when you enter me, but first I need to hold your . . ." Her smile spread, warm and inviting. "I want to hold your buns, dig my fingers into your flesh, and feel you clench that magnificent butt. Now you know my secret. I have a cheek fetish."

Thrain buried his face in the curve of her neck and laughed. *Just laughed.* He felt no overwhelming desire to sink his teeth into her, just a driving need to bury himself in this extraordinary, welcoming woman.

"I could get really involved with your bottom, too. Let's see what we can do about it." Before she knew what he intended, he lifted her to her feet and backed her against the tree next to Molly Carson's headstone.

He didn't have to waste words on directions as she clasped his shoulders to steady herself and then spread her legs. Placing his palms beneath her round little bottom, he lifted her off her feet. She wouned her legs around him, and just before he eased into her, she reached between them to wrap her fingers around his cock and squeezed.

Everything came close to ending right there. The intense sexual stimulus almost ripped him apart. For a few scary moments he thought he'd lose his battle and change right in front of her. Finally gaining control, he buried himself deep inside her. Thrain remained still for a moment, savoring the sensual impact. Tight. Hot. Wet. But then Cindy began to move, and he joined her in the rhythm of sex. She grasped his shoulders, and as he braced her against the tree and drove into her, she cried out her pleasure.

Red. His sexual color. Thrain never understood humans who didn't see colors as part of their erotic enjoyment. As Cindy clenched around his sex, and the tightened coil of his coming sexual release dragged a gasp from him, brilliant waves of shining red colored his universe.

He rose through the red, taking Cindy with him, wrapping her in all the sensual power he'd accumulated in his centuries as a vampire. As he drove into her one last time, she met him with an equal frenzy.

Thrain shouted his triumph as the red deepened until it exploded into black. Even as his orgasm devoured all his senses in that one climactic moment, the black absorbed everything in his world except the one perfect pleasure. And while Cindy's scream joined his shout, the moment of complete stillness took them.

He felt their final merging as they strained, not breathing and muscles locked, trying to sustain the unsustainable, that sensation of physical nirvana that lifted them to a place no other human experience could take them.

Then he was tumbling back through the red again, feeling Cindy's harsh breathing, hearing the pounding of her heart, and realizing he'd never known this intensity of completion before.

He helped Cindy over to his coat and collapsed beside her as they both tried to recover. Only when he was able to think coherently did the realization hit him. *The orgasm had satisfied all of his hunger.* He felt no desire to feed. The wonder of it rocked him.

"You're a special woman, Cindy Harper." She had no idea how special. He could never have imagined finding sex satisfying without the ultimate sharing. Of course, satisfying didn't begin to describe what he'd just experienced.

Cindy looked at him out of eyes that shone with emotion. "I never thought, never knew that . . ." She waved her hand to indicate her inability to explain what she never knew. "Wow is totally inadequate."

Thrain smiled. Fine, so he'd admit to some ego. He sort of liked that she couldn't find words for what they'd shared. "I can't describe the indescribable. You took me all the way to black."

"Black?" She evidently had no idea how huge a compliment he'd given her.

"I see sex in colors, and red has always been the color I see during sex. The deeper the red, the more intense the orgasm." He pushed several damp strands of her hair away from her face. "But I've never gone beyond red. Black is the most powerful sensual color. Black absorbs all other colors, and within the power of black lies the ultimate orgasm. I don't know about you, but I'd say that I experienced black tonight."

"You've given new meaning to 'the black moment.'" She allowed him to help her to her feet and then quickly dressed. Once finished, she picked up her flashlight and then turned to him. "As incredible as you were, I do have one complaint."

He slipped on his coat before clasping her hand. "Let me have it."

She reached up to straighten the collar of his coat. "My eager fingers never got anywhere near your wonderful ass. I had to hang on to your shoulders the whole time to keep from shattering into a million sex-charged particles. Hate to say it, Davis, but you owe me your butt cheeks. Soon."

He laughed, and for this moment, with this woman, everything was right in his world. "Count on it."

As Thrain started to lead her from the cemetery, Cindy paused. "You know, I got so carried away with everything that I forgot to mention something.

From the moment we kissed, I had this strange feeling that I wasn't alone, that someone was in my mind." She cast him a suspicious glance. "It wasn't you, was it?"

"No." Thrain narrowed his gaze as he swept the area with his mind, searching for the one who would dare interfere . . . He stilled when he located the one he was looking for, then he relaxed. Smiling, he looked back at Cindy. "Molly Carson wants me to thank you."

"Molly Carson?" Cindy's voice was an alarmed squeak. Her glance skittered over the tombstone they'd been sitting on.

"She says she hasn't felt that alive since she died. We have an open invitation to come back and visit any time." His grin widened in direct proportion to Cindy's shock.

"I thought you said there weren't any real ghosts here." She narrowed those big blue eyes and those sexy lips in outrage.

"Hmm. I don't think I actually said that. But it was an honest mistake. I was so distracted by other things that I missed Molly." He started to lead her toward the inn again, but she yanked her hand from his and stood with her hands on her hips.

"Do *not* tell me there was a mob of ghosts watching us make love while they ate popcorn and critiqued our performance." She shoved her hands in the pockets of her jacket. Now that his warmth suggestion had worn off, she must be cold.

"Most people are dead wrong about ghosts." He rested his arm across her stiff shoulders as they continued walking. "They think the only spirits who hang around a place are the ones who died violently or suffered an overwhelming loss. Not so. Those kinds of spirits head for the white light as soon as they die. Why would you want to hang around a place where you were miserable? Now, Molly is different. Molly loves these woods in death as much as she loved them in life. She lived in one of the abandoned estates on your land. She's thrilled with what you've done to the inn. She said she's joined your guests quite a few times, and she hopes you don't mind. Do you mind?"

Cindy stared up at him and simply shook her head. But if he wanted to break his promise and peek into her busy mind, he knew he'd find her frantically trying to wrap her thoughts around the idea of a ghost sitting in on her group meetings.

He squeezed her shoulders in what he hoped was a comforting gesture. "But Molly is the only real ghost in the cemetery. Feel better now?"

She met his gaze and blinked. "Feeling better and better every minute you're with me."

Chapter Nine

How could one night's events not only define her entire life but also punctuate it and give it multiple meanings as well? Paranormal events happened, nonhuman entities existed, and her father was alive.

Cindy stood in the inn's hallway and watched Thrain go off in search of Trojan. She had twelve days to fly to Scotland to meet her father at their ancestral castle, and nothing would stop her from going. Within the same time frame, she'd have to come to terms with what Thrain would reveal tomorrow. She wasn't stupid. If his explanation was as simple as a genetic anomaly, he wouldn't have put off telling her.

Slowly, she walked toward the parlor. *And what will your feelings be for Thrain at the end of those twelve days?* She had no doubt her emotions were in the first stages of major involvement, because her level of sexual excitement had always been linked with her emotional connection to a man. And Cindy had absolutely never experienced sexual excitement on the scale she'd felt tonight. But two nights and one real orgasm did not a relationship make. She'd think about Thrain when she was calm and recovered from this night.

Most of her guests had already headed for their rooms, but she'd check in the parlor just to make sure that Gerry, Donna, and Kim weren't there. Maybe profuse apologies and some insincere groveling would save her the cost of a truckload of shoes.

On the way into the parlor, she passed the four men Thrain had labeled as dangerous. They looked like ordinary men until Cindy stared into their eyes. She shivered. Their eyes were cold, emotionless, and . . . hungry. Why hadn't she noticed before?

One of them stopped in front of her. Dark-haired, with ordinary features, he would have earned nothing more than a passing glance if she'd met him on the street. But tonight, something about him caused her to back up a step. Maybe her enhanced senses made her too sensitive to people.

"Your inn is a wonderful getaway, a great place to hunt for the unexpected. You have no idea how much I've looked forward to meeting you and staying here. Maybe we can share a drink before I leave." His smile hinted at hidden meanings and dark intents.

"I'll make sure we do that." Maybe. Even though she suspected her reaction was connected to Thrain's warning, Cindy couldn't warm up to the man. But he was a guest and entitled to courtesy from her.

Once the men had left, Cindy continued into the parlor. The only ones still there were Prada, Horus, and Hathor. Horus and Hathor claimed to be an

Egyptian god and goddess. At the time they'd registered, Cindy had done her usual mental eye-rolls, but not now. No more eye-rolling until she knew who was real and who wasn't.

Prada waved her over, so she joined them as they sat on the rug in front of the fireplace. Cindy was so tired, she didn't think she could even dredge up a pleasant expression, but luckily she had one more smile squirreled away for an emergency. "I hope you enjoyed your night."

Prada seemed to have a never-ending supply of enthusiasm. If she ever ran down, Cindy hadn't seen it. Evidently, sex energized her. And no, Cindy refused to picture the Energizer Bunny in a low-cut black dress.

"Hathor is Horus's consort, and I've been trying to help them work around a few potholes in their sexual journey. I bet you could offer them some great insights." Prada's wicked smile said she didn't think Cindy could offer even one insight, great or otherwise.

Prada was right. Cindy was all out of insights. But she would eat dirt before admitting it in the face of Prada's expectant smirk. "I'll try. What seems to be the problem?"

Hathor pushed her light brown hair away from her face and sighed. "I'm a cow."

"That is absolutely not true." Outraged that anyone would call this sweet, gentle woman a cow, Cindy leaped to her defense. "You have a great face and beautiful hair. Women pay plastic surgeons fortunes to get a body like yours."

Hathor looked puzzled by Cindy's outburst. "No, I mean that I take the form of a cow."

"Oh." Gee, everything was perfectly clear now. "I guess I don't know much about Egyptian goddesses."

Hathor smiled sweetly. "How could you, dear? I'm the Mistress of Heaven and the Goddess of Love, Cheerfulness, Music, and Dance."

"Well, I—"

"I'm not finished." Hathor's smile never wavered.

"Sorry."

"I'm the Mother of Mothers, the Celestial Nurse, the Vengeful Eye of Ra, and the Lady of Drunkenness."

The Lady of *Drunkenness?* She was kidding, right? Cindy glanced at Hathor's intent expression. Nope, she was serious. Oh, boy.

"I'm also the Mistress of Life, the Great Wild Cow, the Golden One, and the Lady of the West. There are several other titles, but I can never remember them all." She waved her hand to indicate the many she couldn't remember.

The Great Wild Cow? Cindy fought to keep from laughing. She figured bad things probably happened to people who laughed at goddesses. "Um, what does the Lady of the West mean?" When in doubt, ask an intelligent question.

Hathor gently patted Cindy's hand. "I'm the goddess of the dead, dear."

Cindy did *not* need to know that. Kick her if she asked another intelligent question.

Horus's amused chuckle shifted Cindy's attention to him. Good-looking, with a sharp, intelligent face and dark, intense eyes, he seemed the antithesis of the sweet and gentle Hathor. The sweet and gentle Hathor who was a goddess of the dead and the Mistress of Drunkenness, Cindy reminded herself.

"Hathor is a very ancient goddess, hence her many titles." He grinned at Cindy. "I'll spare you a list of mine. All you really need to know is that I'm a sky god and I take the shape of a falcon."

Thank you. Cindy's eyes were still crossed from Hathor's litany of goddess duties.

"I'd say this is a classic case of sexual midlife crisis." Prada seemed poised to put on her sexual therapist hat. "Hathor feels that perhaps her cow persona lacks a certain sensual panache, while Horus's falcon embodies all that is strong, virile male. How shall I say this?" She stared into the fire as though mulling over the most delicate way to express herself. "Oh, what the hell. The fact is that other goddesses are coming on to Horus, and Hathor is pissed off about it."

Wow, did Prada know how to handle delicate situations or what?

Hathor allowed herself a soft sob. "Just two weeks ago, that slut Sekhmet, the goddess of war and destruction, put a move on Horus. He didn't exactly fight her off." She cast Horus an accusing glare. "Of course, a lion goddess is a little more spectacular than a cow."

Horus threw up his hands. "Oh, good grief. This is so stupid." He glanced at Cindy to verify that it was indeed stupid.

"Stupid," Cindy agreed.

"Let's not get nasty, people. I think we can work this out, can't we, Cindy?" Prada paused to allow Cindy input.

"Sure, no problem." When Cindy was tired, she'd agree to anything. And right now she was real tired.

"First, what do you think would be the most satisfying way to solve your problem with Sekhmet, Hathor?" Prada waited patiently while Hathor considered her options.

"Yanking her hair out by the roots would give me a warm, fuzzy feeling." Hathor offered them her kind and gentle smile.

"Wrong. Don't you think that's wrong, Cindy?" Prada was so confident of Cindy's yes-man status that she didn't even glance in Cindy's direction.

"Right. All wrong." Cindy was too tired to care.

Horus made a disgusted sound. "I've had enough of this. I'm supposed to be here for some rest and relaxation, not for a rehash of the same old, same old." He started to rise.

"Sit down." Prada didn't raise her voice; she simply stared at him.

Surprised, Horus sat down. Slowly, his startled expression changed to an intrigued smile. "You're one powerful babe, Prada."

"See?" Hathor sounded triumphant. "He's practically drooling. He likes aggressive, powerful women."

Prada sighed, and her expression said that rarely had she seen so much stupidity gathered in one spot. "So let's discover how we can make this work for us." She smiled a particularly predatory smile. "I love guiding couples who feel they're complete opposites, that they have nothing in common, and sometimes even fear each other. Their sexual joining is always more explosive and satisfying because it's fueled by a mixture of so many volatile emotions."

Prada's gaze slid to Cindy and remained fixed on

her. "Sometimes what we fear the most is what we need to complete us."

Fear the most? Cindy didn't doubt for a minute that Prada's comment was aimed at her, and her alone. But she hadn't a clue what Prada meant.

Horus exhaled sharply. "What's your idea? I'm open to suggestions. How about you, love?" He glanced at Hathor.

She nodded, but still looked mutinous.

Prada transferred her attention back to the couple. "I think you should start out with some bondage role-playing. Hathor, you could tie Horus to your bed and have your way with his body."

"Hey, I like it." Horus looked like he was already into the visuals.

Hathor looked unsure. "I don't know if I'd know what to—"

"Of course you would. That's why I'm here." Prada reached down the front of her dress and pulled out several sheets of folded paper. "I'm the creative genius behind the bestseller *Dominatrixes Who Dare*. I'm giving you only the part dealing with ways to drive a bound man crazy with lust. Not only will Horus see you in a new and exciting light, but you'll get a chance to vent a little of your suppressed aggression. In a purely sexual way, of course." She smiled. "And if you find yourselves thoroughly intrigued, I'll sell you a copy of the whole book for twenty-nine dollars and ninety-five cents. No tax."

Hathor snatched the pages from Prada. Her eyes gleamed with excitement, and Cindy realized how beautiful she really was.

"I want to try these now." Hathor grabbed Horus's hand and they both stood.

Cindy watched the happy couple hurry from the room; then she turned to Prada. "Okay, I know you had a reason for dragging me into that little discussion."

Prada glanced down, but not before Cindy saw the anticipatory glitter in her eyes. "Maybe I wanted you to see that even people who feel separated by a sea of differences can use spectacular sex as a bridge."

Cindy had just about had enough of people who wouldn't say what they meant. "So, are you suggesting I tie Thrain up to resolve any issues we have?"

Startled, Prada looked up, her eyes wide with horror. "No. Absolutely not. Never, ever try bondage games with Thrain."

"Why not?" Cindy felt like pulling her hair out. Prada knew something about Thrain and she'd damn well better share it with Cindy.

Prada's gaze slid away from Cindy. "I don't think he'd find bondage sensual. I sense these kinds of things."

You are such a liar. "And what did you mean when you said what we fear the most is what we need to complete us?"

Prada gazed into the fire. "You don't know everything about Thrain, or about any of us, for that matter. You might find out something about Thrain that would . . . upset you. I was just making the point that you shouldn't let your first emotional reaction blind you to the big picture."

"I. Hate. Riddles." Cindy felt like shaking Prada.

Prada sighed. "And I hate keeping secrets." After a brief frown, she brightened. "Let's talk about something else. Every sexual technique isn't right for every couple. I could give you a list of erotic tricks customized for Thrain's particular tastes." She murmured the word *tastes* so softly that Cindy had to strain to hear it.

You don't get off that easily. "I might not know everything about you, but Thrain does. When I told him that you and Trojan were cosmic troublemakers, and that you'd said you were a white cat the last time, he sort of growled. I think he's looking for Trojan right now. I hope I didn't give away a secret." She didn't even try to look sincere.

Prada narrowed her eyes and almost hissed at Cindy. "That was so not smart." She glanced nervously around the room. "I'm really wrung out from helping so many people with their sexual problems. I think I'll go up to my room now."

Helping? How about manipulating? And exactly what connection did Thrain, Trojan, and Prada share? Cindy watched Prada hurry from the parlor. As she rose to follow her, Cindy realized that Prada must have sneaked into her mind at some point in order for her to know anything about Cindy's fears. Cindy was starting to suspect her mind was a well-worn footpath for a whole bunch of entities in the inn. It was a testament to tonight's weirdness that she didn't consider her open-mind policy her major problem.

Thrain had finally found Trojan. The cat was crouched behind some boxes of canned goods in the pantry. He wasn't thrilled to see Thrain.

"I don't know what you want, but save it. This pork chop is calling my name. You wouldn't believe what I have to go through to get a decent meal in this place." He looked up from the chop he was guarding with fierce determination. *"The cook caught me stealing this and tried to chase me with her broom."* Humor gleamed in his eyes for a moment. *"She forgot all about me when her broom turned into a snake and hissed at her."* He looked a little regretful. *"I think Cindy'll have to hire a new cook. As soon as this one came to, she grabbed her purse and ran out the door. Humans have no sense of humor."*

"You might want to stop gnawing on that chop, Ganymede. I wouldn't want you to choke on it." Thrain leaned against the wall and crossed his arms over his chest.

Trojan looked as if the last piece of meat had gone down the wrong way. *"You sure you don't have me mixed up with someone else?"*

"Positive. Let's see if I can remember what Darach told me. You owned the Cosmic Time Travel Agency, and you'd brought your clients from the future to stay at the Mackenzie Castle. Sparkle Stardust, also known as Prada, was your spy. She sneaked around in the form of a white cat ferreting out info about Darach because you wanted him out of the castle. I sort of remember that Darach said you and Sparkle were real pains-in-the-butt, although you did come through for Darach and Blythe in the end. Oh, and this all happened back in seventeen eighty-five. Did I miss anything?"

"Hmmumph." Trojan seemed to have lost his appetite.

Thrain was impressed. He could've sworn that

nothing short of global destruction could have put Trojan off his pork chop.

"You sure know how to ruin a good meal, bloodsucker." He eyed the half-eaten chop regretfully. *"But I'm not going to apologize for being here."*

Thrain pushed away from the wall and squatted down beside the cat. "I guess you can do whatever you want, but know one thing: I won't let you interfere with what I'm doing here."

"And that would be?" Trojan sat up and aimed a steely glare at Thrain. Unfortunately, the ring of pork chop grease around his mouth spoiled the effect.

Thrain couldn't help it; he smiled. Which was probably a mistake, because relaxing around a being with Trojan's power could get you killed. "I don't think your visit is a coincidence, so I assume you already know that Cindy is Darach's daughter. All I want is to help Cindy accept who she is so I can take her to meet Darach. I owe Darach that much for saving my life." Thrain didn't think Trojan knew what part he'd played in Cindy's separation from her father and he wanted to keep it that way. "My turn, now. Why're you and Prada here?"

"In the old days, I was never into the personal lives of humans. I did the big stuff—volcanic eruptions, solar flares, droughts, pestilence. But you know, after thousands of years, all that mass chaos and devastating destruction stuff got old. I decided to go small, try to see what kind of fun I could have messing with human lives." His expression said he really missed the wicked old days. *"I guess I was too good at being bad, because the Big Boss decided to ground me."*

"The Big Boss?"

"Yeah, you know. The head honcho. The guy in charge of

goodness and light. The supreme party pooper." Trojan's cat mouth turned down. *"Anyway, he said I couldn't put a major hurt on humans anymore. He won't even let me off as a bloodsucker. Nothing personal. It was either reform or cease to exist. What kind of choice was that?"*

"Uh-huh. So what does that have to do with Cindy?" Thrain figured that at the rate Trojan was going, it might take him a few centuries to finish his story.

"I'm getting there, okay?" Trojan cast a wistful glance at the now cold pork chop. *"When I got to the castle with my guests, Darach was already there. The Big Boss wouldn't let me do the fun things I'd normally do to get rid of him, so I called in Sparkle to help. She was flying under the Big Boss's radar, so she could do whatever she wanted."*

Trojan cast a thoughtful glance toward the pantry door. *"I think I need something sweet and cold to wash down this pork chop. How about getting me a pint of ice cream? I think I saw Ben & Jerry's Chubby Hubby in there."*

"Named after you, huh?" Thrain grumbled to himself all the way to the kitchen and back to the pantry. But he wanted to hear the rest of the story, and he knew if he didn't feed Trojan, he'd hear nothing but whining.

With his face shoved into the ice cream carton, Trojan continued his story. *"I'd forgotten that all Sparkle cared about was spreading sexual chaos. She didn't care squat about my problems with Darach. In fact, she thought it was a real rush to hook Darach up with Blythe. To make a long story short . . ."*

Thain drew in a deep breath of patience. He didn't

think Trojan knew how to make anything short.

"Sparkle drew me into Darach's and Blythe's lives. And pretty soon, I began to like them. Go figure." Trojan pulled his ice-cream–covered face out of the container and then began trying to clean up the damage with one gray paw.

Thrain figured Trojan's face was at least a ten-paw job.

"Sparkle keeps track of anyone whose sexual life she's ever messed with. She must have a database of millions in her brain. I don't know why she does it. Likes to go back once in a while and gloat, I guess." Giving up on the paw, Trojan rubbed his face against Thrain's jeans. *"She didn't mess with your sex life, but she wanted to, so she kept track of you, too. It took her almost two centuries to realize what you were searching for. When she told me, I decided I had to make sure you did right by Cindy. I mean, Darach lets me take a tourist group to the Mackenzie Castle once a year. I owe him."*

Thrain smiled. "You know, you're really a nice guy under all that bluster."

Trojan pinned his ears back and offered Thrain a silent snarl. *"No one's insulted me like that in a thousand years. You're lucky, bloodsucker, that the Big Boss is keeping tabs on me, or you'd be history."*

Thrain frowned. "I'm going to tell Cindy the truth tomorrow. I don't think she's ready for it, but then, she might never be ready for it. I hope I don't blow it for Darach."

A faint sound from outside the pantry door caught his attention. He stilled, hoping no one came in to find him talking to a cat. When nothing else happened, he relaxed.

"You can count on Sparkle and me if you need character references." Trojan padded to the door with Thrain. *"And since everyone here knows us by our fake names, maybe we'd better keep them until we leave."*

Thrain smiled as he pulled the door open and let Trojan out. Just what he needed, character references from Trojan and Prada, the terrible twosome of cosmic badasses.

Thrain was halfway up the stairs on the way to his room and a good day's sleep when he remembered Sam Pierce's camera. He stood in the hallway trying to decide what to do. The first pale light of dawn was filtering through the window at the end of the hall and he didn't know which room was Sam's. By the time he found out, entered the room, and took care of the camera, the sun would probably be up.

He needed to be in his bed with the curtains drawn by then. Maybe during this next century he'd work on being able to spend brief periods of time in the sunlight. *And since when have you wanted a human ability enough to use your power to get it?* Thrain wouldn't lie to himself. Cindy was used to operating in daylight, and he found that the idea of a walk in the sunlight with her was a real temptation.

Thrain blinked as he found himself standing outside his room. He'd been thinking about the camera and suddenly his thoughts had slid over to Cindy. All without his permission. Shaking his head, he opened his door and went inside.

He'd forget about the camera until tonight. After all, Cindy would already know the truth by the time Sam got a good look at his pictures and spread the word. When that happened, Thrain could plant a few suggestions in Sam's mind to convince him that his camera had malfunctioned.

After pulling the curtains closed, he climbed into bed. After everything that had happened tonight, Thrain figured he deserved at least a few problem-free hours of oblivion.

Cindy stood inside her apartment with her back pressed against the door leading to the hallway. She'd run from the pantry door just before Thrain came out.

She'd heard a voice in the pantry as she was walking toward her apartment and, curious, had gone to investigate. Once outside the door, she'd recognized Thrain's voice. Cindy had only arrived in time to hear Thrain's last comment, but it had been enough to scare the hell out of her. What could he reveal that was so horrible he felt she might never be ready to hear it?

A stronger woman would have stayed outside the door, and when he opened it, she would have demanded that he tell her everything immediately. Cindy had always thought she was strong, but now? Maybe not. Because heaven help her, she didn't want to face any more revelations tonight, didn't want to hear anything that might extinguish the happy glow of knowing her father was alive.

Drawing in a deep, calming breath, she started to walk toward her bedroom. The unexpected knock on the hall door stopped her cold.

Leave me alone. She didn't want to answer it, didn't want to deal with whatever problem waited on the other side. And she had no doubt it was a problem, because no one would be pounding on her door at dawn to tell her they'd enjoyed dinner.

As the pounding continued, she finally gave in and walked back to open the door. The inn was her business, and as much as she wanted to, she couldn't shut herself away from her guests' needs.

Sam Pierce stood outside in the hallway. He clutched a laptop to his chest, excitement glittering in his eyes. "I know, I know, this isn't the time to be bothering you. But you gotta see these pictures." He edged past her, put his laptop on her coffee table, and opened it up.

While he pulled up his pictures, Cindy wondered if the innkeepers' association would yank her membership if she kicked Sam's butt from her apartment. "I'm really tired, Sam. Can't the pictures wait?"

"Nope. These're the shots I took with my digital camera out at the cemetery tonight." He moved away from the laptop so she could see.

For a moment, nothing unusual registered. Okay, so maybe a photo of hovering ghosts and three women dressed as vampires might qualify as unusual, but the photo showed what had been there. "I don't—"

"Look closer." He peered around her shoulder. "Don't concentrate on what you see, think about what you *don't* see."

Sighing, she looked closer. There were the ghosts, the women, her, and . . . *and nothing*. This was the photo Sam had taken while they'd had their backs to him. She was there, but Thrain was nowhere in the picture.

Without waiting for her comment, Sam pulled up

the photo he'd taken as Thrain and she had turned toward the camera. Cindy felt her stomach clench and her breath catch as she stared at the photo of only herself staring wide-eyed into the camera.

"Any idea where the boyfriend disappeared to, hmm?" Sam's smile said he had a few ideas. "Do you know what you have here, lady? You have a whole boatload of weird stuff happening. You're sitting on a frickin' gold mine. And I'm the one who's gonna make everything happen. By the time I get through selling my stories, you'll be famous." His grin widened. "And I'll be rich."

Even as she opened her mouth to respond, Cindy knew her instinct was to protect Thrain. She'd try to figure out the reason for that later. "You could've edited Thrain out of those pictures." For just a moment she felt a stab of relief. That was it: Sam wanted a story so badly, he'd stooped to doctoring his photos.

Sam offered her a sly smile. "But I didn't. And up here . . ." He tapped his head. "You know these are the real deal." He rubbed his chubby hands together. "I can't wait to publish these photos. When I heard about the Jersey Devil sighting, I didn't believe it. But after tonight, I'm not so sure."

Struck speechless, Cindy watched him shut down his laptop, hurry to the door, and then begin humming as he disappeared down the hallway.

Sam Pierce was a greedy, irritating man, and she had to do something to keep him from turning her inn into a media circus. Sure, she wanted to create a buzz about her place, but this was threatening to go from buzz to eardrum-shattering roar.

She could ask Thrain to erase Sam's . . . No, she

wouldn't ask Thrain for anything until she knew what he was holding back. And to keep her sanity until she found out, she wouldn't think about Thrain, his secrets, or Sam's stupid pictures.

All the way into her bedroom and while she undressed, took a shower, and climbed into bed, she was able to keep her mind a blank. It was a handy skill to have, and the last time she'd needed it was with Anna.

During her centuries of life, Cindy had rarely stayed in one place for more than ten years; after that, people started to notice the forever-young thing. But Anna had become a close friend, and at the end of Cindy's ten-year stay, she'd told Anna the truth. Anna had passed no judgment but had simply accepted Cindy for what she was. Cindy still had to move on, but she made time to visit Anna every few months. She'd been there to hold Anna's hand when her best friend died at eighty-five.

Yep, having the ability to erase every damned thought from your mind kept the hurt at bay until it was bearable. Sometimes avoidance kept you out of the local mental health facility.

But as she lay in the darkness, she couldn't keep out the fearful thoughts forever. Like roots from a willow tree, they crept and burrowed into every crevice of her mind.

It was going to be a long day.

Chapter Ten

If her guests were expecting glowing natural beauty from her, they were in for a disappointment. Cindy thought she'd outgrown bags under her eyes seven hundred years ago, but she was hiding under a layer of makeup and concealer tonight. Besides, all women knew that behind every glowing natural beauty stood Estée Lauder.

Cindy had earned those dark smudges under her eyes honestly, though. When she'd finally managed to fall asleep, she'd dreamed of being pursued through the forest by a creature that looked like Jim Kehoe's description of the Jersey Devil. And each time it swooped down on her, it roared, "Come to Papa."

Her sleep, such as it was, had ended abruptly when Hal banged on her door to tell her that Mimi had called to say she quit. Cindy had crawled out of bed to call Mimi. After listening to Mimi tell her that the broom was a snake, the kitchen was cursed, and no, she wouldn't return to the Woo Woo Inn even if her sainted mother came down from heaven and begged her to, Cindy started searching for a new cook.

After finally reeling in Katie Holcomb, a former chef at the Piney Woods Fishing Lodge, Cindy didn't have much time to wonder about brooms turning into snakes. In fact, she didn't even have time to go back to her apartment and change out of her jeans and scruffy Rutgers T-shirt. Hal had to go home a little early, and by then it was late afternoon, so most of her guests were wandering around as they got ready for the night's activities. Strangely, a lot more of them than usual were collected in the library reading books and taking notes. Thrain didn't make an appearance until nightfall, and by that time Cindy had worked up a whole truckload of new worries.

One of her worries had her cornered in the kitchen, where Cindy was trying to help Katie with her first meal at the Woo Woo Inn.

"This is gonna be a helluva night." Sam waved a mini recorder in the air. A bulge in his shirt pocket marked the hiding place of the ever dangerous digital camera. "I've set up an appointment to talk with Leo Varinski. He promised to give me some hot info on wizards. And then I'll hit the forest for a few hours to see if I can scare up the Jersey Devil. Don't worry, I won't harass your guests or make fun of them. After last night, I know this is serious business. If they don't want to talk to me, hey, no sweat." He looked thoughtful. "Do you think Thrain will give me an interview? Maybe explain how he—?"

"I don't know." Cindy had edged her way out of

the kitchen, but Sam continued to stalk her. As she did a quick scan of the hallway in search of possible escape routes, she saw Thrain coming down the stairs. "Why don't you ask him yourself?"

What a wuss. By siccing Sam on Thrain, she managed to avoid confronting two problems. But she had other things to do, other people to see, and other problems to solve.

In fact, she was so busy, she hadn't even noticed that Thrain looked sexy enough to make her teeth hurt. Cindy had too many important things to do, so no way would she have time to pay any attention to his hot male bod clothed in black leather biker pants, scuffed boots, and a snug black sleeveless T-shirt. She wouldn't even take a nanosecond to question his lack of sleeves in October, because she knew from close encounters of the sexual kind how much heat he generated. And she certainly couldn't take time out of her busy schedule to even glance at his glorious mane of Viking hair or hot mouth. Nope, he was a nonhappening for her.

In fact, she was so busy not looking at him that she ran smack into one of the night feeders, the same one who'd stopped to talk with her that morning. Startled, she looked into his dark eyes as he reached out to steady her. She searched her memory for a name to go with the face. Darius.

"Just the woman I wanted to run into." He smiled at her.

His teeth were very white, his smile engaging, but his eyes still looked hungry. She couldn't quite place what kind of hunger. It wasn't an I-think-you're-sexy hunger. It was something else, something that made her uncomfortable.

"You still owe me that walk in the woods." His smile widened. "And I'm not letting you off the hook." He played his trump card. "I'm your guest, and the guest is always right. I won't count this as a successful stay if I don't get my walk."

"Sure. We can do the walk tomorrow night."

Darius was right: He was her guest, and just because he made her uncomfortable didn't mean he was an ax murderer. It wouldn't hurt to walk with him to the ruins of the Hart mansion. She could deflect any kind of romantic moves he might have in mind by keeping up a running dialogue about the dark history of the place. And since she'd already decided to keep her gun in her jacket pocket from now on whenever she went into the woods, she felt pretty secure with her decision.

Thrain had said the night feeders were dangerous, but she was starting to think the real danger might be standing right behind her.

She could feel him. Heat, anger, and a sense of tight control over something just beyond her ability to recognize.

Darius looked past Cindy and his smile faded. Nodding at her, he turned and beat a hasty retreat. Rats.

Accepting the inevitable, she turned to face Thrain. If a man could smolder, Thrain was smoldering. It wasn't a sexy smolder either. He was ticked.

"You won't go for a walk with Darius. He's dangerous." Thrain loomed over her: a big, domineering, overbearing . . . incredibly sexy male.

But she intended to stop his lord-and-master act dead in its tracks. "From what I can see, at least half of my guests are dangerous. *You're* dangerous. I

went into the woods with you and came out whole."
Sort of.

He was almost at the teeth-gnashing stage. His anger and frustration made the air around her vibrate. "The night feeders are vampires. I thought you'd figure that out."

She had to force the lump in her throat down before it choked her. Okay, no walk in the woods with Darius. "Stan, Lisa, and Carl are vampires. You didn't tell me not to walk in the woods with them."

"Would you have gone with any of them after I told you what they were?" His expression said he knew her answer before she gave it.

"No." She hated being predictable. "I'd love to stand here and chat, but I have to check the breakfast buffet. Mimi quit because she said her broom turned into a snake, so I had to hire a new cook today." She started toward the dining room, and he walked beside her. So much for her attempt to brush him off.

He made no comment about the snake-and-broom event. She supposed it was no big deal in the grand scheme of things at the Woo Woo Inn.

"When can we talk?"

There it was. Even though she'd spent almost her entire lifetime hoping to find out about herself, the simple truth was that she was afraid. Afraid Thrain would shoot down her hope that she was human. Afraid he'd reveal something she couldn't accept.

"I'll have time after I finish the nightly meeting in the parlor." Cindy glanced at the buffet Katie had set out. So far, so good. "Now if the broom manages to behave itself, things should be okay."

Thrain smiled at her, and Cindy decided he presented a whole different kind of buffet. But she'd resist; the buffet of the senses he offered, no matter how tempting, could do a lot more damage than the calories in a few pieces of buttered toast. She thought about all the yummy temptations he brought to the table and modified her decision. She'd resist until after she heard what he had to say.

"I think Katie is made of sterner stuff than Mimi." His smile widened. "Katie practices Wicca."

"And you know this, how?" He thought he could shock her, but he was in for a surprise. She felt more secure with a witch in the kitchen who'd be impervious to shape-shifting brooms than with some of the guests who were busy chowing down on the buffet.

Thrain shrugged. "I took a look into her mind. She knew I was there, but it didn't seem to bother her. You might want to ask her to give a workshop for you. She has a lot to share."

"Will do." Cindy grabbed a cup of coffee, then moved toward the parlor with some of her guests who had finished eating. Thrain stayed beside her. He didn't choose anything from the buffet, and she didn't question his lack of appetite.

As they approached the archway leading into the parlor, Cindy eyed the gold-framed antique mirror on the opposite wall. She never looked in that mirror. She wouldn't look in it now. They drew opposite it. She looked.

Cindy's shudder was instinctual, her body's physical reaction to what she'd suspected she'd see but didn't want to accept. Fear tightened her muscles and made her feel clumsy, as though her body didn't belong to her. Maybe it didn't. Maybe it never had.

"Did you see what you expected to see?" Thrain's voice was calm and unconcerned, the same tone he probably would have used if he was asking her to pass the bread. But she suspected he'd never make that request.

"Yes." She'd seen no one but herself, and that was exactly what she'd expected, feared. Never meeting Thrain's gaze, she sat on the couch next to Leo. Thrain sat next to her. Cindy edged closer to Leo, but her thigh still touched Thrain's. She crossed her legs.

"So, I hear you've agreed to give Sam an interview." Determinedly, she kept her head turned from Thrain and her smiling attention on Leo the wizard, a man not to be trifled with when visiting old cemeteries.

"Yes." Leo looked thoughtful. "Droll little man. Perhaps I'll turn him into a frog. Although I hardly believe that will provide as much entertainment as last night."

Alarm widened her eyes. "Please don't. I have enough problems already. My cook quit when her broom turned into a snake, and the cook I hired today practices Wicca . . ." *Shut up, Cindy. You're babbling.*

"Really?" Leo looked intrigued. "I might alter my plans if you'll introduce me to your cook. Do you think she might find me attractive?"

"Absolutely." Cindy tried to ignore Thrain's soft chuckle. "And I'm positive she'd be thrilled to meet a wizard. I bet the two of you have a lot in common."

Cindy silently apologized to Katie, but she'd had to sidetrack Leo's plans to turn Sam into a frog. Although on second thought, Sam as a frog might pose fewer problems than Sam as a nosy writer.

Relieved, Cindy noted that most of the guests had found a seat and were waiting to begin. When she stood up to speak to them, she could move to a different part of the room. She wouldn't have to sit back down next to Thrain.

Thinking logically about her reaction to him, she realized it didn't make much sense. But then, her need to escape from him wasn't too surprising; she'd spent a lifetime always moving away from her problems. She didn't like what that said about her character.

She resisted the temptation to glance at Thrain as she stood. Pasting her cheerful hostess smile on her face, she raised her hand for silence. "Before our discussion begins, I want to make sure you know that a few strange things have happened in the woods over the last few nights. We've seen spirits, a demon, and the Jersey Devil at the cemetery." *Along with a werewolf and a werecat fighting on the back lawn.* Cindy included the demon because she didn't have the heart to embarrass her six fake werewolves by telling them they'd been fleeing from a car. "No one has reported any injuries, but you'd probably be safer if you stayed close to the inn."

Glancing around the room, she saw a mixture of fear and fascination on her guests' faces. Even a few of the nonhumans looked intrigued. The mystery of the woods would draw her guests in the same way a scary movie did. The only difference was that the forest was real, and you couldn't just click your remote to stop the action.

"If you insist on going into the woods, make sure you have your cell phone with you, and I'd suggest traveling in groups." Cindy hoped she was right in her belief that all her guests understood the consequences of harming someone. She would close the inn. And then where would they go to have fun with like-minded individuals? Unfortunately, the Jersey Devil wasn't a guest, so she couldn't influence him. Of course, there was still the chance that Thrain and the others had been hallucinating on the night they saw him. Yeah, like she really believed that.

She strolled over to lean against the wall near the archway. "Now, who wants to share something about last night?" Then she simply listened while carefully refusing to meet Thrain's amused stare. She knew his stare was amused because she was getting good at feeling his emotions, and that was damned scary.

Cindy was only half listening as Clark and his werewolf friends told of their adventures. They were sitting on her furniture dressed in their fuzzy costumes. Why couldn't they find costumes made out of synthetic, nonshedding material? Sheesh. And then Gerry, Donna, and Kim told their harrowing tale of ruined shoes, illogical ghosts, and unfinished manuscripts leading to chocolate binges.

Cindy allowed her thoughts to wander further as she wondered what Thrain would say when they were alone. Did she really want to be alone with him? Maybe they could stay right here, warm and cozy by the fireplace.

A startled gasp from her guests pulled her back into the conversation. "I'm sorry, what did you say, Clark?"

Clark had a book in his hand that he was holding up for everyone to see. "I just found this great book in your library, Cindy. Don't remember seeing it there before. It gives all kinds of unusual summoning spells."

"And you need this why?" Cindy frowned. Her library was extensive, but she didn't remember buying a book on summoning spells.

Clark shrugged and looked a little embarrassed. "Oh, nothing. A few of us just thought a summoning spell was kind of neat. Sort of like a magic tractor beam." He glanced down at the book. "All I said was that it'd be a little tough to find the tail of a werewolf. Unattached. You have to use some really weird things in these spells. I mean, what werewolf would donate his tail?"

"Shut up, Clark." The anonymous voice didn't sound amused.

"Right. I shouldn't have brought it up. Sorry." He gave a halfhearted laugh and sat down. "No way would I want to try a summoning spell, so I guess my tail is safe."

Andrea and Adolfo looked uneasy, while Darren grinned. Adolfo glared at Darren. "The spell would probably work fine if you substituted a werecat's tail." Darren stopped smiling.

Cindy somehow felt left out of the loop. The others seemed interested in Clark's book even if they didn't want him to talk about it. Go figure. "So, does anyone else have something to share?"

"I'd like to know what a guy has to do to get breakfast in this place."

It was Cindy's turn to gasp. An unfamiliar voice. *In her head!*

"For crying out loud, don't scream. It's me, Trojan, your friendly starving cat. And don't answer me, just listen."

Wide-eyed with shock, Cindy scanned the room as guests streamed past her on their way out for their nightly adventures.

"Yo, down here."

She glanced down to find Trojan's ample bottom planted next to her.

"I didn't plan to chit-chat with you, but since Thrain has already made me, there's no reason not to. Look, I know your dad. Great guy. He wouldn't keep me out of his kitchen."

Cindy could only blink down at him. He knew her father?

"Yep, your dad and I've been buddies since seventeen eighty-five. Now about the food thing. I tried to sneak into the kitchen for some breakfast and your new cook made a pitiful attempt to chase me out. I liked your old cook better. This one doesn't scare. She just keeps on truckin' past snakes, large insects, and lots of other scary stuff. I need to eat, and no, I don't do the cat food crap. If you don't want war in your kitchen, you need to get me something to eat."

Cindy looked up to find Thrain standing beside her. "Trojan's talking to me. In my head. I think he's reading my thoughts, too. But then, everyone does that, so I guess it isn't so weird. He says he knows my father, and he wants something to eat. I don't understand any of this."

She looked cute when she was confused. Thrain took her arm and guided her out of the parlor and toward the kitchen. "I'll explain later, but first let's get the bottomless pit some food." Thrain glared down at Trojan. "And I need you to keep quiet. About everything." Reaching into the cat's mind, he succinctly explained to Trojan the unpleasant consequences of blabbing to Cindy about her father. Since all the consequences involved loss of kitchen privileges, he was confident that Trojan's voice would be stilled.

Once in the kitchen, Thrain could see that Cindy

was unsure how to approach the new cook. But he gave her points for courage, because she plowed right in.

"Um, Katie, from now on I'd like you to serve Trojan the same meal the rest of our guests get." She shuffled a few items on the counter, carefully avoiding Katie's gaze.

"At the table, ma'am?" Katie's small, compact body practically thrummed with disapproval.

"No, of course not. I'm sure he wouldn't mind eating in the pantry." Sighing deeply, she met Katie's gaze. "He hasn't had breakfast, so I know he'd appreciate a selection from the buffet."

"Hmmph." Katie rattled plates angrily as she chose items from the buffet dishes she'd brought in from the dining room. "Doesn't pay to pamper a demon. They're never satisfied."

Thrain could almost hear Trojan choking on his anger.

Demon? Did she call me a demon? Even a thousand demons wouldn't be as powerful—

"Oh, stuff it." Thrain had taken about all he intended. He needed to get Cindy alone so he could talk to her.

Cindy and the cook turned to stare at him.

He counted to ten. Slowly. "What I meant to say is that Trojan likes ice cream with every meal. Let's see what you have." Feeling both women's gazes on his back, he walked to the freezer and lifted the lid. "Good. You have Ben & Jerry's Half Baked. I like a flavor that says something about the person who's eating it. Don't bother with a dish, just open the carton and put it on the floor."

Thrain turned and smiled at the gape-mouthed

cook. "Now that everything's settled, Cindy and I'll leave you to it." He kept on smiling even as he felt Trojan's sharp little teeth sink into his leg above his boot.

"That's for the half-baked crack, bloodsucker. You're lucky you're my partner, or else I would've done some molecular rearranging."

Thrain resisted the urge to rub his leg. He wouldn't give Trojan the satisfaction. Knowing it would annoy the cat, he addressed his next question to Cindy as he led her from the kitchen. "Why didn't Prada take care of this? Trojan belongs to her."

Cindy shook her head. "I don't even know where Prada is. She wasn't in the parlor with everyone else." Just before leaving the kitchen, she looked back at the cook. "I forgot to tell you: Leo Varinski, one of the guests, would like to meet you. I think you'd have a lot in common."

Katie nodded tersely. She was obviously still ticked about Trojan.

Trojan's chuckle echoed in Thrain's head. "Your lady just did me a favor. Ms. Kitchen Grump will be too busy with the wizard to hassle me about my eating habits. Oh, and Prada couldn't take care of my stomach because she's busy sexing up Cindy's apartment. She said Cindy has the most boring place she's ever seen. After your crack about Prada owning me, you're on your own with this one."

Cindy stared at Thrain. "He's talking to you in your head, isn't he? Why isn't he talking to me, too? What doesn't he want me to hear?"

Thrain shrugged. "Nothing important. He just said he doesn't know where Prada is. Look, let's go to my room this time. It has fewer distractions."

He thought she might argue, but she merely nodded. She was probably still trying to figure out Trojan's game. Or maybe, like him, she was remembering what they'd shared in her living room and deciding they didn't need that memory interfering with tonight. Either way, his suggestion had the desired effect. He definitely didn't want to be around when Cindy saw whatever Prada had done to her place.

Holding the door to his room open, he watched her walk inside. In terms of physical objects, there wasn't much of him in this room. He wondered how far she'd come in refining her senses. Her reaction to the room would tell him that.

Cindy spun in a circle, studying the room with its faded oriental carpet and antique cherry furniture. Then she raised her startled gaze to him. "I feel . . . energy. The room is filled with it." Moving to the massive four-poster bed, she skimmed her fingers across the wine-colored bedspread. "It's *your* energy, isn't it?"

"Very good." He closed the door and then sat in one of the room's two chairs. "Once you hone your senses a little more, you'll be able to feel the energy of past guests as well."

The line was back between her eyes as she walked to the other chair, a rocker, and sat down. She didn't seem too thrilled with her newfound power.

Cindy looked across the small coffee table that separated them. She stared at him with wide blue eyes. He saw the fear gathering in them, but also the determination. For just a moment, he considered placing a power shield across the door so she couldn't run from the room before he was finished with his explanation. But that would be a denial of the trust he had in her courage. He allowed himself a rueful smile. It would also probably steam her so much she'd haul off and punch him.

"I suppose that smile means you're ready to tell the rest of what I need to know about my father's side of the family." She swallowed hard and began rocking gently.

"Yes." Thrain wouldn't put it off any longer; time wouldn't make the telling easier. He leaned back in his chair, forcing himself to relax. You'd think in a room filled with so much tension, he wouldn't be thinking about sex as he watched her swallow. But he had the sinking feeling that desire would never be far beneath the surface when Cindy was near him.

She nodded and rocked a little faster. Thrain hoped she wouldn't tip herself over when he got to the word *vampire*.

"What I've told you so far is all true. I just haven't told you the complete story." Now he wished *he* had a rocker.

"You only told me the good part."

He shrugged. "It all depends on your perspective. For the most part, I've always been satisfied with what I am."

She didn't answer, but he could see her rolling the words *with what I am* around in her mind. From her expression, he guessed she didn't like the sound of them.

"When we're young, the members of our clan are completely human. During that time, we eat, we grow, we age, and we can die as easily as any human. But somewhere between twenty-five and thirty-five, we change."

He watched her warily as she pushed herself from the rocker and began to pace. "All of our body systems adapt to what we'll be for the rest of our existence. We're immune to all disease and are damn hard to kill."

She paused in her pacing. "Body systems adapt? How? Everything about your body says human. Jeez, I've watched you *breathe*." Her wide eyes pleaded for him to affirm that, yes, everything inside him worked in a normal human way.

"What you've seen are reflex actions retained from before the change. My body remembers what it should do in certain situations and does it." Okay, now for the hard part. "Even if I don't need to do it anymore." He hurried into speech to ward off the horror flooding her eyes. "I'm not dead, Cindy. Only different."

"Different." He watched her swallow hard, trying to wrap her understanding around the reality of *different*.

"With the change comes power. We start out slowly, but our powers increase as we age. Abilities don't come automatically. We stockpile our power for years, and then we use it to gain a new skill. Since it takes so long, we have to choose which abilities are most important to us. For example, your father is interested in regaining certain human characteristics he lost with the change." Thrain shrugged. "I'm more interested in abilities that make me feel secure."

"Okay, okay." She raked her fingers through her dark hair. "I understand the power stuff." Looking up, she speared him with the intensity of her gaze. "Now tell me what I am."

Seven hundred years of pursuit and planning were going to come down to the next few words he spoke. "After we change, we become—"

"*Vampires.*" The word was sizzling accusation, separating them more surely than an electrified fence. "I'm sorry I ruined your punch line, but I had to say it first. It kind of gave me an illusion of control." She stood, feet planted as though to absorb a blow. "You bite people and drink their blood. Did I miss anything important?"

"Listen, Cindy, we—"

"It didn't take a paranormal investigator to put the clues together. You don't eat. You have all these powers. You were a no-show in Sam's photos and the mirror." She drew in a deep breath and her hands shook. "My inn is overrun with vampires. Is this cosmic justice or what? You get what you fear."

"If you'd just listen—"

"I think I've heard all I need to hear. I'm a hybrid, and my vampire characteristics are recessive except for my longevity." She started to edge toward the door. "I'll deal with this. And as long as I don't experience any unusual cravings in the meat section of the supermarket, hey, everything's cool."

Everything wasn't cool. He stretched his legs out in front of him and studied the toes of his boots. First rule when calming any frightened creature: Focus on something else, because direct eye contact may be perceived as a threat.

"Well, now that I know everything, I'll just head on back to my apartment and—"

"You know nothing, Cindy. Sit down." He tried to keep his voice low and controlled, but it was getting harder by the minute.

"You bite people's necks. Don't need to know any more. I'm leaving." She reached for the doorknob.

"Isn't it about time you stopped running? Sit down." *Good job, Davis.* Insult her and then order her around. Bet she'll want to stay now.

Surprisingly, Cindy turned from the door. "You're right." She walked to the rocker and sat down again, but he noticed she gripped the chair arms tightly enough to whiten her knuckles. "Running away was an emotional response. I'm not thinking too logically right now."

Relieved, Thrain massaged the back of his neck to try to rid himself of a little tension. "Don't make the mistake of thinking all vampires are the same. There're many different clans, families, breeds, or whatever you want to call them. Your clan . . ."

She winced. Maybe he shouldn't have used the word *your*.

"I have to keep my intake of human blood to a minimum, so I only feed once every few weeks. I never take much blood from the donor, and I always leave humans with a pleasurable memory of the experience." Thrain watched Cindy's gaze skitter around the room, never quite landing on him. He also noticed that he'd gone from *we* to *I*. It was personal now. "I only drink a small amount of blood at a time, because if I dilute my vampire blood with too much human blood . . ." Uh-oh. Shouldn't have gone there. "Bad things happen."

"Like what?" She stopped avoiding his gaze and fixed him with a narrow-eyed stare.

He couldn't avoid telling her, and maybe it was best that she know the worst right up front. "If I ever gorged myself, I'd destroy the balance of vampire blood in my body. It would make me crave more and more human blood until the bloodlust was too strong to resist. Eventually, I'd become a mindless killing machine that only lived to feed."

"Oh." She said nothing else, but her wide-eyed stare said it all.

Thrain rushed to finish his explanation before she could run screaming from his room. "This doesn't happen often, because we all know the consequences of overfeeding. Those who survive to your father's or my age have too much self-control to fall into that trap."

"Right. Self-control. Is there anything else besides hunger that triggers your need-to-bite reflex?" If she gripped the rocker any tighter, she'd leave imprints of her fingers in the wood.

Don't lie. She needs to know everything. Her need-to-know warred with his don't-want-to-tell. Biting back a curse, he told her the truth. "Sex."

Her eyes grew wider, if possible. "So when we . . ."

"I've successfully controlled my *reflexes* for over seven hundred years." He didn't tell her that she tempted his control more than any woman had in all his years as a vampire. That *wouldn't* make her feel safe.

Only a little more to reveal and he'd be finished. Then the ball would be in her court. "Each of us has to return to our ancestral castle in Scotland once every twenty years and stay there for a month. We have a duty to end the lives of any clan members who come seeking death. Most of the time no one shows up, because the only clan members who seek us out are those who've gone crazy from too much human blood. Even though they can't reason, instinct brings them home. It doesn't matter where they were born or where they are when the madness strikes, they all come home at the end.

Cindy nodded, but with her lips pressed tightly together and her eyes lowered, he couldn't tell what she was thinking. He refused to enter her mind without her permission. "Is that why my father is there now?"

It was his turn to nod. "Darach's duty ends in eleven days. Do you still want to meet him?" What would he do if she said no?

"Yes."

Relieved, he put his worry away.

"I appreciate what you've done to reunite me with my father. Thanks." She sounded distant and formal. "But until I work through what I'm feeling, I don't want to be with you, Thrain." Rising, she walked from the room and closed the door quietly behind her.

Hell.

Chapter Eleven

Ganymede lazily watched Sparkle through half-closed eyes. So wicked, so scheming, so manipulative. What a babe. Her long, black, slinky dress with the slit that went almost up to her earlobe made him want to change into human form. But changing took a lot of time and effort for cosmic troublemakers, and it was almost nightfall. They had mischief to sow tonight.

"You know, it really ticks me off when I'm trying to mess with people's sex lives and they don't cooperate." Sparkle swept angrily from the window where she'd been watching darkness fall over the woods. She stopped beside her bed, where Ganymede lounged. "It's been four days since Cindy exchanged schedules with Hal-the-Happiness-Guy. She knew Thrain couldn't face the daylight, so she gave her assistant the night shift while she took his shift. That is so pathetic. And I'm getting tired of your cat form."

"Yeah, me, too. It cramps my style." Ganymede of-

fered her an amused glance. *"Lusting after my golden-god form, witchy woman?"*

"Sort of." She moved restlessly to a chair and sat down. "Why'd she run, Mede?"

"I think you have to cut Cindy some slack. Thrain clued her in to her vampire connection, and that had to shock the hell out of her. Not everybody has your evil streak to keep them going during the tough times. She must've had second thoughts, though, because I heard Hal telling a guest that she'd be back tonight. Just in time, too. I couldn't take one more night of Hal and his freakin' cheerfulness. If he pats my head one more time and asks, 'How's my cute kitty tonight?' I am going to bite off a finger."

Sparkle smiled, but it was only halfhearted. She was obviously still worried about Cindy. "I gave my all to sexing up her apartment and she didn't say a thing about it even when I got up early so I could purposely run into her. I mean, at least I deserved a few screams of outrage. Then I could've used her anger as a springboard into a meaningful discussion of sex and why she needs to keep doing it with Thrain. But what did I get? *Nada.* It's sort of insulting."

"Maybe she didn't notice." Ganymede stood, stretched, circled, and then lay down again. Exercise done.

"Not notice? Hello? It was, like, so obvious. I put my patented seduction rug right in the middle of her living room floor. When a naked couple lies on it, the fibers deliver minishocks to encourage blood flow and release pheromones to increase sexual excitement. It's bright red, for crying out loud. How could you miss bright red in a sea of gray and white?"

"Yeah, well, maybe she didn't think a rug was worth making a stink about." Ganymede's gaze followed the sway of Sparkle's hips as she threw her hands in the air and continued her pacing.

"You don't think I stopped there, do you?" She prowled the room, a cosmic predator readying herself for the hunt.

He loved her when she was pissed. *"Let's hear it all."*

Sparkle settled onto the foot of the bed. "I hung sexually explicit paintings on every wall of her apartment. I replaced her body lotion with my own special formula guaranteed to arouse unspeakable sexual desire. I put aromatherapy candles at strategic spots where sexual encounters might occur. I filled her fridge with foods meant to enhance the libido. I stuffed her bookshelves with how-to sex manuals and magazines with pictures of buff naked guys. I scattered sensual music CDs unobtrusively around her apartment. I messed with her TV so that it only showed hot movies. I even fiddled with her bed so that when she lay down it would make orgasmic moans and sounds of ecstasy." She sighed. "Where did I go wrong? How could she hold out for four nights?"

"Hmm." Ganymede tried not to laugh. Sparkle really took this crap seriously. *"Maybe she's conserving her anger, letting it gain power and intensity so she can rip your head off when she sees you the next time. And when she's finished with you, she'll probably drag Thrain into her apartment by his hair and have crazy sex with him on your love rug."*

"You think so?" She immediately perked up.

"Sure. Makes sense to me." Now that he'd eased

Sparkle's worries, it was time to move on to the important stuff: fomenting trouble on a grand scale. *"Let's talk about the summoning."*

"I conjured up a bunch of books with fake summoning spells in them and scattered them around Cindy's library. Watching the humans gather the things they think they'll need is a hoot." Reaching down, she scratched behind Ganymede's ear.

He leaned into her fingers. *"The tail-of-werewolf thing was pure genius. The last few nights, you couldn't go anywhere in that damned woods without running into a tail hunter."*

"Mmm. How about the broom-of-witch ingredient?" She skimmed her fingers down his back.

Oh, yes, baby. There were a few perks to being a cat. *"Inspired. I could've told them that trying to steal the cook's broom was a mistake. Of course, I didn't. I was eating dinner when the first idiot made a grab for it."* He paused to savor the memory.

"Well, what happened?" Sparkle stopped petting him long enough to examine one of her long red fingernails. "Remind me to use a different shade of red next time. This color is too bright and girly. I need something deeper, more intense. Something that'll be symbolic of my complete commitment to sex."

"The broom whacked him silly all the way to his room." Ganymede knew it was time to get moving when Sparkle started talking about her nails.

"You mean the cook chased him all the way to his room?" Sparkle stood.

"No. Just her broom. That was one ticked-off broom." Ganymede leaped from the bed. *"The guy checked out this morning. Cindy'll be upset."*

"No kidding." Sparkle walked to the door, then

paused with her hand on the knob. "When should we have the summoning?"

Ganymede padded to her side. *"Soon. If Cindy and Thrain get past their issues in spite of your meddling, they'll be off to Scotland to meet Darach. So the summoning has to happen before they leave, because I'm gonna be right there in Scotland with them. You know how I love happy endings."* A big fat lie, but in this one case, true.

She slanted him a narrow-eyed warning. "I'd like some respect for what I do." Her threat was implicit. No respect, no month of uninhibited sexual excess.

Oops. *"Hey, I respect you to death, cuddle-bunny. Love your meddling. If you meddle with them enough, they'll be so wrapped up in mindless sex, they won't pick up on our plans for the summoning. So meddling is good."*

"Okay, then." She looked mollified. "Why don't we have the summoning on the twenty-seventh, while everyone is still enthusiastic and before anyone decides to check the authenticity of the spells I planted?"

Whew! That had been close. *"Good thinking. It only gives us two more nights to plan, though."* Ganymede watched her close the door behind her; then he followed her down the hallway. *"I think we should hold the summoning on the front lawn. Maximum exposure. And we have to get Cindy and Thrain out of the way so they don't interfere. Oh, and remind everyone to keep quiet around them. We don't want anyone trying to stop us. Not that they could."* This was so great. If he'd had hands, he would've rubbed them together.

Ganymede hadn't had this much fun since he'd caused the last major blackout. With the Big Boss riding hard on him, it was tough to find evil things he could do that wouldn't send His Goodness into a snit. At least the Big Boss had finally given up on trying to keep Ganymede from cursing.

"*Damn, damn, damn, damn.*" Oh, the joy of it.

Sparkle cast a questioning glance over her shoulder.

"*I said it because I can.*"

Cindy had paid a price for avoiding Thrain: She couldn't sleep. But her sudden change in schedule was only part of the reason she'd tossed and turned till dawn.

Each night she'd felt Thrain outside her door. She could sense his restlessness, his *need*. The tough part? She wanted him so badly that everything from toes to teeth ached. After living with Prada's in-your-face efforts to encourage lust-filled thoughts, she was surprised she hadn't thrown open her door and jumped him. Could she both need and fear someone at the same time? Obviously, yes.

Cindy had to give him credit. He hadn't tried to enter her apartment or her mind. Heaven knew she couldn't stop him from doing either. Strange, but she recognized when he was in her head, the light pressure signaling he was there. She had no doubt others rooted through her thoughts, also, but Thrain's presence was the only one that registered on her consciousness.

She couldn't hide from him forever, though. Other than Trojan, he was the only one who could take her to her father. And Trojan was *not* an option. Just the thought of a transatlantic flight spent wedged between Prada and Trojan in his human form was scary. She'd made flight arrangements yesterday, because from what Thrain had said, she didn't have much more time to meet her father at his ancestral castle. *Their* ancestral castle.

Fine, so her return to the night schedule wasn't just about her father. Cindy missed Thrain. But how could you miss someone you'd only known for a few nights? Beyond the sexual attraction, what was there?

When she allowed herself to relax around him, she enjoyed his banter and the feeling of security he gave her. Even though the concept of *vampire* scared her witless, she'd come to the conclusion that she wouldn't be afraid to walk into the woods with him again. She might not trust his teeth near her neck, but she trusted him to keep her safe from other dangers.

And he was at ease with who he was. She admired and envied that. Maybe if he stuck around long enough, some of his ease would rub off on her. *Do you want him to "stick around?"* She was leaning toward a yes on that.

Cindy took a deep breath for courage, locked her apartment door, and walked to the front of the inn. Angela was there to fill her in on what had happened during the day. Angela usually only worked on Hal's days off, but thank heavens she'd been able to come in today so both Cindy and Hal could get back into their normal routines. Angela had also agreed to sub for Cindy while she was in Scotland.

After learning that one guest had checked out after being attacked by the cook's broom, Cindy watched Angela leave. Hmm. Only a broom attack? Must've been a slow night. Angela did have some good news, though. There'd been constant calls during the day for reservations. Evidently, the Jersey Devil story was spreading and growing.

"Decided to come out and face the big, bad vampire, sweetheart?" Even when he was being sarcastic, Thrain's voice was deep, rich seduction.

Surprised at her unexpected spurt of joy, Cindy turned to face him. "I wasn't hiding. I just needed time to figure things out with no distractions."

"But distractions can be satisfying on so many levels." His lips tipped up in a smile, that didn't reach his eyes. "Are you still planning to meet Darach?"

"Yes. I booked seats for us on a flight to Scotland this Friday night, but there's no way we can make the whole trip without your running into sunlight. I assume you have a way to deal with that problem. And I hope your passport is up to date." Cindy knew he was angry with her, but she couldn't quite figure out the flare of emotion she saw in his eyes. It wasn't as though she'd refused to see her father, and that was all Thrain had said he wanted.

"We'll leave on Friday, but it won't be on a commercial jet." He reached out to slide his finger down the side of her face and neck, pausing when he found the spot where her pulse pounded.

Cindy controlled her need to shudder even as she realized her reaction was more about sexual excitement than fear. His touch simmered through her, reaffirming the power of her heightened senses, at least where this man was concerned. She met his gaze. "I wait with bated breath to discover how we'll get to Scotland."

"I'll shape-shift into a giant bat and wing my way across the Atlantic with you grasped in my talons." This time the humor did touch his eyes.

"Thanks for not saying you'd grasp me with your

teeth." She couldn't remember ever finding anything having to do with teeth the least bit funny, but she surprised herself by smiling.

"I hate to disappoint you, but our flight won't have any high drama." He walked with her as she checked on the breakfast buffet and then headed toward the parlor for the first meeting of the night. "Our clan keeps several private jets available for us. Daylight won't be a problem."

Our. For the first time, she allowed the excitement of actually *belonging* to catch at her. "It's nice to know I have rich relatives. You can tell me all about them on the flight."

His soft laughter followed her as she chose her usual seat next to Leo. Thrain sat beside her.

"So, Leo, how're things going with Katie?" She scanned the room, pausing as her gaze locked with Darius. As usual, he and his fellow night feeders were grouped in a darkened corner. Darius smiled at her, and as she returned his smile, she wondered what excuse she could use to get out of the walk she owed him.

Moving on, Cindy's glance found Prada. Trojan lay on her lap. Prada's oh-so-sensual lips lifted in a sly smile. Cindy glared at her. She'd take care of Ms. Sex Goddess later.

"Katie is a marvelously powerful woman." Leo's eyes gleamed with happy excitement. "I've waited two centuries for a woman like her, and I don't intend to let her get away. Katie was going to tell you about our trip, but since you're here, I'll tell myself. I'm taking her to Atlantic City for some fun in the casinos. Prada says Thursday would be the best day to go. We'll be gone all day and probably most of the night." He nudged Cindy. "If I get truly lucky."

"All night?" Uh-oh. If Leo got *lucky*, Cindy might soon be searching for another cook.

"Don't worry about the meals. Katie says her sister, Gloria, will come in to prepare them."

"And Gloria is . . . ?"

Leo grinned at her. "Perfectly normal. She doesn't own any possessed brooms."

"Thank you." Cindy didn't know if she could wrap her mind around the concept of *perfectly normal* anymore. "And I hope you win megabucks at the casinos."

Leo looked puzzled. "Of course I will. I cheat. There have to be some advantages to being a wizard."

"Sure." Cindy tried to settle down and listen to the stories her guests were telling, but her constant awareness of Thrain was like her favorite sexy song played over someone reading the phone directory. No contest.

Her thigh touched his, and this time she made no attempt to move away. In fact, she'd finally decided to admit that she wouldn't mind any part of Thrain's body touching her, other than direct teeth-on-neck contact. It was amazing what kinds of truths were revealed by four nights of wanting and imagining.

"What're you going to do about it?" Thrain's question seemed a natural continuation of her thoughts.

"What?" Startled, she turned to look at him.

"Your nosy writer just finished telling everyone that he was at the cemetery last night hoping to scare up some more ghosts when something really big swooped down on him. He didn't get a good look at it because he was busy running into the woods to escape the attack. When he finally stopped running and turned around, it was gone. But the brief glimpse he got matches the Jersey Devil's description."

Cindy nodded. "Both appearances have been at the cemetery. The creature seems to have strong territorial feelings about the place. I wonder why it didn't appear when we were there with Leo and the three women."

Thrain smiled grimly. "It didn't have a pleasant experience with Trojan and me the first time we met. It might have decided to avoid a second confrontation." He shrugged. "Or maybe it was just sleeping-in that night."

She stood to face her guests. What a difference a week could make. A week ago, if someone had suggested that she'd be warning her guests about the Jersey Devil, she would have suggested a visit to the closest mental health facility. But seven nights had made her a believer.

"Look, for everyone's safety, I'm putting the cemetery off limits until we find out what's going on." She ignored the muttered grumbling and sat down again.

Thrain looked amused. "Now you've done it. All your guests will be sneaking out to the cemetery because you told them not to go there. The forbidden is an irresistible temptation." His eyes said the cemetery wasn't the only irresistible temptation.

She didn't have time to feel flattered. "I know, I know." Cindy rubbed the stress line between her eyes as guests streamed past her on the way to their nightly adventures. "I feel overwhelmed by everything. How much should I tell my human guests?

What do they need to know to keep them safe? 'Stay out of the woods because the Jersey Devil doesn't like you. Be careful with Leo Varinski, because if you make him mad he'll call up a few spirits or turn you into a frog. Don't mess with the cook or her broom will beat you to a pulp. Make sure you don't flirt with Andrea, because you'll have a jealous werecat to deal with.'"

Cindy threw up her hands. "I haven't even mentioned the assorted faeries, gods and goddesses, vampires, werewolves, and perhaps the biggest pains-in-the-butt of all, our resident cosmic troublemakers."

"Did I hear us mentioned in angry tones?" Prada stopped beside Cindy. She held Trojan cradled in both arms. "You know, you really have to keep sweetie here from the Ben & Jerry's. He weighs a ton. Whenever he has to shape-shift into a form he feels doesn't do justice to his magnificence, he compensates by guzzling ice cream. Then, when he changes back to human form, he makes everyone around him miserable for weeks while he sweats off his flab at the gym."

"Why do I put up with this woman?" Trojan's amber cat eyes were narrow, angry slits. *"Just tell me. Why?"*

Startled, Cindy met Trojan's gaze. "Are you talking to me?" She noticed for the first time that Trojan's and Prada's eyes looked the same when they were angry.

Prada's laugh was low and seductive. "You put up with me because there's no one on this sorry planet who can do the things to a man's body that I can."

Okay, don't want to hear this. "Thrain, would you take Trojan into the kitchen and get him a bowl of ice cream? I don't think he's tried Ben & Jerry's Chunky Monkey yet. I need to have a short talk with Prada. Alone."

Thrain's disgusted expression and Trojan's happy purr said it all. Prada set the cat gently on the floor and watched as he waddled away beside Thrain. "Males of all species are so easily pleased. Sex and food. I love the simplicity of their needs." Prada turned to meet Cindy's gaze. "Unlike ours."

Cindy raised what she hoped was a cynical brow. "Oh, you have needs beyond sex? Who would've guessed?"

Prada's smile was sly triumph. "You're mad at me. That makes me feel all tingly inside."

"Yes, well, I guess we get our tingles wherever we can. Now, about my apartment—"

"You noticed. How exciting." Prada clutched Cindy's arm and propelled her back into the parlor.

Cindy dropped onto the first chair she reached and watched Prada perch on the one opposite her. "You know, you shouldn't—"

"How did everything make you feel?" Prada's eyes gleamed with the inner fire of the true zealot.

"Mad. I thought we'd already established that." Somehow, Cindy didn't get the feeling she'd be hearing any abject apologies from Prada anytime soon.

"But how did it *really* make you feel?" Prada seemed intent on wresting some inner truth from Cindy. "As you absorbed the sensual wholeness of your apartment while imagining Thrain's bare, aroused body, what did you feel?"

"Mad." And after she'd gotten over her mad, she'd lit the candles, rubbed the erotic lotion all over her body, soaked up all the sexy visuals, listened to the sensual music, and stuffed all the yummy food Prada had supplied into her mouth. As Prada had no doubt expected, Cindy had imagined her mouth employed in other yummy pursuits. Prada had a lot to answer for. She'd contributed to Cindy's tossing and turning.

Prada sighed, crossed her legs, and tapped one red fingernail on her knee. "Sister, I've been lied to by experts. You don't qualify. Your father is a sensual man, and vampire blood breeds true. So we'll proceed on the assumption that you're a wildly sexy lady."

Prada knew her father, too. It seemed everyone knew good old Dad except her. But Cindy didn't want to get into a new discussion with Prada when she was having so much trouble finishing the present one.

"What's the red rug for?" It crouched in the middle of her living room, a round, fuzzy affront to the room's elegant neutrality.

"That's my love rug. When you and Thrain get so erotically charged you're giving off sparks, it'll be time to have sizzling sex on the love rug. You'll experience orgasmic ecstasy only those from parallel universes have known." Prada leaned closer to Cindy and speared her with a narrow-eyed stare. "And let's do it soon, okay, because I'm not a patient woman. Get over whatever issues you think you have with Thrain and get on with the good stuff."

"Right. The good stuff." If Cindy could get a word in edgewise, she'd tell Prada that during her four nights away from Thrain, she'd resolved all except two issues. The thought of Thrain's teeth near her neck terrified her at the same time the rest of his body gave her sex sweats. Did the Great Vampire Maker have a Thrain model sans fangs? Her second issue was beyond scary. Totally without the permission of her brain, her heart was pounding out a coded message that if Cindy translated correctly meant she was in deep trouble. Her heart was bypassing the teeth issue and going directly to the terrible truth. Cindy liked Thrain. A lot.

"I bet you didn't even use my First Aid Kit for Women Who Waffle during those four nights, did you?" Prada tapped her toe impatiently.

"Well . . ."

"You're beyond first aid. You need major surgery." Prada stood. "Come to my room so I can find some hunting clothes for you. We'll get you out of those jeans and into something lethal." She cocked her head to study Cindy. "I have a red silk dress that's barely there, but what *is* there clings to everything. It'll look incredible with all your dark hair. I'll even lend you my red strappy slut shoes with the six-inch heels. Put a whip in your hand and no man will be able to resist you."

"I . . ."

"What did you think of your bed?" Prada stood.

"I slept on the couch." Cindy frowned. Conflicting emotions about Thrain and her vampire roots battered her, but beyond those, an important question was forming. "Where did you come from, Prada?"

Prada stared at her blankly, and Cindy had the small triumph of knowing she'd surprised Ms. Sexy and Cool. Cindy suspected not much caught Prada off guard.

"Was that a trick question? How the hell do I

know where I came from?" Prada looked completely baffled by Cindy's question. "I just *am*. What does that have to do with anything?"

"Doesn't not knowing where you were born or who your parents were bother you?" The truth slowly unfurled, so simple when she wasn't hiding from it.

Prada blinked. "No. I don't need to know where I came from, just where I'm going."

"That's what *I* thought, too." Cindy followed Prada up the stairs to collect the barely there red dress and slut shoes. "I spent seven centuries denying my past. I convinced myself that only the present was important. I figured my extended life was the result of a genetic anomaly and that modern science would eventually find the answer for me. Every time any kind of thought intruded hinting I might not be completely human, I pushed it away. I rejected the past by concentrating on all that was new and shiny. Then I wondered why I was still dissatisfied."

"And your point is?" Prada opened her door and stepped inside.

Cindy followed her into the room and then stood waiting while Prada rooted around in her closet. "I need to come to terms with my past before I can find peace in the present."

"So? You go to Scotland, fling yourself into Daddy's arms, and achieve peace. Nothing complicated about that." Prada turned from the closet with the red dress draped over her arm and the infamous slut shoes dangling from her finger. "Personally, I think peace is way overrated. But that's just me."

Cindy's father wasn't the complicated part. The tough part was Thrain. She wanted to get close to him on so many levels, and physical desire was a major component of that closeness. But no matter how much she wanted to make love with him, she couldn't get past his vampire nature. Every time he'd touch her neck with his mouth, she'd panic. She had to find a way to overcome her fear. Who would've thought one dog bite could mess her up for over seven hundred years?

Mumbling her thanks, Cindy accepted Prada's offerings and then turned to leave.

"Whoa. Not so fast, sister. March yourself right into that bathroom and change now. I'm not giving you a chance to go back to your apartment, where you can hang that fine dress in your closet and forget about it." Prada's expression was militant.

Cindy decided she'd get out of Prada's room a lot faster if she changed into the dress without arguing. Allowing herself a few mental sighs, Cindy went into the bathroom, stripped off her jeans, top, and shoes, and then shimmied into the little red nothing. Slipping the red sandals with the six-inch man-killer heels onto her feet, she scooped up her discarded clothes and tottered out of the bathroom. Good grief, she felt like a stilt walker.

Cindy was so busy trying to decide how to conquer the fear she'd allowed to fester for seven centuries, she didn't even glance in the mirror.

"Now that's what I call a dress. You're a ticking sensual time bomb set to go off in about five minutes, or as long as it takes you to track down that hot vampire." Prada held the door open for her. "Oh, and you think things to death, girlfriend."

"What?" *Ticking sensual time bomb?*

"Trust me, you'll get to that special moment when

231

your feelings for Thrain block out the sun, and you won't even remember that dog bite."

For the first time in their short acquaintance, Prada's smile seemed sincere, with no hidden agenda.

"How did you know . . . ?" Cindy narrowed her gaze. "You've been in my mind."

Prada shrugged. "Sure. Everyone has." She offered Cindy an encouraging smile. "As of right now, you're Thrain Davis's sexy midnight dream. Go get him." Then she quietly closed her door, leaving Cindy standing in the hallway.

Sighing, Cindy walked back down the stairs and headed for the kitchen. Maybe Thrain would still be there with Trojan. But all she found was Trojan with his face in the Chunky Monkey carton. He didn't bother to even look up when she entered the room.

"Just heard the news. You really got into some major self-discovery crap tonight. Take it from an expert, though, don't let all this self-analysis stuff mess with your head. Sometimes you have to go with your gut feeling."

Cindy accepted the inevitable. "Prada didn't waste any time spreading the news."

"She knew I'd want to know. We have an interest in you, kid." Trojan reluctantly abandoned the ice cream container. *"And Prada's dress is a winner on you."* He winked one amber eye. *"Thrain's waiting outside your apartment door. He's getting impatient."*

Cindy looked directly into Trojan's eyes and for the first time recognized the being beneath the cat form. The power she saw there made her shiver. She sort of liked his greedy, fat-cat image better.

As she left the kitchen, Cindy glanced down at

Prada's dress for the first time. Ack! She could see straight to her navel. But there was no use putting off the inevitable. She marched toward her apartment and Thrain.

Chapter Twelve

Thrain's anger with Cindy simmered just below the surface of his self-control, and no amount of logic would calm it. What was the matter with him? He should be happy, not mad. He'd done what he'd set out to do centuries ago. Darach would meet his daughter.

Propping his shoulder against the wall beside Cindy's door, he tried for some self-truth. In a week's time, he'd gone from a firm determination not to get personally involved with Darach's daughter to where he was now—involved up to his eyebrows.

The scary part of the whole thing was that his anger had nothing to do with sex. Sexual frustration didn't make him mad, it made him hungry. This was something else altogether. It went deeper. And deeper was not a good thing where Cindy was concerned, because it hinted that his feelings for her were edging into a place he'd never gone before, didn't want to go.

Besides, forging emotional ties to Cindy was a formula for disaster. She was afraid of him—or more specifically, she was afraid of his teeth. And the bottom line was that his teeth went where he went.

He pushed away from the wall at the sound of heels tapping toward him. She turned the corner and walked toward him. Thrain didn't believe in fate, but he couldn't control the uncomfortable premonition that destiny was swaying toward him dressed in a short red dress that clung to every tempting curve.

As he slid his gaze down those long, slim legs ending in sexy red heels, desire rose on a sea of shimmering red. Cindy should know better than to look like that in front of a healthy vampire.

She stopped before him, her cheeks flushed and her eyes sparkling with what he could only describe as excited determination.

"We need to talk." He tried to control anything in his voice that might send her scuttling back down the hallway. "Your dress has a head start. It's been speaking to me ever since you turned the corner."

"Really? What did it have to say?" Cindy raised her hand. "No, never mind. I don't want to know. It isn't mine, anyway. Prada lent it to me." She looked down as she smoothed her fingers over the material. "Come in and I'll get you a drink." She frowned as she remembered. "Or not. Sorry, but I don't stock your favorite beverage." She unlocked her door and walked into her apartment.

He didn't reply to her drink comment because he was too busy watching the provocative swing of her round little behind as he followed her inside. "I'll have to compliment Prada on her taste in dresses."

"Yeah, well, Prada thinks that turning me into a sex bunny will resolve all my issues." She kicked off the red sandals and breathed a relieved sigh. "Have a seat."

He was finally able to drag his gaze away from the dress long enough to look around. "Odin's revenge! What happened to your place?"

She smiled at his reaction. "Prada happened. She decided to sex up my apartment on the theory that living with her *subtle* sensual enhancements would turn me into a sex-hungry savage who'd jump your bod the first chance I got."

Thrain returned her smile. "Did it work?" He was almost ready to reward Prada with his priceless collection of erotic literature if her attempt succeeded.

Cindy looked up and met his gaze. "I didn't need Prada's help." Her gaze slipped away from him. "I wanted you all on my own."

"But?" He knew there was a *but* because he heard it in the soft uncertainty of her voice and saw it in the way her glance skittered around the room.

She didn't answer immediately, and for a moment he was afraid she'd refuse to continue.

At last she met his gaze again. "I'm afraid of you." She rushed on to another subject before he could argue with her. "Why are you mad at me? I sensed it as soon as we met tonight."

His smile didn't slip. "Because you're afraid of me." He realized he'd told her the truth. That nasty little secret had hidden in his subconscious until it was ready to pop out and surprise him. People's fears had never bothered him before. The fact that hers did was another warning that maybe he was growing more emotionally attached than was wise. But what he felt for Cindy wasn't about being wise.

She sighed. "You can't possibly be angrier with me than I am with myself." Cindy shrugged. "I guess I'm the only one who can work through my fear, though. Would you like to see the rest of the horror that Prada visited on my place?"

"Sure." He understood her need to avoid the sit-down talk he wanted with her. But she could only put him off for so long. "What's that red rug doing in the middle of your living room?" He scanned the graphic paintings hanging from every wall. It was obvious what the people pictured in them were do-ing, and doing in very creative ways.

Cindy laughed for the first time. "That's Prada's love rug. She says anyone who wants superheated sex should do it there. Prada claims great things happen on that rug."

"Does Prada have a catalog? I wouldn't mind owning that rug." He slid his fingers the length of her back as she led him from the room. "And I'd buy this dress for you. Right now, my emotions are about the same shade of red as the dress." He left his hand on her bare shoulder as she pointed out the candles, the lotion, and all the other Prada touches. Her skin heated beneath his touch while his need darkened, well on its way to blackest black.

They ended up in her bedroom. "If I didn't want you to experience Prada's most creative effort, I wouldn't have let you in here. But this is too good to miss." Her smile was playful, but he sensed the ten-sion behind it.

Thrain glanced around. Other than the usual

paintings of couples doing it and the candles, he didn't see anything unusual. "Where is it?" He sat on her bed, prepared to scan the room a second time.

"Aaaah! Ooooh! Yessss! Please, harder, harder!" Moans of ecstasy oozed from the bed.

"What the hell? The damned bed is having an orgasm." He leaped up and the voices stopped.

Cindy laughed and pushed him back onto the bed. The sounds of sexual bliss took up where they'd left off. "Is this weird or what?" She had to shout to be heard over the rapidly escalating cries of pleasure.

"I've heard enough. The only moans that should come from this bed are the ones we make." He focused his attention on the mattress and visualized the blasted sound box crumbling away. The voices stilled.

"Prada won't be happy that you broke her toy." Cindy's voice had lost some of its playfulness. She bit her bottom lip, and he didn't have to be in her head to know she was considering what it would take for those sounds of pleasure to be theirs.

He didn't intend to give her long to think about it. Reaching up, he drew her down beside him and then lay back on the bed. Reluctantly, she lay beside him, but he felt her tension. "I'd like to say that Prada's decorating genius had worked me into a frenzy, but it would be a lie."

"I don't think this is—"

He put his finger over her lips. "Wise? Maybe not, but I don't care. By the time I get to the color red, it's way too late."

"So what worked you into a frenzy?" She tried to smile, but didn't quite succeed.

At least he didn't see terror in her eyes, only caution. "The red dress. It starts here ..." He leaned over her and ran his tongue across the swell of her breasts, exposed by the scooped neckline.

She shivered and her breathing quickened, but she didn't push him away.

"And ends here." He drew his finger the length of her long, smooth leg and thigh, pausing when he reached the hem of her dress where it had ridden up almost to her spectacular bottom.

He heard her small gasp and the sudden quickening of her heartbeat.

"And it clings to everything in between." He laid his palm flat right below her breasts and then slid his hand over her body. He allowed his palm to rest low on her stomach, right above the hem of the red piece of silk and temptation. "I want to make love to you, Cindy. I've wanted it every night while you were sleeping. By the way, it was pretty weak escaping from me into the daylight." He propped himself up on one elbow and gazed down at her.

"I know. I sensed you standing outside my door each night." She stared up at him with wide blue eyes.

Thrain lowered his lids, enjoying the anticipatory tightening of his body. He smiled, allowing the power of his need to flow over her, shamelessly using the skills of sexual seduction he'd gained through the centuries. "I want you naked on this bed with the only red between us the color of sex in my mind." Fingering the hem of her dress, he edged it higher until he could see the white lace of her panties.

She didn't try to stop him, but he could feel tension thrumming through her. "Only red? I was hoping for black. You disappoint me, Davis."

"It's getting there." He couldn't take this any further until she let her tension go. "I won't bite your neck, Cindy."

She flinched at his blunt statement. "Logically, I know you're telling the truth. But my fear has never been logical."

"You weren't afraid of me at the cemetery." Reluctantly, he pulled her hem down to cover her panties. He had a feeling this wasn't going to be resolved in a few minutes. His body wailed its anguish.

"At the cemetery, I didn't know that you were a—"

"Vampire. Right." It was time to drag her fear into the light, examine it from every angle, and defeat it. "But vampires aren't the only ones with teeth. Every man you've had sex with throughout the centuries has had teeth." *Had sex with.* An irrational part of him wouldn't let him say *made love with* when talking about Cindy and other males.

Something very close to hurt twisted in him as she sat up and then propped herself against the headboard. She bent her knees and wrapped her arms around them in a protective gesture, while her eyes darkened with remembered terror.

"You're right, but humans aren't defined by their teeth. In my mind, the word *vampire* means only one thing—a creature of the night who'll sink his teeth into my neck and rip the life from me just as the dog tried to do." She shrugged but wouldn't meet his gaze. "Reason tells me you wouldn't do that, but fear doesn't reason." Cindy offered him a weak smile. "Even though I can't remember what that dog looked like, I can still remember the terror. I can't make myself get close to or touch a dog." She lifted her hands in a helpless gesture. "If it makes you feel any better, I'd have the same fear of the werewolves and werecat staying here. I'm afraid to get too close to any creature that kills with its teeth."

"I feel so much better knowing you put me in the same class as the family dog." He shouldn't resort to sarcasm, but she'd hurt him, and his first instinct was to lash back. "At least using teeth to kill is honest. Humans hurt each other in more subtle ways that are a lot crueler."

"Anger isn't going to change the way I feel." She raked her dark hair away from her face. "Get it through your head that I can't help myself. What do you want from me?"

I want you to make love with me and look at me like . . . Like what? He wasn't sure. Did he care enough to find out? He admitted he did. He cared enough to try something he never would have considered before meeting Cindy. He just hoped he lived through the experience.

"You're not the only one with an obsessive fear." Could he do this? Could he relive an experience so horrible it had driven him away from all closeness with human females? *Until Cindy.* "I'll make a deal with you. I'll share what I fear most if you let me help you conquer your fear."

Cindy studied him. What could make a vampire who seemed invincible afraid? An army of Italian chefs wielding garlic cloves? Why did she want to know? Natural curiosity was only part of it. Something fierce and protective inside her didn't want him to be afraid of anything, because fear came from being hurt. Surprised, Cindy realized she wanted to lay some serious physical damage on the someone or something that had caused him pain.

She'd tiptoed around her emotions for so many

years that it had become a habit. No more. If facing her own fear was the cost of learning what touched Thrain on his deepest emotional level, then she'd do it.

Cindy nodded, and wondered what she was agreeing to. "I'll let you help me." *Because I want to be close to you without fear, without physical or emotional barriers.*

He moved to her side and leaned back against the headboard. "Groups of human women terrify me. That fear has lived in me since seventeen eighty-five. I could take away your fear by erasing your memory of the dog attack and replacing it with memories of pets you've loved, but I can't erase my own memories."

She shook her head. "I wouldn't want you to erase my memory. It would be an artificial fix. I need the strength to do it myself."

His smile connected them, assuring her they were the same in more ways than they were different. "I'm going to take you into my memory, but this time I'll join you." His smile faded. "I've never revisited that moment, never had the courage to."

Uh-oh. Soft-and-squishy feelings alert. She touched his hand. "Why're you doing it now?"

He clasped her hand. "Because I can never help you with *your* fear if I don't face my own. I don't have a 'do-as-I-say,-not-as-I-do' philosophy."

"If the memory gets too intense, can I break free of it?" She hated herself for asking. That was how she'd always handled life. When things got too uncomfortable, she ran.

"No." He tightened his grip on her hand, a symbolic securing of her soul for the duration of his memory. "You were able to end the memory in the spaceship a little early because I wasn't taking an active part in it. This time I'll be with you, experiencing it with you. Once the memory starts, neither one of us will be able to end it until its natural conclusion."

Cindy felt his fear of revisiting his past horror as a thick river of revulsion coursing up her arm from their clasped hands. She moved closer so her shoulder and arm pressed against him, connecting them in a more physical way and sharing her strength with him. "Will I just be a viewer?"

He shook his head, and something in his smile frightened her. "You'll be a participant. Do you want to back out?"

Here it was, her chance to flee. If it was just about her, she'd be gone. But Thrain needed to face his fear in order to start the healing process. Cindy found she had the necessary courage when Thrain's well-being hung in the balance. "Let's do it." Whatever *it* involved. "Do you have to stare into my eyes?"

"No." He sounded distant, as if he were moving away from her even as he spoke. "When I go, I'll take you with me."

How could he do that? Was she scared? You betcha. Her palms were sweating and the nervous tic in her right eye that only manifested itself during near-death experiences was alive and well. What would it feel like? Would she realize it was happening? Would . . .

She opened her eyes. She'd closed them for a moment to savor the complete joy of total success. Tonight was the culmination of years of planning, and tonight she would finally achieve immortality.

"The sisterhood feels that you should have first choice of the vampires, Elizabeth." Margaret's eyes glittered with suppressed excitement. "For it was your idea to grind the bog myrtle into powder and then release it into the air. Once exposed to it, they became helpless. You also found the man able to create a potion that assured the vampires' sexual readiness whether they willed it or not."

"I thank you for this honor." She must play at being humble, even though she wished only to be rid of Margaret so she could lift her gown and impale herself on the most virile vampire's cock. "But without your spies, we would never have trapped so many of them in one place. All has worked perfectly for us. I cannot believe we have seven to mount this night."

Margaret nodded her acceptance of Elizabeth's compliment. "Ever since the sisterhood found that joining with only one vampire was not enough to achieve immortality, I have renewed my efforts to capture a group for us to use." Margaret nodded toward the center of the great hall. "Remember that you must couple with at least three of them to attain immortality. The potion will assure that they do not lose their erections until we are finished." Brief worry touched her gaze. "I hope they last the night. I fear excessive blood loss and exhaustion might counteract the potion, but we will take from them what we can."

Elizabeth had one remaining concern. "What will you do once we are done with them?"

Margaret shrugged. "We will leave them for the morning sun to find. That way there will be no witnesses to our actions and we can be sure that none of them will pursue us for vengeance."

"You have thought of everything." Elizabeth

hated having to flatter one she felt was inferior to herself, but she must keep Margaret's goodwill if she hoped to rise in the sisterhood.

"I will keep you no longer from what you crave." Margaret gestured toward the seven raised platforms. "Take what you have so rightly earned."

Elizabeth took a deep, anticipatory breath and moved toward the platforms. Seven males lay naked and spread-eagled upon them. All of them were in what must be a painful state of arousal. But she cared not for their pain. They were simply animals to be used as the sisterhood saw fit.

She wrinkled her nose at the bloody cuts that marred their bodies. Unfortunately, once the bog myrtle wore off, the vampires became uncontrollable even while bound. The only way to keep them docile enough for the sisterhood to use was to make them weak through loss of blood.

There was no way to avoid getting blood on her gown unless she shed the garment. This she would not do; it would make her too much like the creatures who lay bound before her. Beyond her need to be immortal, she admitted to a certain enjoyment of the vampires' naked helplessness.

Elizabeth narrowed her gaze as she carefully made her choices. She would pick the most muscular physical specimens to assure the greatest potency. And of course, the biggest and strongest males would feel their degradation more deeply. Males were such prideful creatures. And inside, where truth lay, she admitted what she wished not to admit. She enjoyed the hurting, the humiliating, and the killing of these creatures.

She already knew which one she would use first.

Elizabeth had marked him for her own from the start. A tangle of long blond hair streaked with his own blood framed his lean, hard face. His face was in its vampire form now, but it had not been so when they first captured him. His human face was one women would always feel drawn to—strong, harsh, but softened by startling blue eyes framed with thick, dark lashes. His sensual mouth with its full lower lip was an erotic temptation women would be unable to resist.

Elizabeth tightened her lips at the knowledge that a male with a face and body such as his would never choose her for a mate. She'd accepted that truth long ago. But she would have her revenge on all such males through him.

Standing over her chosen one, she paused to give him time to suffer with the knowledge of her complete control. She slid her tongue over her bottom lip, feeling her sexual hunger rise, and accepting that for her, completion could only come when she knew her victim was helpless and in pain. Curling her long nails into talons, she enjoyed the anticipation of raking bloody furrows into his perfect body as she climaxed. She drew in a deep breath at the delicious thought of inflicting pain.

Lifting her gown, she straddled his hips and then stared down at him, exulting in her power. She thought it a mystery why an animal such as this should have such a beautiful human body. From his broad, muscular shoulders and chest down to his narrow hips and strong thighs and legs, his bare body glistened with a thin layer of sweat that delineated every muscle.

But it was the fury and underlying horror she saw

in his eyes that loosed her sexual hunger. "I will take you, vampire, and I will hurt you while I do so. You will come for me because you cannot help yourself." She leaned closer and smiled at him. "And you will hate yourself for being so weak."

He said nothing, only fought against the bonds that held him spread and open to anything she wished to do to him. And Elizabeth had much she wished to do to him.

Slowly, dragging out his agony, she lowered herself onto his cock, felt the large head slide . . .

Suddenly, her body seemed unwilling to obey her. She felt . . . She felt different, as though a stranger dwelled in her who was battling for her soul. What was happening? She clasped her head with both hands, as though by doing so she could quell the chaos growing within her. Her vision blurred as the pounding of her heart drowned out all other sounds, and her breaths came in agonized gasps. Who was she? Where was she? Why was she here? Her last coherent thought as Elizabeth was anger at being denied her pleasure. She would *not* let this happen . . .

"*No!*" Cindy dragged herself from the memory with a primal scream of fury. She refused to complete the memory, to be the instrument of Thrain's torture any longer. She'd never felt real hate, but she recognized it now. It burned and clawed at her. At this moment, while the horror of Elizabeth's twisted soul was still close enough to chill her, Cindy understood the desire to kill another human.

Cindy swiped at the tears she'd just realized were streaming down her face and turned to look at Thrain. He stared back at her with eyes still alive with his personal horror.

"How did you break free from the memory?" His voice grated with his own silent screams, and Cindy didn't miss the tremor in his hand as he pushed his hair away from his face.

She transferred her anger to him. "How could you think I'd hurt you, even while I was in the soul of another woman?" She leaned close to run her finger along his clenched jaw. "I'm stronger than that." *And I care more than that.* "You feel in color. What color did you feel?"

"At the end? White." His expression was bleak. "The color of death, of nothingness."

Cindy took a deep breath of courage and made her decision. "I understand fear, Thrain. I'll help you deal with it. Not forget it, because no one could forget that kind of savagery. But I want to help you face human women without always seeing the faces of those sick bitches."

Thrain nodded. "We'll help each other." He somehow dredged up a smile, but it hurt Cindy to see how much effort it took. "You saw me in vampire form. Did my face bother you?" Glancing away, he focused his attention on one of Prada's framed sex fests.

Careful. He'd been hurt in so many ways, and Cindy didn't want to add to that. She had to be clear about her feelings. "No. Your face was just an extension of you, and I'm pretty much excited about you in any form. Your eyes were bigger and almost black. Enlarged pupils, I suppose. Nostrils were more flared and mouth fuller because of your fangs. But all in all, it was a great face."

Thrain turned back to her, his relief obvious. "Thanks for being honest. I could've handled it if you gagged, but it would've hurt." Obviously uncomfortable with that admission, he attempted to make light of it. "Vampires have sensitive egos."

She widened her eyes. "Hey, sincerity is my middle name." Cindy desperately wanted to know what had happened to him after she'd torn herself from the memory, but she needed a few minutes to recover, to pull herself together. She'd change the subject until she had the strength to hear the rest of his story.

Thrain's horrific memory had made her realize how little she really knew about him. "You've followed me around through the centuries, so I guess you even know what toothpaste I use. But I know almost zip about you. You owe me a few answers."

"Sure." His expression said he understood the reason for her sudden shift in topic.

"Where do you live and what do you do? Or don't you do anything?" *And who's shared your bed over all those centuries?* Maybe she didn't want to know about the bed-sharing part.

"I have homes all over the world." He reached over and picked up the red velvet box on Cindy's night table. "Not in Scotland. I haven't lived in Scotland since seventeen eighty-five." He stroked the velvet, reminding Cindy of what a wonderfully sensual creature he was. "This trip to see Darach will be my first time back. I can deal with it." He glanced up at her. "With you."

With you. Talk about warm fuzzies. Cindy felt happier about those two words than she had about anything anyone had ever said before. They affirmed that, yes, she was special in his life.

"I own a lot of companies, but I take care of most

communication by phone or e-mail. Not many people ever see me, so I don't have to deal with the problem of never aging. If I keep a company past the span of a normal lifetime, I die, and the company passes to my son." He shrugged. "I could sell all my companies tomorrow and not have to worry about money, but I enjoy the challenges."

Okay, now for the question she *had* to ask, *feared* to ask. But her need to know everything about him drove her. "What happened to you after I left your memory? I mean, I know it's tough to talk about, and I'll understand if you don't want to tell me . . ." She let her babbling fade away without admitting how important it was that he finish his story.

He remained silent for so long, she thought he'd refuse. She could live with that, but she wanted him to trust her completely, and his sharing of that event would demonstrate his trust.

"Elizabeth used me, as did many others. They only stopped when I was too weak to satisfy them any longer." His fingers tightened around the red box until Cindy figured he'd squash it beyond recognition. "I'd bled until I had little strength." He didn't seem to notice that he'd fallen back into the speech pattern of that long-ago time. "When dawn drew near, they left us to die in the morning sun. I was able to free myself, and then I freed the others. We were close to death and desperate for blood."

He gazed at her, and she saw the anguish he didn't try to hide. That was a form of trust as well. Even if he walked away from her after taking her to her father, she'd treasure these few moments of closeness.

"You must understand that members of our clan

are different from most vampire species. We may never drink so much blood that we destroy a life. Once we gorge ourselves to the point that we kill our prey, we ourselves are doomed." He drew in a deep, fortifying breath, a reflex action from a time when he was human. "Killing releases the blood lust, and we are driven to kill more and more until we become mindless creatures living only to feed. At that point, we cannot be redeemed and so must be destroyed. With the instinct to survive, we rose that night and ravaged the countryside. But I was more fortunate than the others. I was able to stop before I went completely mad."

Cindy frowned. "That was good, right? You stopped in time, so you didn't have to be destroyed."

Thrain shook his head, and gleaming strands of his hair, still damp from his ordeal, framed his face. "I was already beyond redemption, but still retained the ability to realize what I'd done. When members of our clan near death, instinct compels them to return to our ancestral castle in Scotland. It is a call imbedded in clan memory and not to be denied. We traveled there together." Distractedly, he fumbled with the catch on the velvet box.

"Go on." Cindy's stomach revolted at the unspeakable cruelty visited on Thrain, but she pushed back the sickness. It was important that she hear him to the end.

"Guilt had kept me from Darach ever since I helped Aesa leave him. But now that I knew my own death was near, I wanted my oldest friend to be the one who ended my life. It was Darach's time to wait at the castle for those of the clan seeking death's release, and I knew he would honor every clansman's wish to die with dignity in battle. He fought and destroyed the others, but he could not bring himself to kill a friend." Thrain paused, and she sensed he was seeing the scene with her father once again.

"In order to survive, I needed blood from a clansman to counteract the imbalance of human blood. I could not bite Darach to fill my needs even though he would have offered himself, because clan law forbids it. I would have died before breaking clan law." He ignored her mumbled comment about stupid laws.

"Fortunately for me, Darach's chosen mate was a wise woman from a far distant future. Ganymede, the one you call Trojan, had brought a group of time travelers to the castle for a vacation in the past." For the first time since beginning his story, Thrain smiled. "She gave me a transfusion of Darach's blood that bypassed the forbidden biting. I was saved. Since then, I have wished to do something that would repay his friendship." He opened the lid on the red box.

"You don't repay friendship, Thrain. It can't be bought or sold. It simply is." Wow, was that profound or what?

"What the hell is this?" He stared into the box.

Speech pattern restored. Thrain was officially back in 2005. Which was good, because she was close to emotional meltdown. "That's Prada's First Aid Kit for Women Who Waffle. According to Prada, a woman who can't commit to unending sexual pleasure with her special man needs something to get her through the tough times."

He held up a video. *"The Pleasure of One?"*

Cindy glanced away. "Umm, I don't think Prada

subscribes to that philosophy, but she threw it in to amuse the stubborn and uninformed."

Rooting around inside the box, he finally pulled out . . . oops. "Explain."

If she got any redder, bullfighters could put her to good use. "A high-tech sex toy. It's a fingertip vibrator. You plug it into your computer's USB port." She had to make one thing clear. "I never used any of that stuff."

He looked intrigued. "I don't have a computer. Maybe I'll get one. We could—"

"No. Absolutely not." She pulled the box from his grip, swung her legs to the floor, and strode to the wastebasket. She held the box high above the can, then dropped it. What a satisfying clunk. Okay, so she was burning her bridges behind her. Who knew when the red box might come in handy? But tonight was a time for uncompromising action.

"I won't need this anymore. This is one woman who's done waffling."

Chapter Thirteen

"I'm searching for signs of sexual bliss here—love ears, duck walk, Opulent Orgasm nail polish . . ." Prada relaxed onto the couch, crossed her long legs, and glanced out the parlor window at the growing darkness. "But I'm getting nothing. What's the problem, sister?" Her pursed lips and narrowed eyes said that Cindy was a major disappointment. "I sexed up your apartment and your clothes. Did I miss something?" Prada's expression hinted that Cindy's sexual failure rested firmly on her own shoulders.

"Love ears? Duck walk? Opulent Orgasm nail polish?" Prada was so far above Cindy on the sexual evolutionary scale that she was out of sight.

"You've lived how many centuries without knowing this?" Prada widened her eyes to indicate how mind-boggling it was that any sensual being could live for so long and know so little. "After an incredible night of sex, the ears tell the tale. Great sex equals red ears. Can't control it, don't even try. The duck walk? After a whole night with your legs wrapped around your man, and all that pumping and plunging and clenching, you're absolutely going to walk a little funny. And your nail polish is a dead giveaway. No erotically fulfilled woman would ever be caught wearing that virgin-pink garbage." She directed a pointed stare at Cindy's pink nails. "I took one look at you and checked none-of-the-above on my sexual success chart. Can we say failure?"

Cindy's first instinct was to tell Prada to buzz off. But Cindy needed to talk to someone, and who better than Prada? Cindy didn't know anyone else who'd understand the weird whirl her life had become. Prada was a major player in that weirdness, so at least she'd believe Cindy. Since last night, when she'd vowed to help Thrain overcome his fear, Cindy had tried to think of ways to deal with her own devils. So far she'd come up with a big fat nothing.

"I'm trying to get to know Thrain better." Would Prada believe that? No.

"He has an excellent package and puts the *aaah* in hot. What else is there to know?" Prada looked sincerely puzzled.

Taking a deep breath, Cindy laid it out for Prada. "Here's the story. A dog bit my neck when I was a kid. I've been afraid of things that bite ever since. Thrain's a vampire, ergo he bites. Result? I'm afraid of his teeth. Come up with a way we can have long-distance sex and I'll run with it."

Prada blinked. "You're kidding."

If she weren't so down, Cindy would have enjoyed Prada's shock. "So unless you have an idea I haven't thought of, I guess you're doomed to fail with me." Cindy had no doubt Prada would rise to the occasion.

Prada firmed her lips. Her gaze turned militant. "I won't let you do this to my career. You will *not* be the mustard stain on my Nicole Miller silk dress, the bent nosepiece on my Gucci sunglasses, the broken strap on my Fendi shoulder bag . . ." She took a deep, calming breath as she fingered the gold chain at her neck. "This is tough. I usually don't have to put so much effort into hooking up people who're wrong for each other. Getting the werewolf and werecat together was child's play. And look how much trouble *that* caused. I loved it. Oh, and I can't forget Finvarra and Aibell. Have you seen any harps or chessboards lately? I think not. All is sensually super with them."

Cindy pictured herself as one of many names on Prada's to-do list. A name Prada was eager to put a check beside. "Any ideas?"

"Hmm. Unusual case. Most of the time I choose my victims . . . er, subjects, do some clever manipulating, and watch nature take its course. Humans are pathetically predictable." Prada speared Cindy with an intense stare. "But you're a challenge. I thought once I got past your disbelief in vampires and Thrain's stubbornness about falling for human females, I'd be home free. I mean, you really did want to find someone immortal like you, and Thrain was hot for you from the beginning. Who knew you guys would test my power?" Her smile was sly calculation. "No one has challenged me in hundreds of years. I needed this. I have to grow and get better if I want to keep my Super Bitch rating in the *Who's Who of Cosmic Troublemakers*."

"And all of this means what?" Cindy didn't have time to waste while Prada patted herself on the back.

Prada tapped one perfect fuchsia nail on her knee. Jeez, how many short black dresses did Prada have? None of Prada's dresses ever got within shouting distance of her knees. Cindy blinked. What did Prada's dresses have to do with anything?

"I wear short dresses because men are endearingly simple creatures when it comes to what attracts them. If a woman has big boobs, long bare legs, and can shake her booty, men will follow her anywhere." Prada didn't even look at Cindy as she spoke. Her expression said she was still focused on Cindy's bite phobia.

Pitiful. Prada didn't even break a sweat while she read Cindy's mind. "Hurry. Thrain should be down any minute." She bit back a frustrated groan as she caught sight of Darius and the rest of his night feeders watching her. He'd probably want her to walk with him to the Hart mansion, and she'd have to find an excuse not to go. Telling him that she didn't go anywhere with blood-sucking fiends would not only tick him off but would lose her four more guests. She'd lost too many already.

"You're crazy about Thrain or you wouldn't be asking for my help. So my question is . . ." Prada's expression said she wasn't used to stepping outside the sexual realm to solve problems. "How much do you love him?"

Love? Even thinking the word stirred . . . what? *Fear.* What if she really did love him? What if she didn't find a way to face her phobia? What if she had to spend forever never feeling him deep inside her again? What if she found Thrain's sword and lopped off her own head? Cindy closed her eyes. Damndamndamn.

"That much, huh?" Prada sounded amused. And very sure of herself.

Cindy opened her eyes. When in doubt, make ambiguous gestures. She shrugged.

"Maybe you need a defining moment in your life, an event during which you experience absolute emotional clarity. Hmm."

Prada's gaze grew unfocused and Cindy could almost hear the wicked wheels turning. How scary was that?

Finally, Prada nodded, signaling that she'd made her decision. "Look, I have people to talk to. How about we meet later and work things out?" Without waiting for Cindy's reply, she rose and wandered over to chat with the night feeders.

Cindy blinked. Well, so much for Prada's help. Maybe she'd try talking to a psychiatrist again. Standing, Cindy crossed the parlor and paused in the doorway. Thrain had just reached the bottom of the stairs when Trojan intercepted him.

Cindy had seen centuries of what's hot and what's not in male fashion, but absolutely nothing compared to jeans and a black T-shirt for wow impact when Thrain was doing the modeling. She watched the two of them head for her kitchen. Looked like her Ben & Jerry's supply was about to take another hit.

Continuing on to her apartment, Cindy spent some time on the Internet deciding which psychiatrist she'd dump her seven hundred years of emotional angst on. She'd make an appointment tomorrow.

Once back in the inn, she started toward the parlor. Breakfast was finished and everyone would be gathered there by now. As she passed a shadowed alcove near the front door, Darius stepped into her path. *No, not now.* She didn't want to stand arguing with the night feeder when she had so many other things to worry about.

"I'm visiting the Hart mansion tonight, Cindy. You'll come with me." It wasn't a request, and something darkly menacing moved in his eyes.

She tried to look away from his gaze, but she couldn't. *She couldn't.* Panic intruded. Cindy opened her mouth to shout for help. Nothing. No words formed in her mind, no message reached her brain. Panic escalated to terror. What the hell was going on?

"I'm simply controlling the parts of your mind that could spoil our little walk in the woods." He smiled, a feral lifting of his lips that revealed long, sharp fangs.

Ohmigod! She was in full fight-or-flight mode, but her arms and legs felt like lead weights.

"After you." Darius gestured toward the door.

Cindy tried to resist. Useless. She walked out into the night with Darius. The other night feeders materialized from the darkness to join them. Silently, they moved through the forest.

Could she call Thrain with her mind? She'd never tried, but she seemed out of other options.

"Won't work." Darius's conversational tone was mild. His threat wasn't. "I've blocked your thoughts. He won't hear you."

Cindy tried to swallow past the massive boulder lodged in her throat. Once they got her to the Hart mansion, they'd attack her. She knew it on a gut level, but she couldn't do anything to stop it.

Pain. Teeth. Throat. Death. With each word, terror

extinguished hope like bulbs burning out on an old store sign. Enough burned-out bulbs and no one could recognize the message anymore. Nausea roiled in her stomach. She shook uncontrollably.

"You're probably wondering, 'Why me?'" Darius moved closer, and it was all Cindy could do to keep from shrinking away from him. So ordinary-looking. *So deadly.* "Actually, we came to the inn for Thrain. All the members of his clan have powerful blood. Human blood is watered down and weak compared to theirs. Thrain's would make us strong beyond imagining, but we knew it would take more than one of us to bring him down. Even outnumbered, he still might destroy all of us. He's that strong. But the chance to drain him and all his power . . ." Darius shrugged. "The temptation was too great."

How to escape? What to do? The questions spun in ever tightening circles as she drew closer to the ruined mansion.

"And then *you* happened." Darius raised his arms to the night sky.

Cindy wondered what dark gods he was thanking.

"We found out that you were the daughter of Darach Mackenzie. All of that powerful blood only a bite away, with none of the danger. Perfect." He looked obscenely pleased with himself. "I'm freeing your vocal cords for any last words of entreaty. I love it when victims beg. Don't you love it, guys?" He turned to the others. They all assured him that they loved it. "I wouldn't waste my energy screaming, though. No one would hear you. All it would do is piss us off and speed up the feeding process." He

smiled at her, a smile filled with hunger and anticipation.

They'd reached the Hart mansion. Spooky, spook-
ier, spookiest. There, she'd described it. On second
glance, maybe she'd shortchanged the old place. The
house oozed malevolence. It hid behind encroaching
vines and gnarled trees, staring at her from black,
empty windows. All it needed was a virgin wearing
a filmy white nightgown fleeing across its lawn. Pure
gothic. Cindy was so glad she'd enlarged on her description. Now the house was scaring her, too. You
could never have too much adrenaline pumping.

Darius probably planned to take her inside to
feed. Nope. No way. Wasn't going to happen. If he
intended to drain her dry, he'd have to do it here, not
inside that creepy old house.

But she wouldn't go quietly. His first mistake was
allowing her to speak. She wouldn't scream, but she
would damn well talk until her tongue fell out. And
then she'd . . . She paused to see if her thoughts got
any reaction from the fiendish four. Nothing.

Darius was so confident that he wasn't keeping
close tabs on her thoughts. Maybe his other victims
had a sacrificial lamb mentality, but not her. She
hadn't survived for seven hundred years by wimp-
ing out. They had no idea how hard she'd be to kill.
Besides, she still had issues to resolve with Thrain.
Now if she could just distract Darius . . .

"Mosquitoes. Have you thought about them?" She
tried to look contemplative.

"What?" Surprise momentarily wiped the self-
satisfied smirk from Darius's face.

"The Woo Woo Inn's been open all summer. I bet

dozens of vamps have stayed here. So what happens when a mosquito bites you guys? Sure, everybody knows Jersey mosquitoes are demons. But are they immortal demons now? Will the whole state become a feeding ground for tiny immortal bloodsuckers, hmm? So what can we do about that? Do you think Raid will start selling itsy-bitsy wooden stakes? Thought-provoking, isn't it?"

The night feeders' eyes were glazing over. Good. She just needed to keep talking while she put out her mental SOS. She'd only get a shot at one or two words before Darius shut her down, so she'd better make it good.

"Wooden stakes would be tough, though. Don't have a clue where a mosquito's heart is. Do you? No, don't answer that. I have a better idea. How about putting holy water in spray bottles?" She tried to look seriously involved in her vampire mosquito monologue while she focused her mind on Thrain, willing him to hear her thoughts. "Not a good idea, huh? Yeah, you're right. It'd be sacrilegious."

Darius growled low in his throat and moved toward her.

"Wait. We could sprinkle garlic flakes all over the house, but then every place would smell like an Italian restaurant. Sure, we could use air freshener, but that would be . . ." THE HART MANSION. "Self-defeating because—"

Darius's eyes widened in alarm as Cindy's thought blasted past him. At least she hoped it had blasted past him. Who knew where her thought was headed. Maybe nowhere. But Thrain would know she was in trouble, because her thought was a panicked shout of, "Yo, get your perfect ass out here and save me." So she'd concentrated all her effort on letting him know where she was.

"Bitch!" Darius leaped for her.

Cindy watched in fascinated horror as he changed to full vampire form. Ick, ick, and ick some more.

"Kiss your immortality good-bye, Darius." Thrain's quiet statement held no anger, no emotion, only cold, deadly intent.

Cindy, along with her captors, spun to see Thrain standing behind them. Whoa, that was quick. This mental communication stuff was great. But how'd he get here so fast when she'd barely sent out her thought? She didn't have the chance to ask him before he pushed his leather coat aside, whipped out his sword, and then launched himself at the night feeders in a blur of motion too fast for her to follow.

Cindy stood frozen in place only long enough to realize that the night feeders, armed with sharply clawed fingers, deadly fangs, and wicked-looking knives, were trying to encircle Thrain. She leaped into action. Sort of. A weapon. She wouldn't be any help to Thrain without a weapon. Frantically, she scrabbled around on the ground, searching for a stick strong enough to do some serious damage.

She was so focused on her search that she didn't hear the pounding of feet until Sam Pierce blew by her. The writer's camera flapped around his neck while he clutched a flashlight in one hand and brandished a wooden stake in the other.

"Aaaiiyee!" With a scream that Cindy guessed was meant to curdle even vampire blood, Sam launched himself at Thrain and the night feeders.

Before she could react, he stabbed Thrain in the back with his stake. "Take that, you murdering, undead slime."

"No!" *Too late.* Sam was already yanking his stake from Thrain's body.

Even as Thrain fell, Sam rushed toward the night feeders. They flung their hands in front of their eyes, for a moment blinded by the flashlight's beam. Sam waved his bloody stake in the air. "Help's on the way. I'll keep these blood-sucking dirtbags busy until they come."

Cindy could hear shouts and the sounds of running feet coming their way. The night feeders looked uncertain. She could almost read their minds. Two puny humans wouldn't be a problem, but what about the shouting mob headed their way? Would there be any werewolves, witches, or wizards with them? Did they have time to take what they'd wanted all along, Thrain?

Over my really ticked-off immortal body. Cindy flung herself onto her knees beside Thrain and eased him onto his back. She dragged his sword to her side. If the night feeders got past Sam before the rescuers arrived, Darius wouldn't find the same shivering, quivering blob of fear he'd taken from the inn. The four fanged lowlifes weren't going to get a shot at Thrain while he was helpless. Failure wasn't an option when the man she . . . Okay, she didn't have time to go there now.

"You're losing too much blood." She'd felt Thrain's blood on her hands when she'd helped him turn onto his back. She couldn't see how badly he was bleeding because of the darkness, but her imagination was supplying gruesome possibilities. Cindy had to stop the bleeding. Then she'd get him to a doctor who could take her blood, give Thrain a transfusion, and not ask any questions. Who? No name came to mind.

Sure, Thrain could replenish his blood anywhere, but the horrors of what would happen if he took too much human blood were still fresh in her mind. He needed blood from one of his clansmen. She might have a mixture flowing through her veins, but her blood had to be a step up from what he'd get at the local ER.

Thrain had changed to his vampire form while attacking the night feeders, and once again he wore the face she'd seen during their shared memory. But this time he didn't look up at her with rage and loathing. Shock seemed to be his emotion of the moment. "I can't believe he stabbed me." Thrain turned his head to see what was happening. "I have to get up. The night feeders will drain him dry and throw away the empty husk."

He had to be kidding. "Let me get this straight. You're bleeding all over the ground and you think you can just bounce up and slay a few vampires? Think again, pal. Try it and Sam won't be the only empty husk floating around these woods." She placed her hand in the middle of his chest to hold him down.

"I don't need any blood. I need to get up and kick some butt." Thrain winced as he lifted his shoulders to see who was riding to their rescue. By Loki's flame, he'd fought barbarian hordes who didn't make as much noise as these people did.

"No. Don't move." Her eyes widened with fear.

For him. When was the last time that had happened? Not since Darach had saved his life. She made him feel . . . important in her world. Did he want to be important in her world? *Yes.* What a revelation to have in the middle of a damned night-feeder attack.

She brushed his hair from his face. "Are you in a lot of pain? I can—"

She didn't get to tell him what she could do, because suddenly a thousand women burst from the forest. Well, maybe not a thousand. Logically, he recognized them as Cindy's scientist friends, but logic had nothing to do with his automatic rush of fear. He dug his fingers into the earth as if by anchoring himself he could deny his memories, his terror.

But the memories came anyway. Naked. Ropes cutting into his wrists and ankles as he struggled. Knives slicing his flesh. Women mounting him over and over again. Their faces blurring into one evil entity. And the morning silence that had left him bitter, shamed, *afraid.*

Then Cindy was touching him. She drew her fingers over his jaw and along his arm. When her hand touched his, he released his death grip on the ground and clasped her fingers.

"Look at them, Thrain. Really look at them. Those are the faces of women who're putting their lives on the line for us." She slipped her free hand under his coat and rubbed calming circles on his chest. "As they run past me, I'm going to cheer them on. If they have trouble with the night feeders, I'll take your sword and join them." She smiled at him. "And then I'll be part of the mob. You wouldn't be afraid of *me*, would you?"

Thrain would be the only one using his sword to kill night feeders, but he didn't bother telling her that as he watched the women. He still gripped Cindy's hand. She gave him strength, and no matter how much power he had or how many years he'd lived, he needed her now. He'd fought the fear alone for centuries, but no amount of logic or self-condemnation had lessened it. He'd thought about getting professional help, but anyone he went to would either not believe him or brand him as crazy. He'd feared ridicule, and so he'd never told anyone about his fear until Cindy.

And because he trusted her, he did as she asked. Instead of looking at the women as one frightening entity, he picked out a single face and studied it. Age about forty, a little overweight, glasses that she kept pushing up on her nose, and short brown hair frizzing in the humid night. Was he afraid of this one woman? No. He moved on to another woman, and another.

Thrain relaxed a little. Was his fear completely gone? Not really. But Cindy had given him a coping skill. He'd never thought of separating the *mob* into its individual components. Maybe with time and a few more coping skills he could put the paralyzing fear behind him. He squeezed Cindy's hand, allowing his emotions to flow over her, enveloping her in his gratitude and . . . It was what might come after the *and* that remained murky.

The women charged past them. Cindy lifted

Thrain's sword in both hands and whooped her support. "Take it to the bastards."

Thrain smiled. Maybe she could handle his sword after all. But his smile faded as he took a closer look at the high-tech weapons their avenging army was waving around. "What the . . . ? Did they bring the whole kitchen with them?"

For a moment Thrain and Cindy didn't say anything as they listened to the clash of knives, forks, pots, and assorted other cooking utensils.

"Uh-oh, someone has the cook's broom. This is *not* a good thing." Cindy glanced around fearfully for Katie. "I hope we can get this stuff back before she finds out it's gone."

Since he was temporarily out of the physical fight, Thrain was preparing to loose his mental power on the hapless night feeders when Prada strolled out of the woods. She held Trojan in her arms and didn't look too concerned about the wild yells or the flow of the battle around her.

"Hey, everyone." Prada raised one hand, realized she needed two hands to hold Trojan's chubby self, and unceremoniously dumped him on the ground. He didn't land lightly. "Show's over. I'm here to take care of things."

She didn't raise her voice, but the fighting stopped. Thrain figured everyone was awed by a woman who could run all the way from the inn on her toes, because that was what it must have felt like wearing heels so high.

Sam the Staker looked horrified. "No offense, but this is a man's job. All of you women need to get out of my way." He puffed out his chest and offered

Prada his superhero smile. "Why don't you sit your pretty little bottom on a log and let me finish this?"

A snort of laughter made Thrain turn his head. Trojan had planted his ample behind next to him.

"Pretty little bottom? What a bunch of crap. Where'd they get this guy?" He peered at Thrain. *"Lying down on the job, bloodsucker? Never mind, I'll get rid of those four fuck-ups. Notice I can curse? Couldn't do that the last time we met. The Big Boss lightened up."*

"The Big Boss?" Thrain turned his attention back to the battle. He winced as Jane smacked Darius upside his head with a frying pan. The night feeders couldn't do much mind controlling with their brains rattling around in their skulls.

"The head honcho. The big cheese. The potentate of all party poopers." Trojan frowned. *"Hope the Master of Sensitivity didn't hear that."* He gazed at the continuing mayhem with a bored-cat expression. *"Since I can't talk, Prada's going to get all the credit. Bummer."*

Thrain looked toward Prada. She raised her arms above her head, which hiked her black dress to right about cheek level, and shouted, "Begone evil night creeps. I banish you from my sight. May you never—"

"Yeah, yeah. Come on, let's do it." Trojan stood, stretched, and then climbed onto Thrain's stomach. Circling twice, he lay down. *"I hate sitting on damp ground. Gives me rheumatism in my butt."*

"The night winds will take you far from . . ." Prada was still going strong.

"She's never gonna shut up, is she?" Trojan yawned. *"She has an audience, so she's good till dawn. I better get rid of Darius and his crew before Prada puts everyone to sleep and they slither away."*

Thrain glanced at Cindy. She was staring, mesmerized, at Prada. He was the only one who could hear Trojan.

Trojan didn't move from his relaxed position on Thrain's stomach, but suddenly the air shimmered and rippled in spreading waves until it reached the night feeders. And then they were gone. No cries, no flashes of light, no booming thunder. They were just gone.

There was complete silence for the moment it took everyone to realize what had happened. Then the women, along with Sam, broke and ran. Jane and company were smart ladies, and they knew when to get out of Dodge. They could probably explain away the night feeders as men wearing clever masks, but not this. Scientific curiosity might kick in later, but right now they were scared.

Everyone raced back toward the inn, leaving Prada staring down at her shoes. "Some lead-foot stomped on my toes. How can any woman disrespect Jimmy Choo shoes?"

"What happened to the night feeders?" Cindy sounded dazed.

Trojan sat up on Thrain's stomach and began washing his face. *"I sent them someplace where they'll be even closer to the bottom of the food chain than they were here. They're dancing with dinosaurs now."* He paused from his washing to look regretful. *"I wanted to turn them into a bonfire, toast some marshmallows, maybe tell spooky stories around the flames, but the Big Boss is still threatening to end my existence if I kill anything. He's not a fun guy. Must be a midlife crisis thing."*

Cindy's bemused expression told Thrain that Trojan was speaking to both of them now.

Prada wandered over to join Trojan. She smiled at Cindy. "You have some good friends, sister. When I told everyone in the parlor that a bunch of creeps in vampire get-ups had kidnapped you, everyone charged to your rescue." Bending down, she scooped up the cat and turned toward the path leading back to the inn. "Let's move our butts, sweetie. There's a fireplace back at the inn calling my name. It's freezing out here without a coat."

"Wait." Cindy scrambled to her feet. "Thrain's hurt. He's losing a lot of blood."

Prada paused and looked back over her shoulder. "He's a vampire, so the wound's probably already closing." She shrugged. "If he needs blood, give it to him. Don't take him to a doctor, though. Too many awkward questions." With that last bit of helpful advice, she disappeared into the forest.

Thrain watched Cindy's chain of thoughts play across her face and saw the exact moment she reached the last link. And realized the chain was welded to her greatest fear.

But before he could assure her that he was fine, that he didn't need her blood, he sensed a presence—ancient, dangerous, *familiar.*

With a grunt of pain, he sat up and then moved back until he'd propped himself against a tree. Thrain had thought he could get to his feet, but Cindy was right, he'd lost a lot of blood.

Ignoring Cindy's worried expression because he'd moved, Thrain turned his head to watch a man step from the forest.

Cindy followed his gaze. Uh-oh. She instinctively reached for Thrain's sword, all the while knowing she wouldn't have a snowball's chance in hell of stopping the man who was walking toward them.

He had to be from Thrain's clan, *her* clan. The man was big and broad-shouldered like Thrain, with the same brilliant blue eyes. He gave the term *dark predator* a whole new meaning. His shaggy black hair looked a little too untamed, his hard face a little too savage for the civilized world. He belonged in some jungle, stalking fleet-footed prey and making the kill with his slashing fangs. *Fangs*. She shuddered.

If you just looked at his short leather jacket, worn jeans, and biker boots, you'd think, okay, this is just another great-looking guy. Of course, ordinary great-looking guys didn't tote around swords like the one he held easily in one hand. But the sword wasn't half as scary as the man's eyes—cold, pitiless, and lethal. He didn't smile as he met her gaze.

"Hey, Reinn. What's up? I could've used your help a few ·minutes ago." Thrain reached for Cindy's hand and pulled her to his side.

Cindy recognized his possessive gesture and didn't try to deny how good it made her feel. "Who're you?" She had to look up a long way to meet the stranger's gaze.

"Reinn Mackenzie." He ignored her to focus his attention on Thrain. "I've seen some half-assed battles in my time, but I don't think I've ever seen four vampires get their butts kicked by a bunch of women with pots and pans. And what the hell is that cat?"

"You stood and watched the fight? Thanks big time for nothing." Thrain's voice had a hard edge of anger to it.

Reinn's shrug casually dismissed Thrain's anger. "You didn't need me."

Cindy had to respond to that. "Uh, maybe you didn't notice, but someone *stabbed* Thrain. Lots of blood? Possible death? How bad does it have to be before you help a friend?" She let the sarcasm drip.

He narrowed his gaze on her but didn't look even the tiniest bit guilty. "When an enemy has his sword poised to cut off a clansman's head, I'll interfere. I like minding my own business." His expression suggested that Cindy would benefit by doing the same. "And I don't have any friends."

His last comment froze Cindy's blood, but she was beyond letting him intimidate her. "Why're you here if you didn't come to help?"

Thrain looked gratified by her hostility. Cindy suspected it had a lot to do with the whole male jealousy issue and forgave him.

Reinn didn't seem to give a damn how she felt. "I'm your pilot. I'll be flying you to Scotland. I thought I'd stay at the inn until it was time to leave. When I sensed the night feeders, I came out to see what they were up to." He speared her with his intense stare. "It was worth the walk. I laughed my butt off." He didn't look like he'd ever laughed in his life. Cindy doubted he knew how.

"Look, since you're here, I need help getting Thrain back to the inn." She took a deep breath and plunged into the most important part. "You have to let him bite you. He needs blood."

"He can't do that, Cindy." Thrain's quiet statement somehow made her angrier with Reinn than she already was.

"Then what the hell *can* he do? Talk about a useless piece of crap." Okay, time to ratchet back the temper. She didn't want to make Reinn so mad he refused to fly them to Scotland.

For the first time she thought she detected a gleam of amusement in his cold eyes. Nah, just her imagination.

"Thrain is your man, so he can bite *you*. Then he'll be strong enough to walk to the inn by himself." And without another word, he strode back into the woods.

"Who crowned him the king of mean? I bet he moonlights as the guy who steals kids' presents from under Christmas trees and all their tooth-fairy money. What a jerk." She tried to hold on to her mad so she wouldn't have to think about what Reinn had said before he left.

Thrain chuckled; he sounded nothing like a man in danger of bleeding to death. Cindy knelt beside him and slipped her hand under his coat to feel his back. Yep, saturated with blood. And there was a dark puddle where his back had been before he sat up. He was obviously delirious and didn't understand how badly he'd been injured.

"Reinn's a loner, but if things had gotten out of hand, he would've stepped in." Thrain frowned. "I think. You never know with him. But he was telling the truth when he said I couldn't bite him. I already explained that it's against our laws for a vampire from our clan to bite another vampire clansman. If I bit him, he'd have to kill me."

Cindy blinked. "I so don't understand that. Look, I left the inn in sort of a hurry, so I don't have my cell phone. I'll run back and get some of the men to carry you home." Maybe she could lure Stan back with her. He was a vampire with no Mackenzie ties as far as she knew. Wouldn't his blood be as good as—

"Don't go."

She'd opened her mouth to answer when he reached up and pulled her down to him. He took her mouth in a searing kiss that branded her with all his unspoken emotions. His tongue tangled with hers, and she tasted the essence of primitive male possession—hot and needy. Evidently, his desires went way beyond just a few pints of blood. Now she felt weak, too. Damn.

"I don't want anyone to carry me back to the inn. I want to walk."

His soft murmur against her mouth heated her blood but sent an icy stab of fear down her spine. "Walk? No way. You're too weak, and I bet you're still bleeding. We'll get you into bed and—"

"No." He seemed pretty definite about that. He slid his tongue over her bottom lip to emphasize his denial. "The wound has closed, but I'm weak from loss of blood. Without blood, I'll be in that bed for at least three days, and we'll miss the chance to catch Darach at the castle. I can't go to a hospital because I'll never even get past the what's-your-blood-type question. Even if I could, they'd try to give me too much human blood at one time."

"Can't you sort of compel someone to come to you so you can feed? Then when you're finished, you can just wipe their memory clean. Sounds workable to me." Cindy knew there were some moral issues involved in her suggestion, but panic tended to disconnect all lines to her conscience.

Thrain raised one expressive brow. "Tossing a sacrificial human to the monster, Cindy?" He shook his head. "It wouldn't work. My body reacts to massive blood loss by making my craving more intense. If I lost control and drank too much, there wouldn't be a happy ending for me or the human."

Okay, now she was segueing from fear into anger. Good. A monumental hissy fit would make him easier to resist. "Oh, but it's fine to drink from me, right? You know, I'm not like a glass of iced tea at your local restaurant. There's no free refill when you've reached bottom. I stay empty." Now he'd get mad at her and say he wouldn't bite her even if she begged. She could feel righteous and guilt-free. Did that thought make her feel better? Well . . . no.

He didn't get mad. His gaze softened. "There're few things stronger than the craving, but what I feel for you is one of them." Thrain smiled, that slow, wicked shifting of his sexy mouth guaranteed to melt metal. "I'm not quite sure what these feelings mean, but when I even enjoy listening to you yell at me, things are getting serious."

"I don't yell." She was yelling. And she was also scared witless. He'd backed her into a corner, and the only way out involved stomping on emotions too new to survive that kind of treatment.

His smile faded. "It has to come from you. If this isn't the time or place, I'll live with that." He firmed his lips as if coming to a decision. "You won't miss Darach. If you can find me some . . ." His expression said he was about to suggest something almost too revolting to contemplate. "Cow's blood, I can get back a little strength. Even if I'm still shaky, I'll make sure we're on that flight. Once in Scotland, Reinn can drive us the rest of the way. By that time, the craving will be more manageable, and I'll be strong enough to hunt without killing."

He was giving her a way out. Why didn't she feel more relieved?

For the first time, he shifted his gaze away from her. "But I'd be lying if I said I didn't want it to be now." He looked back at her, his gaze full of an emotion she couldn't identify. "I guess it all comes down to trust. You'd be putting your life in my hands. You'd have to believe that I wouldn't hurt you." His eyes told her that her trust was important to him. "You'd have to believe that no matter how strong my hunger, I would never hurt the woman I . . ." His voice died, and Cindy wanted to shake that last word from him.

Or did she? Some things were better left unexplored until she had her emotions under control.

Thrain shook his head as if to clear his thoughts. "Never mind. If you're going, you'd better go now before all your human guests check out. Or worse yet, Sam Pierce might come back to reprise his Sam the Vampire Slayer role."

This was it, then. She either had to face her fear or do what she'd done so successfully for so many years—run away. Avoiding dogs for seven hundred years hadn't been any big deal. But now the teeth she feared were attached to a man she wanted more than she had ever wanted any other.

Drawing in a deep gulp of courage, she met Thrain's gaze. "Will it hurt?"

He didn't pretend to misunderstand her. "A brief sting."

"Will you be able to stop if I ask you to?" She

knew her question would probably hurt him, but she had to know for sure.

He gazed at her with eyes that told her how hard it would be to resist the craving, but that he'd do so for her. "Yes."

Did she trust his answer? A little less than two weeks wasn't enough time to really know anyone, but this was where the faith thing kicked in. Yes, she believed him. And if she was wrong, she'd pay the ultimate price.

Cindy didn't feel brave. She had no idea if she could do it, had never thought she'd even want to try. But her new and still evolving feelings for Thrain drove her to say the words.

"Bite me."

Chapter Fourteen

Thrain watched her with his dark vampire eyes. A week ago, she would have called them predatory eyes, but now she saw the man behind them—a man who was vulnerable but strong enough to show her his vulnerability. A man who cared for her enough to expose his greatest fear in the hope that by doing so she could conquer her own night terrors.

He smiled at her, a savage baring of fangs. A shudder rippled through her, but once again she tried to look beyond his teeth to the heart of his smile. She couldn't do it. His smile was meant to put her at ease, and she knew that teeth didn't define the man, but she couldn't tear her gaze from them.

"This won't work, sweetheart." His voice was a low murmur of disappointment. "I have to stay in vampire form to . . ." He hesitated over the word and then forged onward. "Feed, but you're so scared that your eyes take up half your face. I can't do that to you. Go back to the inn and get someone to help me."

Somehow she found her strength in Thrain's willingness to reject his need for her sake. "No. I *can* do this. I *need* to do this." *Because I want you more than I fear you.* That was the bottom line.

Cindy expected him to waste time arguing with her. He didn't. "Help me get my coat and T-shirt off."

"Why?" He didn't have time to undress. "You need to . . ." She couldn't get the word *bite* past her lips a second time. "Do what you do before all my courage oozes away."

"I want to lose the coat and T-shirt first." He sat up, wincing as he tried to get out of his coat without help.

Making sounds of disapproval, Cindy helped him with his clothing. "What's with the bare torso? It's cold out here, and lifting your arms while I slid your shirt off had to hurt."

"You need to touch a human part of me to lessen your fear." Exhausted by his effort, he slumped back against the tree.

This reminder of how weak he really was lent urgency to Cindy's words. "Hello? I don't have to touch your sexy chest to know you're human. Get this straight, oh mighty vampire, you're still you no matter what face you wear." She tried to smile but suspected it looked more like a grimace. "Not that I'll ever pass up a chance to put my eager fingers all over your yummy body."

"Yummy body?" Thrain frowned.

Amazing. Males reacted the same in any form. Evidently *yummy* wasn't part of the studly dictionary of manly terms. She smiled, and this time it felt real. The smile didn't drive out her fear, but it made the terror almost manageable. *Almost.* Cindy wouldn't know if she could get through the ordeal until she tried.

Leaning close, Thrain gently kissed her forehead and then tangled his fingers in her hair. "Both our fears stem from only one incident that happened a long time ago, and yet we allow those fears to dictate how we live our lives."

Put that way, she felt pretty dumb. He gripped her earlobe lightly with his teeth and tugged. She almost didn't notice the teeth or his movement south. *Almost.*

To lessen the impact of *almost,* she flattened her palms against his chest. His skin felt too cool, reminding her there was more at stake than just her fear. But her fear had lived for centuries. It didn't respond to reminders. Tremors that had nothing to do with the cold and everything to do with terror made her wrap her arms around Thrain's waist and hang on.

"Think of what you've missed in life. Bet you never watched *Jurassic Park.* Great special effects." He slid his tongue down the side of her neck.

Cindy was so busy thinking about T-Rex teeth that she almost didn't notice. *Almost.*

"And seven hundred years without ever having a puppy? Can't imagine." His breath warmed the base of her throat. "Warm, cuddly, cute. But you have me now, so I guess you don't need one."

She couldn't help it, she laughed, even as he placed his mouth over the spot on her neck where her pulse beat a frantic rhythm of fear and excitement. "You might be many things, but cute and cuddly aren't two of them."

Thrain didn't give her time to think about what would happen next. Smart. Her vivid imagination was an enemy tonight. He pulled her close, and she had only a momentary impression of fangs sliding across her skin and then a sharp prick.

She'd opened her mouth to scream but shut it almost immediately as a stream of heat and pleasure washed over her. Need curled low in her belly, a hot, moist desire that made her instinctively spread her legs at the same time she clenched around the mental image of taking him deep inside her. Desire burned through her, driving out fear along with every other emotion that didn't feed her sexual hunger.

Wrapping her arms more tightly around him, she gripped his bare, muscular shoulders and moaned her pleasure at the wash of erotic sensations. Moving her hands upward, she anchored her fingers in the tangled strands of his Viking hair and tried to force his mouth closer to her throat when closer wasn't possible.

With the part of her brain still capable of connecting point A to point B, she knew he was manipulating her, replacing her fear with this unbelievable sensory high. Did she care? Uh, no. She'd be crazy to reject this, this . . . wow.

Just as when they'd made love in the cemetery, her senses exploded. The forest breathed with her. She could feel the cool whisper of its breath across her heated body. Sudden wind moaned through the treetops, shaking loose a flurry of golden leaves to affirm that it shared in her emotions. And she knew the clean, biting scent of pine trees would always trigger memories of this moment.

At the instant she felt the unthinkable about to become the inevitable—a bite-induced orgasm—Thrain moved away from her. *No!* Her body clenched around its disappointment, and she felt a compelling need to grind her teeth.

"You can't do that to me." Call her whiny and immature, but she was an orgasm-deprived woman and she had a right to bitch. Absently, she rubbed her neck. Nothing. No puncture wounds, no lacerations, nothing. Cindy fought to calm her pounding heart along with the rest of her outraged body. All concerned agreed that Thrain had cheated them out of their big payoff.

He turned his head to stare into the forest, and when he looked back at her, he was once again in his human form. "How do you feel after your first bite in over seven hundred years?" His smile was easy, but he couldn't hide the worry in his eyes.

Cindy sighed deeply. What a man. He was the sexual and emotional center of her universe—yes, she was willing to admit that—and he thought she was complaining about his bite. Without a clue, thy name is man. "The you-can't-do-that-to-me thing was my perfectly justified resentment bubbling over because you unclenched your teeth right before my ohmigod moment. Am I a sexually frustrated woman? You bet."

Thrain raked his fingers through his hair. "I had to stop. I'd already taken more blood than I should. You remember what happens if I take too much." He still looked worried. "What about my teeth? How do you feel about them now?"

Oh, yes. She remembered. Putting her own needs on hold, she smiled her reassurance. "Don't worry, your teeth and I are cool with each other." To illustrate how cool they were, she leaned forward and slid her tongue across his lower lip. When he parted his lips, she traced the ridge of his teeth with her tongue. "Of course, these aren't the big, bad teeth of a few minutes ago, but you get the idea. Will I suddenly stop being afraid of all fanged creatures? No. I'll have to approach every set of teeth individually and assess their potential for danger. But I've taken the first step." She kissed him hard before leaning away from him. "And I'll never be afraid of you again." A sweeping statement, and one she might regret.

Cindy could feel his relief, and she wondered if he sensed her deep gratitude. She was trying to keep things light, but the realization that he was responsible for that life-altering moment rocked her world. For the first time in all her centuries of life, she'd faced her fear and emerged, if not completely cured, at least much stronger emotionally. "You know, you could just read my mind to find out all this stuff. If you did, you'd know that I might have to kill you if you don't finish what you started. My orgasm is still pending."

"You don't want me in your mind, so I stay out." Thrain tried to make his smile calm, casual, and patient, but he couldn't keep the savage predator out of it. Not when he wanted to take her right here, right now. "Most of the time."

"Oh, sure. Thanks." She frowned as she eyed his discarded coat. "So, what next?"

"Don't even think about it." He pulled his shirt over his head with a lot less pain than when he'd taken it off and draped his coat over her shoulders.

Then he stood. Retrieving his sword, he slid it into his scabbard. "We're not going to finish this on my coat here in the cold." He knew exactly where he wanted to make love with her, and he'd better get there fast before his painfully aroused body decided the forest floor would do just fine.

Cindy would never know the inner battle he'd fought with his vampire nature, the part of him that demanded he take his mate at the same time he fed. Surprisingly, the thing he'd feared most, an uncontrolled feeding frenzy, hadn't come into play. Yes, he'd wanted more of her, but his need to protect her had easily overpowered the feeding instinct.

His sensual arousal was something else entirely. Denying the sexual beast had taken every last bit of his will. The strength of his desire for Cindy shuddered through him. When he was younger, he'd listened skeptically to older clan members describing their heightened emotional and physical responses to their chosen mates. He'd doubted their tales. Sex was sex. Now? He wasn't sure what was happening, but he did know his reaction to Cindy had melted his personal pleasure-meter. His mate? He didn't know.

He helped her to her feet, and she brushed herself off. "I still don't understand how a little of my blood took you from the brink of death to your normal arrogant self. I know you didn't take much blood because I don't even feel dizzy." She walked with him as they headed back to the inn.

Thrain wrapped his arm around her waist and pulled her close. "I wasn't at the brink of death, and the blood of our clan flows through you. Powerful stuff. That's why the night feeders were so anxious to get their . . ." Maybe he didn't need to remind her of the night feeders. "Anyway, your blood has enormous healing properties."

She looked up at him—her hair a tumble of night around her face, her mouth soft and full, and her eyes wide and filled with all her questions, all her emotions. His own feelings were close to the surface, and he needed time to analyze them. *Analyze them all you want, stupid. It won't change a thing.*

"Talking about powerful, I can't believe how fast you got here after I sent my mental SOS. Really impressive, vampire." Absently, she brushed some pine needles from his hair.

"Mental SOS?" He frowned. "I didn't get any message from you. Prada told me you'd gone off with the night feeders, and she thought you might need some help."

Cindy sharpened her gaze. "Prada wasn't anywhere in sight when Darius took me. Wait." She bit her lip as she concentrated. "The last time I saw Prada, she was talking with the night feeders." She narrowed her eyes to dangerous slits. "Do you know what I'm thinking?"

Thrain nodded. "We need to talk to Sam and Jane." They'd reached the inn, and he held the front door open as Cindy strode past him. She practically vibrated with fury, and he didn't doubt she had vengeance on her mind. If what they suspected was true, he might just test how powerful Prada really was.

Sam was holding court in the parlor with a crowd gathered around him listening to his tale of personal triumph. He looked up and saw Thrain bearing down on him, and every bit of color in his face fled to places less likely to get punched.

"We need to talk, Pierce. Alone." Thrain must have looked as dangerous as he felt, because Sam's audience melted away.

"How the hell are you still alive?" He blinked up at Thrain, confusion mixed with terror in his eyes. "I mean dead. I mean . . . I don't get it. Prada gave me the wooden stake to stab you in the back. She told me to aim for the left side so I'd get your heart. Isn't that the way you destroy vamps?" He widened his eyes as his mind caught up with his mouth. Beads of sweat dotted his forehead. "Nothing personal. I was just trying to save the lady."

Thrain aimed his most evil smile at the horrified writer. "Not if the vamp doesn't have a heart." He leaned close to Sam, sending him mental images of what a vampire did when he lost his temper with a meddling human. And he was close to losing it all. "Why did you try to kill me?"

Sam swallowed hard, his Adam's apple bobbing like a cork in rough seas. "Prada said you were going to hurt Cindy. Okay, let's be blunt: suck her dry. A real man protects women." His expression said he was rethinking his hero status. He glanced from Thrain to where Cindy stood with her arms crossed, looking pretty much okay but royally steamed. "I guess Prada was wrong." His shaky voice suggested he didn't believe Thrain was buying into his protector-of-women defense.

Thrain believed him. Sam had shown a lot of guts, running into the woods to take on a bunch of vampires. Brave, but not too smart. Thrain decided to let him live. For now. "You only wanted to keep Cindy safe, so you walk away in one piece this time. But things could get ugly here in a few minutes; you might want to head for your room." He stepped back from Sam and smiled as the man leaped to his feet and edged past him.

"Hey, I'm outta here. Not going to mess with vamps again. They can turn Jersey into Bloodsucker Central for all I care." Sam almost ran from the room.

Cindy broke her silence. "Let's find Jane. She's probably still here. I'm counting on her having too much scientific curiosity to cut and run."

They found her at the kitchen table hunched over a bowl of Ben & Jerry's Cherry Garcia ice cream. The empty container sat beside her. Thrain glanced down. Empty because Trojan had his face buried in a bowl, too. He must have conned Jane into sharing.

Cindy sat down across from Jane. Thrain stood behind Cindy's chair. He clamped his fingers over the wooden back to keep himself from picking Trojan up and shaking him until his little pointed teeth fell out. But he'd save his real temper for Prada.

Cindy put her hand over Jane's, stopping her from scooping up another spoonful of ice cream. "We need to talk."

Jane sighed as she released the spoon. "I suppose so." She stared longingly at the remaining ice cream in the bowl. "I think better when I'm eating." She glanced around the room, finally meeting Thrain's gaze. "Those weren't masks you guys had on, were they?"

"No." Thrain tensed, prepared to catch Jane if she tried to run away.

She simply nodded. "I was afraid of that. Scientifically exciting but personally terrifying." Jane glanced down to where Trojan was methodically licking his bowl. "This whole night's been too weird for words. First Prada tells us we need to grab weapons and run into the woods to save Cindy from a bunch of wacko vampires wearing masks. Then I sit down to a dish of ice cream and hear a voice in my head. The voice tells me I'll turn into Blimp Woman if I eat the whole container, and maybe I should share some with the hungry kitty. I don't see any hungry kitties, only a fat cat. But what the hell, so I feed the cat."

Cindy smiled and patted Jane's hand. "Wow, that's the first time I've ever heard you curse. You must be at the high end of upset."

Jane worked up a weak smile. "No kidding." She stared at Thrain. "When I stop shaking, I'd like to find out more about you." She shifted her gaze to Trojan. "And you, too, cat. I never hear voices in my head. You have some explaining to do."

Cindy stood. "Finish your ice cream. You told me what I wanted to know. Do you have any idea where Prada is?"

Jane shook her head. "I haven't seen her since I got back."

She's in the library planting . . . umm, looking up some info. Don't tell her I ratted on her. She kicks some serious ass when she's pissed. Maybe I'll tag along to see what happens.

Thrain decided that Trojan sounded suspiciously cheerful for a cat whose life hung by a thread. He hoped Trojan wasn't counting on his nine lives to bail him out. Thrain glanced at Cindy, who nodded. She'd heard Trojan.

They hurried to the library with Trojan padding happily beside them. Thrain paused in the doorway, but Cindy had worked up a full head of steam.

Flinging his coat from her shoulders, she strode over to where Prada lounged in one of the overstuffed chairs. "Yo, sex goddess and manipulator of mortals. Get your behind out of that chair and face me like a woman."

Prada looked up, raised one perfectly arched brow, and calmly put down her book. "This book is simply fascinating. Did you know that every year eleven thousand Americans hurt themselves trying out bizarre sexual positions? Personally, I don't think any position is bizarre if it leads to great sex."

Cindy blinked, for a moment taken out of her mad. "I don't have any books with that kind of information in them."

Prada offered her a cat-with-cream-mustache smile. "You do now, sister."

Thrain moved up beside Cindy. She'd need moral and immoral support if she expected to come out a winner against Prada. "You orchestrated the whole scene with the night feeders. They could've killed Cindy. Don't try to deny it."

Prada sighed to illustrate how supremely patient she was trying to be. "Why would I deny it? A plan that brilliant should be celebrated." She frowned. "I made untold sacrifices to pull it off. I ruined a pair of my fave shoes and broke three nails."

Thrain growled low in his throat and moved closer to Prada. He felt the slide of his fangs and fought to hold back the change.

"*Cool it, bloodsucker. This is a female thing.*" Trojan padded from the doorway and leaped onto the back of Prada's chair. "*Think we'll see a catfight?*" Trojan sounded gleefully hopeful.

Cindy narrowed her eyes to furious slits. "How about if I break the other seven nails so they all match? Then I'll dropkick you and your precious shoes out the door."

Prada's mouth fell open. Thrain figured the threat of broken nails shocked her more than the dropkick.

Cindy wasn't finished. "Sam stabbed Thrain, and a whole lot of innocent people almost got hurt. Nothing could justify what you did."

"Does anyone appreciate good deeds anymore? I think not." Prada tucked her hands safely down the sides of the cushion as she asked and answered her own question. She wasn't taking any chances with her nails. "I timed everything perfectly. Thrain was never in danger. I knew the night feeders couldn't touch him, and a little stab in the back wouldn't kill a vampire with his power. You know, I expected a little more gratitude after putting it all on the line for you." Prada tried on a wounded look, but her sly satisfaction leaked through.

Cindy leaned forward until she was inches from Prada's face. "Tell me why you did it, *sister.*"

Prada had recovered from the threat against her nails. Her eyes gleamed with amusement. "Last time I saw Thrain, he looked tastefully pale. Trendy, but definitely in need of a blood bank. Wait, look. Surprise, surprise, now he's all recovered and breathing fire. I wonder what that could mean?" She slid her gaze past Cindy to where Thrain stood glowering. "Yep, bad-tempered but healthy. Someone must've shared her blood with him." Prada raised her gaze to the ceiling and tapped her chin in mock puzzlement. "Since the only someone out in the forest with him was scared to death of his teeth, I wonder if that someone had a moment of absolute emotional clarity. Hmm?"

Cindy looked as though Prada had punched her in the stomach. "You orchestrated all of this so I'd get over my fear of Thrain's bite?"

Prada blinked. "Of course. Hey, I have an obligation to fulfill my destiny. And my destiny hangs on hooking people up. Thrain's teeth were interfering with my agenda, so either they had to go or you had to get over them. You got over them." Her expression brightened. "Instead of getting all bent out of shape, think of the alternative. Would you love him as much if he had to gum his food?"

Cindy curled her lips in the universal *ewww* expression. Thrain wondered if the lip action was in response to the mental image of him gumming his food or Prada's use of the L word. Did he care? Yeah, he did.

"Exactly." She waved Cindy away. "No need to heap praise on me. Just go somewhere and have great sex in my name."

Thrain was frustrated, torn between visiting violence on Prada's deserving head and his distaste for hitting a female. He turned his anger on Trojan instead. "Why didn't you stop her?"

Trojan widened his cat eyes. *"Do I look stupid to you? Prada has one easy-to-remember rule: Get in my way and suffer for a thousand years. Nope, I don't mess with her when she's focused."* He slid his gaze to Prada, and they exchanged a silent message. *"Besides, I have an erotic month in the sun planned when we leave here. It won't happen if I make her mad. Sorry, I'm a selfish bastard. I always put me first."* Trojan's expression said that selfish bastard was a positive cosmic troublemaker character trait.

Cindy took a deep breath. "Look, I hate what you did, Prada, but I can't lie: It worked. Couldn't you have found a less dramatic way to achieve the same result, though?"

Prada looked offended. "How? Anything I tried that involved Thrain's teeth touching your neck would've had all the special effects of a doomsday movie. Would you have gone quietly? Fat chance. I had to create a life-or-death situation to put you in touch with your true feelings. Besides, lots of emotion leads to a need for sexual release afterward. Hint, hint."

Evidently assuming that all was explained, Prada shifted her attention to Thrain's sword. "Have I told you how much I admire your sword, Thrain? So long, so hard, so . . . symbolic."

"Jeez, can you give the sex thing a rest for a few minutes?" Trojan did some irritated whisker twitching.

Prada blinked at him. "Uh, no. It's what I do."

Thrain still thought he'd like to tear something apart, but Cindy tugged at his sleeve. "Let's cancel war at the Woo Woo Inn for tonight. I can't afford to lose any more guests than I've probably already lost. I'll yank Prada's hair out tomorrow. You and Trojan can duel at dawn. Oops. Guess dawn is out for you." She pulled him toward the door. "Let's go back to my apartment and take a break for an hour or so."

Prada offered them a finger wave as they left, then lifted Trojan onto her lap. "Oomph. You're going to have to hire a personal trainer when you take human form again. There's nothing sexy about a tubby troublemaker."

"Forget about my weight. Let's talk about—" He glanced at her watch. After midnight. *"Tonight."* He curled up in her lap. *"And I can't believe they bought that crap you handed them. All you wanted was to cause a bunch of trouble that you hoped would end in someone getting laid."*

"You understand me so well, sweetie." Prada scratched behind his ears. "And it worked. I bet Thrain and Cindy will go back to her apartment and have incredible sex." She shivered with complete joy at the thought. "I feel a red rug moment coming on."

"Yeah, yeah. Whatever." He tilted his head so she could reach that particular spot behind his left ear. *"Is everything set for the summoning?"*

"Couldn't be more ready. I'd just finished planting the last bit of info everyone will need when Thrain and Cindy popped in."

She skimmed her fingers down his back. He resisted the urge to change into human form right here so he could roll around naked on the floor with her. Prada was that sexy. What a babe. But changing now would screw everything. So he settled for some sensual purring.

"I put the last step to the summoning in this book I sort of wrote." She nodded toward the book she'd been reading when he entered the library. "The title is—ta-da—*The Last Step in Successful Summonings.* I'll leave it on the coffee table where some easily manipulated human can't miss it."

"Perfect, perfect. We'll do it on the front lawn, and let's pray it doesn't rain." He thought about that for a moment. *"Forget the praying part. The Big Boss has caller*

ID, and he isn't picking up for me anymore. If it's rain-
ing, I'll just make the rain go away."

She nodded. "Okay, so the place is set. How about
the Jersey Devil? The humans will just be going
through the motions, and you'll be doing the actual
summoning. Are you sure he'll come? I hope you
don't expect me to help you; I don't have that kind of
power."

"No problem, babe. I'm in control." He butted her
playfully in the chest. Great chest for head butting.
Lots of padding. *"And no one here, except maybe
Thrain, is powerful enough to stop me once I've started.
The wizard and witch together might've slowed me down,
but they'll be busy bankrupting the Atlantic City casinos.
I'll send Cindy and Thrain to buy more ice cream for me
from the all-night convenience store. It's far enough away
to keep them busy until we've had our fun. The rest of the
supernatural whatevers don't give a damn about what
happens to humans. They won't interfere."*

Prada frowned. "Once the Devil's done his thing,
are you sure you can get rid of him?"

Trojan narrowed his eyes and flattened his ears.
*"You really know how to hurt a guy, don't you? Hey,
babe, remember? It's me. All powerful. Able to leap tall
buildings at a single bound. Your cosmic love bunny who
can wipe out a planet with a blink."* He whipped his
tail back and forth in irritation. *"Okay, so once the Devil has uprooted a few trees, turned over some cars in the
parking lot, and generally scared the crap out of the audience, I have to send him away before any humans get
hurt. Don't want to annoy the Big Boss more than I have
to."*

"Ow!" Prada pulled his paws away from where

his claws were digging into her thigh. "Sheathe your damn claws."

Trojan forced himself to relax. *"Sorry. I get overstimulated thinking about chaos and destruction. Almost like the old days."* He allowed himself a moment to mourn the old days. The ones before the Big Boss brought his goodness-and-light hammer down. *"You know, this calls for cake and punch. Whatta you think?"* He tried to look hopeful. Too bad cats didn't have many facial muscles. His expression probably lacked any emotional oomph.

Prada smiled and buried her face in his fur. "You're just a big naughty kid, aren't you? We'll drive into town as soon as the stores open and buy a big cake. I'll even make my favorite punch, handed down to me by my grandmother."

If cats could sigh, Trojan would have sighed. *"You never had a grandmother and I was never a kid. I've always been a cosmic troublemaker, who in a far, far distant time had a hell of lot more fun than I have now. By the time the Big Boss got through with his thou-shalt-nots, I didn't have much left to enjoy."*

Prada stuck out her bottom lip and got that sulky look in her amber eyes that said, "Dangerous temper ahead. Do not cross."

"So what if I didn't have a grandmother? If I'd had one, she would've given me this punch recipe. And how can you say you don't have much to enjoy? Sure you do." She uncrossed her legs, and he knew she'd heave him off her lap if he gave the wrong answer. There was no way he could make landing on his head a fun experience.

Prada was magnificent when she was ticked, but he'd had enough excitement for the night. *"Yeah, you're right. I'd trade the joy of melting the polar ice caps for a month of hot sex with you on an exotic island."* And if someone threw in cake and ice cream, he'd be in hog heaven. He figured it wouldn't be too smart to mention the cake and ice cream, though.

Her eyes softened. "I know damned well you gave me the answer you thought I wanted. You're a lying, calculating, manipulative being." She picked him up and hugged him. "That's what I love about you, sweetie."

"Uh, me, too." Now he was embarrassed. *"So everything's set. At midnight we gather all the humans on the front lawn, I summon the Jersey Devil, and all hell breaks loose."*

Chapter Fifteen

Cindy watched Thrain stride to the middle of her living room. She closed the door and then leaned her back against it, keeping all the night's craziness outside.

Without glancing back at her, he stared at Prada's red rug. "You know, tonight I battled four vampires, took a stake to the back and survived, and had a gorgeous innkeeper offer to kick butt for me. A man needs to finish big on a night like this."

He unbuckled his scabbard and allowed his long, hard . . . sheesh. She was starting to think like Prada. He allowed his sword to slip to the floor beside the red rug.

Even when she moved up beside him, he didn't take his gaze from the rug. "Seems to me that Prada owes us a great ending to the night. We deserve it." He finally turned his gaze on Cindy. "I want to make love to you on this rug." His face remained expressionless, but his eyes burned for her.

That's my man, never sneaks up on what he wants.
Uh-oh, where'd the *my man* thing come from? But
even as Cindy asked the question, she knew the answer. It had started the moment he'd walked
through the doors of the Woo Woo Inn and blown
her away with first impressions. It hadn't let up
since.

Most of his traits could be found in ordinary
men—courage, loyalty, humor, arrogance, and, yes,
vulnerability. But she couldn't forget his extraordinary skills, either. His ability to manipulate memories still boggled her mind. And she wasn't sure she
wanted to examine too closely what he did to her
sexually.

His whole package was right . . . for her. Maybe
there was no big, dark secret to love. You simply
sensed it, recognized it on a cellular level.

Love? Was she ready for it? *Uh, brain to self: You've
had seven hundred years of prep time.* Okay, so she was
thinking about it. In the near future. She slid him a
considering glance. In the *very* near future. And with
a life span to match hers, he could truly be her forever lover. How sensational was that?

Cindy shoved away thoughts of her past and future as she stepped into her present. "Love on the
rug. Sounds like a brand-new ice cream flavor, and
just as tempting." Her flip attitude played counter-
point to her pounding heart.

"Did Prada tell you exactly what the rug does?"
His heated gaze told her whatever the rug's power,
his was greater.

Cindy shook her head. "Prada just said it would
enhance our sexual experience." She hoped her

smile wasn't as shaky as it felt. "Enhancing our sexual experience could kill me."

"Hmm." His expression said that wouldn't be a bad way to go.

"Let me do a test lie down." She lowered herself to the fuzzy red rug, lay flat on her back, and clasped her hands behind her head. "It feels . . . strange. Mattress commercials always give us the sleeping-on-a-cloud promise, but this rug really delivers. It's all soft, warm, and . . . ohmigod!"

Her clothes were dissolving! Cindy's blouse and bra disappeared in what felt like a flow of warm water across her chest, leaving behind a tingling sensation that hardened her nipples to sensitive nubs.

She looked up at Thrain, her eyes wide. "Are you doing this?"

He simply shook his head.

She glanced down. "The rug? Can't anyone take their clothes off the old-fashioned way anymore?"

He narrowed his eyes on the rug for a moment and then relaxed into a smile. "I hate it when a rug undresses my woman. If it scares you, all you have to do is roll off it." He moved closer until he was standing as near as he could get without touching the rug. "But there's something very erotic about watching your clothes just slide from your body and disappear." He crouched down to get a better look as her belt slowly faded from around her waist. "I'd bet that Prada designed the rug to be as sexually stimulating as possible. Maybe you should let it do its thing." His voice was a husky murmur. "Freyja knows, *I* find it sexually stimulating."

In a deliberately sensual gesture, he clasped his bottom lip between his teeth and then released it. As he'd probably expected, Cindy couldn't tear her attention from the tempting wet sheen of that lip. Thoughts of the texture and feel of his mouth steered her away from her rug rant and toward the sexual possibilities ahead. In fact, there were so many possibilities that it was tough to concentrate on her clothes.

She could start by using the auto-strip to further her own agenda—driving Thrain Davis into a sexual frenzy. To be honest, she sensed he was almost there already. But you couldn't tell from his expression. Only if you looked into his eyes. Hot and hungry. She suspected they were mirror images of her own.

Cindy arched her back in a lazy stretch even as her jeans and panties flowed away. Her feet were bare, but she didn't remember when that had happened. Didn't care. She wiggled her toes and sighed her pleasure as she slid her palms across her breasts and then touched each nipple with the tip of her index finger to test for sensitivity. Sort of like holding up a finger to assess wind direction.

"You're killing me, woman." Thrain sounded as if he was enjoying the killing process.

She skimmed her fingers over her bare thighs while the warm wash of invisible water floated the remains of her jeans and panties away. The tingling, along with a cool breeze carrying the scent of the sea, followed close behind, tempting her to spread her legs and allow it to touch the heat, the building pressure. Rational thoughts retreated. But then, what good were rational thoughts when her senses had taken charge and had set up command a lot farther south than her brain?

"Mmm." Surrendering to temptation, she spread

her legs and then lifted her hips from the rug—a sensual invitation to play. "This rug is wonderful. Come down and try it out." *Try* me *out*. She frowned as a rational thought intruded. "Remind me never to invite Reverend Turner to sit on this rug."

Thrain's laughter wasn't quite steady. Good. Cindy sincerely hoped she was the cause of that unsteadiness. She gazed up at him through a haze of desire. No, not a haze of desire. The haze was smoke from her patience going up in flames. "Let me rephrase my last command in stronger terms. Get your beautiful butt down here now. Don't make me come for you." Her thoughts were diverted for a moment by the many meanings of *come*.

Thrain took advantage of her brief loss of focus to straighten from his crouch and move away from the rug. And her. She wailed her despair. Fine, so she had no pride left.

"Uh-uh." He slanted her a playful grin while his eyes burned a hotter shade of blue. "If I join you on the rug, it'll all be over in about three minutes. I want you that much. This is going to be slow and spectacular."

Gratified that he really really, wanted her, Cindy admitted they should try to make the pleasure last this time. Okay, six minutes would give them an eternity to extend the excitement. She patted the rug. "Come lie down. I'll try to control my primal urge to leap on you and have my wicked way with your body." She wouldn't try too hard, though.

Thrain stretched, pulling his shirt taut across his chest, if anyone could call that wide, muscular playground for women's hands a mere chest. Smiling, he watched her with the lazy assurance of a seasoned hunter. "Not a good idea. The space between us is filled with so much sexual tension, the air's vibrating. Think I'll strip right here." His smile widened, promising her endless eons of suffering. "And while I'm taking things off, we can talk about sex."

Cindy frowned. This was not a good thing. This would definitely blow her six-minute limit. In fact, watching him peel like a tempting, exotic treat might make her implode before he even got to the rug. She could leave the rug and go to him, but the tingling sensation the rug generated was magic that she wanted to share. Sighing, she surrendered to the inevitable.

"Fine, strip away, if it doesn't bother you to be known to future generations as the late, great Super Tease."

His smile turned wry. "I'll chance it."

He began to unbutton his shirt. Each button took a year, and Cindy mentally heard the ponderous grating of a vault door swinging open as he exposed each inch of skin. She gritted her teeth, wondering if she'd live long enough to actually see his chest.

Finally, he shrugged out of the cursed shirt and dropped it to the floor. He hooked his thumb in his belt and then paused to think about unbuckling it. Arrgh!

"Sometime during this century would be nice, vampire." Cindy hated when she resorted to sarcasm. The rug was revving up its sex-enhancing motor and was now moving beneath her in tiny ripples that massaged her tense body. It felt so good, and she felt so alone on the rug. "Take off the damned belt."

"No, wait. I'm visualizing how it'll be." He began

taking off the belt. The motion could be measured in millimeters, and the time was infinity squared. "I can almost feel the heated slide of your skin, the soft pressure of your breasts against my body." Just in case she didn't know which area of his body he meant, he splayed his hand across his chest and then slid his palm down over his ripped torso.

Cindy was conflicted. Watching him slide his hand over his exposed skin quickened her breathing and pumped up her heart rate. Too bad he had to stop unbuckling his belt to demonstrate, because that really ticked her off. So the whole thing was a wash.

"The belt, Davis." Without thinking, she smoothed her own hand over her breasts and stomach. Her skin already felt damp with anticipation, and as she lifted her gaze to Thrain, his stare scorched her. "Feeling a little frustration, hmm?" She loaded her smile with wicked satisfaction.

Thrain returned her smile. He did evil very well. "Maybe, but when we make love, it'll all be worth it." He finished with the buckle and discarded the belt.

Cindy waited, barely breathing, as he unbuttoned his jeans and slid them, along with his briefs, over his powerful thighs and legs. He kicked them away and then walked, gloriously naked, over to her coffee table.

"Yo, I'm not under the coffee table. Turn and walk directly to the red rug with the panting naked woman on it." He'd already used up their entire six minutes. They should be experiencing the ultimate orgasm about now.

He ignored her. Bending over, he calmly lit the vanilla candle on the table. She didn't even ask how he did it without a lighter, because she had other things on her mind.

Perfect male butt cheeks, an endangered species and rarely seen outside of captivity. Rounded yet firm. No dimples, because vampires should *never* have dimples. He straightened from the candle and turned to face her.

"What're you thinking?" He moved closer.

"That vanilla is the sexiest smell in the world." Other than an aroused male animal, specifically *her* male animal. Of course, that was a shallow thought, and she had dozens of nonshallow thoughts. Like . . . his sexual equipment was a national treasure that belonged in the Smithsonian.

"You like my body. A lot." His voice was all smug male arrogance.

She gave his erection her best slitty eyes. "And you know this, how?"

"Because you haven't looked above my waist since I shucked the jeans." Deliberately, he cupped himself and then wrapped his fingers around the long, hard length of his arousal. "But that's okay, because the interest is mutual. I want to kneel between your thighs, touch you with my mouth, and then bury myself inside you."

Fascinated, Cindy watched his erection swell even larger as he laid out his master plan. "Hey, don't hold back for me. You can tell me what you really want to do." She swallowed hard. It was getting tougher and tougher to maintain her light attitude in the face of his wondrous sexual display and her rampaging lust.

But it wasn't just lust anymore. The revelation

struck with the power of truth. Her need for him was so deep that she couldn't even trace its source. Unnoticed, it had entwined itself with the thing she called self, and she despaired of ever being able to disentangle it. This didn't bode well for her psyche if Thrain decided to walk away from her.

"You've gone all serious on me." His voice had softened and the laughter was gone. "Look at my face, Cindy."

She raised her gaze to meet his. "This is different. I mean, I've had seven hundred years of practice with short-term relationships. I understand all the preliminaries. But this feels different. I think I've run out of smart-mouthed banter."

Still holding her gaze, he crouched down at the edge of the rug. "Good. Because I'm being serious right back at you now." Reaching out, he skimmed his fingers along the side of her jaw.

His touch relaxed her jaw but didn't do much for the rest of her body. She sincerely hoped no part of *his* body relaxed.

"This is how I feel about you. If I were tied spread-eagled and naked on your bed and a dozen women rushed through the door with you in front, I wouldn't be afraid because *you* were there." Hot color seeped up his neck. "And saying that embarrassed the hell out of me."

Cindy realized she was the only one who would understand the gift Thrain had given her. He'd affirmed his trust in her while once again speaking openly about what he perceived as a weakness. She'd bet he never admitted that he was afraid to others. They'd both been born during a time when fear in men was an admission of cowardice. And

Thrain would always have been a strong man in every way.

"Thank you." She clasped his hand and pulled. "Join me. The rug is getting anxious."

He knelt on the rug, and it actually hummed with satisfaction. Cindy tried to ignore the mental picture of a giant Venus flytrap closing around them.

Leaning down, he covered her mouth with his and she parted her lips to meet his passion. As she tangled her tongue with his, she felt him changing—the emerging fangs, the subtle increase of hard muscle beneath her fingers as she clutched his shoulders.

With eyes closed, she explored his mouth, memorizing the taste of him and the way he affected her emotions. He was the flavor of now, not sweet or bitter but a mixture of past sorrow and future hope. His flavor was distinctly his own, and she'd never mistake it for another.

More than his taste, though, Cindy would remember his heat. His warmth flowed to every part of her body, loosening muscles that had been stretched taut with tension and heating her anticipation to simmering.

Carefully, she explored his fangs with her tongue and waited for the expected jolt of fear. None. Sighing, she settled into her happiness. Her body remembered the joy his bite had brought and accepted him.

He broke the kiss, and she could hear the sharp rasp of his breathing, feel the hunger thrumming through him.

Opening her eyes, she met the dark gaze of her vampire. "Why're your eyes so dark when you change?" *Really smart, Harper. In the middle of heat and passion you decide to ask a scientific question.*

"All the better to see you with, my dear."

He leered at her, a savage baring of his teeth that a few weeks ago would have sent her screaming to her therapist. Now she could smile back.

Thrain pushed strands of hair from her face with shaking fingers, a testament to his determination that there would be foreplay even if it killed him. She could've told him that he needn't bother, that she wanted to wrap her legs around him right now and feel him thrust into her, but he wanted to do this for her, so she said nothing.

"When I change, my pupils dilate so I can see in the dark. Vampires have powerful night vision." Leaning down once again, he slid his tongue over her neck, kissed the spot on her throat where her blood coursed strongest, then slid his fingers over the swell of her breasts. "We wouldn't be very intimidating creatures of the night if we spent all our time stumbling around in the dark, would we?"

"Gotcha. Intimidation is important." She panted the last few words as he closed his lips around one of her nipples, teasing it with his teeth and tongue.

Cindy was tempted to lie there like a big pink sponge and soak up all the sensual delight Thrain was visiting on her. But her functioning brain cells, which numbered in single digits right now, reminded her that touching his body would bring pleasure to both of them. And she was all for gobbling up as much pleasure as she could get.

Luckily, he still knelt beside her, so she didn't have to stretch far to reach between his thighs. She cradled his sacs in her palm and then gently squeezed. Remembering the power of her senses, she allowed the tactile impression to flow over her—the smooth, velvety feel of skin stretched tight over such potent maleness.

Strange, but beyond the pure physical pleasure of holding him in her hand was the joy of knowing how completely he'd opened his body to her. She didn't think trust of humans was something he practiced on a daily basis.

He raised his head from her breasts and drew in a deep, rasping breath. His reaction spurred her on. She drew her fingernail lightly over the length of his erection and then circled the head with the tip of her finger. His soft moan excited her, and her desire curled around the pleasure it gave her.

"You might want to remove your fingers from my cock, otherwise this is going to be short and real intense." His warning was grated from between clenched teeth.

She lifted her lips in her cheerleader smile—all teeth and shallower than a mud puddle. "Short and intense sounds a lot better than long and tortured. If I didn't know what an alpha animal you were, I'd suspect you wanted to make this last for, oh, say, ten minutes. Can we say impossible?"

In one fluid motion, he shifted to kneel between her spread legs. "Yeah, I guess ten minutes was expecting too much." He met her gaze and smiled the smile that reduced her to primal ooze. "We'll save that for when we're old and doddering. I know, I know, we'll never grow old and doddering, so it probably won't happen. Too bad, because I have seven hundred years of creative sexual experiments to try out on you."

"Sexual experiments? Seven hundred years' worth?" *When* we're *old and doddering?* The word *we're* held momentous possibilities, but she couldn't concentrate when he was kissing a path over her stomach. And would someone please turn off the music?

Music? She fought past the sensual fog and tried to remember if she'd put on a CD. No. What the . . .

"Ignore it. The rug is serenading us with sexually appropriate music." Sliding his hands beneath her bottom, he lifted her hips and with no warning put his mouth on her.

If she'd had the strength, she would've screamed her pleasure. But the unbearably intense sensation as he teased *that* spot with the tip of his tongue and then thrust into her, reduced her to a pitiful whimper. She was wet, wanting, and if he kept his mouth on her much longer, he'd reduce her to a blubbering blob of hot sauce.

Enough, enough, enough. "No more. Bite me. Come deep inside me." She was speaking in quick gasps and explicit commands. Cindy was vaguely aware that the rug had escalated its motion to frenzied waves that kept time with the low throb of the drums in the erotic musical accompaniment. Various scents she was unable to identify wafted around them. The rug was having a roaring good time.

Everything blurred as she merged her senses and then reached for him. Still supporting her bottom, he rose above her, blocking out the room's light as he paused to spear her with his hot gaze. With his long tangle of hair spread across his sleek shoulders, and the stark and savagely sensual lines of his face drawn tight, he was once again the Viking warrior who'd thrown the ancient world into terror. But he was *her* Viking and she . . .

Cindy didn't get a chance to complete that thought as she felt the head of his sex prod hard between her thighs. Not even making a pretense of defending the castle gates, she welcomed him with open enthusiasm as he plunged deeply into her. Finally finding her voice, she shouted her pleasure even as she wove her fingers into his hair so that she could pull him down to her.

She wrapped her legs around him, clenched her muscles around his erection, and then abandoned all coherent thought as she arched against him, trying to take more of him. No one would ever be able to fill her like Thrain did. No one would ever be able to make her feel this good.

Pleasure so intense could drive her to the edge of insanity, could make her scream with it until her throat was raw, could turn her into a clawing, shrieking she-devil. And she didn't care, didn't worry about anything except the delicious friction of Thrain's thick erection thrusting deep and then withdrawing in his own rhythm of sexual release.

They reached the moment together, exploded over the top of their climaxes, and then hung there at the top of their personal pleasure arcs before plunging back to earth with shouts of triumph.

For long moments she simply clung to Thrain's sweat-slicked body while she listened to her pounding heart and rasping breaths. And when everything came back into focus again, they were five feet away from the rug and, damn it, he hadn't bitten her.

"How'd we get here?" She didn't remember rolling off the rug.

He lay flat on his back, every muscle gleaming from his sexual exertion. Definitely the best kind of exertion. "I'm not sure, but at least we know the rug didn't cause that spectacular finish."

"You didn't bite me." Was that whiny disappointment she heard in her voice? Yep, sure was.

Thrain turned his head to meet her gaze, and she noted he was once again in human form. He didn't smile at her. "I wanted you to know that this was all about us. No bite or rug upgrades. We're this good together. We'll always be this good together."

And now for the cliché women had thought from the beginning of time. Was this just about great sex?

"No, Cindy, this was about a lot more."

She almost didn't hear his soft murmur. And as she skimmed her gaze over his uncompromising male beauty, Cindy knew he was right.

He'd looked into her mind, but he hadn't found her most important secret. In fact, she'd just discovered it herself. Not in her mind, but in her heart.

Chapter Sixteen

"It's midnight. Everyone's out on the lawn. Time to summon the Jersey Devil. And get your head out of the damned punch bowl." Prada offered Trojan her best prepare-to-die glare.

Trojan lifted his head from the bowl and tried to blink away the Mango Madness punch dripping from his furry face. *"What?"*

Prada threw up her hands in exasperation. "Here I transformed myself into a sensual goddess—black leather pants, sexy black silk top, diamond-studded black slut shoes—and all you can think about is your stomach. I can't believe you were drinking from the bowl. Just because you've taken an animal form doesn't mean you have to act like one." With a small huff of outrage, she turned away from Trojan and walked toward the front door, the *click click click* of her heels proclaiming she was royally steamed.

Reluctantly, he abandoned the punch to follow her. *"Forgive me, oh human with two hands and ten fin-*

gers. I don't see anyone holding a glass to my parched lips." He continued to grumble as he stepped onto the porch, tripped over the welcome mat, and fell flat on his face.

Alarmed, Prada stared down at him. "Are you okay?"

"Yesh." Climbing to his feet, Trojan stalked off the porch with stately if exaggerated caution.

Prada narrowed her gaze as she watched his progress toward the humans gathered on the lawn. A wobbly walk. Noticeable weaving. She hurried to catch up with him. "Did you spike that punch?"

"Yesh. Punch isn't worth crap without a bite." He burped loudly.

She glanced at the humans, who'd begun their useless spell. They'd built a small fire on the lawn. Cindy would go ballistic when she saw it. "Are you too zonked to summon the Jersey Devil?"

Trojan blinked owlishly at her. *"Me? I'm terpect . . . uh, pectfer."* He hissed his frustration. *"I'm perfect."*

"Sure. Perfect." Anxiously, she watched the humans. They were rapping to some primal rhythm and moving in a circle. Amazing. None of them had even questioned the book she'd planted that said they had to chant "Mary Had a Little Lamb" to a rap beat while doing the bunny hop. "You'd better get started on the spell. They're about to perform the last step—sacrificing a bowl of broccoli to appease the gods of the forest."

"Broccoli?" Trojan stared at her. *"And you think I'm drunk?"*

It was a testament to her state of mind that she

didn't even worry about breaking a nail as she scooped Trojan up and shouted into one twitching ear. "Start. Summoning. Now!"

"Okay, okay. Put me down so I can whip up the biggest badass spell you've ever seen." He ruined his take-charge attitude by hiccuping.

Relieved, Prada placed him on the ground and went to sit on the porch until he was done. She didn't even bother listening to his thoughts. If she knew anything, she knew that even half crocked, he had the power to do whatever he chose to do.

Trojan stood staring intently toward the forest. The humans had grown quiet and were moving restlessly around the lawn.

Prada noticed the stillness first. If this quiet could take physical form, it would be a malignant black cloud. There was nothing natural about it. She held her breath as night mist seemed to ooze from the forest, crawling across the lawn and weaving around the humans like ghostly snakes. The humans were now huddled together in the middle of the lawn. But this was one time they wouldn't find safety in numbers.

Suddenly an unearthly screech echoed through the woods. Prada gasped, a gasp that was repeated by all the others. Except for Trojan. He was still doing his thing.

And then she heard the beating of monster wings. Whatever was coming must be gigantic to make that kind of noise. The whimpers coming from the crowd said that maybe this hadn't been such a good idea. Prada smiled. *Too late now.* Let the scary stuff begin.

Screaming its fury, the Jersey Devil arrived on a rush of wings wide enough to cast the pitiful group on the lawn into their shadow. Branches bent as it swooped down from above the trees. Prada widened her eyes. Cripes, Trojan hadn't told her how huge it was . . . or how big and pointy its teeth were. Some ancient god must've been as smashed as Trojan when he made this sucker. The creature looked like some horrific cross between a bat, a horse, and a T.rex. Ugh. No wonder it was ticked. If she looked in the mirror each day and saw that face, she'd be cranky, too.

The humans broke their shocked silence as the Jersey Devil made his first pass at them. Everyone scattered and ran. Terrified screams grew in volume as the creature turned over several cars, uprooted a few trees, and broke three of the inn's windows while pursuing the fleeing humans.

"Hey, sexy lady. Gotta go inside for a minute. Be right back." Trojan's eyes looked a little crossed.

Prada frowned. "Umm, maybe you should send the big guy back to where he came from first. He's tearing up the place pretty bad. Cindy's insurance company might not pay out for Jersey Devil damage. And . . ." Her voice trailed off as the *big guy* flipped her beautiful, expensive car onto its beautiful, expensive roof. She forgot about Trojan.

"You son of a bitch! Get your creepy ass over here so I can bite your big, ugly head off." She shook her fist at the creature. It ignored her in favor of swooping toward a chubby real estate agent it obviously felt offered a more substantial meal. "The insurance company's going to total that sucker and I'll never get my money out of it." The Devil didn't care.

This had to end before that prehistoric pinhead ate

all the guests and leveled the Woo Woo Inn. Cindy would *not* be amused if she and Thrain came back with Trojan's ice cream only to find the inn was no longer turning a profit. And the lawsuits? There'd be many, many lawsuits, and Cindy would be very, very pissed. Prada definitely didn't want to get her behind kicked out of the inn before she'd successfully completed her work with Thrain and Cindy.

She'd just make Trojan send the Jersey Devil away. Then she'd try to calm down the guests and pick up a little before Cindy got back. She glanced at the destruction. Okay, so picking up a little wouldn't get it done. At least she could offer the guests punch in the hopes they'd fall into a drunken stupor and forget all about the Jersey Devil.

Prada glanced around. No Trojan. Irritated, she watched the Devil uproot a giant oak in an attempt to reach the little old librarian hiding behind it. The real estate agent must've been too slippery for the creature. Figured. Big teeth, tiny brain.

Prada stomped onto the porch and kicked open the door with criminal disregard for her designer shoes. The librarian stumbled in behind her. Ignoring the woman's hysterical screams, Prada went in search of Trojan.

She found him passed out in the punch-bowl. Too bad she didn't have time to call down a few ancient curses on his punch-soaked head. She could almost visualize the scenario. He'd wake up and . . . oh wow, someone had stolen his balls. Hey, you snooze, you lose.

Prada dragged him out of the bowl and left him sprawled across the table. She paused to listen to the escalating screams outside. "Do we have a situation? I'd say yes. And where is my cosmic dumb-ass partner?" Her dumb-ass partner burped so she couldn't miss his location.

What to do? Most of the guests couldn't make a run for the inn because there was too much open space to cross. The Devil would pick them off. They were better off hiding behind the dubious protection of trees and bushes.

She didn't have enough power to get rid of the Jersey Devil. The only one she knew who could reach the inn fast enough to stave off complete annihilation was Thrain. Frantically, she ran to the parlor where Cindy kept her cell number posted beside the phone. She quickly punched in the number.

Cindy drove while a silent Thrain sat beside her in the passenger seat. That was okay, because if last night had been anywhere near as life-altering for him as it had for her, he needed some quiet time to think.

But the silence from the brooding beast in the backseat wasn't acceptable. Reinn's silence made her nervous. And so she continued her attempt to engage him in conversation. "What made you decide to tag along with us, Reinn?" Cindy had found that only questions aimed directly at him earned any kind of response.

"Needed toothpaste." Reinn didn't waste words. The word *I* was unnecessary vocal effort.

She smiled. "Ah, yes. I hope you bought a brand with whitener. Have to keep those fangs shiny and bright, don't we?" Cindy hoped she annoyed him to tears. Probably mission impossible. She'd bet that

Reinn had never in his whole existence cared about anyone or anything enough to squeeze even one tear from those icily beautiful eyes.

"Right the first time, lady. If you don't care, your enemies can never use that caring to make you weak." His husky murmur held no emotion. "And if you stay far away from people, you're never tempted to care."

Cindy thought about telling him to stay out of her mind but decided it wouldn't make any difference. She shivered. She'd never met anyone quite this cold in her whole life. "I guess I feel sorry for you then."

His soft laughter held no humor. "Don't bother. I like what I am just fine. In fact, being a cold bastard just got me a promotion." For the first time emotion crept into his voice, but the bitter mockery she heard chilled her. "For a thousand years I've made sure no one wanted to be around me, but they still couldn't leave me alone. They hunted me down and made me the clan's Guardian of the Blood."

"Guardian of the Blood? What's that? And who're 'they'?" She wasn't really surprised when he didn't answer.

But Thrain did. "The clan council appoints the oldest and most qualified member of the clan to replace a Guardian of the Blood who's died. Since we're immortal, that hasn't happened in nine hundred years. But it did happen two months ago."

Cindy mourned the finality of the Guardian's fate but couldn't deny a morbid curiosity. "How'd the last Guardian die? Did he drink too much of the wrong blood, then wander home to Scotland and get whacked by whatever vigilant clansman was on duty at the family homestead?" How heartless was that? She wasn't sure she liked the Mackenzie traditions.

Thrain cast her a probing glance. "No. Love destroyed him. A Guardian of the Blood has to meet certain criteria. He has to be at least a thousand years old to prove he can survive. He can't have any emotional ties that might make him vulnerable. And he has to be totally ruthless." He returned his gaze to the road. "The last Guardian fell in love with a human. When a band of night feeders took her from him, he rushed after them." Thrain shrugged. "Love made him careless. The night feeders used bog myrtle to render him helpless, fed from him, and then took his head."

The story was scarily similar to her night feeder experience. Cindy didn't want to think about Thrain's vulnerability. Just like the Guardian, he'd leaped into battle against the night feeders only to be caught unaware by Sam. Her stomach knotted and she felt nauseous at the thought of losing Thrain that way. Fiercely, she swore she'd always be there to watch his back. *Right. And you'll do this how?*

Drawing in a deep breath, she guided her thoughts in a less disturbing direction. "What does a Guardian of the Blood do?" Personally, she thought it sounded sort of out there.

"Our blood is the clan's strength. But the same blood that gives us enormous power can also destroy us. The clan has two laws no one can break. First, clan members can't bite each other unless they're married. Couples are allowed to share each other's life force because it's part of the sexual joining."

"I don't understand." *It's part of the sexual joining.*

She didn't have the dental equipment to give him the complete pleasure a woman of his clan could. The thought saddened her.

"There's something in our blood that over a period of time causes addiction. Your father gave his blood to save my life, but he got around the law by sharing it in a transfusion. And because I only took his blood once, it didn't addict me." His voice was clinical, unemotional. "Since you're half human, your blood is diluted enough so that you wouldn't come under the law."

"But what happens if two members of the clan marry, and say the wife is killed?" She was almost afraid to hear the answer.

He shrugged. "The addiction is irreversible. Her husband becomes insane and either destroys himself or preys on other clan members."

"Loving a Mackenzie comes at a high price." Cindy was safe from the blood addiction, but there were many kinds of dependencies. A woman would have to think long and then love strong before marrying Thrain.

"We're worth it." His teasing eased her tension.

"I bet you are." She tried to keep her tone as light as his. "Tell me about the other law."

"The second law forbids any act that would alter our blood." Thrain peered through the windshield at the thickening mist. "I can't believe you went out at this time of night to hunt up ice cream for that cat."

"Forget Trojan. What happens when someone breaks these particular clan laws?" She glanced in the rearview mirror at Reinn. The blue eyes that stared back at her were the same as Thrain's, but his were hard, eyes that belonged to someone who wasn't a stranger to violence, someone who would kill with cold efficiency.

Once again, Thrain answered. "The Guardian of the Blood destroys them."

For the first time, Cindy wondered if she really wanted to rush into the welcoming arms of her family. "Let me get this straight: Someone is always waiting at your ancestral castle to kill any crazy clan member who drinks too much of the wrong blood and then makes the mistake of coming home. And if a clansman breaks one of your blood laws and is smart enough not to go home, then the Guardian of the Blood hunts him down and kills him. Not a particularly loving family, are you?"

The mocking laughter from the dark demon in the backseat affirmed her growing suspicions about the Mackenzie clan.

Thrain tore his attention from the gathering mist to look at her. "The clan laws have remained the same for thousands of years. The council has discussed changing some of them, but until they're changed, we have to abide by them. The laws have kept the clan strong." Her scowl told him what she thought of those laws.

"Uh-huh. Tell me more about the second clan law. What would warrant a clansman having his head lopped off by Reinn the Ruthless?" She didn't try to hide her contempt.

"Your woman shows no respect for powerful immortals, Thrain."

If Thrain didn't know better, he'd almost think that Reinn was teasing him. Impossible. Reinn's dark humor didn't include anything as playful as teasing. Thrain decided to ignore him.

"There are certain species we're not allowed to mate with, because the sexual act involves feeding. Humans are okay because their blood is weak, and as long as we take only a little blood, no harm is done. Human blood would never be strong enough to compromise who we are. But we're forbidden to mate with any kind of shape-shifter or demon. Werewolf and werecat blood is powerful enough to change our essence, and the clan can't afford to lose its identity."

"Okay, got it. No mongrels allowed." She frowned. "But *I'm* a mongrel. Does that mean I need a green card to mix with the pure of blood?" She glanced away from her driving for a second to meet his gaze. "It's a good thing I love your body, because some of your laws seriously suck." *Liar. You don't just love his body.* "When I meet good old Dad, do I address him as Darach the Destroyer?"

Thrain exhaled sharply. He couldn't argue with her because he didn't believe in the blood laws either. At the very least, the council should be funding scientific research into the blood addiction. If they could find a way to cure the addiction, they wouldn't have to kill their own. And mating with another species didn't deserve death. "The clan has only had three Guardians of the Blood during its whole existence, so I don't think you have to worry about Darach becoming the fourth."

"Yeah, Darach's safe." Reinn had abandoned mockery and returned to bitterness. "I know how to survive, so I'll be holding down the guardianship for a lot of centuries. And friendship can't compromise me because I don't have any friends. Love and friendship make a man vulnerable." He said the word *vulnerable* as if it were a terminal disease.

Silence filled the car. What did you say to that? Thrain wondered. Sure, love made you vulnerable, but it also made you stronger in ways that Reinn would never understand. For example, since he'd met Cindy, he . . .

Listen to yourself. Do you know what you're saying? Thrain smiled. Yeah, he did. He loved Cindy Harper. And with the admission came joy. He wouldn't look past the joy. It was enough for the moment.

Thrain glanced back at Reinn. "Thanks, old pal." When, not if, he convinced Cindy to marry him, neither of them would ever have to be alone again.

Reinn looked pained, as if the word *pal* was a venomous insect bite. Thrain laughed.

Cindy's cell phone rang. Thrain rooted around in her purse, pulled it out, and handed it to her. He watched the expression on her face turn from puzzled to horrified as she listened to what the caller said. By the time she handed the phone back to him, she was pale.

"What's the matter?" Damn it. This new love thing made him super-sensitive to anything that worried her.

Cindy glanced over at him with wide, frightened eyes. "That was Prada. Some of the guests got together and summoned the Jersey Devil. It's destroying things and threatening the guests." She stomped on the gas. "She says you're the only one who can stop it."

He frowned. "What about Trojan? He's powerful enough to take care of it."

She shook her head. "Trojan's drunk. He passed out in the punch bowl."

Reinn's bark of laughter surprised all of them, probably Reinn most of all. "I really love this place."

Thrain and Cindy ignored him as she burned rubber turning into the driveway. As she took the last curve leading to the inn, they got their first look at the disaster.

Cindy screeched to a stop and they leaped from the car and ran for the porch, where Prada waited. The Devil didn't notice; it was trying to flush Clark and his other fake werewolves out from the small crawl space under the corner of the inn. As the Devil battered the building with its wings, the werewolves screamed their terror.

Thrain closed his eyes for a moment. Great, just great. Then he looked at Prada. "Go into the inn and tell everyone left inside to get their butts out here. Now."

Prada took one look at his expression and hurried inside.

Reinn glanced at the chaos and shook his head. "I'm going to brush my teeth while I think about what a useless piece of crap I am." He followed Prada into the inn.

Cindy clutched at Thrain's arm and shouted to be heard above the noise. "What're you going to do?"

"Damage control, sweetheart. Damage control." He turned to glance at the group of fearful guests Prada was herding outside. "And before you ask, yes, I do need everyone out here when I take care of this problem."

Something in his heart tore loose and floated free as Cindy nodded and smiled at him.

"I trust you, vampire."

Thrain strode to the middle of the lawn, waved his arms at the Devil, and shouted, "Hey, forget about the werewolves. They're bad takeout. Come and get a midnight snack that won't hide from you." As soon as he had the Devil's attention, he drew his massive power to himself, centered it, and wove his memories like a giant spiderweb over the creature and all the humans. But not Cindy. He wanted Cindy to know what he'd done. A man wanted the woman he loved to admire him. Yeah, so he was showing off.

The Jersey Devil abandoned the werewolves and rose into the air. Flapping its massive wings, it soared above Thrain, ready to begin its deadly dive. He continued to focus on the memories.

Suddenly, he realized that Cindy had left the safety of the porch and braved the creature to stand beside him. Pride filled him. He'd embraced the modern world, but at heart he was still a Highlander. And the savage soul of his warrior past exulted in his woman's bravery.

Without losing his concentration, he reached out his hand to Cindy. "Take my hand and give me your strength." Sweat sheened his face and his breath came in gasps as he approached the pivotal moment that would spell victory or death. Because he didn't for a minute doubt that the Jersey Devil recognized him as a danger and would kill him if it could.

Cindy's eyes were wide with fright, but she didn't

flee to safety. "I don't have any strength to give you. I can't do anything."

His power surged and triumph filled him as she placed her hand in his. He didn't look at her as he stared up at the creature above him. "A woman always gives strength to the man who loves her."

Energy exploded from him, moving in waves that captured old memories and replaced them with new ones. The wind howled and sizzling sparks of blue light lit the darkness. Then it was over. Weakness washed over him as he watched the Jersey Devil circle the lawn once and then disappear into the night.

The humans wandered dazedly around the lawn. Clark walked over to them and shook his head. "Wow, did you see that tornado? It could've killed us all. You're lucky it didn't take out the inn, Cindy." When Cindy didn't comment, he wandered away.

"What did you do to the Jersey Devil?" Her voice was quiet, controlled, and sounded like there was something else entirely on her mind.

"From now on, he'll remember how much he fears humans because of their strength and cunning. He'll also remember that to stay safe he has to fly away whenever he senses humans nearby." Thrain acknowledged his exhaustion. He couldn't even work up enough energy to kick some cosmic troublemaker butt. Cindy's guests didn't have enough power to summon the Devil. This had Trojan's pawprints all over it.

"And you gave the guests the memory of a tornado roaring through here. They're not even questioning a tornado in October. Clever. I'm just thankful no one got more than a few cuts and bruises." She glanced across the lawn and parking area. "I'll have to plant some new trees and replace a few cars and windows."

His weariness was now laced with despair. Cindy didn't love him. She'd decided to ignore his admission, because there was no way she could have misunderstood what he'd said.

"Let's go inside." There wasn't anything else left to say. He'd take her to Darach and then fade from the picture. Would he get over it? Sure. He'd survived for over seven centuries. Would he ever be the same? No. Cindy would always own a part of him, and without that part he'd never be whole.

She followed him inside and then paused in the hallway. "That took a lot out of you. Sleep with me, vampire." She didn't smile at him, but her eyes swam with emotion. "Because a woman gives strength to the man she loves."

The man she loves. He froze, letting the power of her words fill him with happiness and dispel the loneliness of centuries. Strange, but the only words that came to him were from the land he'd abandoned more than two hundred years earlier. " 'Tis a wondrous gift ye've given me. *Tha gaol agam ort.*"

"*Tha gaol agam ort?*" She moved closer to slide her fingers across his chest. "I hope that doesn't mean, 'I'm married with five kids.' "

He pulled her roughly into his arms, all the emotion of so many lost centuries sweeping everything before it. "It means 'I love you.' "

Her hands were a little unsteady as she cupped his jaw. "I'll have to learn a meaningful Gaelic phrase for you."

"Not now. We have the rest of our lives to say all the words that need saying. Now is for the senses.

Let's go to your bed and explore. Remember all of those sexual experiments I talked about?" He lowered his head and nipped her neck.

She laughed as she raised her mouth to his. "I thought you were exhausted."

He offered her a look of mock surprise. "You won't believe what just happened. I've gained another power. Suddenly, I realize I have superhuman sexual energy. Amazing."

As he covered her mouth with his, she murmured, "Take off your red cape, vampire, and come to bed."

Chapter Seventeen

The final chapter of her incredible journey. There'd be a whole lot more books in this series, but today she'd close the pages on this particular one. Today she'd meet her father.

Cindy paused beside Thrain as she looked across the stone footbridge linking the island on which the Mackenzie castle stood with the mainland. Still isolated from the usual tourist routes, the castle was a stark black silhouette against the Highland's night sky. Only a few lights in the narrow windows promised that it wasn't just a haunted memory of centuries past.

"Let's go." Thrain put his arm around her waist and pulled her close.

His heat and strength gave her confidence. He'd insisted on returning to his clan's home wearing the same kind of clothing he'd worn when he left. Evidently, it was a tradition that clan members dressed in kilts during their stay at the castle. That was fine with her. A great-looking man in a kilt was seriously hot.

"Does my father know we're coming?" She walked beside him across the footbridge. Stopping before the massive doors, Cindy felt the first quiver of unease. What if Darach didn't believe she was his daughter? What if he didn't want any reminder of his first wife? What if Stepmommy Dearest hated her on sight? *What if he couldn't love her?* That was stupid. Of course he wouldn't love her. She'd be a stranger to him. But maybe with time . . .

"No. I wanted it to be a surprise." Thrain didn't sound worried as he pressed the doorbell. The doors were so thick that they couldn't hear if it rang inside. "The old castle didn't have any modern conveniences like bells the last time I was here."

He frowned, and Cindy knew he was remembering what had caused that last visit—his pain, despair, and humiliation. She knew that only his love for her would have brought him back to face his demons.

"Thanks for coming with me." She stood on tiptoe and kissed his cheek.

He turned to smile at her, but his expression was shadowed. "Love is a powerful motivator. For over two hundred years, I've refused to stay here for the month all clan members are expected to give. This is a step I needed to take. Besides, this isn't where it happened. I don't know if I'd ever revisit that place. It probably crumbled away centuries ago, anyway."

All conversation ended as the doors creaked slowly open. And there, standing in the doorway with the lights of the great hall behind them were . . .

"Prada? Trojan?" Why were *they* here? Cindy's

most recent memories of them involved some really ugly accusations and threats tossed back and forth. The proverbial last straw had come when Thrain said he intended to put a shield around the fridge that would keep Trojan from getting near it. Prada had called a cab, and they'd left in a huff. Cindy had never expected to see them again.

"How'd you get here before us?" Thrain's glare should've left a smoking hole in the middle of Prada's forehead.

Prada ignored the glare and offered him her best sex-kitten smile. "Wow, you are *so* hot when you're mad. We didn't travel by . . . conventional means." She looked down at Trojan, who crouched beside her. "We got here just a little before you, so cuddle bunny didn't have a chance to change into human form." She frowned. "Oh, and before you start shouting again, we have every right to be here. Darach and Blythe are our friends." She didn't try to hide her sly triumph. "Besides, we have an engagement gift to give you guys. We *are* invited to the wedding, aren't we?" Her expression said that, invited or not, they'd be there.

"Cuddle bunny? You're kidding." Thrain stared at Trojan, then laughed.

"Shut up, bloodsucker." Trojan evidently didn't feel the need to guard his tongue here. "And we don't need the aliases anymore. From now on we're Ganymede and Sparkle Stardust again."

Cindy felt her smile beginning. It was too weird listening to that big male voice coming from the gray cat. "What's your agenda? I know you didn't show up because of our deep and abiding friendship."

Sparkle stuck out her bottom lip and blinked as

though she was fighting back tears. Uh-uh, wouldn't work. Sparkle just didn't have the knack for looking hurt.

Ganymede made a rude noise. "Soft and sensitive isn't you, so give it up. You're cunning, manipulative, and wicked. That's what I love about you, babe."

Sparkle heaved a deep sigh and shrugged. "We came because we have too much invested in you. We were here when Darach saved Thrain's life. We helped save Darach from the same women who got Thrain. We want to see everything." Now she looked militant. "We *deserve* to be here."

Thrain opted for not arguing. "Where's Darach?"

"Darach and Blythe are in the great hall. Let's go and surprise them." Ganymede looked up at Thrain with bright, eager eyes.

Now Cindy was really getting nervous. She wiped her sweating palms on her suit jacket. Had the suit been the right choice? What did you wear to make a good impression on a father you've never seen? She stepped into the great hall beside Sparkle.

Thrain and Ganymede fell behind a few steps. They were talking quietly, but Cindy couldn't hear what they were saying. Besides, she'd focused all her attention on the man sitting at the long table near the fireplace. He rose at their approach.

Across the span of seven centuries, she stared at a man who looked young enough to be her brother but Cindy knew was her father. Tall and hard-muscled, Darach Mackenzie had the same black hair and blue eyes as she. She was vaguely aware of a blond-haired woman rising to stand beside him.

" 'Tis glad I am to see ye again, Thrain. Who did ye bring with ye?" Her father talked to Thrain, but he never let his gaze waver from her face. The beginning of recognition moved in his eyes. "Who are ye?" This time he spoke directly to her. Unlike Thrain, he must have lived most of his life in Scotland, because he'd kept his distinctive Scottish burr.

Thrain moved up beside her, and Cindy knew he was preparing to tell her story. She put her hand on his arm to stop him. This was her father and her story to tell.

"I'm Elina, but I haven't used that name for a long time. Now I'm Cindy Harper. Aesa was my mother. She only talked about my real father once. She said they were planning to marry when she got pregnant. He abandoned her, and her family disowned her because of the disgrace. After hearing that, I decided not to ever look for you." Cindy glanced over at Thrain, grateful for his support. "Thrain told me a very different story. I wanted to meet you." Lord, had she said the right words? Had she sounded too cold, too detached? Would he expect more emotion? *Would he reject her?*

There was nothing hesitant about Darach as he strode from the table to stand in front of her. Blythe remained by the table, her eyes wide and concerned.

He spoke to Thrain even though his eyes devoured Cindy. "'Tis your skull I'll be cracking for not telling me ye thought I had a daughter."

Cindy sensed Thrain's shrug. "I wasn't sure, and I didn't think you needed that kind of disappointment. Losing your child once was enough."

Darach laid his palm against her cheek, and Cindy watched his eyes grow moist. "She named ye after her sister. Aesa didna realize the harm she caused. If I'd known ye lived, I would have come for ye. I suppose 'twas what she feared." He lowered his voice. "I would have loved ye. But 'tis never too late for love. Welcome home, Elina Mackenzie." Roughly, he pulled her to him and wrapped his arms around her. "Welcome home, daughter."

Okay, getting all weepy here. Cindy wiped the tears from her eyes as Darach released her.

"Don't wipe the tears away, Elina. Enjoy them. Life doesn't hand out many second chances, but you and your father beat the odds." The blond woman clasped her hand. "Darach is too busy pretending he's not crying to introduce us. I'm Blythe, your wicked stepmother. And even if you were the step-daughter from hell, I'd love you for giving a piece of his life back to your father. He always mourned your loss." She grinned. "What do you want us to call you, Elina or Cindy?"

"Cindy." She didn't hesitate. Elina was part of a lost and unhappy time. Cindy was who she was now, the person who loved Thrain.

As if by agreement, they all migrated to the table and sat down. Now it was Thrain's turn to look nervous. "I hunted for Cindy through the years because if I hadn't helped Aesa run away, you never would have lost your daughter."

Darach slapped him on the back but still couldn't bring himself to stop staring at Cindy. "Ye were not to blame."

Cindy knew by the determined look in Thrain's eyes that he was about to tell her father they were getting married. Sparkle leaned forward, an excited glitter in her eyes. Ganymede leaped onto the table.

"I love Cindy. She loves me. And we're getting married."

Cindy blinked. Wow, was that brilliantly poetic or what?

Darach surged to his feet, becoming vampire even as he rose. "Did ye hear that, Blythe? I just got my daughter back, and the bloody reiver is stealing her away." He lifted his lips from his fangs in a snarl. "Come out to the courtyard and we'll discuss this stealing of daughters."

Blythe put her hand on Darach's arm and, still growling, he dropped back into his seat. She smiled at Cindy and Thrain. "Darach wishes you all the happiness in the world." Blythe turned her smile on her husband. "Don't you, dear?"

"Aye." But Darach still glared at Thrain. "We'll discuss his worthiness later."

Blythe winked at her, and relief flowed through Cindy. This woman would be her friend.

Ganymede plunked his impressive bulk in front of Cindy. "Hey, this whole thing was a blast from beginning to end. Okay, so maybe I didn't need all this mushy stuff, but I had a super time raising hell at the inn. And I always love coming back to this castle. All those bad memories—the crazy vampires, the rampaging Highlanders, and those bitches who almost killed Darach. Can't have enough bad memories." He was on a roll.

"Me and Sparkle got you guys an engagement present." He narrowed his amber gaze on Sparkle. "She wanted to give you dumb stuff like your own personal sex trainers." Ganymede ignored everyone's startled expressions. "But I said, nah. We needed to give you the gift that would keep on giving. Go get their gift, babe."

Sparkle cast him a slitty-eyed look that said she'd

be giving him the pain that would keep on giving when she got him alone. Then she left the hall.

Everyone remained silent until she came back. Cindy figured they were all a little suspicious of any gift Ganymede gave. He seemed to go in for the scary and spectacular. If he gave her a Jersey Devil egg, she'd break it over his head.

She didn't have any more time to speculate on what it might be. Sparkle leaned over and set the gift she'd had cradled in her arms onto the table in front of Cindy.

Cindy was eyeball-to-eyeball with a fuzzy brown puppy. The puppy yawned, exposing tiny puppy teeth, but teeth nonetheless.

For just a moment, she considered jumping away from the table, putting some distance between herself and those miniteeth. But then she felt Thrain's hand covering hers, reminding her that beings with teeth had a lot of love to give, too.

"He'll grow up to love and protect you, Cindy." Thrain's voice was a low, soothing murmur. "Look at him and see all the years of love he'll give you." The puppy demonstrated his undying love by piddling on the table.

And Cindy laughed. She couldn't help it. Scooping up the puppy, she turned to where Ganymede and Sparkle stood waiting for her reaction. "Thank you. Fine, so maybe this makes up a little for the overturned cars and uprooted trees. And I'll name him . . ." She considered possibilities. "Trouble. Every time I call him, I'll remember all the . . . interesting times we had."

Satisfied, Sparkle and Ganymede headed toward their room, where Cindy had no doubt Ganymede would change to human form. Sparkle wore her I'm-looking-for-a-sexy-guy expression.

But just before leaving the great hall, Ganymede paused to look back at them. No one else noticed because they were busy talking. For a moment, Cindy thought Ganymede was staring at her, but then she realized he was focused on Trouble. Deliberately, he winked at the puppy. Cindy shifted her gaze to Trouble in time to see the puppy return Ganymede's wink.

Hmm. She narrowed her gaze on her small new companion. Trouble wagged his tail and offered her a happy puppy grin. Cindy relaxed. He was just a cute puppy. Trouble yipped his agreement.

Darach and Blythe soon followed Ganymede and Sparkle out of the great hall, with Darach still muttering dire warnings if Thrain didn't treat his daughter like the princess she was. Blythe told them which room to use and then took the puppy with her so that she could find something for it to eat.

Once she was left alone with Thrain, Cindy's thoughts turned to the sensual. How could she help thinking erotic thoughts when she was sitting next to the hottest Highlander in all of Scotland? And the miracle of his love would never cease to be a wonder.

"I hope you know how to find our room because I want to strip you naked and do incredibly stimulating things to your yummy body." She gave him a coming attraction by sliding her fingers up his bare inner thigh.

His eyes gleamed a darker blue in the flickering light of the single candle left burning. "Sounds like an invitation I can't turn down."

"Uh-huh. And I finally memorized a Gaelic

phrase for you." She tangled her fingers in his long Viking hair and pulled his head down so she could whisper in his ear. *"De th'ort fo d'fheileadh?"*

He threw back his head and laughed before standing. Clasping her hand tightly, he led her toward the stone steps spiraling up the tower. "Let's go to our room so you can see for yourself what I wear under my kilt."

Nina Bangs
Master of Ecstasy

Her trip back in time to 1785 Scotland is supposed to be a vacation, so why does Blythe feel that her stay at the MacKenzie castle will be anything but? The gloomy old pile of stones has her imagination working overtime.

The first hunk she meets turns out to be Mr. Dark-Evil-and-Deadly himself, an honest-to-goodness vampire. His voice is a tempting slide of sin, and his body raises her temperature, but when Darach whispers, "To waste a neck such as yours would be a terrible thing," she decides his pillow talk leaves a lot to be desired.

Dangerous? You bet. To die for? Definitely. Soul mate? Just wait and see.
